Ben Pastor, born in Italy, became a US citizen after moving to Texas. She lived for thirty years in the United States, working as a university professor in Illinois, Ohio and Vermont, and currently spends part of the year in her native country. *The Night of Shooting Stars* is the seventh in the Martin Bora series and follows on from the success of *The Horseman's Song, Road to Ithaca, Tin Sky, A Dark Song of Blood, Liar Moon* and *Lumen,* also published by Bitter Lemon Press. Ben Pastor is the author of other novels including the highly acclaimed *The Water Thief* and *The Fire Waker,* and is considered one of the most talented writers in the field of historical fiction. In 2008 she won the Premio Zaragoza for best historical fiction, and in 2018 she was awarded the prestigious Premio Internazionale di Letteratura Ennio Flaiano.

# THE NIGHT OF SHOOTING STARS

## Ben Pastor

**BITTER LEMON PRESS**
**LONDON**

BITTER LEMON PRESS

First published in the United Kingdom in 2020 by

Bitter Lemon Press, 47 Wilmington Square, London WC1X OET

www.bitterlemonpress.com

This edition published in agreement with Piergiorgio
Nicolazzini Literary Agency (PNLA)

Translation of Friederich Hölderlin's 'Der Ister' on p.11
by Richard Sieburth, from *Friederich Hölderlin: Hymns
and Fragments*, Princeton University Press, 1984

A CIP record for this book is available from the British Library

ISBN 978–1–912242–28-3
eBook ISBN 978–1–912242–29-0

Typeset by Tetragon
Printed and bound by the CPI Group (UK) Ltd, Croydon, CRO 4YY

*To everyone else who resisted,*
*but nobody remembers*

# MAIN CHARACTERS

**Martin-Heinz von Bora,** Lieutenant Colonel in the German
army
**Nina Sickingen-Bora,** his mother
**Benno von Salomon,** Colonel in the German army
**Bruno Lattmann,** Major in the German army
**Max Kolowrat,** journalist, traveller, former war correspondent
**Arthur Nebe,** Head of the German Criminal Police (Kripo)
**Claus von Stauffenberg,** Deputy Commander of the Reserve
Army
**Willy Osterloh,** civil engineer
**Emma "Emmy" Pletsch,** Staff Leader in the Reserve Army
**Margaretha "Duckie" Sickingen,** Bora's sister-in-law
**Florian Grimm,** Detective Inspector in the Berlin Criminal
Police
**Albrecht Olbertz,** Nazi physician
**Ida Rüdiger,** hairdresser to the Party wives
**Berthold "Bubi" Kupinsky,** a shady character
**Gerd Eppner,** jeweller and watchmaker
**Roland Glantz,** Sternuhr Verlag publisher
**Gustav Kugler,** former Kripo officer
**Namura,** Lieutenant Colonel in the Imperial Japanese Army
**Sami Mandelbaum, a.k.a. Magnus Magnusson, alias Walter
Niemeyer,** clairvoyant and stage magician

# GLOSSARY

**Abwehr:** The Third Reich's military counter-espionage service

**Alex:** Nickname for Berlin's Alexanderplatz, used here mainly to denote the police headquarters

**Brownshirt:** Member of the paramilitary SA (Sturmabteilung)

**Einsatzgruppen:** Special SS paramilitary death squads employed on the Eastern front

**Garde-Regiment zu Fuss:** The 1st Foot Guards, a Prussian infantry regiment

**Heimat:** German for native land, homeland

**Kripo:** Contraction of "Kriminalpolizei", the German Criminal Police

**NSKK:** Short for "Nationalsozialistisches Kraftfahrkorps", the military transport corps which provided drivers, mechanics and motorcycle riders

**OKW:** Short for "Oberkommando der Wehrmacht", the High Command of the German Armed Forces

**Old Warrior (German "Alter Kämpfer"):** term for members of the NSDAP who joined the party before 1933

**Ostarbeiter:** A prisoner from the occupied territories of Eastern Europe, used as forced labour

**Ostjude:** Eastern European Jew

**Revoluzzer:** Derogatory name for a revolutionary

**Ritterkreuz:** The Knight's Cross of the Iron Cross, a coveted military and paramilitary medal

**RSHA:** Short for "Reichssicherheitshauptamt", the Reich Security Central Division

**Schejner Jid:** Yiddish, "a real Jew"

**SD:** Short for "Sicherheitsdienst", the SS Secret Service

**Shtreimel:** Mink hat worn by observant Jews in Eastern Europe

**Sonderausweis:** Special orders papers, issued to soldiers travelling for duty reasons

9

**Stulle:** An open sandwich

**TeNo:** Contraction of "Technische Nothilfe", a paramilitary technical emergency corps

**Verlag:** German for "publishing house"

**Zdravstvutye:** Russian, a polite "Hello" or "Good Day"

*Es brauchet aber Stiche der Fels*
*("But rock needs splitting")*

FRIEDRICH HÖLDERLIN, 'DER ISTER'

# PREFACE

Berlin, Sunday, 9 July 1944, *Deutsche Allgemeine Zeitung*

The solemn state funeral of Dr Prof. Alfred Johann Reinhardt-Thoma, who passed away suddenly in his residence on the evening of Friday, 7 July, will take place tomorrow at the Kaiser Wilhelm Institute in Dahlem.

Until 1933 head surgeon at St Jakob's hospital in Leipzig, Dr Prof. Reinhardt-Thoma was the founder and director of the Clinic for Children's Welfare and Health, a private institution in Dahlem. His wife, Dorothea Reinhardt-Thoma, née Baroness von Bora, daughter of Field Marshal Wilhelm-Heinrich von Bora, hero of the Seven Weeks' War, preceded him in death two years ago. Saskia Reinhardt-Thoma, adopted daughter of the illustrious deceased, is unable to attend due to a grave illness. His sister-in-law, Nina Baroness von Sickingen, widow of the late lamented Maestro Friedrich Baron von Bora, has arrived from her residence in Leipzig; and shortly to arrive from the front, where he is heading up an assault regiment, is her son, Lieutenant Colonel Martin-Heinz Douglas, Baron von Bora, bearer of the Knight's Cross with Oak Leaves, nephew of Dr Prof. Reinhardt-Thoma.

Honouring the departed with their presence will be His Excellency the Head of the Party Chancellery, Martin Bormann; Dr Leonardo Conti, SS Group Leader, Secretary of State for the Interior and Director of the National Health Department; the Lord Mayor of Berlin, SS Major General Ludwig Steeg; and the former Lord Mayor of Leipzig, Dr Jur. Carl Friedrich Goerdeler. Also attending will be Dr Karl Gebhardt, President of the German Red Cross and Chief Surgeon to the SS and Police; Dr Max de Crinis, Chair of Psychology and Neurology at the Friedrich Wilhelm University; and the illustrious colleagues of the departed, Drs Matthias Göring, Karl Bonhoeffer, Hans-Gerhard Creutzfeldt, Kurt Blome and Paul Nitsche, along with many others. Lieutenant General Dr Siegfried Handloser, Head of the Armed Forces Medical Service, will deliver the funeral address.

In accordance with the testamentary disposition of the late Dr Prof. Reinhardt-Thoma, no religious ceremony will follow, and no funeral procession. Burial will take place at a later date in the family plot at the Waldfriedhof Dahlem.

Born in Halle an der Saale in 1878 and educated at the universities of Leipzig, Jena and Berlin (where he also held the Chair of Internal Medicine), Dr Prof. Reinhardt-Thoma will be remembered as a star of the first magnitude in the firmament of medical research and practice. Through the many years of his distinguished career as a paediatrician, experimenter and academic, he received the highest awards in the Fatherland and abroad for his studies of congenital and perinatal malformations.

The Führer and Chancellor of the Reich, Adolf Hitler, always solicitous in remembering every comrade who has honoured the German Fatherland, sent a personal note of regret for the grave loss brought upon the family.

# 1

*Great events usually come unexpectedly,*
*and whoever expects them only delays them.*

JOSEF ROTH, HOTEL SAVOY

## APPROACH TO SCHÖNEFELD AIRPORT, NEAR TELTOW, MONDAY, 10 JULY 1944, 6:38 A.M.

The ink in his fountain pen was running low. The last sentence on his diary page was of a watery blue, and, providing that he found the needed supply for sale somewhere, Bora would have to rewrite it to make it legible. The blotting paper was hardly needed; he replaced it as a bookmark and rested the diary on his knees. He felt the aeroplane bounce through the layer of clouds as it descended. Lazily, the metal body met air pockets and seemed to let go, only to be buoyed back up. It was banking now, lining up with the runway, regaining some altitude. Then came the vibration and change in pitch of the engine at the final descent, the short racket of the landing gear coming out, the wind resisting before it gave way. The wheels touched the grassy ground with a thump.

Flying in from the Italian front, Bora considered it fortunate that there was no window from which to see the condition of the terrain traversed. He was all too aware of recent air raids, but somehow not seeing their actual results helped a little. So he had not seen the state of Berlin from the air – but soon he would have to go out and look around.

While the aeroplane taxied towards the hangar, he reread what he'd jotted down in his diary hours before, when he had anticipated reaching his destination before nightfall, as false a hope as could be had that summer. The presence of enemy fighters had forced the cargo plane to stop over in the first airfield available within German borders, and that's how it was that dawn had broken with them still in flight.

Entry begun on 9 July in a northern Italian airfield, while awaiting a flight to the Fatherland. The occasion is a sad one. Uncle Alfred's death comes as a surprise. Nina (whom I spoke to briefly by telephone, and thankfully will see soon) says she heard from him on my stepfather's birthday in June; Uncle was sixty-six, but hale as far as we knew, busy in his clinic caring for young patients shocked by the air raids, as well as for those physically wounded. The former would, in his opinion, suffer longer-lasting effects.

Civilians and soldiers use words very differently. The adverb "afterwards" is one I more and more tend to avoid. Is it superstition? In Stalingrad, one of my commanders forbade the use of the word "tomorrow" in his presence. We were under siege, and soon 84 per cent of us would fall into enemy hands, dead or prisoner – or wounded, which meant dead. Less than twenty months ago, Colonel von Guzman did not want to hear the word "tomorrow". Imagine what neologisms we had to invent, to indicate the day after. Nothing has been heard of him since. Did he fall into the meat grinder at the close of 1942? Is he languishing in a Soviet prison camp, where tomorrow truly does not exist, or – God forbid – has he joined those who have betrayed the Fatherland out of desperation or cowardice, like our own commander-in-chief on that front? That field marshal's name is truly one I refuse to write.

I do say "tomorrow", even in the harsh face of reality. I believe it will come, in some form. "The sun also rises", we read in Ecclesiastes. Whether or not I will see it matters less to me at the moment than the horn button clasping my shirt collar.

I force myself to write to my family (I am "the only one left", my mother Nina reminds me without faulting me for it, a year and a month after my brother Peter died). How can I explain to them, to Nina or to my 74-year-old stepfather, that every letter sent or received costs me a great effort, because it confirms my ties to them? No ties means freedom, because even hope is not so necessary when you are alone.

PS Added the following morning, 10 July, en route. Ink failing. I still enjoy writing to Professor Heidegger and Captain Ernst Jünger. The dialogue with them is entirely abstract, and does not hurt as much. I even received a letter from my friend Bruno Lattmann, seriously injured but thank God alive and recovering near his native Berlin. Meeting him (if at all possible), and especially Nina, is a consolation at this time of family loss.

"We made it, Colonel," the co-pilot called out to him. "But this is as close to the city as we can get, couldn't obtain clearance for Tempelhof this morning."

That they'd landed on grass, not a paved runway, Bora knew already.

"Where are we, then?"

"Schönefeld."

"I thought there were some paved runways there." Ever the counter-espionage officer, asking questions was his second nature. And Bora had a schedule to keep to.

"There are three. But they're not long enough to manoeuvre on, and this old lady will need to take off again."

"Thank you." The diary found its place inside Bora's briefcase. "It feels like a storm is coming. Is it raining outside, by any chance?"

"Why, no."

The car expected to take Bora to the south-western quarter of Dahlem was probably waiting for him in town at the civilian Tempelhof airport, kept open as an exception the night before

17

for his military flight. Now the change in schedule, with the official start of the ceremony in two hours, left little hope of securing a ride there in time, from this patch of countryside at the south-eastern edge of Greater Berlin. Bora used the telephone in the control tower to communicate his delay; it turned out that the driver assigned to him had been informed and was already motoring towards Schönefeld.

KAISER WILHELM INSTITUTE, DAHLEM, 8:55 A.M.

Bora hastened to the crowded university hall just before the authorities walked in. He barely had a moment to greet his mother before all had to rise for the Head of the Party Chancellery. Bora had frantically clasped and clipped on his medals as he stepped into the building, where someone who introduced himself as Dr Olbertz – who evidently had been waiting for him – briefly detained him. He'd only whispered a single sentence in his ear, but one that Bora couldn't get out of his head. Army and party greetings, nods, handshakes seemed strange and misplaced after hearing those words. And it still felt like a storm was brewing, when odours grow stronger and hues grow sharp, and there is an ominous sense of expectancy in the air.

The beribboned wreaths around the coffin gave out an exotic aroma, as if perfume had been sprinkled on branches and flowers that possessed no scent of their own. It was the same sweetish, artificial, sugary odour of carnival confetti. Bora breathed it in from the front row, telling himself that he was grateful to be standing side by side with his mother – much more than for the public display of a state funeral. Contravening general practice, if not etiquette, she had lifted the black mourning veil, exposing the serene firmness of her grief. It was a typical Nina-message. *I get my gutsiness from her*, he thought. Even without Olbertz's hasty, unasked-for revelation, he'd correctly and a little anxiously read the hints emerging from the newspaper article, where the list of Party guests ran longer than the dead man's biography. He hadn't expected them to mention Reinhardt-Thoma's adopted son, a resident of America for the past eight years; but pointing out the year 1933 as the end of his uncle's tenure at St Jakob's, and Saskia's tactful illness (requiring hospitalization, to be credible!) drew a picture of political unreliability. Not of disgrace, however – because you do not disgrace an acclaimed physician, whom even the Führer's "great heart" honours with a personal message.

Dr Handloser, sombre in his lieutenant general's uniform, read from a typewritten sheet, which he held up like a royal decree. "Let us bow our heads and lift our proud spirits. Let us impress our virile pain upon the great colleague, teacher and seeker – before the *medicus amabilis* who, for the benefit of science and mankind, has over three decades of dedicated work adorned the name of our German Fatherland ..."

Yes, the wreaths smelled like confetti. They seemed enormous, like great wheels leaning against the chariot of a fallen hero, actually the luxurious coffin provided for the send-off by the Association of National Socialist Physicians. In comparison, his brother's burial in Russia had been rushed and understated; these days, one learned to evaluate the political reliability – or otherwise – of the deceased by the ostentation of his funeral. To Bora's right, his meaty neck stuck in his shirt collar making him look like a mastiff about to attack, stood the Head of the Party Chancellery himself. Along the front row were lined up the Doctors Conti, Steeg, De Crinis and Göring (all of them wearing Party uniforms). Old Professor Bonhoeffer appeared moved. As for Goerdeler, who'd spoken to Nina upon his arrival, he had slipped out before the funeral oration. How far at the back of the hall stood Albrecht Olbertz, behind state officials, bureaucrats and Nazi doctors – whose whisper "Ein nicht so freier Tod" gave the lie to this day? It felt like a storm, a great storm, was coming.

"… A reverent and heartfelt gratitude stirs in all of us, his collaborators and friends, for we recognize in Alfred Reinhardt-Thoma the virtues of our race and of medical science, incarnated in the highest degree …"

"Ein nicht so freier Tod." If a "voluntary death" was the German euphemism for suicide, what was a death that came "not so freely"? Bora's well-concealed anxiety was justified. Oversized hall, massive wreaths, guests of great consequence … Things (and circumstances, and events) seemed bigger these days. Unless the opposite was true, and he simply felt crushed by all that was happening. But he honestly didn't think so. Wounds and the military situation notwithstanding, he had the same energy as always, the bold and slightly arrogant pluck his regiment put so much trust in. "I'm serving with Bora" (or "under Bora", depending on their rank) was what the men wrote home or told colleagues from other units, and "my Commander" was said with the reflected pride that all in the regiment apparently shared – except Martin Bora. For him, in the summer of 1944, along the embattled Apennines where Germany was playing her last card in Italy, such faith only added ballast to his sense of responsibility. Without ever saying it, he thought, with a dose of realism, *I'll do my best, but we cannot all be saved.*

"The foundation that bears the name of his devoted spouse, now and for ever a beacon of excellence, spurs us on to continue along the trail he so selflessly and brilliantly blazed …"

*All my men want – officers included – is reassurance. For the rest, I have no answers. Uncle Reinhardt-Thoma is dead, and a storm is coming.* It wasn't as if he no longer hoped: without hope he'd have died in Stalingrad, or by the dirt road where a partisan grenade had taken off his left hand, or when Dikta, without asking him, obtained the annulment of their marriage. Yet where did his hope come from? In the last four months, he hadn't even bothered to pray. Thirty years on earth, seven as a soldier, five spent at war. Martin Bora's hope existed as long as he didn't try to imagine a clear future for himself.

"The heavens above contain fleeting meteors and eternal, fixed stars. Our colleague, our comrade, Alfred Reinhardt-Thoma has secured his place in the immutable firmament. Alfred Reinhardt-Thoma is not dead. He lives for ever in his legacy."

Bora and his mother were separated at the end of the ceremony, as colleagues and friends flocked to them to express their formal condolences. Nina barely had time to tell him she'd been offered a ride to the Adlon, and would wait for him there. Within minutes, when the crowd and the authorities – who'd naturally been the first to take off – had left the hall, the man who had identified himself as Olbertz once more came up to him. "My apologies for approaching you earlier," he said curtly. "You don't know me, Colonel, but I used to work with your uncle. Earlier I spoke somewhat in the spur of the moment; I simply said what was on my mind … it was merely an impression."

*We, his relatives, never even entertained the possibility of suicide*, was on the tip of Bora's tongue – where it stayed. He waited courteously, but showing no friendliness, not least because the physician did not wear a uniform. This lack of a reaction must have taken Olbertz aback, because he made a curt gesture, as if impatient with himself. "What the devil – no, look, Colonel, I know for certain it was suicide. I'd spoken to your uncle just the night before."

"I see. And did my uncle express an intention to kill himself?"

"Not wholly of his own free will. This is what I feel like saying – do what you will with it. But I'll deny that I ever told you."

Again, Bora did not react. These times called for restraint. It meant watching out for traps and provocations, not responding in the way the other might expect. Grief, anger, even outrage lay out of sight, where his army intelligence work had trained him to keep them. But he could think of at least three reasons why what Olbertz said could have come about: Reinhardt-Thoma had refused Party membership, with all that it implied from 1933 on; if, thanks to his international fame, they hadn't dared to destroy his career, he was still precluded from high-ranking government posts. The other reason was that he had adopted the children of two colleagues who had died in disgrace, one of them a Jew – unacceptable in today's Germany. Years earlier, the young man in question had been shipped off to study in America, where he safely lived to this day. Incidentally, it'd be a complicated matter to inform him of the death of his adoptive father: perhaps only Grandfather Franz-August could manage it, thanks to his old contacts in the diplomatic world. Judging by Olbertz's discomfort, the third reason would be the least acceptable of them all. Bora wouldn't let himself dwell on it, because he remembered all too well a couple of uncomfortable visits at his uncle's house, after Poland. *Ballastexistenzen* – "dead-weight lives" – was a term he'd first learned then, in reference to medical practices the old man had protested against and refused to apply. Yet the highly respected physicians in attendance today, Karl Bonhoeffer and Leonardo Conti among them, theorized or supported that research. For all he knew, Olbertz might be Gestapo, or an informant, or be lying outright.

Attendants must have opened a back room behind the hall, because a draught swept across it carrying that artificial confetti smell from the wreaths around the coffin. Could it be a sign of the approaching storm? Bora cut matters short.

"Thank you, Dr Olbertz."

"Well, we'll see each other then," Olbertz grumbled just as drily, and turned his back on him.

"See each other ..." In Berlin, according to army colleagues who'd been there on furlough, the commonly accepted farewell nowadays was "Stay alive, will you?" The moment Olbertz was gone, before walking out into the street, Bora removed the Knight's Cross from around his neck, and all other medals; he only left the campaign ribbons.

Warm and sunny weather reigned over the region: "Führer weather", toadies called it, just as in the Kaiser's days they'd called it "Hohenzollern weather". In the fifth year of war, it meant that there was no storm in sight – whatever he might have felt – and gave the green light to enemy pilots. For Bora, freshly arrived from the south of Europe, the temperature was comfortable, especially in the shade of the aged linden trees in full leaf. He took the tram from Thielplatz to Leipziger Platz, from where he'd continue on foot towards the Adlon. Along the way he decided to look around, as if this were not the city he knew so well, the city where he'd attended a good part of his military schooling and met Dikta so many times. *This*, he thought, *is what it is: a place I'm visiting for the first time, over which I pass no judgement.* The details stood out even more than the massive damage to entire blocks, more than the mutilated ministries and gutted embassies, those scars he'd seen in other cities, for which German bombs were often responsible: weeds growing rank among the ruins in the summer heat, debris that had been punctiliously swept aside, glass fragments shining like icy fangs; there were vegetable gardens in lieu of flower beds, solemn cornices topping nothing, perhaps a single fallen tile, or a sea of tiles, a nakedness of sky. Last night, while waiting for the second leg of the journey, the co-pilot, a Berliner, had blandly recited a long list of what had been totally or partially destroyed. "In Mitte and the surrounding quarters it's easier to count what's still standing. We did all we could, but we couldn't ..." He stopped there. "My brother was a pilot too," Bora had told him. "Tomorrow it'll be thirteen months since he died over Kursk. I don't doubt you've done all that is in your power." During this war, there had been times when the place he found himself in got under his skin, fascinating or awing him. Spain, Poland, Russia, France, Italy. Even those few days in Crete: every front echoed in his mind, and often in his heart. Not now. Not even in Berlin. These days he moved from his command post to this or that sector along the defensive line like one who knows that he is only passing through and must neither hate nor fall in love with his surroundings. Seeing everything, closely observing the details, but passing through.

The truth was that he'd begun pulling away from things. As he pulled away, he was worried by it, because attachment to something, to someone, had kept him alive. But attachment also hurt; once you let go it'd be easier to fight, to resist, so long as you didn't necessarily expect to survive. Maintaining control was all he could do, so that others wouldn't notice – neither the teenaged soldiers who regarded him as an adult, nor the commanders in whose eyes he was still a lad. Strange that some of his colleagues still thought him agreeable: Bora felt anything but agreeable. He acted according to strict education and training, never revealing himself except in some pages of his diary, which, however, he often tore up.

12:15 P.M.

In the square where he got off the tram there was some kind of confusion. The fire service and bomb disposal troops blocked both Hermann Göring Strasse and Leipziger Strasse. They were removing, it seemed, an unexploded bomb left by the air raid from three weeks earlier. Bora had to backtrack on foot down Saarlandstrasse and around the immense block of

24

the Air Ministry – so much like an unimaginative schoolhouse built for Titans – to reach Prinz Albrecht Strasse. A minor incident that had occurred on the tram was still upsetting him, and he now had to make a detour past the infamous Gestapo building and SS headquarters into the bargain, to regain Wilhelmstrasse.

The battered parade route, lined with state buildings, had not escaped the bombs. Bora walked without focusing on anything, staring ahead, determined to keep what Olbertz had said from his mother. Why worry her? Mourning added on to mourning is like unfairly targeting a house already struck.

He'd walked beyond the courtyard of the Air Ministry, and north nearly as far as the crossroads with Leipziger Platz (at this end, too, blocked by an armed patrol), when he heard the sound of boots quickly approaching from behind. Bora was one of those whom the front line makes stoic, not excitable, and he did not turn to look. Whoever it was, he would overtake him and go past. A grip on his elbow, however, was another matter altogether: physical contact made him react immediately. It took him a pinch of fraught seconds to identify the newcomer as someone familiar, wearing the uniform of the German General Staff.

"Bora, I *thought* it was you!"

Bora had heard somewhere that Benno von Salomon had made full colonel at last. A whole year had passed since their days around Kursk. Bora saluted, and the look he gave the hand grasping his left arm was his only display of irritation. The hold was released, but the anxious quality of the approach remained.

"I urgently need to talk to you. *To talk to you*, understand?"

"But Colonel —"

"Ssh, ssh … Please, act normal."

Bora *was* acting normal. It was Salomon who was staring at him with a bewildered look, and although Bora had already seen him fight his, in the man's own words, "inner demons" in Russia, this time it wasn't fidgety nerves: it bordered on panic. A step back created enough space between them to make Bora feel more comfortable.

"What is it, Colonel? What happened?" he asked, although for some reason he doubted that he wanted to know.

Once more Salomon hung on his arm, which downright annoyed Bora.

"Let's walk. Walk on this side. Let's cross. Act normal. There, to Kaiserhofstrasse." They did cross the street in that direction, but Bora failed to see why. The ruins were high as hills on the other side; of the once imposing Hotel Kaiserhof, only a gutted shell remained – landfill material, with its scalloped entrance canopy hanging down, smashed and empty. The gilded lettering on the lone-standing front wall had about as little to do with an "imperial court" as the street and the establishment that had once borne that name. On the other side of the road, beheaded young trees were nothing but stumps.

"Quick, Bora, answer me: are you familiar with the full meaning of the word 'oath', of the concept of *loyalty*?"

Bora could hardly believe his ears. It was out of place here and now, but it wasn't the obviousness of the answer that troubled him: those emphases did.

"Yes, of course."

"They are not unambiguous, you know. There isn't just one kind of loyalty. That is precisely what complicates the lives of men, of officers … of us all. In the end, they are nothing but words."

*I studied philosophy – don't try to teach me nominalism,* Bora thought. The moment that principles decay into simple verbal expressions, a moral danger awaits. He didn't answer, because an opinion doesn't necessarily demand an answer. He realized that his silence might make him appear like a young politicized officer, something he wasn't, or was only in part. But he had no sympathy for unconcealed fear. Stepping aside, he freed himself of Salomon's hold.

"I need to —" The dog-faced former lawyer stopped in mid-sentence, squinting in the sun. He didn't tan, even at the height of summer; Bora remembered that detail about him. Today, if anything, he looked green. "I must speak to you."

Bora tried not to stare. It was undeniable: he felt a change in the weather, as he had in Ukraine in the summer of Kursk, when citadels of dark clouds rose so far away on the horizon that they seemed harmless, though the atmosphere was nevertheless already electric, as if saturated with lightning. The fact that he was now facing his former commander without encouraging him to speak would either keep the man from embarking on uncomfortable confessions, or else push him to hasten and speak at length.

Salomon wiped the perspiration from his upper lip with a starched handkerchief, and when he tried to put it away he at first missed the pocket in his breeches. The General Staff officer's red band on them, Bora knew from his Roman experience, meant both privilege and limitations. Occasionally risk, if one was ready to take it.

"I absolutely must speak to you in private, Bora. When did you arrive? How long will you be in Berlin? Where are your rooms?"

A lie was better than a partial truth. "I don't know yet where I'll billet. I'm only here for a matter of hours, so it's better if we speak now, Colonel. We're in the open, there's no one around; it seems like a safe place."

"No. Not here. And 'safety' is only a string of meaningless letters."

More nonsense. It was impossible for Bora not to take his turn to ask the obvious.

"Are you feeling well, sir?"

"I've been throwing up three days in a row. Worse than in '41." The starched handkerchief surfaced again. "You be the judge."

Given the premise, the least advisable thing for Bora to do would be to ask if there was anything he could do. He remained silent, trying to understand where Salomon's personal exhaustion ended and a real threat began. With a man like him it could be anything, from a private little scandal to a shameful disease, to the most unthinkable extremes for a war-weary German officer in 1944, which Bora did not even want to graze with thought. Those summer storms in Ukraine returned to mind, the way you couldn't ignore the coming of bad weather. *Please tell me what it's all about,* he was on the point of urging.

The colonel saved him the effort. "I was approached by Fritz-Dietlof von der Schulenburg."

Those few apparently neutral words, pronounced in a strangled, low voice, put Bora on high alert. As far back as 1941, he'd been warned (in Crete, of all places) about the left-leaning Schulenburgs; Fritz-Dietlof was serving as governor of Lower and Upper Silesia in those days, and his father as ambassador in Moscow. He'd had orders to monitor their telephone calls at the embassy. Had he not – rather coincidentally – been expelled from the Soviet Union, he'd have done just that.

"… The younger Count von der Schulenburg heard your name from Colonel Claus von Stauffenberg. It's a godsend, meeting you here today."

Time to put his foot down. "Forgive me, sir: for what reason would Colonel von Stauffenberg mention my name to Fritz-Dietlof von der Schulenburg? I don't know either of them in person. Claus von Stauffenberg and I only met once, during a sporting competition years ago."

"You're aware he is the deputy commander of the Reserve Army?"

"I am, Colonel, but still fail to see why he should mention me to Count von der Schulenburg or anyone else, or why the fact seems to trouble you."

Pink dust rose from the spectral Kaiserhof, as a brick noiselessly fell from a window frame. Salomon provided no answer.

"I'm staying at the Adlon – or at least I was until this morning. You too, right? I heard your lady mother has rooms there as well."

"Your lady mother ..." These old-fashioned niceties, so out of place in a street that looked like the moon. Bora acted no less inscrutably than he'd done with Olbertz. "As I say, I'm due to leave Berlin very soon, Colonel. Please, if there is anything private or urgent you wish to share with me, do it now. I am in a hurry."

"No, no. I am not going to tell you here, not going to tell you now. Leave it be. This evening ... You're not leaving before tonight, are you?"

"I believe not."

"I'll find you."

Bora watched him hasten down the street towards what remained of the Trinity church, zigzagging like a hare before the fox. This, on top of everything else. Just what he needed, now that he was back in Berlin for the first time in years. Returning for a death in the family, he had found the city in this state, they'd sprung on him the news that his uncle might have been forced to commit suicide, and, as if that weren't enough, his former commander on the Russian front seemed close to mental collapse. It made him even more impatient to see his mother, because she, too, would be leaving soon, as soon as a train could set off with a modicum of safety towards the south-west, and the city of Leipzig.

Bora gloomily continued past destruction old and new; right and left, what the bombs of 8 March had not accomplished in the quarter, those fallen on 21 June had. Hardly a ministry survived intact, not to speak of the two Chancellery buildings; and it'd been more than a year since St Hedwig's – the Catholic church attended by the Bora family when they were in Berlin – had burned to the ground.

## HOTEL ADLON, PARISER PLATZ, 1:10 P.M.

The Adlon, at least, was still standing. The bricked-up ground floor, a solid wall that completely obliterated its famous glazed archways, gave it the appearance of a graceless Chinese fortress, set in a sea of ruins. Were the smiling stucco masks that had once decorated the arches still there, behind the bricks? This was another place it was safer to look at as if it were for the first time, given the memories of Dikta for ever associated with it. At the beginning of the war (while Bora underwent Abwehr training, and later guest-lectured at the Military Academy), boys and girls seeking autographs used to gather by the entrance to the hotel. Avid readers of *Signal* and *Der Adler*, they collected the autographed likenesses of the most successful flyers, and of soldiers decorated with the coveted Knight's Cross. Like poker players, they leafed through photographic postcards and spied on the officers entering and leaving the Adlon. Photos were worth more, apparently, if those portrayed later died a hero's death. Bora had grown to loathe the myth. It irritated him that, when he'd received the *Ritterkreuz* in Kiev, they'd published an article about it in all the Leipzig dailies. But it was hard to avoid, with a grandfather who was a publisher – if for no other reason than that the journalists wanted to please him. A gentleman, his stepfather preached, should appear in a newspaper only at birth and when he dies.

These days, there was no demand for autographs; few school-age girls were in sight, only a handful among them reasonably well dressed; and even these wore outfits too short or too tight for them, to which lace hems and cuffs had been added to make them last another season. Bora was struck by seeing these Berlin women wear whatever they could, even evening-gown material, satin and other shiny fabrics. But then, a quarter of them no longer had a roof over their heads, let alone a wardrobe. Among those he'd noticed from the tram, walking or in queues outside shops and warehouses, the harlots stood out like tropical birds. Silk or nylon stockings, high heels, a brief glimpse of a lacy underskirt as they climbed onto a bus – the pretty arsenal so favoured by men (Bora included) was now all too often seen on girls who brazenly passed their tongue over their teeth after touching up the rouge on their lips. His stepfather disparagingly spoke of the "whorement" – a word of his own making – of French girls during the Great War; at that time he was already a Catholic convert, and – newly bigoted – pining for the young widow Bora, who took her time before saying yes to remarriage. To General Sickingen, all women, save his wife and sisters, were potential whores.

Was that what it was? Though he had spent a good part of his life in army barracks and at the front, "whore" was a word Bora seldom used: perhaps because he thought that you couldn't apply such a term to a woman if there wasn't at least one man on the scene.

Inside, despite its dimness, all in all the hotel still gave an impression of sophistication. The concierge was the same from his stays with Dikta – only greyer, with the disenchanted, resolute look of a skipper whose ship may be sinking but who would never haul down the flag. He remembered Bora; his greeting had that special quality of recognition devoid of servility, and was impeccable. Each was quietly surprised that the other hadn't died in the meantime. With a soldierly nod, the man answered Bora's enquiry by saying that yes, Baroness Sickingen was in. Should he phone her room?

"Yes, please."

"Your key, sir."

The fact that he had been provided with a car at the airport (albeit the wrong one) and a bed at Berlin's premier hotel courtesy of the Interior Ministry was so out of the ordinary that Bora began to think it might truly betray a concerted attempt to make Reinhardt-Thoma's death appear natural.

"Please advise me as soon as there's a call for me from the Schönefeld airfield," he said.

The Blue Room, once so brightly lit, looked rather drab, despite the wall sconces doing what they could to make up for the obscured French windows. It was there that Bora paced the floor as he waited for his mother. At the funeral, they'd merely stood side by side; but this was a *meeting*: there was no avoiding the difficult chasm created by Peter's death, the mutilation. It had to be bridged somehow.

Nina found him in the middle of the room, where he stopped at once and turned to greet her. She walked up to him; he clicked his heels and kissed her hand. Those formal steps were necessary for him to let go enough to embrace her. Thankfully, the looks they gave each other sufficiently expressed what would have been too hard to say with words. Nina couldn't help but ask, "How are you, Martin?" He promptly answered "Fine", and she did not persist. What followed were a few solicitous phrases, the sharing of news expected in those circumstances. How things were at home – and, yes, how suddenly Uncle Reinhardt-Thoma had been taken from them. Words floated like useless debris over real feelings. For Bora it was very sad seeing her in black, for Peter and now for his uncle too.

She led the way to a small table where the graceful armchairs were those of old, making this meeting in a bombed-out city less absurd.

"They've told me that the burial will take place as soon as possible," she said. "At night, along with those of others."

Briefly, the mirrored squares above the fireplace reflected her slender neck and shoulders as she walked past, and for a moment it was as if her delicate double were crossing a phantom room next door. "I must go to see Saskia next, if I can."

"I'll go with you."

"Best if I go on my own, Martin. Frau Sommer, your uncle's secretary, is coming to fetch me in half an hour, and will accompany me to the Wilmersdorf hospital. Saskia is in the infectious diseases ward, you know."

Bora, who was standing a few feet away from her, went to the door and closed it.

"Why, what's wrong?"

"I imagine it was the only way she could think of to avoid attending the funeral. Times have not been easy for them lately."

This would have been the right moment for Bora to report Olbertz's gossip, but he decided against it; he sensed that Nina had herself heard something whispered by the nurses, which she was keeping from him for the same reason. He hoped to capitalize on the little time he had with his mother in Berlin, but he understood that there were things she had to take care of in Dahlem.

She sat down, inviting him to do the same.

"Martin, before the funeral Dr Goerdeler entrusted me with a message for you."

"Did he?"

Bora wouldn't usually admit to being surprised, but in this case he could afford to. Nina was discretion itself. Like her small handbag, her gloves, the light touch of face powder, everything about her derived its elegance from understatement.

"Yes. Tonight at nine you're to report to the office of Arthur Nebe, chief of the Criminal Police." She drew a small breath. "Carl-Friedrich was not concerned, so I believe it may be routine ..."

This time Bora found it difficult to stay impassive. *Routine? How can it be routine that the head of the Kripo – who, incidentally, is also a general in the SS and presides over the International Criminal Police Commission – is summoning me?*

"Did he say anything else, Nina?"

"Only not to worry, and to use the service entrance."

It made less and less sense. If his mother was frightened (and she might well be), she was concealing it for his sake. Bora, too, kept his composure.

"Very well. We'll see what Group Leader Nebe wants."

In fact, his heart was in his mouth, especially after meeting Salomon. He knew about Nebe from the days of Einsatzgruppe B and its death squads in the East. It did not give him any pleasure to march into his office of his own accord. He wished that he could tell himself that he hadn't got himself in any trouble, but it'd be a lie – although the trouble he had got himself into fell under the Gestapo's oversight, not the Criminal Police's. The one element that reassured him a little was the messenger: Carl-Friedrich Goerdeler, a former official who wasn't in the Party's good graces. If Nebe had entrusted the message to him instead of one of his uniformed thugs, there was a reason for it. Olbertz's whispered words came back to him; and although he didn't share them with his mother, he did say: "It could have some-thing to do with Uncle, Nina. If his clinic and residence are still standing, who knows, perhaps there was an attempted break-in overnight."

"Do you suppose so? Maybe."

They were sitting in such a way that, by slightly leaning forwards, they could have reached for each other's hand; but Bora would not initiate such a contact, which might undo the effort Nina was clearly making to control her emotions. They sat and looked at each other – she treasuring him, he treasuring her, but aware that even now, even in her presence, he was pulling away from things. He forced him-self to keep to polite topics: enquiring about his stepfather, the General (whom Nina referred to as "your father"), his grandparents' health, Peter's wife and the baby, bombed-out friends staying at the family home in Borna … It surprised him to hear that his sister-in-law had moved out of the house on Birkenstrasse.

"She returned to her parents' place in Esterwegen, Martin."

"Ah. It's safer, in the countryside out west."

"True."

"And the Bora Verlag's Berlin branch … ?"

Nina removed her gloves without haste, resting them in her lap together with the small handbag. "As we expected, the June raid completely destroyed the office in the Zeitungsviertel, and Grandfather Franz-August's townhouse has been badly hit. But the printing facilities out in Potsdam are still functioning. Leopardi's *opera omnia* is coming out next month, with a preface by the poet Ungaretti."

"Ungaretti, right. He's teaching in Italy now, isn't he?"

"In Rome, I believe."

Bora nodded. He found it difficult to relax his shoulders or look away from her. "Pulling away from things" offered no absolute protection from pain. From one moment to the next, words could feel insubstantial or unbearably heavy, easy or entirely impossible to pronounce. The fuller the heart is, the less it is able to empty itself. Oddly, the more distanced he felt, the more beautiful his mother appeared to him – a compliment Bora wasn't able to pay her; he feared that whatever he said would only hurt her. Especially if he asked about her grief. His brother's death was another reason for him not to talk about himself.

"Make sure you give my love to Saskia."

"Of course."

"And ask her if she needs anything."

"I will."

His own wounds, the end of his marriage, knowing that he was politically at risk, seemed paltry compared to the loss that Nina, that everyone in the family, had experienced. *She has lost one of her two sons, and I will for ever be "the other one" – I became "the other one" when it happened, and will always be the one who should have died instead of Peter. If I cannot forgive myself for it, how can my parents forgive me?* The thought overwhelmed him, and Bora braced himself against his emotions. He was seldom moved to tears, and the fact that it'd happened in Rome, weeks earlier, filled him with shame, even though it had been brought about by extreme stress and anguish. If he remembered correctly, his mother had last seen him weep when he was maybe twelve years old. It amazed him that *she* wasn't crying; he believed that his sitting here, while Peter was dead, must be intolerable for her. *If I'd been the one to die they would still be a complete family – father, mother, son. Now we are two families – my mother and the General, my mother and myself – doubly mutilated.*

"Have you heard from our friends in East Prussia lately, Nina?"

"Not directly. One of the Modereggers wrote that they're all well."

When Nina opened the handbag to put away her gloves, he caught a brief glimpse of a dainty cigarette case inside it. She never used to smoke, so she was clearly contravening one of the General's diktats about healthy living. Bora liked her even more for it.

Here they sat, the relatives of a man whom the regime may have destroyed, while a bomb from an aeroplane was being defused a few blocks away and with a summons from Arthur Nebe for tonight, and he was courteously enquiring about friends. *Well, we all protect ourselves as best we can. She is waiting for me to say something, and knows I can't, so she waits without prompting me.* Bora looked at his mother's hands with admiration and a sense of gratitude, of comfort. She rarely wore jewels, and this was neither the place nor the time to put on a display. On her right hand she only wore her wedding band and an ancient family ring, the same one she'd intended to give Dikta the day of her church wedding to Bora. The General, who'd never approved of the match, had forbidden it. Now Bora wondered why she'd given in to him that time, since his mother was not the sort of woman who took imposition lightly. *It's because she didn't care for Dikta either. Even in this I let her down, just as I did by not having children with my wife ...* Then he realized – and it was a raw awakening – that Nina might have known about Dikta's abortions and never told him. *If the General had found out he'd have thrown it in my face, like he did in Krakow five years ago when he spoke ill of Dikta's behaviour before she met me. If he hadn't already been aboard the train then, I don't know if I could have controlled myself. I held a grudge against him for months, and in truth I still do today. Yes, Nina must have known of the abortions, or at least she'd suspected. When she wrote to me before Stalingrad that "Dikta isn't feeling well", it was because she was pregnant. Of course. And since nothing came of it she must have suspected that, unless she had suffered a miscarriage, Dikta had chosen not to carry the child to term. Dikta herself told me all about it in Rome – so that it'd be the final blow, the one that would make me break away from her, set her free. So now she is free, and I'm not.*

Bora contemplated his mother with a humiliating need to admit his pain, one he would not give in to. *"The fuller the heart is …" Whatever happens, whatever today's strange meetings portend, I'm heading back to the front after this; let's face it, we may not see each other again in this life.* He used the same arguments on himself that he employed as an interrogator on captured enemies, which all came down to variations on "You had better start talking now."

Above the fireplace – which had been blocked, so that smoke and debris from air raids would not come down the chimney – the mirrored tiles reflected the opposite wall. Above them, reaching nearly to the stuccoed ceiling, a painted scene showed two girls reclining in an impossibly idyllic landscape. Bora looked at the delicate décor, and kept avoiding the heart of the matter between them. Finally, he said – as one who begins to acknowledge the necessity of getting to the centre, but starts at the furthest point of the spiral – "Somehow I was sure that Peter's wife would stay with you. I hope Dikta's leaving had nothing to do with it; I realize how close the two of them were." It was another way of saying, "I hope Dikta was not a bad influence on her, at least in your eyes."

"The girls were close," Nina agreed. Too tactful to add a comment, she did use the moment to say, without looking directly at him, "A few months ago, when you wrote to me and asked me to, I did ask your wife, 'Do you love him?' At first Benedikta just smiled. You know her smile. Then she answered, 'Of course.' 'But enough to have children by him?' I insisted. 'Nina, I don't think we're ready to have children.' 'Martin is.' 'I'm not. But I do love him. Do *you* love your husband?'"

Bora was painfully jarred by finding himself so suddenly at the spiral's core – another reaction that he strove to conceal. He said something under his breath, and when Nina's glance indicated that she hadn't caught his words, he repeated, "A disrespectful comment on her part," as if her impertinence had been the centre of the spiral all along and he could now simply back out of it again.

"That was Benedikta, Martin. Then, in September, when you were wounded in the ambush, it was the last straw as far as she was concerned. She was even more distraught than during the Stalingrad days, because you were so severely injured. I was hoping they'd repatriate you. But your father informed me that you'd asked not to be, that you'd chosen to be hospitalized in Italy, and added, 'He's right. He's a soldier, he doesn't want to risk being returned to Germany and being reassigned to a desk. I understand him, and support him.' Then Benedikta told us quite plainly that it could not go on like this, and that she'd already started the paperwork for an annulment. In fact, that was the reason for her forthcoming journey to Rome. 'I already wrote to him,' she said. 'Martin knows why I'll be there, and it's better this way.' Your father became so enraged, he slapped her."

"He should have never done that."

Nina absent-mindedly passed her fingers along her cuff, as if smoothing over Bora's criticism. "But as we now know, the letter did not reach you. The rest – we are sadly familiar with."

"Yes, we are."

He'd stepped out of the spiral again, having avoided the centre. But then Nina – whether because she now felt able to speak more freely or because she was seeking to distract him – admitted: "We are having some difficulties with Margaretha at the moment, your father and I."

Ah, yes, Duckie was moving out of her in-laws' home, where both women had spent their married lives. Was there more to it? Nina and the General seldom called their young wives by their nicknames, like they did their sons: thus Dikta remained Benedikta, and Duckie was Margaretha. Bora jumped at the chance to forget the topic of his failed marriage.

"How so?"

"She has changed so much since Peter was shot down over Russia. Grief, bitterness. She has *soured*, Martin."

Nina looked down. Bora had the brightness of his eyes from her; he saw himself in her act of dimming them quickly, to shield herself, as if she felt responsible for the behaviour of those around her – another trait she and he shared.

"Margaretha is … Oh, it's become quite difficult to relate to her. For the first six months after her little girl was born, she spent entire days in bed with the curtains drawn. She was angry at the world, at all of us. Since this spring, she has been seeing one of Peter's former squadron colleagues, who is on an assignment at headquarters." Bora wanted to ask, *Is that the problem?*, but his mother anticipated him: "It is understandable. I know, I have been a young widow myself. But those were other times, there were different rules: even in mourning, time moved more slowly."

"Not now," Bora said. "Is there anything I can do?"

"No, my dear. Anyway, that isn't the problem. She is free to do with her life as she wishes, after Peter. The fact is, Margaretha always wanted everything to be rosy for the two of them. She expected it. Her sweetness depended on the continuation of their love story. Because they were so much in love, you know. We were awaiting Peter in Leipzig for the birth,

and then …" Nina straightened her back, facing the recollection. "I can never thank Benedikta enough for the role
she played when you called from Russia with the terrible
news, thirteen months ago. The women were down in the
garden – the birth was only days away – and it was enough
for your father, distraught as he was, to look at Benedikta
from the window, for her to understand that disaster had
struck, and that it concerned Margaretha. She was able to
put on a good face, I don't know how, and in her sensible
way convince her sister-in-law to go out for a long walk.
She did this so that we would have time to grieve alone for
an hour or two without her knowing. And so Margaretha
found out only a month later when all the risks had passed,
concerning her health or the baby's."

"I didn't know."

"In the weeks after the incident Benedikta was superb.
She was such a help to me, Martin. She kept the secret by
telling Margaretha that all furloughs had been cancelled,
and thus capably kept her away from your father, who was
silent and withdrawn."

She always knew how to say the right thing. Bora stared
at the floor.

"Benedikta hasn't told you this?"

"No."

"I am sorry the two of you are no longer together."

Hearing it made Bora utterly grateful, and it nearly
broke his resolve. To say that he was sorry about it, too, was
impossible. The subject caused him physical discomfort; she
noticed it, and fell silent. If he had been in a better condition
of spirit, he'd have mentioned Mrs Murphy in Rome – his
crush on a married woman who'd said no but understood,
and he knew that she understood him, and this consoled
him against all hope; although, rationally, he knew it was an
infatuation that could have no future.

"I also have to tell you, because you must have been

wondering: before Stalingrad, her symptoms were so similar to Margaretha's ... and, well, Margaretha *was* pregnant. After Benedikta's trip abroad with her mother, the symptoms had gone. Young women's health is capricious; you understand that it was not enough to assume ... and then Peter's wife demanded most of our attention. While you were in Stalingrad, I simply could not ..."

"Thanks for not telling me then, Nina."

It was minutes before their attention was recalled by a discreet knock on the door. Not a bellhop, but the concierge himself, captain of the brave ship *Adlon*, cracked the door open to announce that a Frau Sommer was here for the Baroness.

"Thank you," Nina said. "I will be with her in a moment."

Bora sprang to his feet and offered to escort his mother to the car, to prolong their meeting for as much as he could. In the hotel lobby, about to walk out into the glare of day, she hesitated and turned to face him. In her native English, she said in a small voice, "Your father warned me not to ask, but – he did not suffer, did he?" Which meant: "Please tell me that Peter did not suffer."

How she must have longed to ask for the past half hour, but spoken about her living son instead ... For her, Bora would have lied in the face of death.

"He did not suffer, Nina. He really did not. You don't suffer when such things happen."

She was careful not to glance at the gloved fist that had replaced his left hand. "But you must have, terribly."

"If I did, I forgot." It was true that he did not recall the pain of the incident itself, but it'd been unbearable at the hospital, in the days that followed. Playing down personal hurt was something Bora had been taught at home, so she might not believe him.

"Will I see you later today, Nina?" Which meant: *Please, I need to see you again. We haven't said everything yet.*

Nina came close to smiling, a way she had with her eyes rather than her lips.

"I will be back before six."

Bora waited on the pavement until the Volkswagen motor car – provided by the Charité hospital and driven by Frau Sommer, his uncle's trusted secretary for the past twenty years and more – had disappeared from view. He'd always been protective of his mother, but not nearly as demonstrative in his affection as Peter. His brother had been a hugger, which annoyed the General but probably made Nina glad. Inhibition was a mistake when life turned precarious, Bora realized: he couldn't help his reserve, but looked forward to sitting with her before they parted ways again.

The Adlon lift was out of order, so he decided to climb the stairs to his room after asking the concierge to place a phone call to the Beelitz sanatorium for him. "I'll take it upstairs," he told them. As he left the desk, he had the impression that the man had paused when he'd noticed the absence of a wedding ring, betrayed by a pale thin circle against his tanned skin. Or maybe not. Bora was self-conscious about it, because the last time he'd spent the night at the hotel with Dikta they were still married.

The long flights of steps notwithstanding, the knee he'd injured during the partisan attack did not hurt. Bora gingerly climbed the stairs. The dry, distinct odour of freshly pressed sheets and towels hovered in the stairwell. Given the intermittence of the electricity supply, the luxurious hotel must have resuscitated the use of charcoal irons. It was the same toasty odour of the large room behind the kitchen at Borna, of the farmhouses in Trakehnen. A faint signal from the past, recalling that there had been peace once and, God willing, would be again. Bora was not in a recollecting mood and had no desire to consider the toll that peace would exact, being among those who had paid for it in advance.

One more floor, and he had reached the hallway of his meetings with Dikta – for years her mother had kept a suite here, rarely occupied but always ready. It was here that she'd rendezvoused with SS Colonel Tilo Schallenberg before her divorce; it was here that Bora and Dikta had, God knows how many times ... He blotted out the thought, hastening up the next flight of stairs.

Around the doorknob of the room next to the one assigned to him, a sign read "Do not disturb", and a pair of officer's riding boots of excellent workmanship waited nearby to be picked up and shined to a mirror. Japanese, Bora guessed, by their size and style. He noiselessly let himself into his room. Just inside, so close to the threshold that he stepped on it, a folded piece of paper (no envelope) lay on the floor. Even before sweeping it up and unfolding it, the certainty of its origin provoked him.

In his punctilious solicitor's language, Salomon was urging him to keep the evening free, "as agreed this morning".

*I never agreed to anything.* Bora seethed. In Russia, it'd been Salomon's habit to demand his company for dinner or even late into the night, because he was bored and an insomniac and wanted to lament the loss of his family home in East Prussia. More than once, Bora struggled not to fall asleep while hearing the tale of Polish infamy during the Great War, because – unlike his commander – he had to be up and at the Russians at dawn.

*I'll give a piece of my mind to the concierge for blabbing my room number to him.* Bora prepared to jot down a note to have placed in the colonel's pigeonhole, claiming previous commitments and the limited time he had in Berlin, all too aware that – whatever the time of his return from Kripo headquarters (assuming that he would return, though one never knew) – Salomon was likely to pester him into the morning hours. In a capital city where refugees huddled in every available space, he'd even have risked leaving his comfortable hotel quarters, if he hadn't been so firmly set on seeing Nina off in the morning. Only the firing squad (or a carpet-bombing) could keep him from that commitment.

It was only after taking out his fountain pen that he recalled that he had no ink left in it. Mindful that using his notebook pencil to write to a superior contravened military etiquette, he resolved to wait for the phone call and then borrow a pen at the desk downstairs.

Within minutes, he was speaking to the head nurse at the Beelitz sanatorium. She confirmed that Major Bruno Lattmann was indeed still a patient there. "If time really represents such a constricting factor for the colonel," she added, "a call outside visiting hours is possible." Bora confirmed that he expected to leave Berlin by mid-morning the following day at the latest, and offered to come at once; *how* to accomplish it was another matter. Beelitz lay at a good distance from the centre of Berlin.

Public transport was regular, but punctuality was not. Taxis were hard to come by, low on fuel and unlikely to commit to long drives. Bora had noticed that, in addition to ration books, people carried colour-coded cards for every facility and service – and this was not an occupied country, where you could commandeer what you needed. The front line spoils you, that way. It was true, as he had heard from the co-pilot, that ready cash gave access to most goods – from bottles of French wine jealously kept in the cellars of restaurants and hotels, to supplies stacked in military depots, all the way to the most exclusive brothels. And if, officially, army intelligence – the Abwehr – had melted like snow in the sun after its disbandment by the Gestapo months earlier, Bora still had a few friends in the "shop" he could count on.

He set aside his concern about Salomon's hysteria and the worrisome police summons; his next step was to call up the concierge and instruct him to secure a bouquet of roses ("Best if they're red, at least twenty-four") and have it arranged in his mother's room. Also to dig up "a bottle of high-quality Russian vodka and blue Pelikan ink for a fountain pen" in the next half hour. The concierge expressed no surprise at the requests: this *was* the Adlon. Now came the trickiest part: Bora phoned an old Abwehr colleague presently serving as liaison officer in the Air Ministry: "How are you? It's Martin Bora. If I make it on my own as far as Dahlem, what do I need to do to get hold of a quick transport to the Beelitz sanatorium?"

That done, he again called the concierge. "Make it *two* bottles of high-quality Russian vodka."


2:40 P.M.

Thirty-five minutes later – and although he hadn't eaten since he'd grabbed a bite the previous night, before the last leg of his flight to Berlin – Bora decided to skip lunch in order to visit Bruno Lattmann. At the desk, he heard that all the requested items except for the blue ink were available.

"As for the bouquet, the best that could be done was twelve 'Crimson Glory' rosebuds, Lieutenant Colonel, greenhouse-raised here in town. I took the liberty of requesting the addition of twelve red peonies."

The concierge laid a sealed envelope, bearing his name and rank typewritten in red ink, on the counter. "And this came for you, sir."

Bora stepped away from the desk to open the envelope, angry at what he assumed was a second message from Salomon. "Did you give my room number to any of the guests?" he asked, looking over his shoulder.

"Why no, sir."

But the Gestapo had up-to-date lists of the hotel residents, of course, as well as informers among the waiters, valets and chambermaids. Names and indiscretion were other things ready cash could buy.

The note, on a sheet from which the upper segment containing the letterhead had been removed, consisted of two typed lines, simple but enough to cause concern: *It is necessary. At least come to terms with it philosophically, and good luck.* The signature was only a capital G. Bora folded the sheet and replaced it in its envelope with pretended unconcern. *Has to be Goerdeler,* he told himself. *What's got into his head, that he should first approach my mother and then send an obscure note of this sort? What is supposed to be "necessary"? For me to undergo police interrogation? Thank you very much; it's a blow on the chin as far as I'm concerned, and anything but necessary.*

"Who delivered the message?" he asked the concierge.

The man shook his head. "I am mortified. It must have been posted by hand in your pigeonhole while I was personally checking the quantity and quality of the flower arrangement before sending it up."

Bora's friend at the Air Ministry was better than his word. In the habit of considering out-of-the-blue requests by colleagues as indicative of urgency, counter-intelligence officers went out of their way to anticipate the callers' needs. Bora was walking to the underground stop with two vodka bottles wrapped in tissue paper inside his briefcase, when an unprepossessing grey-blue car with a young airman at the wheel pulled in alongside him. "Lieutenant Colonel von Bora, bound for the Beelitz Heilstätte? Please climb in, sir."

The road to the sanatorium was the same as the old route that led to Leipzig, leaving to its left the Wannsee villas and the citadel of the film studio at Babelsberg, the lakes and artificial rivers formed by the Havel. Flies, gnats and other small insects flew to their deaths against the windscreen, leaving streaks of yellow and red. South of the city, the countryside had for decades been honeycombed by artillery ranges, army training grounds, landing strips and convalescent homes, now joined by High Command offices relocated from the bombed-out

Berlin quarters. The army, and until not long ago the Abwehr, lay in the relative safety of parks and leafy copses, disguised as rural holiday homes and farms.

When the driver, who was voluble for a private, informed him that he would have to return the vehicle to the ministry by 6:30 p.m., Bora answered that he understood. He recognized the excited, empty chatter as a side effect of amphetamine use – Pervitin or another brand – common fare among flyers for the battling of fatigue from long hours in the air, and of fear. It made him indulgent, though in other circumstances he'd have confronted the airman over his drivel. He lent an uninterested ear to the man's pointing out of this and that villa, owned by film actresses, members of the government, high-ranking officers. In its uselessness, the prattle had a calming effect on his nerves. Occasionally, craters that spoiled the young woods and were readily filled with rainwater marked the spots where bombs had missed their target or were discharged by enemy planes returning to their bases.

At Michendorf they turned off the highway and headed west.

# 2

*He who enters the smokestack should not mind the smoke.*

GERMAN PROVERB

## BEELITZ SANATORIUM, 3:45 P.M.

In his striped pyjamas, Lattmann did not look well; he'd lost weight, the tendons showed on his once bull-like neck, and freckles stood out like stains on his fair skin. His foul-mouthed sense of humour, however, was unchanged. When Bora asked about his wound ("Fucking sniper bullet through the lung on my last day in Russia"), he described in detail how "close to kicking the bucket" he'd come: "They clung on to me by my red hair, Martin, and with my cropped head it wasn't easy. Thank you so much for coming. What are you doing here in Berlin? How long are you staying?"

"A relative's state funeral; it's a few hours' stay."

About himself, Bora added nothing. He handed the vodka to his friend and sat down across from him in the great turn-of-the-century hall. In other days, the smell of cleaning fluids and alcohol and the quality of screened daylight would have affected him. Now he acknowledged them with a level-headed lack of reaction, convinced as he was that showing nothing might eventually become *feeling* nothing. Lattmann looked him up and down, stood the vodka bottle up on his knee and turned it slowly. His eyes fixed on Bora's prosthesis. He wouldn't let him get away with silence. "So, what else are *you* keeping from me?"

Bora kept mum. He turned to the windows overlooking the garden. There, in a wheelchair, sat a man whose legs had been amputated above the knee. The man was staring grouchily in this direction, as if envious of a physical loss that must seem minor to him, so Bora returned his attention to Bruno Lattmann.

"Dikta left five months ago."

"Ah, blast. That's too bad." Trying not to appear too intrusive, Lattmann pretended to read the Cyrillic label on the bottle. "I suppose it's indelicate to ask how it came about."

"You know we never even set up house together." Bora stretched his legs and crossed them at the ankles. "We told each other we weren't made for domesticity, but perhaps in the end we were happy with what we gave each other."

"Well, did you ever do anything together, aside from shagging?"

"When there was time. But it's true that we essentially remained lovers. Dikta reminded me of it in Rome, when she came for the annulment in February."

"Is she stupid, or what?"

"She's not stupid, and I have my faults. When we met nine years ago, we were young."

"You were *too* young. You're barely thirty now."

"Thirty-one in three months. Anyhow, we kept taking and leaving each other. It was only after my return from Spain that we became serious about it. She grew tired of me, I think."

"And you of her?"

"I don't know. Look, Bruno, I'll tell you about it some other time." Bora smirked as casually as he could. "Would you believe that this morning a Berliner actually got up to offer me his seat on the tram? I couldn't blow my top because the gentleman was twice my age and meant well, but Christ almighty, I'm not crippled."

Nurses were within earshot, so they didn't engage in conversation of a more serious nature.

"You tell *me*," Lattmann groaned. "I sit here all day. Doctors won't let me as much as walk around, because a fragment of the bullet is still there, too near the heart for comfort. Sooner or later they'll operate. From now on, at best it's home service for me, and not necessarily in a uniform. Bothers me a little. But I'm not like you, I've had enough of the front line. The wife, of course, is ecstatic — Oh, sorry."

"No, no. I'm glad to hear about Eva. Your two children …?"

"Three. We finally got the little girl she wanted. All well. Out in the suburbs, the only real problems are those arsehole refugees who fill your home and don't even know how to flush a toilet, and those who roam at night – escaped POWs and other runaways, plus your horny foreign workers. I'm teaching Eva how to use a handgun."

Bora sympathized. *Dikta and I too would have three children now, if things had gone the right way.* But would that have been the right way? He was surprised to find that the pain was no longer lacerating, like that of a fresh wound – more like the lingering pain from a hard blow. Ever since Dikta had left him, his soul had felt bruised.

Once the nurses moved away, the superficial chat between colleagues was no longer necessary. Jealously cradling the bottle, Lattmann said, "This liquor must have cost you. The last one we shared – where was it? Borovoy? I'm sorry we lost sight of each other. Lots of water under the bridge, in the span of a year."

"Especially as far as the 'shop' is concerned."

The sentence officially opened the way for a frank exchange.

"Right." Lattmann sighed. "The hare-brained defection of our man in Istanbul to the Brits couldn't have done a better job of ruining us. The 'Stapo was just waiting for a chance to put us out of business. After they shut down the Abwehr, there weren't too many in our outfit who were retained by the new management. Luckily that fucking Russki sniper spared me the choice, in case I was offered one. And you?"

"I was in Rome when news came that the chief had been dismissed. 'Smiling' Albert Kesselring got me out of trouble in the Ukraine with an assignment to Italy, where I was kept on ice but never officially laid off. The new owners never asked me, either."

"Are you still in touch with them?"

"That's how I got a lift here. Charity among castaways, until they blow us out of the water." Bora turned slightly, to avoid the stare of the man in the wheelchair. "What about the chief?"

"Seems that after his cashiering he was given a sinecure as Head of the Special Office for Economic Warfare; other than that, he broods at home with his basset hound. When you've been a naval hero, an admiral, and have led German army counter-intelligence for umpteen years, it's either that or a bullet in the head."

It would have been the perfect cue to mention Dr Reinhardt-Thoma's suspicious death, but Bora had something else in mind.

"I saw Salomon a few hours ago."

"Ooh, old House-in-Masuria! I heard he finally made full colonel. I thought he never would. Is he in town?"

"Apparently. He sought me out."

"What for?"

"He's beside himself."

Lattmann knew Bora better than anyone, including his family. He immediately caught an edge in his words. "Well, Benno von Salomon is forever hysterical about something. Is it his 'demons' again?"

"Don't know. He wants to meet again tonight. Not that it makes much difference to me. Whatever he's after, I'm scheduled to leave Berlin in the morning. It's just that he looked even stranger than in Kharkov. I don't know, I had the very unpleasant impression that he might be angling for help – I thought maybe you heard something."

"You see where I am. Something like …?"

"I have no idea. Some pickle he got himself into. But I'll probably know tonight, whether I want to or not."

"Martin, you're not telling me everything. You wouldn't even mention that crackpot if there wasn't something else."

"He dropped names, claiming that they mentioned me to him."

It was warm in the hall, as if it was a spa or a Roman bath. The fact that the man in the wheelchair seemed to be dozing relaxed him enough to glance his way and count his blessings.

"What can you tell me about Claus von Stauffenberg?"

Lattmann set the bottle on the floor next to his chair. "That he's Chief of Staff of the Home Army. That he suffered disabling wounds in Africa, but since he was groomed from the start as a General Staff officer they didn't hurt his career. If anything, quite the opposite. What else? He's bright – Junkerish, for a Swabian. Those who know him either love or intensely dislike him, which can only be said of interesting people. Full stop."

"Supposedly it was he who mentioned me to the younger Schulenburg, who then spoke to Salomon."

In Russia, Lattmann had been in the habit of chewing his fingernails to the quick. A month in the sanatorium had cured him of the practice, as the chest wound had cured him of his pipe-smoking. He lay back in the lounge chair with a pensive, slightly troubled frown.

"Dunno. Schulenburg was always an administrator of sorts. Berlin's deputy police chief under Count von Heldorff before the war. I think you'd call him a 'Prussian socialist'. All I know is that he partied with some of those who 'became unavailable'" – (the standard euphemism for being jailed) – "after the exposure of the foreign currency scheme, with which he helped Jews who left the Fatherland. That cost us our own General Oster last year, and Moltke, too. But such associations have more to do with rank and status than with politics. Didn't you serve at the German embassy in Moscow when old man Schulenburg headed it up? That's probably how Fritz-Dietlof knew about you. Why, are you really worried about this?"

Bora uncrossed his flawlessly booted legs. "I received a summons to the Criminal Police headquarters, for tonight."

"Wait." Lattmann waved his hands as if the words were coming in too fast. "Wait, wait, wait. Let me understand — no, hang on, wait. Sister!"

A sour-faced army nurse, in a seersucker smock and white apron, approached from the other side of the hall, and then stood there as if the two men were uninteresting shrubs in a flower bed. Lattmann asked her to bring glasses and a bottle opener for the vodka.

"You shouldn't be drinking, Major."

"Well, I shouldn't have been wounded, either."

"Only one."

"Cross my heart and hope to die."

After the bottle was uncorked, she remained there with her arms folded, to make sure the officers poured no more than one drink. She even went as far as to take the vodka away as soon as the glasses were half-filled.

Downing liquor on an empty stomach shot a flush through Bora's system. He quickly emptied his glass, to get it over with.

"I should also tell you that my dead relative – my late paternal aunt's husband – was always an … independent thinker, shall we say. He staunchly opposed the 'lives unworthy of life' programme, which he helped to close down with his petitions and complaints. For this and other reasons – like adopting Dr Goldstein's orphaned son in '35 – he stepped on several toes through the years. I won't bore you with details, but no sooner did I arrive than a colleague of his confidentially suggested the possibility of a forced suicide. There's nothing much I can do about it here and now, Bruno. Besides, it's nearly impossible in these cases to prove whether one has killed himself freely or not."

"Well, we Germans are melancholy by nature: when you add political ostracism, personal losses and bombs over your head, the mix can push one over the edge. How well did you know your uncle?"

"He was our paediatrician when Peter and I were children, though I suspect the General considered him far too liberal and freethinking for our own good. In my adult years I seldom saw him."

"So why should the head of the Kripo want to discuss him with you? If politics was involved in your uncle's end, I wouldn't bet any money that it's a reason to call you in. Was it a written summons, or did Nebe send someone?"

"Neither. Carl-Friedrich Goerdeler told my mother before the funeral."

"And what does *he* have to do with the Criminal Police? Isn't he a manager at Bosch?"

"As far as I know." Bora took out the note from his pigeon-hole at the hotel and showed it to him. Lattmann read silently, moving his lips.

"Why does he follow up a spoken message with a written one, which incidentally adds no information?"

"Exactly. I don't want Nina to worry, but you understand …"

"And how. Nebe is SS: he and the 'Stapo must be thick." Lattmann finished his vodka and passed his tongue around the inside of the glass to gather the last drops. "On a positive note, I recall rumours that. in Russia, he inflated the number of those given 'special treatment' in his jurisdiction. They say it saved lives."

"Yes, I heard the story as well. Forgive me if I don't believe it."

"Well, Nebe could have lied simply to get the most credit with the least effort. The end result would be the same, if not the humanitarian intentions behind it. The 'Stapo and SS were like door-to-door salesmen those days, vying for efficiency bonuses."

"It does not change the fact that, like the Gestapo, the Criminal Police is now part of Kaltenbrunner's Reich Security Service."

"The RSHA? That applies to what remains of our 'shop' as well. Martin, has anything happened in Italy to make you so skittish?"

"Nothing that hasn't happened elsewhere. Except for the partisan grenade, of course."

"You know that's not what I mean."

"And you know I clam up if you push me."

Lattmann screwed up his mouth. "Just as I thought. Blast. I'm stuck here and powerless like a lump on a log. I don't know what to tell you about the Kripo, but stay away from Salomon, whatever is ailing him. Such frantic blabbermouths spell nothing but trouble. *No.* You don't work for him anymore, Martin. You owe him nothing. Stay away —" He interrupted himself: "See that nurse? Andreas is the name. She's a sneaky one, planted here to spy. If she looks this way, look amused, as if we were just chatting casually."

The nurse in question was crossing the floor with heaps of bloody cotton in an enamelled tray. It was a duty Bora had last seen Nora Murphy carry out in Rome; he'd been hopelessly heartsick but unwilling to let her know. Luckily the nurse was in a hurry, because he didn't feel much like pretending.

"The good one," Lattmann resumed, "is Sister Velhagen, the one who grumbled but let me drink. I'll tell you what, Martin. There are so many of us vegetating here that rumours can surface if you know how to ask. I have access to a telephone. When are you supposed to meet Nebe? Nine o'clock? Fine. If I learn anything, I'll pass it on before then. My advice, in any case, is *not* to meet House-in-Masuria."

"Thank you. I'll avoid him if I can."

Lattmann saw through Bora's composure, and worried about him.

"You had better."

Flippancy, his personal antidote to serious turns of events, was not always well timed, but he tried it.

"Say," he added familiarly, and it was like a verbal wink, "out with it before you go, Martin: now that Dikta is out of the picture – have you got someone new?"

"No."

"I could introduce you to someone."

"No."

"Why? I could …"

"I don't want to meet *someone*. Drop it, Bruno. I'm not in the right mood."

"Oh. You mean you don't feel like sex?"

"I feel like it. I'm simply not in the right mood."

"What nonsense! Is it because of the hand?"

"What do *you* think?"

Lattmann disregarded Bora's crossness. "You're wrong, and I'm sorry for it. Anyhow, the girl in question needs to get laid, or I've lost my knack for observation."

"Guess what, she's in luck: there are lashings of available men in Berlin."

"But I'd bet good money that she hasn't had a shag in a while. Her boyfriend is here, in a coma, so you see that a little impairment is altogether negligible."

Bora stood, ready to leave. "Christ, listen to yourself. I should slip under the sheets of a defenceless man? You know me better than that."

"I do. And I agree with you: we haven't yet sunk to such a level of barbarism that meeting a woman means jumping on top of her. Still, one night in Berlin and then back to the front without a bit of fun … Snuggling a bit always did it for me."

"No. Thank you all the same." Bora's time at Beelitz was running out. With the car expected back at the Air Ministry in an hour and half, he had to leave now if he wanted to make it. "I have to go, Bruno. Get well soon, and give my love to Eva and the little ones."

Lattmann clung to Bora's hand. "Will do. It was good

seeing you, too. I wish we had more time to catch up. See that you take care."


5:00 P.M.


When Bora returned to the car, he found the driver slumped in the front seat, fast asleep. This too was an effect of Pervitin: you functioned frenetically for days, and then collapsed. The car window was open, so he knocked energetically on the windscreen until the young man started awake with a mumbled series of apologies. Bora did not wait for him to open the car door; he climbed in on his own and said drily, "If we do not arrive according to schedule, I'll hold you responsible."

Easier said than done. Shortly before the Michendorf turn-off, a Field Police patrol halted them. They were searching, they said, for Russian prisoners who had escaped hours earlier after cutting a sentry's throat.

"So?" Bora shot back. "We certainly do not have them on board. I am expected in Berlin, let us through."

"As soon as the dogs are done tracking along the side of the road ahead, Lieutenant Colonel."

Recently shorn German shepherds accompanied the policemen. They were busily pulling on their long leashes up and down the paved road and across the wooded countryside. Ordering the driver to push ahead, around the police vehicles, was not advisable. In the heat of the afternoon, Bora opened his door and rested his foot on the asphalt. Moments dragged by before one of the dogs, with a singularly ferocious look, scented something in the air and started away from the others. He dragged his handler in the direction of the air force vehicle. He would have lunged against it, had he not been restrained, which was more than enough for the patrol to pay attention to it.

"Please, Lieutenant Colonel, you'll have to get out," the leading NCO urged. "And you too." He gestured to the driver.

This was no time to make things worse by resisting. Bora got out of the car, and remained motionless and unresponsive when the dog circled him and sniffed his riding boots and their steel spurs. The airman's dusty ankle boots drew the attention of a second dog, which was soon keen to enter the car so that he could sniff the pedals under the driver's seat.

It was evident there were no other passengers on board, but the policemen still threw open all four doors to allow the dogs to search inside the car, and ordered the airman to unlock both the boot and the bonnet. Bora wondered what that scatterbrain might have done while he was inside the sanatorium with Lattmann. He anticipated the Field Police's question.

"Have you met someone in my absence or left the vehicle unattended?"

The young man looked mystified. He replied that no, he'd met no one and hadn't walked away, though at some point he'd just stepped away to urinate in the bushes. "I'd been drinking coffee all morning, Lieutenant Colonel."

Plausible though it was, the statement forced an annoyed Bora to explain to the Field Police where he had gone, and why. A vigorous questioning of the driver ensued, because now they wanted to be shown on a map where exactly he'd relieved himself near the gate of the Beelitz Heilstätte.

After a seemingly endless time, the policemen concluded that the runaways had probably separated after escaping, and that one of them at least had paused or spent the night in the scrubland around the sanatorium, right where the driver had stood the following day.

"Maybe Ivan pissed in the same spot," one said to the other; then one of them addressed Bora more formally: "Sorry to have held you up. But there are women living alone in the countryside, Lieutenant Colonel, and we can't risk their safety with such filth running around."

*Right – that's why Bruno is teaching Eva how to use a gun. And all of this in the heart of Germany.* Sitting in the car once more,

Bora had no need to berate the driver. They took off like light-ning, so that they reached the Air Ministry two minutes early.

"The only reason I'm not turning you in is that I'm in haste," Bora said grouchily. He left the vodka bottle for his old friend with a thank-you note, and continued on foot towards the Adlon.

The removal of the bomb from the quarter was turning out to be more complicated than expected. Bora watched another fire engine approach and slowly take a left on Voss Strasse. It stood to reason that all the vehicles blocking the streets in the morning were still there, which meant that they would continue working overnight.

Meanwhile, Nina had returned from Dahlem. There were no messages in Bora's pigeonhole; no one had sought him (not even Salomon or Lattmann), so he asked the concierge to telephone his mother's suite and ask if he might come up.

When in Berlin, Bora's parents usually stayed in Grandfather Franz-August's apartment in Zehlendorf. Nina, however, had taken rooms at the Adlon before; and she happened to occupy the same suite this time as on her last visit, when she'd come to say goodbye to Bora, then bound for the German embassy in Moscow.

As he climbed the stairs, Bora anticipated a typical Adlon combination of well-appointed rooms, with an ample archway trimmed in cane work separating the bedroom from a parlour, no different from the haven he and Dikta had known so well. Bora fondly recalled the bathroom with its ornate turn-of-the-century tiles, where Dikta would soak in the tub after making love. Or before, joining him in bed drenched like a mermaid.

The sight of a middle-aged chambermaid met him at the top of the stairs. She was pushing a dinner cart from a door at the end of the hallway to the dumb waiter; her weary looks – long hours, little money, perhaps loneliness too – diverted Bora from his recollections, so inopportune before meeting his mother. On the cart, the leftovers on the plates (these days, too, with rations so restricted for all!) rudely reminded him how hungry he was: another embarrassing reaction he swore to conceal from Nina if they dined together later.

*Later? Christ, later I have to go to the Criminal Police, a branch of the same service that purged us.*

Before knocking he made sure, with a sweep of his fingers across shirt and collar, that he looked impeccable.


7:15 P.M.


Even though she affectionately thanked him for the flowers, tightly clasping his right hand, Nina seemed more anxious than in the morning. Bora assumed that she had heard rumours about his uncle's suicide from Frau Sommer or Saskia, and regretted not informing her when he'd first learned about them.

Wasting no time, he asked, "How is Saskia?"

"Distraught. To all practical purposes, she is now alone in the world. It's her intention not to leave the hospital for another week, or until Uncle is buried. He'd been in fine health, and she cannot understand how death could have come so suddenly. The evening before it happened, she was at the house of family friends; it was only in the morning, when they phoned her there from the clinic, that she heard that he was absent from work, and she was worried at once. She supposes he may have suffered from heart failure, because they haven't had an easy time of it for several years, as you know."

"What do Frau Sommer and his colleagues at the clinic think?"

"They are keeping quiet, Martin. They thought the world of the 'Herr Doktor Professor', but would rather not speculate."

Nina sat down at one end of a small sofa. Its delicate chintz upholstery paled against the blaze of roses and peonies that dominated a spindly round table, on which her enamelled cigarette case created the only other spot of colour.

"May I join you?" Bora asked, and took a seat at the opposite end of the sofa. Soberly, he added, "It might not have been a mere cardiac arrest, Nina. I beg you to consider it as a possibility, that's all."

For a moment she seemed tired, more so than he'd ever seen her. Not older, not less beautiful: only very tired. She averted those brilliant blue-green eyes of hers from him for as long as it took for her to accept his words. Slowly she nodded, wordless and poised, diplomat's daughter and wife of a German general that she was. Bora saw pain travel across her face, recognizing from experience the hurt you feel when you try not to display it.

"It will be best not to share this with Saskia for now," she said, pressing her lips together afterwards as if to underline the need for silence.

His taking her hand and kissing it was, for them, a gesture so intense and so tender that they both drew enormous comfort from it.

"Is everything all right, Nina?"

"Yes."

"Are you sure?"

"Yes, dear."

"I'm not worried about tonight, you know."

"Of course not."

"It's just routine. I anticipate being back for dinner."

"I'll wait for you."

They still looked at each other in suspense, because she clearly feared for him. But he sensed there was something else, too. The *unsaid* anchored them to their seats; it all depended on who would break the bounds of restraint first. Bora would not. On the contrary, he regained complete control of himself. Turned slightly towards her, he evaluated her beauty with the serenity of a man who, feeling no sexual attraction, has a clear eye. Despite her fifty years, she struck him as surprisingly young, even younger than he was – and now about to travel back to an empty house where an old man had withdrawn from everything because his son had died and his stepson had been mutilated. Out of the blue, he thought of the French bar where, sitting across from him, La Mome had asked him in her liquid voice (she was a singer and a whore), "Do you think it's fun, letting an old man fuck you?"

*Why am I thinking that? How dare I think such things in the presence of my mother?*

"I invited Saskia to come and stay with us in Leipzig, Martin, but I doubt she will. Her annuity allows her to retain the house in Dahlem; all her memories are there. Incidentally, it seems that Uncle's papers were at least in part entrusted to a colleague, whose name however is unknown to her."

"It's better like that, Nina."

*"A colleague." Olbertz, or someone else? Surely Uncle had left instructions; it could be counterproductive if Saskia enquired about his papers now.*

Faced with his mother's beauty, Bora wondered how she felt about his imperfections, those she knew well and the more recent ones. The way one of his incisors slightly overlapped the other (which Dikta, however, had found irresistible), the first grey hairs ("thirteen, fourteen", the army barber had informed him, unasked, two weeks earlier, when a trip to Berlin wasn't even in God's mind – or maybe in God's mind alone) … the visible scars – the Polish one across his temple, the fresher ones on his neck – and especially the glove shielding the artificial left hand. Bora was acutely aware of the useless guilt he felt for giving her back, damaged, the body she had formed whole. He was far from right – Nina felt nothing but love for the son who had survived and was still in mortal danger. But because of the intensity of his admiration for her, Bora could not – for all his facility with concepts and words – explain himself to the woman who had given birth to him. It was for this reason, and not because he thought it inopportune, that he'd told her nothing about Dikta at the start, not even of their civil wedding. Even now, after Dikta had thrown him away, he found no means to share how he felt. He settled for giving her an impression of solidity on which she could count, now that her husband was lost in mourning and Peter's young widow had emotionally withdrawn from her. After all that had happened in the last two years, Nina was now the true reason why he felt that he should live. Dikta had been, too, until the year before; and the unreachable Nora Murphy had seemed so, too, fleetingly, in Rome. Bora sat there with his mother, while just outside a world – their world – had been thrown into upheaval and in good part destroyed. He'd say *I will take care of you*, if only he believed that events would allow.

Nina clasped her knees with her hands, staring in front of her. "I saw an old friend again last night. He came to fetch me at the station."

A few words, in her impeccable native English. Bora heard them sink into him like a self-evident formula, a code needing no interpretation. He had something like a flash of knowledge, and with it came a sense of unique privilege that gave him goosebumps.

He did not ask her anything. But when Nina nervously reached for a cigarette from the enamelled case, he took out his lighter (it'd been Peter's, so he held it in his fist to keep her from recognizing it, and grieving), and lit it for her.

She really did not know how to smoke; it was only her small act of rebellion.

"With your permission, I'll have one too," Bora said. He usually went without, but always kept the Chesterfields in his breast pocket. It was his only luxury at the front, and now he lit the small flame again with a click. After a drag, he quietly observed: "It isn't easy to live with the General. I know full well."

He was referring to Sickingen's aversion to smoking, naturally. But also to the rest. Nina seized the opportunity, and cautiously followed his sophisticated balancing act. "It would not have been appreciably easier for you with your natural father, Martin. What I loved about him – his being *temperamental* – would have been an obstacle between you."

"I'm a damn difficult son." Bora smiled as he said it. "And this time I was even late in arriving. Forgive me. I'm pleased they came to fetch you at the station."

"Yes, I was glad also."

Her *nearly* telling him more moved him deeply. They had never been so close, never conversed so intimately. Too introverted to speak about himself and his affairs, mannerly and laconic, he was nevertheless the son who, when asked how he was, invariably answered "fine".

"Do I know him, Nina?"

"No."

"Well, I'm pleased anyway."

They smoked silently for a while. He reckoned the measure of her loneliness by the fact that she had broached such a private subject with her son; she had probably never even told Grandmother Ashworth-Douglas, her own mother. Bora did not presume to deserve her confidence, but felt honoured, and certainly passed no judgement. He was not jealous of her, because he knew that nothing could come between them.

"His name is Max Kolowrat."

Bora nodded in acknowledgement. He was a renowned journalist and traveller, a former war correspondent who'd lived in half the world, and had during the Weimar days severely criticized the prevailing culture. Bora had read his thrilling African chronicles from the Italian campaign of '35.

"He now lives in Berlin." Looking at him with her head slightly inclined towards her shoulder, she seemed sad – but in a different way from her mourning. "I detest feeling powerless. And I should not saddle you with this."

"You *should.*"

Blushing, Nina once more turned away. "He travelled to Leipzig when they gave you up as missing – or much worse – at Stalingrad. I had not seen him in years, perhaps twenty-five or more. He asked how he could help. How? My first-born was lost: no one could help me. But I appreciated his asking. I don't know if it was out of vanity that I allowed him to speak to me. I always thought that if you listened to a man … if you let him know that you were listening … Vanity is morally wrong and tasteless in equal measure. I have always tried to be mindful about these things. The impression we women give, at times – perhaps we should be more aloof than engaging."

"Nina, most of us males aren't worth such worries. You alone are the judge of whether *he* is worth it."

"Oh, Martin. You were lost. After Stalingrad fell, the General spent his days locked in his study, speaking to no one. Peter of course was still in Russia, we didn't know where exactly, but … Margaretha had just found out she was pregnant, and she unexpectedly panicked. I was dealing with it all as best I could. The only one to keep her wits was Benedikta. And not because she didn't care for you. She helped me run things, to keep up the expected social obligations – and the pretence of serenity; because as long as there was no official word, you might still be alive. That was when your father had a row with her, because he knew better than most what it was like in Stalingrad, how unlikely that you'd survived. 'If Martin is meant to come back, he will'– that was the extent of her answer. And she would not let him see her weep."

*What a mess we left behind at home, even at Stalingrad.* It was Bora's turn to avoid his mother's eyes.

"You should know … I never wanted to be the one who came back, Nina. I very much hoped it'd be the opposite."

"The opposite? Please, stop thinking in those terms! Do you really believe that if you had left your life in Stalingrad" – she couldn't bring herself to use the verb "die" in reference to her sons – "Peter would be spared? It isn't so. I am so deeply grateful that you *did* come back. Seeing you at the hospital in Prague was like giving birth to you all over again. But I left you to Benedikta in Prague, because you belonged to each other and needed each other."

"For all the good it did me."

Bora felt sad for his mother and, like Max Kolowrat, he, too, wondered how he could help. He said, "I believe you must go beyond grief, Nina; even beyond serenity, and try to live as happily as you possibly can." The cigarette in her hand was burning out, so he gently took it from her and extinguished it in the ashtray. "Old men is all you've known."

"In 1915, after my two years of full mourning, Max was there, convalescing from a war wound. Formally, and insistently. Never once alone with me. But I'd promised the General I would marry him."

"Because he courted you before the Maestro, and because when he died the Maestro asked him to take his place? Come now, Nina!"

"Those were different times."

"Yes, times have changed."

Again that pain, that restraint on her part, that sense of obligation Bora knew so well. "Martin, I cannot do this to your father."

"Which one of the two? … Anyway, you can. Dikta didn't believe me when I told her I'd always been faithful to her; so you see, it isn't worth it. There are many other forms of betrayal." He had to look her in the eyes when he said it. "Whatever you decide, Nina, whoever you choose, I am on your side."

This was something he could tell her. Peter couldn't have; he would never have encouraged her so calmly. But Bora's loyalty was to his mother. He relished being on her side – a serene and secure complicity. Not that he was angry at the General – not exactly. But, between the two, he knew who to choose. He'd sworn no oath to *him*.

66

"Time for my appointment," he said lightly. He put out what remained of his cigarette in the ashtray, and rose. Without hurrying, he retrieved his cap from the sofa where he'd placed it at his side, and put it on. "I'll be back soon," he said, smiling.

8:30 P.M.

Once outside the door, however, he was seized by panic. He paused at the top of the stairs and closed his eyes in order to calm himself down quickly – fear will come in through the smallest hole, if you let it. When he'd offered himself to his mother as guarantor and protector, he'd unexpectedly laid himself open to fear. *Is this the coming storm? Christ, I must pull away. Pull away from all things, even from my sixth sense. Regain some emotional distance. I've been in storms before – but the way I feel now, if Salomon has the unhappy idea of waiting downstairs to collar me, I may not be able to restrain myself.*

Fortunately for both of them, Salomon was nowhere in sight. Bora stopped at the desk to ask if anyone had called for him from the airfield, or if there were any other messages (there were none), and to deposit the diary from his briefcase in the safe. Once out of the hotel, solemn and battered, he turned right on Wilhelmstrasse; the fifteen-minute walk would give him time to collect his wits before he reached Nebe's office by the Spree.

It was still light outside, despite the hour; the sky was clear. It was past closing time, and the quarter seemed deserted – but Bora wondered how many people might still be working in the beehive that was the government offices: a world inside a world, with a remnant of quiet, invisible activity. The wide pavement stretched before him like a starched ribbon.

He arrived at the once glorious Wilhelmplatz; the Foreign Ministry stood there looking ominous after being damaged by fire. The raids had not spared the Chancellery, either:

its narrowness belied its true dimensions, which extended the length of Voss Strasse and made it a citadel impossible to miss from the air. A temporary brick structure, a shelter or storehouse, rose across from it. The haphazard combination of the stately and haphazard unsettled the eye, and where superb city planning had given way to a shanty town the effect was of an oversized maze. In the evening silence (silence, in Berlin!), all you could hear was the faint noise of the men and vehicles working on the unexploded bomb a block away. The tramlines ran across the street like scars. Bora stopped a moment to compose himself, because he was still too edgy.

Every gate and entrance was manned; there were sentry boxes one after the other, and yet the impression was of a street lined with sepulchres, such as the Romans erected outside their city gates. In front of him, the Air Ministry blocked out the luminous western horizon. Beyond it, the nerve centre in which the offices of various authorities – the SD, the State Police, the Criminal Police, the Gestapo's counter-espionage division – were stacked on top of each other, forever reporting to the Reich Security Service. *Things could be worse: they could have summoned me to* that *building.* From his occasional errands at the Prinz Albrecht Palais, he recalled the grand staircase and the gallery around the handsome inner court. But in the basement, in the rear wing, there was a prison block where the inmates died.

Bora was trying not to brood on it, but everything inside him was tense and alert. He expected – for no other reason than that he'd left early – to be stopped by a patrol at the corner of Voss Strasse, and he was.

They were SS, but this too he'd expected – it was their neighbourhood. Since he was turning east, in the opposite direction, Bora hoped to be able to dodge their questions. If Goerdeler had suggested a certain amount of caution (he'd said Bora should use the service entrance), there had to be a reason for it; it did not necessarily mean that he should *lie* to the patrol, but —

"Your papers, please."

*I wish I had a mark for every time I had to show them.* Bora did as they asked.

"Where are you going, Colonel?"

"Französische Strasse."

"For what purpose?"

"My duty. I'm expected."

It might be enough, or it might not. He was actually going beyond it, to Werderscher Markt. They'd probably wonder why he hadn't stated the exact address or identified the official who'd scheduled such an appointment after hours. The SS patrol held on to the documents, and were on the verge of asking for further explanation. How well Bora knew that puckering of the lips, the officiously slow turning of the pages. *They don't even need a reason to withhold permission for me to proceed. They're like the shorn police dogs near Michendorf, sniffing me for evidence of wrongdoing and waiting for me to flinch.*

"Expected in which office, Colonel?"

An earth-shattering blast from the direction of Leipziger Platz interrupted the SS men, Bora's thoughts and everything else. They all instinctively hunched, as if rounding their shoulders would save them from destruction. Panes exploded from high-up windows and came down in a shower of fragments. Chunks of metal and plaster pelted to the ground like hail, and tiles plummeted down, shattering into pieces on the ground or landing on the roofs of the cars; one of the SS men was struck on the helmet, staggered backwards and fell. For a stunned moment, Bora was back in Rome, when another deadly explosion had brought about swift reprisal and more deaths. *The bomb just went off … sounds like a medium calibre, but still, more than enough to kill those who were working around it.*

"Go, go." Suddenly no longer interested in him, the other SS man gestured like a traffic policeman for him to move.

Bora did so only after retrieving his papers. *Thank God I'm not as consequential as a bomb.* He walked away into the controlled chaos that always followed such events; those working late at the Transport Ministry looked out of their shattered windows, called to one another and pointed at the pillar of smoke, invisible from the ground, rising behind the tall buildings. Soon ambulances would come wailing along.

Bora would not have easily cleared the patrol's scrutiny without the blast. As it was, no one minded him, because in those days an army colonel was not yet a man you went after when a bomb exploded.

Once past the skeletal Kaiserhof, where further collapse caused by the explosion had loosened a cloud of dust the colour of face powder, he was glad to be turning off the avenue. He left behind the wail of sirens, the confusion. During his Berlin Sundays, he'd often taken the underground to Mohrenstrasse, bound for the narrow street that once led to St Hedwig's, a neighbourhood of venerable churches, none spared by the bombs in May. Towards the east, where the sky was shaded a more intense blue, Werderscher Markt lay in silence.

It was from there that Nebe ran his empire. The Kripo headquarters were across the river, on Alexanderplatz. They said his office had an exit useful for quick getaways which led to an outer court, but Bora didn't know which one it might be, or if the general's door was in any way marked. Those of high-rankers with secretive duties often weren't. *What will I say if they ask me why I'm here? Do they know I'm coming?*

His worries were, paradoxically, those of a fly that fears it may miss the spider's web. At the service entrance, in his senior officer's uniform, Arthur Nebe himself was waiting for him.

He invited him in with a nod, turned and walked back in. In ten seconds or so Bora had reached the threshold. Finding himself in an empty workplace, to all appearances a secretary's room, he recalled Bruno's words about a trap; but it was too late to do anything about it, so he took a deep breath and remained standing there. *If I'm lucky, they'll shoot me straightaway.*

But Nebe was looking out from a second doorway, which opened on an inner office, as if wondering why Bora hadn't promptly followed him inside.

"What are you waiting for? Do come in, Colonel von Bora."

As soon as Bora entered, the Chief of Police turned the key in the lock behind him. "That was a nasty boom, wasn't it?"

"Yes, sir."

At first sight, there was nothing martial or police-like about Nebe's features. As far as Bora knew, he belonged to the middle class, yet his careworn face reminded him of certain proletarian non-coms, whose hard daily lives were imprinted across their brows. He was gaunt and dark-haired, and his prominent nose looked squashed, as if it'd been broken and never quite regained its shape. At this moment, the misshapen cartilage cast a shadow over stretching lips, the ghost of an arch smile.

"Please." Nebe pointed to a chair, and took his place at his desk. This display of courtesy after being locked in only succeeded in troubling Bora even more. Once he sat down, he'd be with his back to a third door, and he wouldn't be able to keep an eye on it. He sat down, ready for anything. And at that "anything", his heart bled at the idea that he might never see Nina again.

"You and I have something in common, Colonel." Nebe turned a framed photo towards him, in which he was mounted on a horse, about to leap over a hurdle. "Marvellous sport. Here you see me in action. I was in the Eternal City, the year you received the Roma riding award from Il Duce's own hands, and – if I'm not mistaken – also the Premio Speciale Arnaldo Mussolini."

*So?* Bora nodded, but remained suspicious. This wasn't the first time he'd faced SS personnel who smiled at him as they sprang the trap. His award-winning year of 1935 coincidentally marked the time when General Sickingen had displayed his antipathy for the regime, by resigning his command of the 14th Infantry Division, Gruppenkommando 3 – Dresden, along with his commission, greatly upsetting his sons. Especially Peter, who was still in school and sought refuge in his brother's room to weep, from anger and shame. Bora expected nothing less from his contrary stepfather, and had swallowed the bitter pill. To academy comrades who enquired about it, he drily answered, "You'll have to ask the General," and that was that.

Nebe kept staring at him. A desk lamp cast a milky glare on him through the greenish opalescence of its glass shade. From outside came the muffled wailing of ambulance and fire engine sirens racing west towards the evacuated, cordoned-off blast area. Probably too many vehicles for an isolated incident, but bombs always unnerve politicians, who would like to see themselves as immune in their palaces. Nebe, however, was indecipherable, focused.

Under his scrutiny, Bora wondered how much the tense officer sitting in these boots resembled the one who'd just spoken to Nina, and before that to Lattmann, Olbertz and the Berliner co-pilot. *Am I really the same man whose heels the police dog sniffed at four hours ago?* It surprised him that it had all belonged to the same day, which, however, was not yet over (*Noctem quietam et finem perfectum* ... even the old Catholic prayer, asking for a peaceful night, admits that to its very end a day can bring surprises). What if Nebe brought up Dr Reinhardt-Thoma's "not so voluntary" death? Would the Reich's chief criminal investigator choose to meet after hours to discuss it? Bora could not forget that, on this man's authority, death squads carried out exterminations in the East. *Christ, in the course of two years on that front I reported every episode I learned of to the German War Crimes Office* ...

Nebe punctiliously folded and put away a typewritten sheet. Deliberate gestures, Bora knew from his days as an interrogator, are a way of making your counterpart aware that you have all the time in the world to make people cave in and confess.

"Do you believe in the stars?"

"In the stars, Group Leader?" Bora repressed a nervous need to smirk.

"In the stars, yes. In the heavenly orbs. In destiny."

"Not much, to tell the truth."

"That is *perfect*."

Not knowing where to look without seeming impudent, Bora contemplated the photo as if waiting for Nebe's horse to jump over the hurdle at last.

"I am telling you this, Colonel, because it is my intention to introduce a topic that requires scepticism."

Bora raised his eyes to the general. "I should premise that I am not exactly a sceptic, Group Leader."

"I know, you were raised a Catholic. But you do not believe in the stars."

"No."

"Then you can investigate the death of Walter Niemeyer, whose name you probably haven't heard before."

Straight-backed in his armchair, Nebe had the slightly laborious breathing of someone who has been ill, or functions under great psychological pressure. Both things could be true. Bora stared back at him. *Investigate? What the devil ...?*

"I haven't," was all he said.

"But are you familiar with Magnus Magnusson?"

"Not at all."

"What about Sami Mandelbaum?"

"Less than less, Group Leader."

"All dead." Nebe placed the photo back its original position on the desk. "But in fact they comprise a trinity; they are three in one and one in three, two aliases of Niemeyer's. Thus, there is just one corpse. It simplifies matters, in a murder case."

"I am not sure I understand, Group Leader. My flying visit to Berlin is due to a sad loss in the family."

"I know why you are here. And it's because you're already in Berlin that I have summoned you."

Bora asked none of the questions that crowded his mind. From his confusion a vague glimmer of interest slowly surfaced, which was so unwelcome here and now that he grew apprehensive again.

Whether Nebe, as an expert in crime, saw through his puzzlement, or merely took for granted that he would accept the task, he continued: "In case you're wondering what the victim's profession was – Mandelbaum was an *Ostjude*, a third-rate actor from the depths of Galicia. Magnusson was of Scandinavian descent and earned his fame as an astrologer. And Niemeyer, finally, was none other than the Weimar Prophet."

The Weimar Prophet – it rang a bell. Bora might have read the name on placards or in the press when he attended the Military Academy in Berlin. The temptation to feel relieved because he was not himself under investigation gave him a thrill that bordered on pleasure, but God only knew if it was well founded.

Did Nebe know he'd snared him? He squinted as though he were satisfied. "Niemeyer was found dead as a dodo at his sprawling mansion in Dahlem a week ago, blasted twice through the upper body with a twelve-gauge hunting rifle." The jargon grated on Bora's nerves, reminding him that he was in a police station, in the presence of Germany's leading detective. "No eyewitnesses, although there are some potential suspects. You were too young when our man rose to fame, but piles of newspaper articles were written about him, and there are his two lengthy autobiographies."

Despite himself, Bora began to feel curious.

"Plus a few police reports, no doubt."

"Those are available to everyone, Colonel. Me, you." Nebe turned on the intercom and spoke into it: "The Niemeyer folder."

Whoever was at the other end of the wire must have had it in their hand, because almost immediately the door behind Bora opened and a non-com walked in with the folder. "Give it to the colonel," Nebe said.

Bora saw the dossier slide onto the desk in front of him like a menu – at a restaurant where they could feed you or poison you. He waited before he flipped it open.

"Am I allowed to ask questions?"

After the non-com had left the office, Nebe stood up and went to lock that door as well. "All but one. Go on, ask."

"Why hasn't the case been assigned to someone in the Criminal Police?"

"That is precisely the one question you will receive no answer to."

*Imagine that.* Bora watched Nebe return to his desk. "I expect it would be pointless for me to mention that my regiment is under attack every other day, Group Leader."

"It *would* be pointless. Besides, a week will make no difference. Who cares about the Italian front? Italy is lost anyway."

"We dare to think that it may not be. Not yet, at least."

"Leave it, Colonel. Do as you're told." Nebe had abruptly become cross. "What is it with these young colonels, who dig their heels in like schoolboys?"

*This bad-tempered reproach is meant for someone else,* Bora told himself. *Not for me. I wonder whom he's thinking of.* Without observing that he wasn't in the least digging his heels in, he said, "Forgive the banality, Group Leader, but why choose *me*?"

"Because you were recommended to me."

Bora bit his tongue. Whatever was behind this, someone other than Goerdeler must have mentioned him to the head of the Criminal Police; when Goerdeler was mayor of Leipzig, he had resigned over the removal of a "Jewish monument" (Mendelssohn's statue) from a city square. Colonel Kinzel, his Abwehr superior in Leipzig and Paris? He had since conveniently transferred to Kaltenbrunner's RSHA. Familiar with his lack of scruples and his maliciousness, Bora's mouth went dry at the thought of having to deal with him again. *No. It wouldn't be Kinzel, he would have summoned me directly to Prinz Albrecht Strasse.* Could it be the head of the Berlin police, Heldorff? Bora didn't know him at all. Nonetheless, he said, "Won't enlisting an army officer in a police inquiry be seen as undue interference by Count von Heldorff?"

"This is a criminal case, Colonel von Bora. Limit yourself to carrying out your orders. Be discreet; should you run into any significant hurdles, you will report only to me." Nebe pushed a calling card with his private phone number across the desk towards Bora. He then opened and closed a drawer without taking anything out of it. "You are fortunate, because you will enjoy privileges that not even millionaires can afford in today's Berlin. You'll have a car at your disposal, a driver, and nearly unlimited access to fuel. Do not overdo it, but make whatever use of it you must. The driver is one of my own, a faithful Old Warrior who will follow you like a shadow."

"Shadowing" was an expression Bora disliked. They'd "shadowed" him day and night in Moscow, before the war against the Soviet Union began. Whether it was a Soviet or a National Socialist, it meant constantly having someone at your heels. As for Old Warriors, street thugs from the early days, there was scarcely one among them who hadn't personally committed murder, political or otherwise.

He continued to gaze at the closed folder. *The case must be a controversial one, an important one. Is this the storm I felt in the air? Much as I've been grieving for my uncle, I suspected there was something else all along: pulling a regimental commander out of a war zone, for whatever reason, is unusual.*

In the blinding sunlight of the heights north of the Arno, Bora had shared with his staff the urgent summons signed by Lieutenant General Greiner, head of the 362nd Infantry Division. Scrambling to secure transportation to the valley, and from there to the nearest airstrip, he'd delegated Major Luebbe-Braun, who was faithful but like the rest worried sick by this sudden recall to Germany.

"I must send a personal message to my second in command."

Nebe impatiently tapped the top of the desk with his open hand. "Yes, yes, whatever. You can notify your second in command or whomever you want. Open the folder."

Bora obeyed. On top lay a direct order signed by Field Marshal Kesselring, commander of the German army in the Mediterranean, countersigned by no less than Field Marshal Keitel, commander-in-chief of the OKW. "See, Colonel? We all knew, except you."

Bewilderment and having gone nearly twenty-four hours without food dulled his senses, but not to the point that Bora couldn't stake a small claim of his own. He placed the calling card in his left-hand chest pocket. "I will do as I am ordered, Group Leader. Naturally, solving a murder case in a week might not be easy."

"I'd say it's rather impossible, from my professional point of view. But I expect you to give it your best shot. If your final report reaches me *after* you've left Berlin, so be it." This sounded mysterious: he was given a week's time, but invited not to rush? The phrase "so be it" was out of place in a policeman's mouth. And why did Nebe say "left Berlin" and not "returned to your post"? Was he implying something?

By the end of the meeting, an overwhelmed Bora knew that two boxes of documents (including newspaper and magazine clippings, plus the magician's two autobiographies and unspecified "other items") awaited him in the boot of the car.

"You will receive further instructions tomorrow at 8:00 a.m., when your driver will report for duty. His name is Florian Grimm."

"Is he at all acquainted with the case, Group Leader?"

"He found the body."

Nebe accompanied Bora to the same door through which he'd let him in, and unlocked it with a jailer's swift turn of the key. "Do you have all you need, Colonel?"

"Yes, for the moment."

"Not true." From his pocket, Nebe took out a bottle of blue Pelikan ink, which he put in Bora's hand.


9:38 P.M.


Bora made his way back to the hotel in a field-grey Mercedes, imposed on him notwithstanding the short distance, with the boxes of documents and "other items" in the boot – which would stay there until morning, because it hadn't been decided whether he'd stay on at the Adlon or not. The man at the wheel was not Florian Grimm; he would join him the day after. The sun had just gone down; shortly after sunset, the first stars pierced the muted blue. An immense ruin punctuated the avenue of the East-West Axis, which was wider than most run-ways: at its Pariser Platz end, the Brandenburg Gate, with its camouflage netting, seemed distant and forlorn. As they drove past the checkpoint by the Interior Ministry, the burnt, metallic odour of the explosion hovered in mid-air like an invisible mist.

Thanks to the police's sophisticated equipment and his high-priority clearance, Bora had been able to radio his regiment from Nebe's headquarters. Luebbe-Braun, loyal to a fault, sounded as if he was acutely aware that there had to be a pressing reason for the commander not to return as planned. In fact, given this rather official journey back to the hotel (even the SS let the car through without stopping it), why the farce of secrecy surrounding his summons? There had to be more to all this.

Through the open car window, he looked up. Above a gaping, jagged skyline worthy of a Caspar David Friedrich painting, there really was no sign of coming rain; the stars weren't hazy, like they are when moisture fills the air. Can a storm brew unseen?

Pragmatism set in. He had orders, he'd follow them. Luckily, Sergeant Major Nagel had insisted that he bring along two uniforms. Ever since Stalingrad, Nagel had been not only a trusted non-com, but also the personal guardian of his commander's impeccable attire, which went well beyond decorum; it was the very sign that all was under control.

*At the moment, all I have control over is the fact that I brought along two uniforms.* When they reached their destination, Bora did not wait for the driver to open the door for him. He ordered him to unlock the boot so that he could grab the topmost folder from one of the boxes, and walked into the Adlon with it under his arm.

No messages for him at the desk, either from Salomon or from Lattmann. Not even from the Schönefeld airfield – but Bora now knew why. He wolfed down a sandwich before joining Nina upstairs for a late dinner, because he was too embarrassed to show her how hungry he really was.

She'd been very anxious about him. When he said, "All's well, simply routine," she accepted his brevity; although in the course of the meal, Bora in a roundabout way broached a subject he very much wanted to discuss but had saved for last: the suggestion that the entire family spend the rest of the summer in Munich.

"How long since you last stayed at the house there, Nina? It would be a nice change. And since you keep in touch with the Modereggers, why not let them know they would be better served being with their sons in Königsberg – and more comfortable – rather than all the way out in Trakehnen?"

Implying that Leipzig, not to mention East Prussia, was no longer "comfortable" was Bora's way of telling her how serious the situation was on the Eastern front. Normally he would trust the General's foresight in military matters, but the latest developments may have escaped the man in his distracted state.

Nina smiled. She calmly told him that as far as her parents were concerned, they would not leave their home in

Probst-Heida. "It's not because of the works of art or the property, Martin. They simply decided that they will both stay. We have refugees staying with us at Borna, and I already invited Irma Moderegger to join us on Birkenstrasse … we'll see if she accepts. As for your father, he is a Prussian general."

"Tell him to take you to Munich, Nina. Or go on your own."

"We'll see."

The end of the evening threatened to turn sad, so Bora told his mother about the sleepy air-force driver racing towards Berlin as if his tail was on fire, and whatever else came to mind that was light-hearted. Before retiring, he asked if he could have breakfast with her in the morning, and said he'd already booked a taxi to the train station.

Nina thanked him. She did not bring up the subject they'd so tactfully concluded in the afternoon, but, having himself been very much in love, Bora could intuit just by looking at her that Max Kolowrat had also asked to see her off in the morning. To him, it meant leaving his mother outside the station and losing the last precious moments with her. All the same, as he already stood on the threshold he casually said that it would be impossible for him to stay with her until the train took off. "I am truly unforgivable, Nina."

She would see through him, but Bora hoped that she'd let him render her this service. When Nina she asked him to bend down so that she could kiss his cheek – her way of showing unspoken gratitude – it seemed the right time to tell her how much he had grieved, and how much he still grieved.

She took his face between her hands, and looked into his eyes.

"Martin, how do you feel, *really*?"

"Fine, Nina. I'm fine."

Updated in Berlin, at the Adlon, 11:58 p.m. West of the hotel, five bomb disposal men lost their lives in the explosion, caused it seems by a time fuse. Had they known, they could have simply waited for it to blow up on its own.

I am writing in brand-new blue ink, even though I made a bit of a mess refilling the fountain pen with my one hand. At dinner, Nina did a wonderful job of not staring at it, although my occasional awkwardness with the cutlery must have distressed her. I tried to laugh it off – saying that it isn't much different from when I had a broken arm in Russia – but I don't think my attempt was very successful.

Anyhow, a godsend from her: two tailored army shirts and hand-sewn underwear. Things she used to provide me with before I married, and with her characteristic discretion refrained from sending during the years I was with Dikta; now the clothes actually come in handy, because I wasn't equipped for more than a short stay. I feel so far advanced into adulthood that I sometimes forget I'm her boy, and that she still looks after me.

Enough said. Twelve hours ago, I was leaving Uncle's memorial service; twenty-four hours ago, we were stuck near G. because of an air raid over the German border. Not for the first time, my orders changed en route, or, for all I know, had changed even before I set off from my post.

Just like I deemed from the start that taking leave at this point in the war was improbable, I now wonder about this task. Of course, we who belonged to the Abwehr are at present like the ancient Japanese warriors without a master – ronin, as they were called. Whether we deserve it or not, we are mistrusted, but have useful skills.

Group Leader Nebe forbade me to ask why the inquiry into a charlatan's death is being contracted out. He has men, informants, every type of means at his fingertips; so does his counterpart in the Berlin police, Count von Heldorff; yet, at least formally, I am to work under the aegis of the Kripo, whose paperwork and logistic support I am being provided with. In the hour or so I spent at Nebe's office, I got the strong impression that he knew all about me, and spoke to me as he did because of that. It's no secret that some of those I have worked for, as well as those I've had disagreements with, talk to one another. If they haven't fallen in battle in the meantime, the latter still have an axe to grind with me. Speaking of axes, Colonel (now Obersturmbannführer) Kinzel has buried his hatchet with the Reich Security Service. Not he, not any one of them, would recommend me. Who, then?

It doesn't matter. A lieutenant colonel can hardly argue with special orders that come from two generals and two field marshals. In lieu of my three-day pass for a loss in the family, I can now produce a Sonderausweis not even St Peter could object to.

It's been a long day and I should be tired, but I'm not. Hearing from the concierge that Salomon has been out since midday and did not return to the hotel for dinner is a relief. Collegiality aside, I'm not in the mood to hear him gripe or fantasize. In Russia, he had a tendency to imagine threats and dangers where none existed. Let's put it this way: whatever it was that he was so impatient to discuss with me, he has either forgotten about it, or else it has killed him.

So what? I told Nebe I'm not a complete sceptic, but I can be cynical. Back to my task – here's a brief outline:

Last Wednesday, 3 July, the same day when, on the Southern front, Siena (not my sector) fell to the damn French, Walter Niemeyer, born 11 November 1900, was shot to death in his luxurious residence on Lebanonzederpfad, in the south-western quarter of Dahlem in Greater Berlin. Two twelve-gauge slugs were fired, the calibre used on hefty game like deer. From a rifle, which you can hardly carry around concealed about your person. No sign of forced entry, no visible traces on the scene. The photos attached to the file show a half-naked man sprawled on his belly in what seems to be an entrance hall. No bathrobe, just a towel around the waist. Either he had just left a shower or bath, or else he slept unclothed and the killer surprised him when he came downstairs after hearing an alarming noise. Judging by the considerable damage, the first shot was fired from no more than two or three yards away, and the second was inflicted when he was already lying on the ground.

A.k.a. Mandelbaum and Magnusson, he was officially engaged in his "profession" (the Jews use an appropriate term for people like him: Luftmenschen, "men living on air") from 1915, when he literally ran away to the circus, to 1941, when he retired from the scene to "recharge his psychic energy" (his words).

From 1941 until the time of his death, he continued in private practice, mostly acting as a counsellor of sorts and holding hypnosis sessions with hysterics, at the highest levels. A partial list of his clients reads like the Almanach de Gotha of Weimar (and post-Weimar) society and politics. Despite the war, his lavish parties drew the cream of the Berlin crop, as they had ever since 1930, when he built his villa.

He was married at least twice, once to a Bulgarian acrobat (forsaken after six months, with the excuse of an extended tour abroad), and later to an affluent widow twenty-five years older than him. The latter suddenly died of an asthma attack during a trip in a sailing boat to celebrate their first anniversary, leaving Niemeyer a rich man. He was investigated pro forma, and cleared.

Judging by the gaps in the paperwork I have read thus far, he must have run into some sort of problem in the mid-1930s. I have my own ideas in that regard, and am leaning towards a political matter, but I need more details. Because of his difficulties, he kept away from Germany for a year, touring South America.

The most intriguing element of this man's life, namely his strange choice of aliases, is what fascinates me. Passing himself off as a Scandinavian, and before that as a Galician Jew! It boggles the mind. There was only one image of

Niemeyer in this folder (the rest are sitting boxed up in the boot of the car). The portrait, I believe, is an enlargement of his passport photograph, and shows a man in his forties, with rather anonymous features. Given a good disguise and the right accent, I do not doubt that he could masquerade as anybody, except only as an African or Chinese man.

The folder lists four names of possible suspects (three men and a woman); no details, and no probable motive for the murder. More stuff to find inside the boxes, I suppose. I do not believe in the stars, as I made clear to Nebe, notwithstanding the coincidence that Niemeyer and I share the day and month of our birth, thirteen years apart.

Time to turn in. Nina leaves at six in the morning and I won't miss my chance of seeing her to the train station. Should Colonel von Salomon knock on my door in the dark hours, I will turn a deaf ear.

PS A curious episode tonight, as I reached my floor. I distinctly heard someone sobbing in one of the rooms: a man, not a woman. This in itself is highly peculiar. Hounded as I was by the thought that Salomon might try to pin me down, I recalled that I saw him weep tears of frustration at least twice on the Eastern front, in both cases for minor incidents which most of us would shrug off. Was he by any chance boohooing to himself somewhere? Imagine my surprise when, as I approached my door, I realized that the sounds came from the room next to mine, occupied as far as I know by a Japanese officer. I thought the Japanese never cried!

PPS Sometimes it'd be better if they, and men in general, did.

# 3

### HOTEL ADLON, TUESDAY, 11 JULY, 7:38 A.M.

Bora was not in a good mood when he heard at the front desk that Salomon had called his room several times, beginning at six in the morning.

"He also left word that he will lunch with you here at one o'clock, Colonel."

The concierge wasn't at fault in the matter, so Bora acknowledged the message, careful not to show how angry he was. Though he'd been away from his family for over ten years, he felt homesick for his mother after seeing her off; that, too, played into his present disposition. If he knew himself, it'd take him an hour or two to regain his comfortable state of a loner.

"Where is Colonel von Salomon now?" he asked.

"Out for the morning, sir."

*Well, for one who is dying to speak to me in private, he does make himself scarce.*

In little more than a quarter of an hour, the car and driver supplied by Nebe would be at the entrance. Real coffee was available at the hotel, so Bora ordered a cup while he waited. From Anhalt station he had taken a circuitous way back, walking south and then back along Kochstrasse, where – at the heart of the Zeitungsviertel, the newspaper quarter – the damage caused by the bombs of 21 June was particularly severe. The building that for the past seventy and more years had housed the Berlin offices of the Bora Verlag was simply no longer there. It was as if a large tooth had been extracted from a line of teeth in various stages of decay. Nina said that for a whole day after the raid everything that had survived, including typewriters and filing cabinets kept in the basement for safety's sake, had been watched over by the employees, so that it would not be stolen. It now sat in temporary storage at the printing press in Zehlendorf. It was all "very unpleasant", in his family's typical understated formulation, but at least there had been no loss of life. Sipping his coffee, Bora wondered which pieces of their art collection his grandparents would have to sell this time, in order to rebuild. According to Nina, all stipends continued to be paid, because you couldn't simply throw the men and women who'd been with the firm for so long out on their ear.

After the bombs, the Party-owned Deutsche Verlag offered to buy the Bora trademark and its Leipzig and Munich publishing branches, but Grandfather Franz-Augustus graciously refused. As an old diplomat, he could afford to be gracious; the General, who understood nothing about publishing but was anything but diplomatic, spluttered that "if the Brownshirts get their grubby hands on the firm, they'll turn it upside down and shake out the whole catalogue". It was the sort of talk that had for years caused friction with his sons. How it must haunt the old man that Peter had argued with him the last time they'd spoken. Usually Bora was the obstinate one. In Kiev, two weeks before being shot down, his brother had told him, "Father gets on my nerves, Martin. I can't stand it when he says such crazy and traitorous things, such as that the officer corps ought to take over." Bora remembered replying: "That generation of old men had their chance to take over twenty years ago, and didn't." Now Peter was dead, and Bora still felt the same way.

Three minutes before eight o'clock, a lumbering fellow in civilian clothes and a garish American tie, every inch a Party henchman, stepped into the lobby. After a quick scan of the vaulted space, he saw Bora, walked up to him and raised his arm in the Party salute: "Lieutenant Colonel Baron von Bora – Lieutenant Florian Grimm, reporting for duty."

The first name gave him away as most likely Austrian or Bavarian, but the accent was pure Berliner (Treptow? Neukölln?). A detective inspector, with probably no more than a middle-school education; physically speaking, Bora judged him capable of felling a man with his fist. He was built like a wrestler or bodyguard, his arms hanging awkwardly down at the sides of a large torso; a bulky ring on his left hand circled the finger so tightly that you'd need to sever the gold band – or the knuckle – to take it off. No doubt, as a typical Berliner he proudly saw himself as *schlagfertig*, always ready to strike.

Florian Grimm had small, slanting eyes that made him look like a bull terrier, and the same well-planted, sturdy stance. Bora had the impression that he might have served on the Eastern front under Nebe. They sniffed one another like kindred dogs who'd been in Russia together, but not necessarily dogs that got along. There is a vast difference between an armed reconnaissance unit and killing missions behind the lines. Bora nodded an acknowledgement. When Grimm offered to carry the briefcase for him, he declined. Before climbing into the car – an Opel Olympia OL38, lovingly kept when compared to the battered and dusty service cars and taxis, which often had all windows smashed in by explosions – he knocked on the boot as a sign for Grimm to open it. Only after choosing a handful of newspaper clippings from one of the boxes did he take his place next to the driver. He'd have sat there in any case, but the back seat happened to be occupied by maps, folders and a hefty Berlin phone book.

"Where to, Colonel?"

"To Lebanonzederpfad, Dahlem."

Grimm looked at him.

"That's where the crime took place, isn't it?"

Having laid the briefcase on his knees (last September, it'd saved him from getting a bellyful of fragments from the grenade), Bora used its surface like a table and leafed through the clippings.

"The house was destroyed by fire, sir."

"We'll see what's left in the grounds. You were the first on the scene, as I understand."

"Yes and no."

Grimm started the car. Dodging the street cleaners still busy removing masonry hurled all the way here by yesterday's bomb, he explained: "On the fourth, a crew from the gas works was due to check some faulty pipes at the victim's residence, at his request. When no one came to open the door, naturally the men thought the leak had turned deadly, and alerted the fire brigade. They forced a window open to enter the property, and verified that there was no perceivable gas leak. But a dead body lay in the hall, so they went no further; they called the local police station from the nearest public phone, and they in turn called us."

"Well, what were your first observations?"

"That he'd been shot dead the evening or the night before. That he was caught off guard just as he'd finished bathing. What struck me most was that I knew the man under a different name."

"Not 'the Weimar Prophet', or 'Magnusson'?"

"Not even close. In the days I saw him perform he was 'Sami Mandelbaum, the Son of Asia'." When Grimm smiled, he showed a golden canine. "I used to attend magic shows at the circus as a boy. Like most boys, I expect."

Bora said nothing. During their childhood, he and Peter had been forbidden to attend the circus, because of the circuses' treatment of "captive wild creatures". It'd been a painful ban, because all their friends went and came back with enthusiastic tales. The Circus Gleich's human cannonball being shot out of a Great War field gun was something Martin would have given an eye tooth to see. But paternal vetoes were the way of life in their household. The garish tie around the inspector's neck – yellow, with purple swirls – would never make it past a Prussian threshold.

Grimm's driving was surprisingly agile for a big man. His familiarity with the state of the streets meant that he took perfect detours to avoid roadblocks and checkpoints. He continued his report.

"No signs of breaking and entering, except for the window forced by the firemen. The front door had a deadlock. Either the victim let the killer in, who then simply pulled the door behind him when he left, or else he had a key. He must have worn gloves, because we found no fingerprints."

"Was anything stolen?"

"Well, see – that's a poser. There was so much stuff in the house, the disappearance of a single item would be obvious only to the owner. When we opened it, the safe was empty. It was one of those small ones used to store documents."

They were heading south-west. Grimm, wedged behind the wheel, spoke as he drove, minding the road when Bora looked at him but secretly staring at Bora when he thought that the officer was engrossed in his papers. Bora, self-conscious about a small razor cut on his jaw from a hasty shave, felt Grimm's eyes on him. It seemed to him that the policeman slowed down when they'd crossed Uhlandstrasse. There, not far from the bachelor's flat belonging to Dikta's hedonistic stepfather, a glum building housed Department IV B of the RSHA – which dealt with the enemies of the regime – and "Gestapo" Müller's dreaded office. The car virtually crept along in front of it. *Is Grimm giving time to those inside to see who's riding with him, and in which direction we're heading? I'd put nothing past the Criminal Police.*

"Tell me, Inspector, have there been similar high-profile murders lately in that neighbourhood, or elsewhere in Berlin?"

Grimm glanced at him.

"No. The last major case was the Ogorzow murders four years ago."

"The 'S-Bahn murderer'? I remember. I was in Berlin then."

"A whole different kettle of fish from this case. The victims were all women, none of them were shot. The crazy thing is that I knew Paul Ogorzow before he started working for the railway. He never did like women, but who ever thought … It's very satisfying when something you personally know about a fellow helps you to solve a case."

Jowly, double-chinned, with his small eyes and short bristle, from this angle Grimm resembled a happy pig more than a bull terrier. "I recalled that Ogorzow underwent treatment for gonorrhoea in our storm trooper days together, so even after he was discarded from the first batch of suspects, I kept thinking about him – that the disease could have *really* made him go off women. And I was right. No, sir. This killing here is one of a kind."

Bora remembered something. "I thought there was another world-famous clairvoyant murdered in town years ago?"

"Steinschneider the Jew, who went by 'Hanussen'?" Grimm shook his head. "He wasn't killed in Berlin. And when we found him near Zossen days later, you could hardly tell what had happened to him. The case remains unsolved."

"Two victims in the same line of work: could we not be facing the same killer?"

"Begging pardon, Colonel. I don't know what kind of experience you have with criminal investigations" – *I shouldn't even be here* was on the tip of Bora's tongue – "but it's always tricky if one starts with a ready-made idea."

"I believe I was given a ready-made list of four suspects," Bora pointed out. Just then, something in the set of clippings relating to Niemeyer's career drew his undivided attention, and he went quiet. What he singled out was a lengthy article signed "Kolo". The night before, he'd noticed an "M. K." listed among the highbrows who frequented Niemeyer between the wars; in both cases, it was likely to be Max Kolowrat, who often wrote under that pen name. Bora folded the cutting and pocketed it.

The bulk of the press material, filling a number of albums and folders, would take hours to sift through, adding to the dimension of his task. The articles he had in hand dated back to the 1920s and 1930s and were in no particular order, but showed just how many people had come in contact with the Weimar Prophet. Photographs accompanied written testimonials from celebrities ("Rosa Valetti and Gussy Hall, fresh from their successful cabaret shows"); others portrayed a tuxedoed Niemeyer at the Coq d'Or, at the Allaverdi and other Russian émigré haunts, with Ernst Kerek of "Jonny spielt auf" fame, and Duke Ellington at the time of his "Chocolate Kiddies" show. Even "HRH the former King of Albania" figured among those who, as Nebe put it, believed in the stars.

Every time Bora glanced up from the papers, his eyes met demolition, ruins and makeshift buildings, long queues and shabbily dressed girls. Weeds growing along the kerb. He obstinately kept to his reading until they reached Grünewald.

"Well," he said then, "let's have it. Ready-made or not, bring me up to date with the profiles of the four possible suspects."

"With famous people, Colonel, there's a queue of loonies who want them dead for some reason." Grimm loosened the knot of his tie. "It was that way with the Jew Steinschneider, and it's the same in this case. Most loonies would never act out their spite, or couldn't if they wanted to. Three out of the four on your list, however, three at least, had access to the house."

"Are you suggesting they could have let themselves in any time they pleased?"

"Two of them, definitely. A former lover – Ida Rüdiger, a hairdresser by trade, who kept a set of keys to the villa – and a well-heeled watchmaker named Eppner, whose wife spent more time with the victim than with him. She was apparently in the habit of slipping in through a back door conveniently left unlocked for her … but for my money, she had a key to it. Then there's Kupinsky, a queer with a shady past who did the gardening for the magician. The last person of interest is Roland Glantz, publisher and proprietor of Sternuhr Verlag, whose business went under thanks to Niemeyer reneging on a deal he'd already been paid for."

"But did the four of them have access to a hunting piece?"

"Let's just say they all know how to shoot."

"It's not the same. I find it difficult to imagine a hairdresser or a book publisher —"

"Consider the fact that before the war the hairdresser habitually went hunting with her husband. The watchmaker belonged to a shooting club for years and served as fusilier in the Great War. Kupinsky's communist father kept an arsenal for the Spartacists, in the old days, and as far as the book-man, when he had money he spent it on African safaris." Aglow with perspiration, Grimm's pink face looked like he was saying *Well, how about that?*

"Have they been brought in for questioning?"

"Not yet."

"Who then collected enough material about Niemeyer to fill two boxes?"

"Those come from the villa. A good thing, too, that we took them along, because the library went up in smoke with the rest."

"But the victim had a police record, correct?"

"Under his three aliases, correct." When Grimm reached for a folder in the back seat, he revealed a glimpse of a concealed holster and the a sweat-stained shirt front. "Here it is."

Bora looked through it. "It's very slim. Some of the items are copies of the dossier I read overnight."

"Not everything goes on file, Colonel." Grimm's expression suddenly precluded further questions.

But a scowl could only intimidate civilians under interrogation. Bora frowned back. "Not every*one* goes on file, you mean. In the dossier I saw initials used in lieu of full names."

"During the Republic, people with enough influence succeeded in never having their surnames entered in, or extracted from, police files. The file is as it was."

Bora slipped the folder inside his briefcase. *Great. I'll have to work with a censored file. And I'm willing to bet that if Niemeyer had Party representatives among his recent clients, their names do not appear anywhere in these papers; they appear somewhere else, in dossiers out of my reach.*

Aside from bomb damage to a church and the local post office, in Dahlem the war seemed to be far away. In order to reach their destination they had to drive past the Kaiser Wilhelm Institute, where Uncle Alfred's funeral had taken place; Bora had read in the morning paper that a physics lecture by Professor Heisenberg, entitled "What are the stars?", was scheduled for the following day. Somehow the topic seemed singularly appropriate to his task. Grimm drove on until they reached a shady lane. Despite its name, there were no cedar trees along Lebanonzederpfad, it was just one of those labels applied to affluent residential developments; signs at street corners recalled exotic flora that ranged from sumac to date palms. The chain that usually denied cars access to the lane hung limply at the side. When Bora rolled down the Opel's window, a balmy air wafted into the car from among the trees. The season seemed mute compared to the Italian summer – without that endless song of the cicadas, which across the southern wilds gave the almost painful impression of a whistling in one's ears. He listened closely but could only hear crickets, and swallows chirping as they swept low over the fastidiously trimmed hedges.

"You'll see, there's nothing left," Grimm insisted.

According to a *Junggeselle* article Bora had read overnight, Niemeyer's villa had been built nearly fifteen years earlier, in expensive Polish lumber from the Białowieża forest. The exterior, constructed with utmost precision, was devoid of nails. Iron had been proscribed inside, too, if the woman columnist was telling the truth: "As was done in the temples of the ancient gods," she wrote, quoting the proprietor's boast. Instead, bronze, copper and silver took the place of iron.

All else was wood – perfect for a blaze. And it was true, there was nothing left. Through the windscreen, Bora saw a building razed to its concrete foundations. Rather isolated from the other residences, the layout of the grounds indicated that a driveway had once led behind the structure; tall shrubs and a garage at the rear would have ensured complete privacy for the owner and his guests.

Grimm opened the car door and hauled his bulk out from behind the wheel. The fire, he said, had devastated eighty per cent, at least, of the building; the rest had been demolished and carted off for reuse or landfill. With the photos of the scene of the crime in his hand, Bora walked up the footpath and looked around. Judging from the scorched greenery skirting the perimeter of the walls, the blaze had been impossible to quench. Not surprisingly, perhaps: the *Junggeselle* article described furnishings of highly perishable materials: rattan chairs and Tibetan prayer flags made of paper, and everywhere silk hangings, wooden prayer wheels, straw mats and gauzy curtains. Still, an entire mansion had *gone*. Had he not known how difficult it was to secure fuel of any kind, Bora would have suspected foul play.

"Is there a thorough report by the fire service?" he asked.

"The flames started in a pipe in the gas fireplace, Colonel. All you need is a spark. With air raids every other day, damaged pipes frequently cause conflagrations. It's routine."

"Of course, phosphorus dissolved in carbon disulphide would do the trick too."

"Why? If the killer wanted to, he could have burned the place down right after the murder. The house was empty."

"The Reichstag was empty, too, when it caught fire, Inspector. Please secure a copy of the fire sergeant's report."

Bora crossed what had once been the threshold, and was soon straddling a collapsed granite pillar, roughly hewn to represent a troll or other misshapen giant. In the images illustrating the *Junggeselle* article, it originally shouldered the vaulted roof of a vast, fern-filled hall. A cartouche reading "A POSSE AD ESSE", which used to be visible over the pillar, had gone along with the rest. The floor surface was the size of at least three tennis courts. No wonder that Niemeyer's motto was "From 'it is possible' to 'it is'". Drops of molten lead and glass were all that remained of what, according to Bora's sources, had been three large Jugendstil windows. Transferred here from a Viennese hotel Aryanized in 1938, they had once faced the mystical east.

The scene of the crime could not teach him much, Grimm was right. He stood there watching Bora, elbows out, his thumbs in his waistband and that brash tie of his looking like the last night's dinner puked up.

"In five days' time," he called out, "with the authorities' blessing, our zealous Berliners picked the place clean. They'd removed the still useable stone and tile flooring as late as yesterday. See how they swept the ground afterwards: you can eat off it. Down there," he added, pointing to a small heap of rubble, "there was a hearth you could fit a dinner table in. On the mantel, the magician kept an urn with his mother's ashes. As I said, it was a gas fireplace, so when it blew up it caused the whole upstairs to cave in. Went up like a match. I arrived after the fire engine, and such flames were shooting out of the windows, the men couldn't even get close. There, see? That spot over there is more or less where the corpse lay when I saw it. If you look at the photos, you'll see the hall was a cross-beamed space in the middle of the villa, from which you could climb upstairs. The bathroom used to be there, where you see pipes sticking out. The tub was half-filled with soapy water when I found the victim." Grimm gestured to the screen of leafy garden plants, still coated in powdery grey. "By now Mama's ashes must be scattered all over the neighbourhood."

"So the bathroom was on the ground floor. If the victim heard a noise, he only had to step out of the tub to meet his killer. The garage was in the back?"

"Yes, separate from the house. It was rickety and they had to tear it down, along with a small storage shed. Luckily the cars inside the garage survived, and have been requisitioned. Because of the limitations on fuel, three of them hadn't been driven for some time. There were five in all."

The back of the grounds, beyond the driveway and the garage, overlooked a small artificial lake surrounded by birches. Its surface was overgrown with water hyacinths – they may have purposely let them spread these days, to hide the shimmering water from the planes.

Bora walked over to it. Grimm followed.

"We dredged it in search of weapons, but no results. Well, not exactly *no* results. We found the wreck of a Duesenberg Model J car, with the remains of two greyhounds inside it. Ah, and those of a Negro as well. American licence plate, under water for the past ten years at least." He squinted in the sunlight. "The detail seemed odd, until we learned that in the old days some Negros had rented a place down the street, during the tour of their revue *A Bird in the Bush*. So raunchy, the show was, that we eventually shut it down. I read about that Duesenberg. It cost a fortune, more than a plot of land with a house on it and everything. And a Negro owner was driving it!"

"And the neighbours? Didn't anyone hear the shots?"

"No. You've seen how large these places are. The other houses are made of brick and stone – they have thick walls and proprietors who love their privacy. They certainly can afford it. Cash is so plentiful in these parts, the premises are still occupied by single families."

They had retraced their steps to the middle of the ground floor when a silver-haired woman, in elegant linen trousers and blazer, interrupted her constitutional to stare at them from the edge of Niemeyer's garden.

"Do you have permission to be there?" she demanded to know.

When Grimm pulled back his coat to show the police badge, she raised a jewelled hand, hunched over a little and turned her head as she walked away, to signal that it was all right then, and no longer of interest.

"Lives next door," the policeman told Bora in an undertone. "Name's Wirth. Her husband's an administrative bigwig at the Charité lunatic ward."

The surname was not new to Bora. Under Max de Crinis, Gero Wirth led the cadre of politically engaged hospital administrators who had allied against his uncle and embittered his final years. "Wait here," he told Grimm, and caught up with the old woman as she strolled to a sprawling house buried among tree roses.

"A word with you, Frau Wirth."

She ignored Bora, and carried on walking until she'd reached her garden gate. Only when her hand was on the latch did she glance back. "I've spoken to the police. I have nothing to add."

Typical. War and hardship hadn't affected this area enough to make these professionals, Party upstarts and commercial parvenus any less arrogant. No evacuees huddled in these attics and basements! Bora could have imposed himself on her by taking Grimm along. Instead, he decided to follow Frau Wirth across the lawn; as she let herself into the house, he inserted his cavalryman's build into the doorway so that she couldn't shut the door on him.

Not that he gained much from the tetchy answers he received. The neighbours had seen little of Professor Magnusson lately – "But doesn't everyone mind his own business these days?"; before the end of 1942, during the days of his grand parties, countless luxury cars with distinguished plates would be parked up and down the street. "We were *always* invited. But you understand – my husband is an eminent scientist, and has a reputation to uphold."

"Do you mean you continued to receive invitations from him, despite the fact that you always turned them down?"

"Until the end of '42, yes. After Stalingrad fell, the lavish parties became scarce, and then ceased altogether. I'm sure he saw clients and friends, women especially. At least three of them committed suicide because of him. Professor Magnusson was a fascinating man."

Fascinating? Perhaps Frau Wirth had been tempted to attend the gatherings, and only her husband's position at the Charité had kept from it. Though clearly annoyed by the interview, she was enough of a gossip to tell a colonel what she might have kept from a Party minion.

"As everyone knows, he was deeply cultured: only not very scientific. He was Swedish, and a Swedenborgian scholar, you see. If you've read his books on mysticism you can't help but appreciate the depth of his understanding."

She was surprised by Bora's lack of reaction. Why, wasn't he familiar with them? Where had he been? Everyone across Germany had devoured the essays. "Especially the treatise on the runic symbolism of the Round Table."

"That has nothing to do with Swedenborg."

Her dismissive tutting was meant to put him in his place. "How can you know, if you haven't read Magnusson?"

"I've read Swedenborg."

"Anyway, as I told the police, neither Dr Wirth nor I heard anything unusual on the night of the crime. With all those horrible Russians and Poles and Italians creeping around in the dark, we don't stay away from the windows. When the blaze started in the dead of night, two days later, we saw the glare through the shutters. Dr Wirth phoned the fire station … but not immediately."

"Why not?"

"Because every day this spring a car would linger for hours on end in different shaded spots in our neighbourhood, so naturally we assumed that Professor Magnusson was under government protection."

*Or surveillance*, Bora thought.

"Still, to be on the safe side Dr Wirth decided to do his duty and give the alarm anyway. After all, the breeze was blowing in our direction. That is all."

Judging from the annoyance in her voice, she was about to give him a terse *Will you go now?* However, what she said instead, eyeing him up and down, was: "Are you from around here? You look as though you might be from around here."

Bora did not care to be accepted as a suitable member of this exclusive neighbourhood. "I'm not," he answered drily. "But I knew Dr Reinhardt-Thoma, over on Dohnenstieg."

A pause, then a reticent little smile. "Ah. The doctor with a son in America." Her tone was colder now, which Bora had fully expected. "He passed away."

Those bourgeois euphemisms. Only privileged civilians could indulge in them these days. "Yes, he died last week. Your husband must have known him."

All at once, reticence became defensiveness. "Well, not really. They were colleagues; it's not the same thing." Guessing from Bora's straight face where he stood, politically, she added, "No religious funeral," with a virtuous shake of the head. "Not even his adopted daughter was present. Dr Wirth only attended because he and the others *had* to. The last thing anyone would expect was for the authorities to give him such a send-off, given the bed that Reinhardt-Thoma had made himself and slept in for years."

"I'm sure my uncle preferred it to sleeping in bad company, Frau Wirth."

Bora watched her blush. He stepped back enough for her to think that she could shut the door in his face, so when his steel-capped boot blocked the door she panicked.

"If you don't … if you don't leave this minute, I will call the police!"

"I came with the police, remember?"

Bora only let Frau Wirth get away with nothing more than a bruised ego because Grimm was waiting for him (and because he knew that his cousin Saskia would continue to live in this neighbourhood). Joining the policeman in the Niemeyer driveway, he asked: "Was the victim under surveillance of some kind? The neighbours noticed a vehicle parked within sight of the villa recently."

"Surveillance? Not by us. Not anymore. We observed him for a few months eleven years ago, after the Reichstag fire, as we did other clairvoyants who came up with sham predictions during that election period. It was then that horoscopes and similar mumbo jumbo were outlawed. Our man officially gave them up, and toured South America. Five years later – when all astrologers had to leave Berlin – he stayed abroad elsewhere another month or so. Practising 'psychic medicine' per se is not forbidden, so that's how he was able to come back and elude the prohibition." Grimm took out a greasy notebook and scribbled something into it.

"The Wirth woman said nothing about a parked car before."

"She thought he was under official surveillance."

"Well, I'll check and see if he was kept an eye on by some other government agency. Say, Colonel, I'm walking over to the fire station to see what they have on the blaze. Care to come along?"

"No, I have to do some more reading. I'll wait."

In this generally quiet neighbourhood, Grimm had left the car unlocked. As soon as he was out of sight, Bora climbed in and reached for the phone book in the back seat. There was only one *Olbertz, A.* listed, a medical doctor; he noted down his office number, 962175. *I will not let him get away with vague hints at a funeral: if he knows something about Uncle Alfred's death, he has to meet me and tell me more.* He then opened the glove compartment and looked through it. A torch, a short truncheon, a six-pack of SA-produced Trommler cigarettes and a box of paper clips shared space with a loaded Mauser HSc. This did not mean the inspector might not also not carry another similar pistol in his pocket, and a larger calibre – a PPK, maybe – in his shoulder holster.

Bora put everything away as he found it, and as he leafed through the folders in the back seat he saw that they belonged to other, unrelated cases. A further search of the car revealed nothing else of interest; the only thing Bora left untouched was the thin, sweaty pillow on the driver's seat.

He'd worked with policemen before – one never knew with them. Trusting them was necessary to getting things done, but also highly inadvisable. During their drive from the Adlon, Grimm spoke of a hunting rifle – loud, unwieldy to carry, but guaranteed to kill – as if its possession weren't impossible in wartime Berlin. Of course, he spoke from experience. Still, Dahlem was out of the way for most city dwellers: you didn't simply take a train or a tram there with a rifle in your pocket or your handbag. In the city centre, phosphorescent paint revealed the ghostly presence of pavements and street corners after curfew, but in the wooded garden quarters visibility must be close to nil. Even assuming he or she had a motor vehicle, a prowler would at some point have to proceed on foot, shouldering the gun and with a torch shaded with red paper or paint as his or her sole aid.

*Of course, leaving aside the list of four, a local killer would have a much easier time of it. Neighbours mind their business, and would only cover for one another at a pinch. The victim might have let in a friend, but would he open the door without a stitch on? Let's not forget that Niemeyer's married girlfriend apparently stole into the house through an unlocked back door. What if the weapon was brought to the property during the day, and kept hidden in the garden until the time came to use it? There is a gardener among the suspects.*

Increasingly puzzled, Bora went to rummage in the boot for more documents. Most of the material was promotional; no private correspondence whatsoever, although you'd expect lots of it. Requests for advice, thank-you notes, love letters, even threats or insults ... If Niemeyer's personal mail had gone up in smoke along "with the rest", as Grimm put it, the loss could include irreplaceable clues. Inside a cardboard sleeve, Bora found a blueprint of the villa. He spread it across the bonnet of the car, and Grimm found him poring over it upon his return.

"Take a look, Inspector: if this discreet little door opposite the garage was ajar, entering unseen through it would've been child's play."

"The back door? Yes. Except that it was closed and locked from the inside when I arrived on the scene. Say the killer found it open: since it couldn't have locked itself, before leaving the scene he'd have to have locked it from the inside and used the front door. Maybe. I think he entered and left through the front door. Here's the fire sergeant's report, Colonel."

The account was not as skimpy as Grimm had suggested. It detailed the time of arrival, equipment used, the ineffectual operations undertaken to douse the fire, and the minor injuries sustained by two crew members. It listed a gas leak as the probable cause, without actually discounting the possibility of arson: the blaze had raged to the extent that no precise answer was forthcoming.

Bora kept any comment to himself. He folded the blueprint and got into the car, and when Grimm plonked himself behind the wheel and asked "Where to next?", he only said, "Tell me about the gardener."

Unexpectedly, the policeman reached under his haunch and pulled out a file from beneath the pillow, where Bora hadn't looked.

"Take it." He started the car. "No need to read my notes about him. Berthold 'Bubi' Kupinsky. As a youngster, he sold his tail at three marks a throw for a living, but a few months in jail after the Fritsch affair straightened him out. At the time he was a waiter at the Café Mexico on Alexanderplatz."

Bora opened the file. *How convenient*, he thought indignantly. *A disreputable café right by the Criminal Police headquarters, where they could readily pick him up and use him to bring scandalous, trumped-up charges of homosexuality against General Fritsch.*

"And now?"

"Now he mows lawns and does the gardening in this neighbourhood. He also looks after domestic pets for their masters. Niemeyer had a house full of them."

"What sort of animals?"

"The feathered kind, especially parrots. The big ones, with a blue tongue." While they spoke, Grimm found a shady spot to park the car. "The zoo has them now. Kupinsky would be close to the bottom of the list of suspects if he hadn't had the bright idea of disappearing after the murder. Talk about a bird taking to the bush!"

Bora did not smile. "His last known address is near Hermannplatz. Is he being actively sought?"

"As actively as possible. At present, due to the air raids, house numbers count for little. He has no family in town or elsewhere, so he could be just about anywhere in Berlin."

"Does he know he's wanted?"

"Only if someone informed him when we delivered the subpoena to the Neukölln address."

"So we don't know where he is."

"For the moment."

In the next ten minutes, Bora learned that in the days of the Republic Kupinsky's parents ran a sweet shop and a dilapidated cinema in Neukölln. Left-wingers, they'd become embroiled in the riots after the Great War, with the result that they lost their businesses, and thus their livelihood. Bora could imagine the bowls of sweets tossed out into the street, the windows smashed by truncheons and rocks. A cinema called Spartakus must have been a red rag waved in front of the SA bulls. The street gangs set it on fire at the end of February 1930, with no thought for the tenants living upstairs. The final count of the victims came to thirteen dead and sixteen ill with smoke inhalation, but a couple of SA lost their lives when they were shot at from the blazing building.

"The end of February 1930 – was it connected to Horst Wessel's death?"

"You bet, Colonel. The Reds killed the best man among us; we couldn't simply grin and bear it." Crowding his passenger, Grimm took out the cigarettes from the glove compartment. He stuck one in his mouth and offered the pack to Bora, who said no. "Anyhow, little more than six years ago Kupinsky surfaced again, and we brought him in as a witness. The Fritsch affair, as I mentioned. It must be said he didn't identify the general as a client, but he was the only one not to."

"General Werner Baron von Fritsch was cleared of all charges by the military court."

Grimm did not dare reply, but from his expression you could tell that, to his mind, a soldier tried by fellow soldiers is likely to be acquitted anyway. He lit the cigarette and carefully blew out the match before tossing it out of the window.

"Kupinsky spent six months in a cell at Moabit. After that, he did odd jobs of all kinds, including distributing leaflets for vaudevilles and other shows. That's how he first met Niemeyer. As you've seen from his photo, when you clean him up you can almost make him look like he's not a pervert."

Without asking, Bora placed the Kupinsky file inside his briefcase. "It's a long way from Neukölln to Dahlem. I suppose the wages he received here made it worth his while. Given that he did regular weekly chores at Niemeyer's house, and given his past, it's understandable that he's in hiding."

Grimm stared at him through a cloud of tobacco smoke. "His past – meaning Kupinsky's or Niemeyer's?"

"Kupinsky's, naturally," Bora fired back. "What are *you* implying: that Niemeyer's sexuality was questionable, too, or that passing himself off as a Jew was in itself reprehensible?"

"With all due respect, that *is* reprehensible in itself, as far as I'm concerned."

"What concerns you or me, Inspector, has nothing to do with this case."

A small gilded insect flew into the car from the thick shrubbery; Bora swatted it away. "Why would a homosexual with a police record kill his employer?"

"I don't know yet *why*. As for *how* – he could have stashed away one of the rifles from his old man's arsenal. Years ago, I did my share of rounds of the places where those Red low-lives congregated, and I wouldn't put any crime past a deviant."

"Kupinsky had better surface soon."

"He will."

Unasked (Bora's curiosity was of a different brand), he added, "I'm from Neukölln myself. I can tell you, it used to be a rough neighbourhood before 1933. My old man, who was a shoemaker by trade, moved us all from Munich to Berlin at the end of the Great War. Seven of us, to Neukölln. I swear, as a boy you faced a simple choice there in those days: you either became a juvenile delinquent or joined the police."

"It's clear which path you chose."

"But only after serving in the storm troops for a spell. Being able to wear shiny boots was what drew me in to begin with." He stole a glance at Bora's riding boots. "First thing I noticed about you, Colonel – top notch, hand-sewn. Not German."

"They're English. Pre-war."

"I thought so. Anyhow, the SA did me good. As a Brownshirt, I learned most of the skills I needed to apply for a job in the Kripo."

*Yes*, Bora told himself, *and you were able to indulge in all the bullying like a juvenile delinquent, without paying the price for it.*

"Did the Russians do that?" Grimm was referring to his injury.

"No."

"The Americans, then? The English?"

"No." For all his sternness, Bora was seldom gruff. But he rather resented being asked about it, and had to force himself to go beyond monosyllables. "It was partisans, the day I arrived in Italy. You can be sure that they've never caught me off guard since." He glanced at the watch on his right wrist. It was 10:30 a.m. His appointment for a late lunch with Salomon was two and a half hours away. Whether he wanted to or not, he should head back to the city centre. "Let's see which suspect we can interrogate today. The Rüdiger woman?"

"For sure. Rüdiger, Ida, 47." Grimm finished his cigarette. Leafing through his dog-eared notebook with his big thumb, he read: "Hairdresser to the élite. Lives across from the post office on Landgrafenstrasse, in the Zoo quarter. The most high-ranking Party wives send their chauffeurs to pick her up when they need her."

"Let's hope none of them is having her hair done now. Does she own a shop?"

"Looks as though she works from her apartment. She was bombed out of her Ku'damm shop last November. We don't have an official photo, because she has never been arrested." Grimm's choice of those words – instead of saying "She never broke the law" – was pregnant with meaning. "Although she teamed up with Niemeyer, she's still married to a member of the Border Guards. And, as I said, she's familiar with firearms."


LANDGRAFENSTRASSE, 11:10 A.M.

*Friseurin – Coiffeuse.* The rich lettering on the third-floor door led to an elegant waiting room, where a petite girl in a light-blue smock told the visitors that she would fetch Madame for them.

Naturally, neither Bora nor Grimm waited. Through an archway, they glimpsed the unfamiliar sight of a particularly female space. Partitions covered in abstract wallpaper separated the different stalls, each of them supplied with a hairdryer consisting of a metallic contraption on a stand with a long, flexible tube, and from the ceiling hung what resembled a lamp dripping with wires, used for the "permanent" curling of hair. Everywhere sinks and taps, shelves lined with bottles and containers of all kinds, towels in every shade of pastel. No clients, but three young hairdressers, who had time to squeal their surprise at this male intrusion before a gleaming white French door opened to reveal a very altered Ida Rüdiger.

"What is the meaning of this?"

Her perfumed, stylish person looked unimpressed when Grimm followed his usual badge-flashing with a mumbled "Criminal Police".

"This way," she said, directing them into her quarters.

The atmosphere there was smart and airy. Ida Rüdiger made it clear to the visitors that she would not be intimidated by the law or by military rank. "I have two ministerial secretaries' wives and the sister of a field marshal coming shortly," she declared. "I hope there's a good reason for your barging in like this."

Women may be quicker to respond than men, but once they've rallied their wits men often overreact.

"The 'reason' is Walter Niemeyer's murder," Bora said, without flinching. As for Grimm, he did an about-turn and pushed the door open.

"How completely stupid and outrageous! I warn you, sir, there'll be consequences." Swathed in a tailored, low-necked scarlet gown, the manicured and aggressive Ida Rüdiger reminded Bora of the painted figurehead on a sailing ship. She was the sort of self-assured entrepreneur who in the old days would have advertised her shop as "catering to crowned heads". And judging by the photos of some female members of the old imperial family on the walls, she probably *had* arranged their curls, years before.

She stood her ground. "Don't think that you can frighten me, Colonel. I have influential friends, and can afford the best of lawyers."

Bora was suddenly both angry and amused. He removed his cap and cradled it in the crook of his arm. "Why would I think of myself as *frightening*?"

"As if you didn't know! Your size, your uniform ... you can't fool me." Critically tilting her head, she added: "Who cuts your hair? A tad too much of the razor ... but I can live with it."

"The regimental barber will be thrilled."

"There is nothing to smile about! My space is being brutally invaded. I demand an explanation."

"Frau Rüdiger, to start with, I don't *think* of myself frightening – I have the authority to *be* frightening. Second, it is *I* who demand to hear when you last saw Walter Niemeyer, whether there were any serious disagreements between you – and if so, why – and whether you have access to firearms."

Her well-drawn eyebrows rose critically. "Firearms, plural? Isn't one enough for you?"

"It depends. Tell me."

"There's nothing to say. The possession of firearms is forbidden, as you are well aware."

Bora thought of Bruno Lattmann, teaching his wife how to shoot. "Some women illegally secure guns and practise shooting for personal protection."

"Ha! Have your minion search the premises. I don't need guns. And in case you're wondering, let me disabuse you of the idea that there were any weapons in Walter's home. He detested hunters and bloodshed in general." She arranged a curl behind her ear, as if she were standing in front of a mirror. "It's true that my former husband collected guns old and new. But that was before the war, when grousing was not yet against the law in Silesia."

"'Former' husband? I was under the impression that you're still married."

She gave him a spiteful look. The scarlet dress, trimmed in emerald green, struggled to contain her outrage.

"So young and already so hidebound." ("I'm not hidebound," Bora interrupted.) "I met Walter for the last time on Saturday, the sixth of May, at Kranzler's. I couldn't forget the date if I wanted to: the following day the café was wrecked by a bomb. We argued. As always, he tried to avoid the subject, which was his latest flame – he spun me a tale about feeling destruction all around us, and hearing the shattering of windows all along Ku'damm. I'd had more than I could take, so I tossed my iced tea in his lap. Well, so what? It's no secret that I was furious with him for his continuous cheating, especially given his intolerance to cheating on my part. What's good for the goose is good for the gander – if you get my meaning."

"I'm not hidebound," Bora repeated.

"Whatever."

She suddenly pulled something out of her plunging neckline that resembled a mother-of-pearl compact but was actually a card case.

"Here's the name of my solicitor. I know my rights. I have friends, even in law-enforcement circles."

Nebe's and Heldorff's names were just two among the hoard that she flashed at him, loosened from the elastic band that held them together.

"Had I wanted to get rid of Walter, I'd have turned him in for drafting horoscopes in violation of the law. The night he died, Colonel, I was with this gentleman." She took out the card of an assistant to the Propaganda Minister. "Surprised? I dress Frau Magda Goebbels's hair, and lovely Reichsmarschallin Göring's as well. Don't waste your time here: go ask the hag Walter's been bedding lately. Or rather, ask her husband. Eppner's the name." She tapped her chin with her manicured finger, as you do when you call another's attention to his own face. "Know what, though?" she commented. "You shouldn't do your own shaving."

When Bora and Grimm left the apartment, the policeman trailed an odour of lotion and slightly singed hair down the stairs, from his interrogation in the salon. "I told the three young helpers to remain available," he said, "and I've phoned the station and told them to send two men for a thorough search of the premises. They will be here in half an hour, but I doubt there's much to be gained from it."

Bora quietly noticed that Grimm was holding a folded piece of paper in his right hand. "Well, what do you think overall?"

"Other than that she wears costly Italian shoes? She does well for herself, and there's no sign of a man's presence in the flat." Grimm stopped on the landing, where an open window let some air into the stuffy stairwell. "Her young helpers are intimidated. By her, not by us. Not that they would tell, but for my money they really have no idea what Ida Rüdiger does once they leave work – incidentally, the girls all live together, since two of them are evacuees. Their homes were bombed out. They can't tell if or when Madame went to visit the victim, although they're aware that she'd lived with him. The other tenants are respectable state employees and pensioners, and when we sent for him the block warden had nothing to report about them or Ida Rüdiger. The penalty is severe, if he's found to withhold information, so it must be that she's very prudent, or on the level."

Bora nodded. The scrupulous cleanliness of the stairwell contrasted with the loss of plaster here and there due to bombs having fallen nearby. "She declares that she spent the night of the murder with an official from the Propaganda Ministry. Here's his card. Above our station, I'm afraid. Freely admits she knows how to shoot a rifle, and claims Eppner the watchmaker is our man. What do we know about her estranged husband?"

"He's serving at the front in France. There's also a grown-up son, under arms and assigned in the east somewhere."

Bora started down the next flight of steps. *Somewhere. That's how they referred to us when we were in Russia. "In the east somewhere." Why not? We often didn't know ourselves where we were.*

"An interesting titbit, Colonel, is that pansies come to get their hair done here as well." Because Bora was watching him, Grimm kept the slip of paper in his hand, rather than putting it into one of his pockets. "The wealthy ones who've got good protection, anyway. I showed the girls Kupinsky's photo and they burst out laughing because of his forelock. They've never seen him."

"Is the Rüdiger telephone being monitored, by any chance?"

"Was. The 'service' was discontinued months ago, after a request from upstairs. Obviously a side effect of her cheating on Niemeyer with high-ranking government blokes. As for the Niemeyer residence, his extensions were obviously all tapped."

"And?"

"Waste of time. Too clever to discuss anything controversial down the line." Grimm slowly crumpled the piece of paper. "I supervised the installation of listening devices in Greater Berlin for a while. Before the war, it was easy to pass yourself off as a telephone company worker. For the past five years everything's had to be done in the absence of owners or tenants, because the moment you enter a house wearing overalls or carrying a toolbox they know what you're there to do."

This wasn't news to Bora. Wherever he travelled, he was in the habit of checking the room where he stayed, looking for signs of concealed microphones. He'd removed or put out of operation several of them, and – like Niemeyer – never spoke of topics that could be used against him. At the Adlon, he'd inspected Nina's suite before chatting with her, and both had lowered their voices when discussing Uncle Reinhardt-Thoma.

"What about Eppner, Inspector, is he around?"

"More's the shame – another evacuee. I'll have to go back to headquarters to track him down." Grimm halted on the step, pulled out a pocket watch and contemplated it. "Might as well do that next. Drop you somewhere for lunch?"

"The Adlon, please."

Noticing that Grimm was lagging behind, Bora turned. He saw him conceal the paper along with the watch inside his pocket. Caught in the act, the policeman automatically took it out and showed it to him.

It was a note, scribbled in a girl's childlike handwriting. "Since we were there, I asked one of the helpers for a recipe. My wife needs a fixer you can make at home."

Bora read: *Hydro-alcoholic preparation – rectified alcohol, 2.8 millilitres, Lavender water 3.2 millilitres, water 20 millilitres, sodium borate 20 grams, glycerine 30 grams.* "She says it can last months, once you bottle it. You use it with an eyedropper."

A weathered limousine was pulling up to the kerb as the two men left the house. Here came Ida Rüdiger's clients: a trio of middle-aged ladies with heads of improbable colours and impossibly tight curls. How women got themselves up, even in times like these... *Not my mother*, Bora thought, *British in this as in many other regards, who wears her naturally wavy hair parted on one side. Nor Dikta, who let hers down only when she came to bed.* The thought of his women could have made him melancholic, but his attention shifted to a man in civvies, standing on the doorstep of the post office across the street. The attitude, lazy and stock-still, was not that of a mere onlooker. Keeping an eye on a high-ranking official's lover, or her clients, or ... ?

Bora glanced at Grimm, who headed for the parked Olympia seemingly unaware of the observer. But the fact that he was acting oblivious didn't mean that he was.

Before they pulled away from the kerb, the policeman turned the car radio on. They'd missed the midday news broadcast by a few minutes. The pretentious notes of Liszt's

'Prelude' were already fading into the usual report from the High Command: "Das Oberkommando der Wehrmacht gibt bekannt ..."

"Leave it on," Bora said.

News about the battle around Minsk made his stomach sink. He saw through the sober euphemisms and was not deceived: place names did not lie, and they spelled a rout. Having trundled on horseback through Belarus three years earlier at about this time of year, when German progress seemed unstoppable, he knew the course that the loss of Bobruysk and the crossing of the Pripet marshes would draw on the map. *Our family place in East Prussia is twice as far from Berlin as it is from Minsk.*

"Just you watch, we're letting them approach before we spring the trap on them," Grimm said, boldly turning the car around on the soft asphalt.

Bora had nothing to say.

Predictably, Salomon changed his mind. At the front desk of the Adlon, Bora found a sealed envelope containing the scribbled address of an open-air restaurant not far from the hotel. Free of Grimm's presence until two, before emerging once more into the heat of the day, he spoke to the concierge: "I don't know if I will stay on here. I'm expecting a telegram from my mother, so please put it aside for me. Don't assign my room to anyone else yet. If necessary, I'll be back later to retrieve my things."

In the lobby were stationed a handful of General Staff officers, chatting among themselves. Bareheaded, they were clearly hotel guests congregating before lunch in the dining room below. Was their presence the reason why Salomon had chosen to eat elsewhere? Two of them glanced over, rather nervously, in Bora's opinion. They replied to his nod in a hurried, mechanical way and ostensibly turned their backs again. It was what you do to send a clear signal that you're not inviting familiarity.

Bora had seen similar edginess before, something between the clannishness of classmates and the hostility of a pack of wolves.

He walked out, baffled rather than hurt. *What is going on?* Naturally, there might be worse news from any one of the three endangered front lines, but the officers' response had a different flavour, somehow immediate, closer to the skin. At the "shop", they'd taught him to "mark the day and hour" whenever he noticed uncharacteristic behaviour among colleagues, for future reference. And that was what Bora did: *12:30 p.m., 11 July 1944.*

12:57 P.M.

The difference between the haves and the have-nots had not been so blatant in years.

Gone were the days of river cruises for labourers and excursions abroad for lower-class youngsters, of the affordable amenities and mass participation in the German good life. A few blocks away from where Bora sat, coupons and queues for simple foodstuffs represented the daily grind, jarringly incidental to this *all'aperto* restaurant shaded by camouflage netting. But even in the handful of remaining luxury spots in Berlin, menus contained more and more unprecedentedly homely dishes. Cabbage, potatoes, pork and the ubiquitous *Eintopf* (which contained everything but the kitchen sink) had ominously made their way to this once charming establishment.

Bora's mind was focused not on the lunch, however, but on the reason for this meeting. He waited for his table companion, caught between annoyed curiosity and the temptation to resume the interrogator's habit of wheedling the truth out of his counterpart. Truth be told, he wasn't sure that he wanted to learn what Salomon might have overheard, and perhaps misread, at headquarters.

He watched the colonel appear on the restaurant terrace in a summer suit – officers in civilian clothes were a common sight in Berlin. The now disgraced General Oster had made a practice of it. What troubled Bora was Salomon's guardedness, so obvious that it made him stand out even more.

The edgy General Staff officers at the Adlon came back to mind. Bora knew headquarters, its rules and foibles, the danger of entropy. He'd served under certain members of the General Staff; others he'd known for other reasons, not all work-related. The years spent in military counter-espionage meant that he'd learned more about his colleagues and superiors than he cared to know. He'd stumbled on baffling wire-tap transcriptions, reports, recordings of radio exchanges (coded or not), titbits like fragments after a shipwreck or a blast: unrecognizable and irrelevant unless one kept them in mind to piece together later.

Thus, he knew all too much about some of them: about the Schulenburgs, from his days at the embassy in Moscow, between 1940 and '41; about others – like Oster – he recalled disquieting tales, hints dropped over cognac at the officers' mess, ever since returning from Spain in 1938. But among comrades and brother officers, often of the same social class, mouths remained shut, no conjectures were made. True, a few openly expressed their feelings about the war and even politics. In Russia, he once overheard a general grumbling to his aide, "That arsehole, Hitler ...", but griping is typical of soldiers. Surely Labienus complained about Caesar at times during the Gallic war. And eventually Labienus did betray Caesar.

Salomon saw him rise from his chair. He ordered him to sit down again with a short nod, like a nervous tic. Bora counted the seconds as he watched him approach tentatively, until, as God willed, he reached the haven of their table.

"At ease," he whispered, to keep Bora from greeting him. "I thought you were leaving Berlin. Have you ordered? No?

Order at once – anything. No wine for me." He sat down and immediately took out a round little box, whose contents he emptied out on his plate: at least five different pills, which he arranged in a row according to size. "I don't know if it's harder for me to fall asleep or to stay awake."

It was typical of the colonel to ignore others during his tormented moments. If he noticed Bora's mutilation, he disregarded it completely. After Bora had ordered, he waited impatiently, darting quick, distracted glances across the table-cloth. When the waiter arrived with bottled water, he asked him to pour at once, and swallowed all the pills together.

Bora waited. Outwardly unflinching, he read with increasing concern the signs of mental strain in Salomon's grim silence. The first course came, and still the colonel said nothing. Yet Bora judged the open-air restaurant reasonably safe: he couldn't exclude the presence of government agents among the customers, but the tables were spaced far apart enough to permit free conversation.

"Sir, I have exactly forty minutes," he began. "Please tell me what is happening."

It was not at all the preamble he had been planning, but never mind. Better be direct.

"Are you mad?" Salomon scolded him. "As if I could tell you what is happening!" He spoke under his breath, but emphatically, looking over his shoulder like a schoolboy who fears that someone will copy his paper.

*Hasn't shaved since yesterday*, Bora noted, *and probably hasn't slept in his bed at the Adlon, either. What the devil is with him, and how do I get him to talk?*

"In that case, sir, acquaint me with the circumstances that led the officers you mentioned yesterday to speak my name. I have a right to know."

"Fritz-Dietlof heard about you —"

"This I'm aware of, and also from whom he heard. Tell me where, and why."

The food could have been cardboard, for all the distraught Salomon cared: he ate merely to keep his countenance. Between apathetic mouthfuls, he lost himself in innuendos, metaphors, but Bora was beginning to separate the wheat from the chaff.

Knowing the man, he was not yet ready to worry. Aware of the effect a listener's attitude can have on a nervous speaker, he calmly interjected, "You did not answer my question. At any rate, I fail to see how a few discouraged words from men exhausted by long working hours can in any way implicate you. Have you considered asking for a furlough?"

Salomon nearly choked as he drained his glass. "What are you saying? Don't you understand? It is … It is about *high treason*, and they saw me!"

Bora went ice-cold. "They saw you – where?"

"At Home Army headquarters." (*Yes, of course*, Bora thought, *in his capacity he would visit the Bendlerblock from his office in Zossen.*) "The two officers I spoke of are privy, more than privy …"

*Jesus Christ, I can only play things down, and keep my head while he loses his.* "And what do I have to do with it?"

They fell silent while the waiter brought the second course. Salomon refused it with a disgusted wave; not Bora, who was hungry, and continued to eat under the colonel's resentful stare.

"The same arrogance," Salomon hissed. "The same overconfidence that will ruin us all. But remember that 'Rebellion is worse than murder, and is the gravest of sins. Neither injustice nor tyranny justify rebellion.'"

As a Protestant, he'd naturally appeal to Martin Luther. Bora swallowed his mouthful, dabbed his lips with the napkin and for nearly a minute simply stared at the colonel. He might well have given an impression of condescending haughtiness, but in fact he needed that pinch of time to sketch out a plan.

"I have no knowledge of the *things* you're referring to," he stated. "I am a soldier, and my duty is to fight." As a sign of

117

unconcern, he allowed himself to watch an attractive woman walking by. "Did you simply wish to inform me, or is there something else?"

"Don't toy with me." Salomon vibrated with anxious rage. "Whatever the reason is for your presence in town, I'm *on to you*. Clear? You served under me in the Ukraine. I'm not blind."

The fork Bora had in his hand noiselessly came to rest on the edge of his plate. "Anything you think you know about me, Colonel, is certainly no mystery to the secret police. And here we are. You sought me out, you said what you wanted to say. Did you simply wish to inform me, or is there something else?"

Just as quickly as he'd lost his temper, Salomon caved in. Tears filled his eyes. He had to sham a coughing fit to conceal his turmoil. But he was crying out of fear, and something had to be done quickly. Bora summoned the waiter to pat the colonel's back, as is customary when a morsel sticks in someone's throat. Then he took the situation in hand; he rose from the table and firmly steered Salomon towards the men's toilets. There, he compelled him to rinse his face and remain seated on the toilet for a few minutes. If there ever was a room where a listening device could be hidden, a toilet was it, so Bora commanded silence by placing his forefinger on his lips.

Aloud, he instructed him: "Now we'll go back to our table and order a digestif. If you have something for your hay fever with you, it is best if you take it now." Another pill emerged from Salomon's pocket, and was gulped down at once.

Whatever the medication contained, together with a shot of brandy it ended the crisis. Bora calmly finished his meal, declined coffee and liquor, and since his drowsy colleague kept rummaging through his pockets for his wallet, he paid for both.

As they parted ways, he expected to hear from Salomon anything other than what the man said: "You must help me to escape from Germany."

# 4

*Cassandra did not change the fate of Troy, and the living demand their due.*

MAXIMILIAN SLADEK, 'OUR SHOW'

1:59 P.M.

"How did it go, Inspector? Did you find Eppner?"

Bora sounded controlled, almost easy-going, when they met in front of the Adlon. Grimm nodded. Perspiration was streaming from his closely cropped skull down his forehead; only a pair of tobacco-coloured brows kept it from dripping into his eyes. "Looks as if he ended up at his sister-in-law's at Bergholz, out in the sticks."

Bergholz, in fact, was not far from the Beelitz sanatorium. Although the ten or so minutes Bora spent calming himself after confronting Salomon had failed to obliterate the traces of his irritation, he needed to consult with Lattmann again. "No time like the present," he said, getting into the car. "Let's go."

During the first part of the trip he read more of the Niemeyer material, setting aside the items that deserved a closer analysis. He tried to remind himself that Salomon was a pessimist, prone to let his imagination run wild; he'd been placed under medical observation after his nervous breakdown years earlier. High treason! Undoubtedly, he'd heard a couple of indiscreet High Command colleagues say *something*, and his tendency to jump to conclusions had probably done the rest. Still, in his present state he was a loose cannon who could create complications. Having served two years at the Abwehr headquarters, Bruno Lattmann was likely to have privileged information he might be convinced to share. *Why was he so*

*insistent that I stay away from Salomon? And why do I keep think-*
*ing of the jumpy officers at the Adlon, and the man watching from*
*the post office on Landgrafenstrasse? I shouldn't do what Salomon*
*does – make mountains out of molehills. All the same, I need to hear*
*what else Bruno has to say.*

Near Schöneberg's central police station, they had to wait for
the manoeuvring of some heavy equipment ahead. Grimm
turned off the engine and sat wedged behind the wheel, fan-
ning himself with a folder.

"Gerd Eppner," he informed Bora, "is only distantly related
to the famous watchmaker brothers who had their shop on
Charlottenstrasse, but he's done well for himself. Anything
you need to know about his wife's affair with the victim is in
this folder, courtesy of the Dahlem police department." He
gave Bora the contents of the folder, keeping the cardboard
cover so that he could continue to fan himself.

When the officer returned the police report after reading
through it, Grimm replaced it in the folder. He then left the
car to chat with the policemen down the road, and when he
returned he said, "It'll take a while. We might as well make
ourselves comfortable."

"Are there no alternative routes?"

"No. Now there's a house-to-house search ahead too. We
have to wait."

Whether to kill time, or to contribute to the case with a
personal recollection, he then said, "You know, from my days
in Neukölln, I can tell you lots about the Son of Asia."

"I'm listening."

"Sure, he went by Magnus Magnusson later on, but at the
start of his career, roughly from '22 to '32, we all knew him as
'Mandelbaum the Son of Asia', a Galician Jew."

"I'd heard."

"Ah, but you may not know that he passed himself off as
a lapsed Jew who'd been turned out by his folks because he

broke the Sabbath and such. Matter of fact, he told how his old man once found him eating a piece of sausage with a Polack child his age, and beat him black and blue. But it was all a story, understand? All made up. He was not a Jew!"

"This I also know."

"Can you imagine an Aryan who pretends to be a Jew, who makes up a whole past in a shtetl, complete with your fallen-down huts and noisy neighbours, your pious *rebbe* and suffering at the hands of those mean Polacks?" Grimm snorted. "You had to hear his sing-song: 'I was born twelfth of twelve children, like the tribes of Israel!' During the Republic, Jewish quacks and magicians were all the rage, and he tugged at the heartstrings of his public with those tales. All lies, but after the war the fat merchants, the profiteers and those who'd stabbed the Fatherland in the back … well, they liked to sit in their warm furs and listen to the woes of the poor little Jew Mandelbaum, who owned nothing in the world but his 'great gift'. You almost felt like you were there, with him in that muddy handful of huts, with the shul at the end of the street where the geese honk, and the overbearing Polack farmers on the other side. I myself, who was then an apprentice and a regular of circuses and cabarets, drank up all those lies of poverty and redemption … By God, you almost wanted to be there with him, in the filthy shtetl with a father who's a tailor and ruins his eyes at the sewing machine, and on holidays slaps the ratty *shtreimel* of wild mink tails on his head. We ate it all up, us dumb Aryans. Me, he didn't fool me too long. Those days, me and my Party comrades broke heads in back alleys when it was called for. I don't scare easy. I performed a tour of duty in Russia and have no problem admitting that I killed my share of real Jews in the East." Grimm interrupted himself, because Bora said nothing. "You aren't batting an eye, Colonel. Don't you like to hear comments like this? You may belong to the old-fashioned army, but we each have the experiences we have."

"There is just one army, and it's the German army."

"Right you are. Anyhow, you won't believe this – or maybe you will – it was the Yids themselves who unmasked him one fine day. My favourite story! It must have been late in '31, at Oppeln, where the Party had sent me. He was already famous there and soon he would be even more so, as he'd predicted. What he didn't foresee was that there would be two real Jews from Lodz in the audience. At some point they'd had their fill of all that bullshit about the shtetl, so they up and asked him one or two questions of the kind only a Yid can answer. Well, Mandelbaum didn't know the answer. He tried, but failed miserably. With the entire hall in a hubbub, at the end of the show there was so much confusion that the Yids – they were strong like bulls – were able to catch him and pulled down his pants, to see how much exactly he descended from David. And he didn't! By God, he didn't! He was no *schejner Jid*! The roof all but came down, people were laughing so hard. That too was a show, and of the most amusing sort. Anyway, when all was said and done, it ended well for our hero. After a week spent in a cheap little hotel to lick the wounds sustained by his self-love, he got a call from the folks at the Circus Kludsky, and shortly thereafter by a big impresario who even back then already knew the difference between Christians and Jews. The Son of Asia had the bright idea of making a confession of sorts before his next show – he published it as a booklet, and distributed it widely. He explained how the popularity of the Yiddish singers and entertainers from the Pale of Settlement had convinced him that *that* was the only way to obtain favour with the public. Cripes, did it work! I wasn't present, but I know some who heard that public confession, and it went over so well that a couple of females started bawling. After several cases of beer had circulated, we all went to beat up the Yids living in the neighbourhood, just to teach them right from wrong." Grimm sighed at the fond recollection. "That was how we learned his 'true life story', which was every bit as interesting as the first one. Magnus Magnusson was the son of a poor sailor from Sweden, who'd worked his way through a university degree. Except that he wasn't from Scandinavia at all; he just fed us more bullshit. But at least, given that things were starting to change in Germany by then, he never tried the Jewish ruse again." He watched Bora, who seemed unmoved. "This was just a long story to explain to you what went through my mind when I heard he died. So many lies. That's what he died of."

"Lies, and a couple of shots from a hunting rifle."

The traffic slowly began moving again.

BERGHOLZ, 4:02 P.M.

The cottage had a vaguely oriental appearance, due to the way the gables sloped and then curled up at the bottom edge, over the gutter. A semicircular porch lined with ivy formed a two-storey front part, whose upper floor resembled a glorified dormer with four windows; a short flight of steps led up to the entrance; the rest of the façade was dressed in bright green creepers. It was the type of spacious porch where wicker furniture and flowerpots are arranged in the good season; none were present now, perhaps for fear that they might be stolen.

When Bora neared the entrance, the furious yapping of a small dog intensified within. Grimm followed half a step behind, to his right, as he probably did with a partner on patrol.

In those days of intermittent power supply door-ringing often came to nothing, and the Eppners had solved the problem by installing an old-fashioned bell, complete with a shiny brass chain and an ornate little plaque that read *Please pull*. The single toll aroused a paroxysm of barking, which a woman's gentle, accented voice tried to soothe. The door opened; the girl standing there with a pug in her arms did not look German. Her round face, with its high cheekbones, blushed with astonishment on hearing Bora address her in Russian.

"Zdravstvutye," she answered, after a moment. To the question of whether the Eppners were in, she answered that "Mistress" wasn't, but "Master" was.

*Twenty-seven years after the October Revolution, more or less her age – and here she is, calling those she works for "masters".* Bora pointed this out to her with a smile, and she grew more confused than before.

"No need to announce us," he added, urging her to take a step back to let him in. There was no question that the bespectacled man of around sixty, in shirtsleeves and with a callipers in his hand, was Herr Eppner in person, come to scold the girl for speaking Russian. At the sight of the strangers, he went from crossness to alarm.

"Get out!" He dismissed both maid and dog. "Gentlemen … ?"

On principle, Bora didn't usually stand on ceremony with civilians: imagine a murder suspect in a satin house jacket. He curtly explained what they were here to discuss, and once Grimm had identified himself Eppner had no objection. He led the visitors beyond a well-lit breakfast room, to what he called his "laboratory".

The room, clearly a former parlour, was now crowded with metal shelves on which odd instruments of all kinds, lathes, vices and boxfuls of wheels, screws, knobs, tweezers, magnifying glasses and miniature anvils shared space with finished clocks and watches, all deadly still.

They all marked different, silent hours, as if in more than one sense time had stood still. *At each of these hours something happened or will happen to me,* Bora told himself. *If I really knew how to read these clock faces I would understand what, remember what. It was 16:27 when the grenade struck the car last September. I'd just checked my wristwatch, and it's the last thing I remember. When the shooting was over, it seems I sought my wedding ring in the dust,*

*because my hand was no longer there, and neither was the wristwatch.
It's true what I told Nina, that I don't recall any pain. But each of
the hours on these clock faces, randomly, matches a precise time from
my past and future, and everybody's.*

"You're wondering why I don't wind them," Eppner volunteered, "but you see, we ourselves are guests here, and my
sister-in-law's nerves fray easily. This is a temporary accom-
modation for us. Our home is far more spacious. I assure you,
however, that every one of these instruments is functioning,
very much functioning."

Was he making conversation to gain time? Bora did not
look amused, so there came a generic apology: "I really don't
know how I can be of use to you, gentlemen. I am not even
acquainted with the person whose death you are here to
discuss."

Bora was on the verge of saying, "Your wife knew him
well enough." But he had no time for games. "Where is Frau
Eppner?"

"At our shop on Breitenbachplatz. Someone has to mind
the shop while I recover from colic. What does Frau Eppner
have to do with — whatever the name of the deceased is?"

Bora quickly listed Niemeyer's aliases, and since the watchmaker still pretended not to understand, he added, "Well,
Walter Niemeyer was killed, and for reasons possibly obscure
to you but not to us, you are among the possible suspects."

Eppner rested the callipers on his cluttered worktable.
"What? I live out here in the country, how could I ever —"
He stopped, because Bora had never mentioned the victim's
address. He awkwardly tried to correct himself. "If as you said
they called him the Weimar Prophet he must have lived in
Weimar, no?"

"Not at all." Bora took out his notebook. "According to our
information, after leaving your bomb-damaged home in the
centre of Berlin, you spent ten days in the quarter of Steglitz."

"Ah, then the crime happened in Steglitz."

"No, not in Steglitz. In nearby Dahlem. Don't you read the papers?"

"I do not."

Bora stared at a series of carved clocks from the Black Forest, decorated with an array of dead hares and pheasants, stag horns, game bags and hunting guns. "But you listen to the radio."

"No."

"And you never even go to the post office, the bakery or the tobacconist's …"

Eppner stiffened. When the satin cord around his house jacket came undone, he swept it up before it reached the floor. Brandishing it like a whip, he carefully picked his words: "I do not engage in gossip with shopkeepers. The chores I leave to the servant, or to my lady wife."

"A foreign worker is not a servant," Bora snapped back, "and I rather doubt your wife is a lady."

Grimm, who was poking around the instruments on the shelves, burst out laughing at the words.

Bora's briefcase came to rest on the worktable, scattering the diminutive tools. He took out a typewritten sheet. "Here's a complaint for disturbing the peace, filed at the Dahlem police station on Cecilienallee. Your name is on it. You may not have known Niemeyer as thoroughly as other members of your family, Herr Eppner, but you still parked not one but six times in front of the victim's property, 'repeatedly', as you can read here, 'activating the car-horn instrument known as *Schalmei* at all hours, causing not only annoyance but outright alarm to the whole neighbourhood'." Grimm laughed; Bora turned around crossly, but the policeman was having such a fit that he had to leave the room. "Furthermore, a witness testified that at least on one occasion you threatened to kill your wife *and* Niemeyer. Before you deny it, consider that it was your wife who shared the threat with someone, who then reported it to the police station down the street from here."

A punctilious Eppner tried to put his disarranged table in order. "That *someone* is my sister-in-law, who cannot be trusted. I deny …" Without glancing back, Bora could read on his face that Grimm must have quietly come back in, and replaced laughter with a look of physical threat. "I *do not* deny" – the watchmaker had changed his tune – "that past indiscretions have led to a misunderstanding with my wife. But I resent that idle gossip is deemed more credible than the word of a faithful taxpayer and Party member." While he spoke, he tied the satin cord around him with three knots, tight enough to make it virtually impossible to undo. "As for my family situation, unless you're married, you can't understand —"

Bora cut him short. "Enlighten me, then."

It took an agitated Eppner a good half hour to provide an alibi and tell his version of the story, while Grimm disappeared again to search the house. Bora heard drawers being yanked out, the trampling of feet overhead; the little dog, relegated to a closet somewhere on the ground floor, alternatively whined and scratched at the door to be set free. At one point Bora summoned the Russian girl to fill in some details.

The tiresome narrative of the watchmaker's self-defence ("Spoiled wives, when their men work as hard as I do … three shops in Berlin alone … The so-called Prophet was a true hoodwinker, let me tell you …") was winding down when the policeman marched back in and placed a Sauer automatic and a box of ammunition in front of Bora. "They were stuck inside a disconnected boiler, wrapped in cellophane. The gun's loaded. The ammo is a mixed bag. One of them" – he did not say which – "matches."

A sudden change came upon Eppner. "Match? Match? Match *what*? Give it back!" He uselessly tried to snatch the gun from the policeman. "You are looking at a second lieutenant in the Berlin Garde-Regiment zu Fuss, who earned his right to bear arms thirty years ago! I will be goddamned, do you hear me? I will be goddamned before I give up my self-defence and let anyone harm me and mine, in my shops or in my home!"

Grimm sneered. "Liar. In the time it'd take you to fish the gun out and unwrap it, an intruder would riddle you like a sieve. This," he said as he weighed the pistol in his fist, "and the fact that you violated the law on foreign workers by keeping an *Ostarbeiter* in your home, is enough for me to take you to Alex for a talk."

Bora examined the pistol and returned it to the policeman. It was not the murder weapon, and until a rifle was discovered on the premises he'd lost all interest in this lead, thanks to the alibi provided by Eppner in his long-winded tale. From the breakfast room, Grimm phoned the closest police station to get men sent over for a thorough search of the house. Eppner frantically scribbled the names and addresses of those who could verify his alibi on a slip of paper. "They're all neighbours, Colonel, all respectable: one of them is the rector of the local parish ... Do you think they'll let me call a lawyer?"

Bora said he didn't know.

The local police took less than ten minutes to arrive. Grimm gave them their orders, and while the pug barked up a storm in the closet, the young Russian saw him and Bora to the door and out into the garden. She must have been frightened by the goings-on, but had enough sense to stay quiet and lie low, like all small animals intent on survival. Bora stopped to converse with her by a flower bed, in the full sun, asking questions and receiving answers. *She savours her sweet mother tongue as she addresses me; and yet her eyes are fearful because of the police, and because my knowledge of Russian tells her I'm one of those who invaded her country.* It reminded him of another day, little more than a year earlier: another garden and another farm girl, looking at him with trepidation. Nyusha, her name had been, and she had been taking care of his father's old lover,

Larisa Vassilievna. *Ten months since we pulled back from Kharkov. I wonder what happened to them. Did Nyusha, whom Larisa loved well enough to bequeath everything to, protect or betray her? And this clear-eyed girl – even if she survives the war, what will happen to her if the Red Army should reach Berlin?* He felt a sudden, inexplicable pity for her. Although there was no one around who could understand them, he bowed his head to whisper in her ear, "Do not let anyone convince you to go back home. I know what happens to those who go back."

Grimm waited for him at the gate. He still held the Sauer in his hand, and kept fingering the safety catch. "What did the Russki tell you just now?" he enquired.

"That Eppner and his wife lead practically separate lives under the same roof. The sister-in-law was so nauseated by the tense situation that she took a job as a tram conductor, so that she could be out of the house as much as possible."

"And what did you tell her?"

Bora calmly watched the play of fingers on steel. "That she is lovely. For a Russian, that is. Are you going to put that away, or should I take mine out too?"

Grimm pocketed the pistol. "The moment they find the hunting rifle in this house or in one of Eppner's shops, he's done for."

"Well, there are some calls we need to make before we leave the neighbourhood. This is a list of three people who supposedly were with the Eppners when the murder took place."

To Grimm's disappointment, the first two of the three guests confirmed the watchmaker's alibi, a birthday party that lasted all night because of the curfew. Bora tried to think of a way to make a detour to the Beelitz sanatorium, without Grimm wondering why.

He had to consider that there was a fair chance the Criminal Police had kept an eye on him ever since the funeral. *They might have simply placed someone at the Adlon, timing my arrival and then my departure, when I travelled out of town to visit Bruno.*

129

*There's nothing out of the ordinary in going to see a wounded colleague. If they clocked me in again at my return, all I did then was meet Nina at the hotel, and from there I went straight to Nebe's office. Grimm took over the shadowing this morning, so he most likely only knows what I'm up to when I'm in his company. However, if Nebe, for whatever reason, decided to have me closely followed, he will be aware that Dr Olbertz approached me before Uncle's funeral, and – worse luck – that I met Salomon twice in the space of twenty-four hours. Consorting with a former commander is not suspicious per se, unless, as an SS Group Leader, Nebe is on that blabbermouth's trail as well, for political reasons. I say "Nebe": what if it's the Gestapo?*

The possibility made him cringe. Suddenly he realized that the plan to travel to Beelitz next was foolhardy, and scrapped it. Bora settled for checking Eppner's alibi with the rector a few streets away, while he devised a pretext to be on his own for the time he needed to track Goerdeler down and ask what was really going on.


6:50 P.M.


After the rector confirmed the alibi of the two Eppners, the investigators returned to Berlin. Crossing Bülowstrasse, Grimm said he needed to make a phone call. "I'm expecting a colleague's report on Kupinsky's whereabouts and details about a parcel deposited at Anhalt station."

Bora wondered why he hadn't been told earlier. "Is the parcel in Kupinsky's name?"

"No, the editor's, Roland Glantz. He sent the receipt to himself at general delivery, poste restante, but we easily traced the parcel to him all the same." Grimm saw a telephone booth and braked. Finding that it was out of order, he said he'd make his call from the police station on Linkstrasse. "It might take a bit, Lieutenant Colonel. No need for you to come in, unless you want to."

Linkstrasse, in other words, was Potsdamer Platz – and from there it was a short walk to the Potsdam and Anhalt train stations. Bora saw his opportunity to seek Goerdeler out, away from Grimm's watchful eyes. "I have plenty of reading to catch up on," he answered. "I'll stay."

He waited in the car until the policeman turned the corner. When he was still serving at Abwehr headquarters on Tirpitzufer, he'd known the names of those in the ordinary police and Criminal Police who informed for the Gestapo. But four years had gone by. Oster and Canaris had been thrown out one after the other; the Abwehr itself as Bora knew it was gone. And now Nebe had paired him up with a former thug from the SA. "A faithful Old Warrior", in Nebe's words, could only mean that during the Night of the Long Knives ten years ago he'd turned up and taken arms against his own comrades.

He left the car and started out on foot. The sun was still strong, throwing pailfuls of blinding light onto the street. In the immediate vicinity of the stations, where prostitution had thrived years before, Bora could name at least six hotels from memory, although it was difficult to say how many were still standing after the November raid. One day, at the beginning of the war, he'd casually run into Goerdeler at the clinic at the Askanischer Hof.

Asking the front desk about a guest could be problematic or impossible, depending. Concierges were required to exhibit their registers to the Gestapo, but not to an army officer; trying to buy the information could result in a formal charge, or even arrest, if plainclothesmen were present. Bora decided to try a third option.

Since the clinic was still standing and open for business, he simply entered and said that he had a business appointment with Dr Carl-Friedrich Goerdeler. He was told to leave a written message. This did not in itself prove or disprove Goerdeler's presence, and the concierge's discretion could also indicate that the guest had asked not to be disturbed. Bora did not want to leave messages; on the other hand, he could not any waste time there. "Never mind," he said casually, "I will call again."

He fared no better in the other hotels nearby, although at the Stuttgarter Hof they at least told him there was no guest registered under that name. Three quick and fruitless visits later (the destruction of other establishments spared him further calls), a disappointed Bora walked back to Linkstrasse to wait for Grimm's return.

He did so just in the nick of time, because the policeman soon rounded the corner with his flat-footed step, wiping sweat from his sunburned neck. "Aren't you warm?" he asked, as he crashed behind the wheel. "You sat in the car all this time and you're not warm?"

"I'm not warm."

"I'm as uncomfortable as hell." Grimm loosened his wilted tie around his fat neck, and ran his soaking wet handkerchief between cloth and skin. He removed his badge and tossed it into the glove compartment.

Bora looked away from him. "What news from your colleague?"

"Kupinsky has been seen in his old neighbourhood, near the bus depot by the cemetery. The depot is over in the Treptow quarter. He has friends on Persiusstrasse, working at the municipal garage across the Spree. He's drifting. I wrote down his movements across the Horst Wessel quarter all the way to the city slaughterhouse. You know where that is?"

"Vaguely."

"They're working overtime butchering eastern cattle," Grimm went on. "That's why in Berlin you find more meat nowadays than you did a year ago."

The thought of stockyards and what went on there was depressing to Bora. "So, do we have a precise address?"

"We pinned him down to a square block in Neukölln. Won't go anywhere between today and tomorrow." Grimm mopped his face with the handkerchief spread open, as if he were trying to print on it a holy shroud of sweat. "We should look into the matter of the parcel at Anhalt station now, instead. It's actually a small trunk, left there in Roland Glantz's name on Friday, the seventh of July."

Bora slipped the papers he pretended to have been reading in Grimm's absence into his briefcase. *Surely the phone call to headquarters did not last more than fifteen or twenty minutes, but he was gone nearly twice that time. What else did he do at the police station? I bet that he didn't insist on taking me along because he was going to report to his superiors about our day so far, including my talking to the Russian girl.*

"Fine, I'll walk from here," he announced.

Grimm's scowl trailed him as he left his seat. Bora heard the engine start and assumed the policeman would drive to the station ahead of him. The Olympia overtook him, however, and halted a few feet away, where it was already shady at this time of day. A resigned Grimm got out, and began to walk.

6:37 P.M.

The goods-and-freight section of Anhalt station was in ruins, and so was the locomotive depot at the nearby Potsdam station. The surviving service areas, though the worse for wear, remained relatively busy. Uniforms outnumbered civilian clothes, and among the civilians the majority were women. Signs of hasty maintenance – the odour of plaster, paint, freshly cut timber and plywood – filled the greasy air. Behind the counter of the luggage deposit, a policeman stood waiting for Grimm and Bora, with the parcel at his feet. Twenty-five or thirty inches in length and half that in width and height, it rather resembled a shoemaker's box, or another sort of toolbox. It featured no visible lock, but was bound up in wire, here and there secured by lead seals. After a brief confabulation, they agreed to carry the parcel out of the station and find a vacant area where they could open it.

The policeman suggested that a bomb disposal crew handle the job. Bora remembered the explosion of his first evening in Berlin; no matter how careful you are, at war disaster can strike. "It was safely taken down from the shelf, wasn't it?" he said, impatiently. "The wire is not connected to the interior in any way, so cutting it could never prime a charge." But he granted that the presence of a time bomb could not be ruled out.

For the moment, they settled on a careful transfer to the empty plot south of the Potsdam depot. There, Bora – who was slipping more and more into one of his "I don't care what happens" moods, and had enough of tiptoeing caution – stared at the innocuous-looking container on the mangy grass. It annoyed him that they might think he was showing off, because he had better reasons than most to fear a blast, but he really saw no reason why a bankrupt editor should leave an explosive device of any kind in a luggage deposit.

"How much would you say it weighs?" he asked the policeman, who'd grudgingly carried the parcel under his arm.

"Box included, maybe ten, eleven pounds, Lieutenant Colonel. We'd better wait before we open it."

"No. I'll open it now. Step back."

Grimm, hitching up his pants with hooked thumbs, did not say anything. He had the face of one who had decided that, if he could not call Bora's bluff, he could at least let him know he didn't care either way. He nodded to the policeman. Both withdrew to a distance of twenty or so yards, under a sky that seemed immensely wide and serene.

Bora crouched by the box and used his fingers to unwind the wire. As expected, nothing bad occurred. He easily opened out the hinged cover, and all he saw inside was firmly packed wood shavings. They weighed close to nothing and the box had thin walls, so the heft and bulk belonged to the object or objects nesting below. He put his hand inside and fumbled around, wondering if Cleopatra had felt as fatalistically carefree as he did right now, when she reached for the asp among the figs. He, who supposedly no longer cared for his surroundings, was suddenly aware of every detail around him. For ever lost to trees felled God knows where, the blond and frail wood shavings swam around his fingertips; a scent of forest still rose from them as they spilled over and fell onto the mangy grass. Faint city sounds floating across had the muffled quality of noises heard in a dream. Above, the summer sky would soon change colour as the day began to drain from it. *I see, hear, smell everything, yet I'm ready to leave it all behind.*

The object was metal, at any rate. And wood. And under his fingertips it felt like a strange kind of rifle barrel.

The three of them were soon observing a disassembled weapon neatly arranged on Grimm's store-bought, sweat-stained jacket; Bora had some familiarity with it, but had never used it.

"*Nee, so was!*" The policeman whistled. "If that doesn't top it all. It's a combination rifle."

"A huntsman's Drilling. But not for civilian use." Grimm pointed with a stick at the letters punched onto the breech. "It's marked L. W."

Bora had nothing to add. His brother's bomber crew had occasionally carried it on board over southern Russia, although it was at first only issued to downed pilots in Africa and the Mediterranean, to defend themselves against wild animals. The weapon's peculiarity was its three barrels, a pair of twelve-gauges and, below them, a rifle barrel for a rimmed 9.3 cartridge. Stags, boars and even lions could be brought down by its fire.

"Both calibres were present in Eppner's house too," Grimm mumbled.

"Are the editor's fingerprints on record anywhere?"

Grimm told Bora he'd have to check. Surprise had given way to a sort of wild glee in his small eyes, a vicious foretaste of victory. "I'm taking this to headquarters, Colonel. By tomorrow morning at the latest we'll have what it takes to place Glantz under arrest."

Still shaken, the policeman wanted to put in his twopenn'orth of wisdom. "You really shouldn't have risked it, Colonel. Could have been an explosive device." Bora nodded at the words, but his attention was still on Grimm's malicious expression. *I shouldn't have touched the barrel, that's what I shouldn't have done. Grimm used his handkerchief to handle the weapon, and the policeman never laid his hand on it. Now my fingerprints, or part of them, are readable on the metal shaft for future reference. Christ. No wonder the minion is smiling.*

He watched Grimm start out for the Potsdamer depot, trailed by the policeman with the box still under his arm.

"Should I take you back to the hotel before I head out to HQ, Colonel?"

"Yes, please."

A handful of the wood shavings lying in the grass trembled when a breath of warm wind swept the empty plot. Bora stooped to pick them up as if they were in need of salvation, but then crushed them in his fist. Walking unhurriedly behind the policemen, he thought, *I would not hesitate to kill him, if needed. There is a considerable feeling of freedom knowing that you could – without making it into a question of conscience – eliminate the man at your side. Especially when, as in Grimm's case, the feeling is reciprocal.*

8:09 P.M.

At the Adlon, two messages awaited Martin Bora. A telegram from his mother, confirming her safe arrival in Leipzig, and a verbal communication from the concierge, looking unusually contrite. "A reservation has been made for you at the Leipziger Hof, Lieutenant Colonel. Herr Adlon himself took the phone call."

136

So that was where Arthur Nebe wanted him to stay. Bora did not comment. An apologetic Louis Adlon, who'd known his natural father during his glorious musical tours in Berlin, stepped out of his office to say, "We're sorry to lose you and regret the inconvenience, Lieutenant Colonel Baron von Bora. We will of course look after the transfer of your luggage first thing in the morning …"

"No inconvenience," he replied politely, "and no need to transfer my luggage. I'll see to it tomorrow."

The Leipziger Hof was a small, elegant hotel that never cared to compete with the large establishments in Berlin. Bora had assumed it'd been bombed, because of its proximity to the main rail line to the south, but if it was indeed standing and serviceable, it might just be where Goerdeler was staying. Located in the neighbourhood of the Heinrich von Kleist Park, it looked on Potsdamer Strasse where the latter became the wide, old highway leading to Magdeburg and Leipzig. Behind it, the imposing civil and criminal court faced the park, along with other government offices, a classical colonnade and that abominable leviathan that was the Pallasstrasse's multi-storeyed concrete bunker.

Once he'd retrieved his diary from the hotel safe, Bora showered, changed, called down to have his laundry done and ready by morning, and descended to the lower level for dinner.

The clique of staff officers he'd seen nervously chatting in the morning was occupying a long table at the end of the room. They seemed to be having a much jollier time now. They ate, drank and conversed in a jolly mood that looked like relief to Bora's eyes. *They act like schoolboys who dreaded flunking an exam, and instead passed it with flying colours. Or … No. No, something slightly different: like students who heard that the exam was cancelled, or postponed.* There was nothing forced about their merriment, quite the opposite. If anything, it ran through the table like an electric current.

Bora sat alone, as always taking care that he faced the hall and the people in it. He'd taken along his briefcase so that he could read more of the printed matter on the Weimar Prophet.

Gossip, starry-eyed reviews and photos of pre-war parties were the side dishes to his meal. He saved the lengthy article signed by "Kolo", Max Kolowrat's pseudonym as a journalist, for last. Like all other press items featuring Niemeyer, the article was stapled to the cover of the magazine it'd been published in, in this case the November 1923 issue of the *Berlin Illustrirte*, priced one billion marks at the height of inflation.

The piece, apparently one of a series covering the esoteric aspects of Berlin during the Republic, bore the title "*Stars over Berlin* – Part 7: Sami Mandelbaum". The synopses of subjects already dealt with were listed in italics under the title: "How mysterious are Berlin's Mysterious Places?"; "Erik Jan Hanussen: Forecast or Fraud?"; "The Capital's Dubious Horoscope: The Disappearance of Berlin's Ghosts"; "Nostradamus in a Skirt: The Seeress Elsbeth Ebertin"; "Jazz: Crimes, Champagne and Predictions". All promised a fairly cynical and amused point of view.

Bora began to read:

Berlin is a metropolis where the young woman about town can, on the same morning, munch on *Stullen* in her favourite café on the Ku'damm, have her best pair of stockings mended at the "Stocking Clinic", and listen to a man who will disclose her sentimental destiny to her. Empires may crumble, financial tides may rise to wash over Atlantis many times over, but to the young woman about town in this capital city all that seems to matter are the morning treats, the precious silk hose repaired for another turn of the fox-trot, and Sami Mandelbaum's predictions. No, she will not enquire about the bond market, or starvation in China, or women's rights. The crime rate and the moral state of the

Nation do not concern her. She longs to learn if the gentleman in whose company she danced the night before is "the right one". If one thinks of it, all her morning errands lead to this momentous question: the sugar lumps that will charmingly round out her figure, the stockings returned to tip-top shape, and a magic key that will unlock the door of the future.

But what if the magus, the man of the stars, the clairvoyant from the East tells her that no, in her chart there is no reference to Herr Perfection? Disillusionment? Disaster? Will concerns that are more important barge in to trouble her mind and soul? No danger. The Son of Asia will not disappoint a woman in love.

But who is our snatcher of mystic secrets, the seer who claims a descent we do not hesitate to define as biblical? In our first article, we gave an account of his less than glamorous beginnings. Since then, this writer has sat with him for a week, and can report here only a small part of his countless observations ...

The interview that followed belied the introduction's sarcasm. Bora found the contents so significant that among all the articles about Niemeyer, tawdry in their nature and useless to him, Kolo's writing stood out as potentially vital to his investigation. Bora set it aside with care. Meanwhile at the other table, with the complicity of several toasts, the staff officers had reached the stage when merriment gives way to nostalgic sombreness. When he left the dining hall for his room, some had reverted to the jitteriness of the morning, others were resting their foreheads on their clasped hands or sitting back staring into space. *No, they definitely did not pass the test, whatever it was: the examination was only postponed, and they will have to face it again soon.* Before retiring, Bora asked the concierge for the Berlin phone book, and the first of several home numbers he sought was Max Kolowrat's.

In his room, it took just minutes for him to pack his things,
ready for the transfer to the Leipziger Hof in the morning.
The evening was airless, but what made Bora uncomfortable was that after weeks of reprieve he felt feverish. It was
Stalingrad's gift. Ever since he'd suffered typhoid pneumonia,
his temperature still rose at the close of day, even though he'd
officially regained his health. Sitting, still dressed, on his bed,
he felt sore, weary and strangely inadequate.

Reconstruct a man's life? He, whose job as a soldier was
to dismantle, had, in every case entrusted to him, done just
the opposite of taking things apart. He rebuilt, from what a
victim left behind, the substructure of deeds, relationships
and secrets that permitted understanding and the solving
of the crime. There had been times when he knew so little,
and time was so short, that only his imagination had allowed
him to connect the dots and create a picture. This case
was a variation on the theme: Niemeyer left not one, but
two autobiographies (unreliable, but full of details); stacks
of monographs and scientific articles covered the twenty
years and more of his public career; he'd met thousands,
given countless interviews, and studio photographs and
snapshots accompanied him from his cheap vaudeville days
to the glitter of his latest performances. Sifting through all
that would take months. Bora had one week. No point in
wondering if among the crowd of delirious admirers there
were one or two dissatisfied enough to kill; the question he
had to answer was, why had the murder taken place there
and then? Not that it was a guarantee of success: Erik Jan
Hanussen, the acclaimed seer who'd supposedly foretold
the coming of the Third Reich and paved the way for
Niemeyer, was killed at the time of the Reichstag fire; yet
no reasons were ever given for his murder, and no culprit
found.

Niemeyer might be too clever for him, even in death. Everything was hazy about the man who went by at least three different names and had credibly "passed himself off" (Grimm's words) for years as a Polish Jew. Grimm seemed to believe the incident of his unmasking was casual, but someone like Niemeyer was astute enough to realize that the political times were changing. The dramatic revelation in his second autobiography (as fake as the first), that he'd been forced to assume a Jewish identity by post-war circumstances, could paradoxically have worked in his favour. It was risky, however, and perhaps his penchant for living dangerously played a role in his demise. According to the papers, Niemeyer was married two, if not three, times, changed residence often, and during his early career stayed over in countless private homes and dosshouses. In his Jewish incarnation, he wrote that he'd married a Gentile woman and was cursed by his family. Actually, though the girl existed he had apparently never married her, and it was her family who'd disowned her for marrying him.

In the boxes occupying the small anteroom, Bora had separated the worthwhile from the worthless material. Niemeyer's autobiographies, of little practical use, were *Up From the Shtetl: My Life As a Luftmensch*, published during the Republic (which had later seen all copies withdrawn from libraries and bookshops around the country), and *Magnus Magnusson: Clairvoyant From the North*, which sold like hot cakes and was in its fifth edition. Two magazines founded by him, the monthly *Beyond Ostara* and the quarterly *Siegfried Lives On: Reincarnation in Today's Germany*, could still be found for sale at newspaper stands. Bora sat and dutifully searched through the Prophet's "visions" ("prediction" was not an acceptable term in Hitler's Germany): "The Führer will never die but be 'translated' into another form, remaining vigilant like Barbarossa on the Kyffhäuser; though that won't happen until 1984 ... Germany will expand, to the extent of creating the United

States of Germany, large enough to reach the Pacific Ocean and 'come to touch the American continent' through the Aleutian islands ..." Bombed-out regions would become particularly fertile, "thanks to the phosphorus in the explosive charges, phosphorus being used as a fertilizer"; this would allow the cultivation of fruit and vegetables never before available in northern climates. "Orange groves will extend from the Oder to the Elbe, Saxon and Pomeranian farmers will make their wealth from mangoes and bananas." It was an exercise in futility to look for intimations of his death. Niemeyer laboured under the delusion that he would live for ever, or else he was superstitious – or simply very careful not to give anyone any ideas.

Bora didn't know what usual proportion of correct answers to a given set of questions might be, but in retrospect Niemeyer, as a clairvoyant, seemed to oscillate between 25 and 30 per cent, which could not be much more than you'd obtain by guessing wildly. *It is true he did forecast some events correctly, like the lightning-quick victories at the start of the war, and the rapid collapse of France. I'll defer judgement on the creation and use of an atomic bomb "by the Japanese thanks to German technology", on a war between the United States and Russia lasting into the 1970s, and unmanned aeroplanes that will deliver the mail, let alone a new constellation shaped like a German Cross to be discovered in 1965.*

The last issue of *Beyond Ostara*, from May 1944, was printed on excellent paper, notwithstanding war restrictions (paper weight and quality were something Bora was accustomed to noticing, given his family's editorial practice), and featured as always a brief note about the Prophet's person, to the left of the table of contents. Nothing whatever hinted at possible risks, or worries about the immediate future. The cover, printed using the expensive four-colour process, showed a Nibelung of sorts standing on the prow of a long ship under a starry sky. Bora found an article exposing the fraudulent "street magicians" and "circus clairvoyants" intriguing. Niemeyer went so far as to lambast them as anti-German. Since he'd plied both those trades in his "Jewish" days, his gall was incredible.

The room was stifling, and he was definitely running a fever, but if he opened the window the lights had to be off, and Bora wanted to update his diary. So while the cool air outside drifted freely through the bedroom, he sat on the edge of the bathtub with the bathroom door closed, a torch he'd secured from the concierge casting enough glare for him to write.

What a full day, this first day of the investigation. Could it also be the last? It appears that the case is solved, and it's none of my doing.

The discovery of the "Triplet" rifle deposited at Anhalt station implicates Roland Glantz nearly beyond doubt; and the last shade of doubt will disappear tomorrow, as soon as his fingerprints are matched to those he most likely left on the steel of the three soldered barrels. According to Grimm, Glantz is familiar with big-game stalking, having travelled to Africa when he's had the means. So it was a German hunting weapon first designed in the last century, resembling an elegant double-barrelled shotgun with a third barrel flush beneath, that brought death to the Weimar Prophet!

If everything goes as it should, my Berlin stay will thankfully be short. I might be flying back to the front twenty-four hours from now, and can't say I'll regret it.

Note: regarding the Sauer M30 Drilling, Luftwaffe model. As far as I know, only two or three thousand such combination rifles were produced for our air force; the number 342 punched on its metal means that it was produced in 1942. Glantz will have to explain how he came to have it, but that will be the least of his problems.

All done, then? Most likely. But – for the sake of precision, and to make a record of it – I would be remiss if I did not mention the two suspects Grimm and I actually confronted.

While Ida Rüdiger's high-ranking alibi may remain stuff for the chief to check into, Eppner the watchmaker is slipping to the bottom of the list of suspects. A quick sketch of the man: viscid and supercilious, he has the annoying habit of reinforcing adjectives with emphatic predicates: "working, very much working", "true, very much true", "capable, very much capable". Well, there is no doubt that he is rancorous, very much rancorous about Niemeyer and his cheating wife. According to him, Frau Eppner is a "romantic old girl" who "falls in love every other year" and then comes back to cry on his shoulder.

"Doesn't it annoy you?" I couldn't help asking. It does, but through the years the couple reached a compromise: Frau Eppner's flings, all told, aren't to last more than a month. Niemeyer reportedly "bewitched" her by evoking the shade of her first beau, a poet who is supposed to have died of privation at the turn of the century! "You understand, it was unacceptable, very much unacceptable being betrayed by a dead man, especially when his astral body entered the flesh of a charlatan very much alive!" I'd have laughed, had I been in the right mood.

Once the allotted month of the fling was through, Frau Eppner couldn't bring herself to leave the mystic marriage, hence her husband's horn-honking charivari. As it happened, the clairvoyant's bedroom on Lebanonzederpfad had soundproof walls, so it was the neighbours who bore the brunt of the fracas. Were other rooms in the villa similarly insulated? It would explain why no one heard the gunshots. The Dahlem police records indicate that the rivals refused to file written complaints against each other on each occasion. It was a concerned neighbour (Frau Wirth, who else?) who had signed the grievance I showed Eppner.

Thus it appears that the conflict between the two men was mainly a ritualized give and take of provocation. Odd, but possible.

Could the watchmaker kill? It is my opinion that we all could (or do), given the right circumstances, but this former Foot Guards lieutenant is the type who would act from a safe distance or through a hired assassin. I have difficulty believing that you could presently hire someone for that purpose in the capital of the Reich, notwithstanding Frau Wirth's "awful Russians, Poles, Italians" walking around at night.

Does this impression in itself exonerate Eppner? Not in the least. His alibi does. He swears he was with his wife and sister-in-law the night of the murder. Not only that; there was company, it being Frau Eppner's birthday. One of the guests is the esteemed rector of a local parish. Grimm and I drove to his residence, and he confirmed the story, listing the many delicacies scrounged for the occasion. Paulina Andreyevna Issakova, the foreign worker who had to stay up until dawn to clean up after the party, also confirms the account. As for the handgun meant for personal protection at the shop, the excuse is believable, although it gravely violates the law. Grimm was disappointed. Seizing the weapon was all he could do for the moment. If he drags Eppner to Alexanderplatz, it won't be for murder, but for the concealed gun, and for allowing a Russian national under his roof (they have to return to their camps at the end of the working day).

My reaction? After the find at the train station, it would appear that the Kripo does get its man.

PS Regarding my little exploit out there by the depot: I was damn sure there was no charge inside the box, otherwise I'd have never risked my good hand in opening it.

# 5

*What is rational is real, and what is real is rational.*

HEGEL, *ELEMENTS OF THE PHILOSOPHY OF RIGHT*

## HOTEL ADLON, WEDNESDAY, 12 JULY, 5:20 A.M.

Early this morning, even before I was fully awake, the concierge rang up my room, with the message that the radio was broadcasting an air-raid warning. In private homes this is followed by a precise routine, which Nina explained to me: turn off the power, water and gas, open the doors and windows, make the necessary preparations for going down to the basement or to the closest air-raid shelter. At the Adlon, within five minutes you could hear the hubbub of those who rushed down the stairs to seek refuge at the Pariser Platz air-raid shelter, easily reachable from here.

I admit I had no desire to join the herd, partly because I hoped the bombers were not aiming for Berlin. I simply opened the windows (sorely tried by narrow escapes from previous air raids) and walked out into the hallway.

Everyone seemed to have fled below, so I sat to wait at the top of the flight of stairs. All the doors were wide open, except the one of the room next to mine, where I assumed a Japanese officer was staying. I'd heard him retire last night, thus I was sure that he was still inside. Worried that for some reason he hadn't been warned, I knocked on his door. He opened nearly at once. Like me, he wore uniform breeches and boots, but he was in his shirtsleeves. Without a need for explanations, we nodded to each other, and he came to sit with me on the step.

From the pack he had with him, he offered me a flavoured, incredibly strong cigarette, and while we smoked we began talking. What else was there to do? We could be dead at any time. So, as people do on trains with perfect strangers, he told me titbits about himself, in a flawless German. He is a *chusa* or lieutenant colonel, and his family name, as I later learned, is Namura; he's slightly older than me, having been born in the forty-third year of the Meji Era (1910); he studied in Berlin; has served in the 2nd Cavalry Regiment of the 2nd Division (the Sendai), and owns a horse named Shimpei, which in Japanese means "Recruit". To these mundane facts, he unexpectedly added that his wife died in an air raid three weeks ago. They were married just before he left for an assignment at the Japanese embassy here. He didn't bat an eyelid while he spoke of his loss, surely unaware that I had heard him sobbing the night before last. Waiting for bombs to fall on our heads, it could have been the right occasion for me to share my troubles with Dikta, but I didn't. I find it difficult to open up to others; besides, I didn't want to give the impression that I meant to compete with his grief. I simply listened.

He is such a committed smoker that his forefinger and thumb are yellow with nicotine. At one point, serene but wholly serious, he told me, "I have every intention to die, which explains my behaviour at present. And you?"

I knew how to reply, but didn't.

He surprised me when, after we finally introduced ourselves and shook hands on the step, he said, "You too wish to die, Lieutenant Colonel von Bora, but have too many things to do first."

Is he wrong?

He isn't.

The air-raid alert came to nothing, and "those about to die" in the stairwell had that advantage over everyone else:

147

they only had to wear their shirts in order to begin their working day.

6:00 A.M.

Given the fingerprint business to attend to at headquarters, Florian Grimm wasn't going to report for work before nine o'clock, "or a bit later". Three hours for Bora to use as he chose. He thought that he could not reasonably expect to find Dr Olbertz in his doctor's office yet, or Max Kolowrat out of bed (he was wrong on this count); other phone calls would have to wait as well. He began by giving instructions for transferring his things – mostly boxes of Niemeyer material – to the hotel luggage deposit, in anticipation of his move to the Leipziger Hof.

At this early hour, only a handful of guests were up and about in the lobby. Two talkative young pilots waiting for a lift reminded him of his brother, chatty and exuberant in the face of daily risk; the recollection was so painful that Bora had to look away from them. A few steps away, motionless, with his back to the exit and a newspaper under his arm, stood a lieutenant colonel, one of the smug staff officers he'd seen the day before, so tense that his mandible seemed nailed to his upper jaw.

Bora judged the colourless character sitting in a corner with nothing to do to be the inevitable hotel detective.

He'd just left his room key at the desk when he heard a voice address him from behind. "'Morning, colleague. Sorry to impose on you: can you tell me what time it is?"

Bora turned. He had not expected to be approached by the General Staff officer, and in such a harried, husky undertone, too, for a rather mundane request. What made it even stranger was that the wall clock, visible to everyone, functioned perfectly. Yet he automatically replied, "Five minutes after six." A distracted nod was all the acknowledgement he received. The tight mouth and seamed countenance of the man wheeling away from him could have been Salomon's: the face of one who lives holding his breath.

Salomon – right. Had he forgotten about him? After the embarrassing scene at lunch the day before, his former commander had said something about securing a medical certificate and "going back to his room to rest". Bora decided to leave before he ran into him and had to explain why he was moving out of the Adlon.

Stealing away, carving fragments of time out for himself, was something he hadn't been able to do in months; his short presence in Berlin seemed even less promising in that regard, but here he was, nearly three hours richer than he had a right to expect. Unlikely as it was for any taxi to be on hand already, one happened to be stationed at the entrance of the hotel. In the cool, clear mid-July air, Bora directed the squirrel-faced cabbie to the quarter of Zehlendorf. Three turn-offs later, he realized that a dull grey car was following the taxi, with the "hotel detective" at the wheel. The licence plate was civilian, yet suddenly nothing could disabuse him of the idea that, by asking him the time, the General Staff officer had set him up or even pointed him out to a Gestapo plainclothesman. *Damn it, he shook him off by calling attention to me.*

Everything about the lovely morning changed its colour, smell and taste. The squirrel-faced taxi driver, too, was aware that they were being tailed. "What street did you say again, Colonel?" was his tactful way of inviting his passenger to change destination, if necessary.

Bora unhesitatingly repeated the approximate address he'd first given. "Leave me on Machnowstrasse."

## BISMARCKSTRASSE, ZEHLENDORF

When Bora got out of the taxi and entered a stationer's on the busy Machnowstrasse, the grey car drove on. He whiled away close to fifteen minutes before leaving the shop and continuing on foot towards nearby Bismarckstrasse.

A bomb – or fragments of one – had randomly struck his relatives' charming house along the tree-lined thoroughfare. Half the roof had fallen in, leaving the walls intact; it was partly inhabitable, and you could enter it from the street. Inside, collapsed beams from the upper floors studded the once elegant entrance hall and stairwell. Whatever the enemy had dropped from the air had burrowed a large hole in the tiled floor, smashing through pipes and sandy soil; you could hear water running at the dark bottom of it.

Through the years, Bora had seldom frequented this family's pied-à-terre – not large but beautifully appointed, on two floors, plus a garage below and an attic. The attic was precisely what now occupied most of the stairwell. He had to keep close to the wall as he climbed to the first landing, where a door led to an apparently untouched apartment. Wreckage obstructed the flight to the second floor.

Squeezing past metal shafts and rubble, Bora worked his way to his grandfather's front door, blown open by the explosion. Things intact and things crumbled to dust stared back at him from the interior, where part of the ceiling had caved in. The internal staircase was leaning, tangled, off to one side, isolating the upper rooms. All that could be removed from the spaces readily accessible had been stolen. Skirting a large roof beam and a heap of roof tiles, Bora reached the library and peered in. The sombre curtain shading half of the shattered windowpane suggested that his relatives must have visited at least once after the air raids started. In fact, the destruction was so recent that there was no appreciable rain damage, and birds had had no time to come and build their nests and soil the floor. Bora scrabbled through debris to get in.

In bookcases nailed to the walls, some of the books were still in their place; piles of them lay on the floor. The sight of an old armchair was like a friendly face in the midst of ruin. After Bora had wiped dust and plaster from it, he saw that it had not otherwise suffered. It was Grandfather Franz-August's "fauteuil", the same he'd had in his student room at the ancient family seat in Borna half a century earlier. There was nothing special about it, except that the old man was fond of it. English-made, it had originally been covered in leather, but at some point he'd had it reupholstered in damask. The structure below remained intact, so that one could feel the leather buttons through the cloth of the backrest with one's fingers. Heavy and cumbersome as it was, not even scavengers could haul it out.

Bora, who had a bittersweet recollection of his own regarding the armchair, ran his eyes around the room. If he recalled correctly, it was shortly after the great 1933 book-burning that Grandfather had this furniture moved to Berlin. He felt an ache just short of nostalgia, just short of fear. Everything seemed to be breaking apart. Buildings, relationships, people. It mostly happened from fatigue, although the worst – he was convinced – was yet to come. Wounds, illnesses, family crises were not ends in themselves; they were symptoms of a larger malaise, recognizable by those, like his stepfather and grandfather, who lived through the Great War.

*Whom will we blame this time? How many times can the same nation claim that it had been stabbed in the back? We reap what we sow.* The most disturbing thought was that all would have to pay, the innocent along with the guilty. *There might be no lands to the west left to escape to, and those in the Baltic may never be able to escape. Fear of the Russians drives them, and they don't even know how much more afraid they should be. Those of us who served there know. Those of us who tried to stem the violence, who disobeyed orders and even flatly refused to carry out unspeakable crimes, know.* Bora stroked the armchair as he would a beloved animal. He did not want to dwell on the panicked thousands who were huddling or running around in circles to escape East Prussia, the Sudetes, and the Banat. *We at the front are fortunate that we can keep busy without agonizing about tomorrow. For us, as the Gospel of Mark says, Sufficient unto the day is the evil thereof.* Bora found feeling powerless particularly insufferable, so he forced his mind away from such thoughts. The prospect of returning to war in the mountains was attractive, to the extent that it left him no time to envision the future. Ignored thus far by looters, on and off the shelves were books on travel and the natural sciences, read by his father as a young man. Leafing through a nineteenth-century text by a Jewish astronomer, his glance fell on the name *Friedrich Bora*, written across the end page in a boyish hand, as youngsters do when they practise an elegant, "grown-up" hand. His father was obviously trying to impress a certain character on the letters, especially the flourish of the *F*, and the way the final *A* turned on itself like a snake or a tendril and swept back in a loop to meet the staff of the capital *B*. It didn't appreciably differ from the Maestro's autograph, such as Bora had seen on musical scores and portraits.

Where the chapter "Comets" began, a folded piece of paper marked the page. It was blank, which disappointed him (Bora always looked for messages or signs), but graced by the watermark of a long-tailed star. *Is this why it's been placed there, or did Father simply stop reading at this point?*

Behind a door at the bottom of a corner bookcase, yearbooks, annual reports and catalogues chronicled the last ten years of the Bora Verlag. Behind these, looking for nothing in particular, Bora spied a set of shabby-looking volumes, so unlike the rest of the collection as to make him wonder, but not for long: by their suspiciously singed edges, he knew what they were even before he opened one, and then another. Heine, Proust, Gorky, a copy of *The Magic Mountain* clumsily covered in the jacket of a different book, a brochure from the Buddhist Centre in Berlin, which his Scottish grandmother had helped to create decades ago ...

He gloomily crouched in front of the bookcase. In Krakow, five years earlier, he'd sat in a Jew's requisitioned flat, reading. He forgot the name of the man, a playwright, but remembered that room vividly, even the scent exhaled by the oiled furniture. Who could foresee that today, in a library strangely like that other one, and just as forlorn, he'd find similarly outlawed books?

He would have stayed away, had he known about them. Now the titles his grandfather had saved from the Nazi bonfire changed this simple visit into something potentially incriminating for them all, when they least needed it.

*Jesus, what am I doing? What are we all doing? I should have never entered the apartment.*

He rose to his feet with the astronomy book in his hand. Through the window, visible past the ragged blackout curtain, he saw the grey car turning into the boulevard at walking pace, as if looking for someone. Why? There was nothing here for the authorities, unless they knew about the proscribed books ... or him. His famous father's name, so unlike his own bold and unadorned signature, stared back at him from the old page.

*I, who come after my elders and, compared to them, signify very little, have long ago signed my death warrant,* he thought with a surprising lack of concern. The car crept to a complete stop in the abundant shade of an elm across the street. Bora watched it from the blighted room and his unconcern gave way to anger. He was angry with those spying on him, but – unexpectedly – also with his imprudent grandfather, with the officer who approached him at the Adlon, and those who – if Salomon wasn't lying – might be maladroitly conspiring to end what they had helped to create. Could soldiers who allowed looting, political murder and deportation be credible?

Most of all, he dreaded the idea that Salomon might be telling the truth. It tasted like blood in his mouth. *If it's true, and if they should fail, there will be mayhem of the kind we helped unleash in Stalin's Russia, when we fed his paranoia about the Red Army and precipitated the Great Purge. Trials and bloodshed which the Weimar Prophet never predicted in his "visions".*

... Or had he? Bora stepped back from the window. What if the officers who spoke freely before Salomon had secretly consulted Niemeyer? Why had he not thought of it? Seeking oracles was not beyond desperate men. At the time of the Reichstag fire the clairvoyant Hanussen was consorting with the powerful, knew too much, talked too much, and died. Bora held his breath.

He had things to do (the Japanese *chusa* was right), and not much time. Before leaving the apartment, he pocketed a few papers from his grandfather's study. He then gathered up the armful of forbidden books, carried them through the rubble down three flights of stairs, and dropped them down the deep hole in the entrance hall.

When he came out of the building, the car was no longer stationed under the elm. In the tram on the way back, no one seemed to be following him, unless that dark green saloon with three hatless men inside had taken the place of the grey one.

At eight o'clock he tried to phone Olbertz, not from the Adlon but from a booth at a discreet distance from the hotel. He failed to reach him. Either the physician was still out of the office, or else chose not to answer. The rest of his phone contacts – journalists who had interviewed Niemeyer and followed his career through the years – he would call up from the Adlon. He headed back there while the city started its wartime working day in earnest.

Aside from the Jews among them – who had long since disappeared from the Berlin phone book, if not altogether – six out of the seven magazine contributors on Bora's list weren't able to satisfy his curiosity. He heard that two had since died; one was serving at the front; three were decrepit, had no memory of those days, and did not understand who was calling, or why.

Only Max Kolowrat, left as a last resort, answered promptly, as if he'd been sitting by the telephone waiting for someone to ring him up.

Bora immediately liked the cheer in his voice. And he immediately fought hard not to sound embarrassed while he identified himself and his reason for calling. Even if there was a remote possibility that Roland Glantz had not shot Niemeyer with his Drilling rifle, it was but a thin excuse for a phone call – given that he was Nina's son.

Kolowrat, however, did not sound overly surprised. "The *Berlin Illustrirte* articles," he said, "of course, Lieutenant Colonel. I keep the entire series here at home. I frequented the so-called Weimar Prophet for a time … For professional reasons, during the decaying Babylon that was our Republic." He laughed, and his laugh was also pleasant. He waited for Bora to say something, but Bora – who seldom felt awkward – was feeling very much like a tongue-tied boy. He hadn't said why he was interested in the articles, or in Walter Niemeyer, as it was best not to give details over the phone.

He regained his aplomb, as if he'd slapped himself awake. "Mine are professional reasons as well. I would be grateful to read through the material as soon as possible, sir."

It was Kolowrat's Austrian lilt, barely there, like a repressed form of mirth, which gave his voice an amused inflection. "You are welcome to view them all; I'm not sentimental about those titbits of 'asphalt literature', as I believe such urban tales from the Weimar days are dubbed." Bora had the distinct impression of a smiling man at the other end of the line. "Besides, there is much from my interview with the Prophet that I left unwritten, but I recall it perfectly to this day." A pause followed, during which both men strove to conceal

155

that they knew what this call was *really* about. Did Kolowrat conclude that Bora's pretext for approaching him was not groundless? "Let's see," he continued, "I'm an early riser, and my days are free at this time. Shall we meet, so that I can give you the material?"

It was what Bora had hoped (and in a small way feared) to hear. "Yes, please. The directory lists Drakenstrasse in the diplomatic quarter as your residence. Will I find you there?"

"No, thanks to the British air force I have become a West Ender of sorts." Kolowrat gave a Barbarossaplatz address in the so-called Bavarian quarter. "I will be out this morning, but home by the late afternoon."

Bora was sure he could shake Grimm off by 7 p.m., and suggested a meeting half an hour after that time. He hung up, unsure that he'd done the right thing, feeling guilty for mixing the requirements of his investigation with something else that was difficult to define, because it had to do with Nina. It was not curiosity on his part, much less a desire to check on his own mother – but it was, undeniably, the firm intention of letting Kolowrat know that she was not defenceless.


8:58 A.M.


The hotel staff would never disclose information about guests, save perhaps to the Gestapo. However, personal maids, helps and retainers did not qualify as guests. When Bora asked about the man he'd seen in reception and then in the grey car, the head concierge's young understudy replied that he served as a chauffeur to a retired army general. Neither the general's name nor other details were forthcoming.

Bora had jotted down the grey car's licence plate while riding to his grandfather's; as a last resort, he was prepared to ask Grimm about it. For the moment, he said he would like an opportunity to meet the retired general.

156

"Sorry, sir. His chauffeur picked him up at 8:15, and he's gone."

"For the day?"

"The general left the hotel, sir."

"I see. What about Colonel von Salomon, then? We were to meet this morning," Bora lied.

"The colonel too left the Adlon."

This could be good or bad news, depending. It relieved Bora of his pestering presence, but potentially let a disturbed man loose in a city where his penchant for confession could result in a disaster. "Well," he said, rather more irritably, "where has *he* gone, then?"

"He left no forwarding address, Lieutenant Colonel von Bora."

If Bora was in a contrary mood, Grimm mirrored his feelings. He arrived ten minutes after nine in a brash green tie with red zigzags, frustrated because there were no identifiable fingerprints on the Drilling other than the slight smears caused by Bora's touch.

"Nothing of use, then?"

"No. The fact remains that Glantz had an air-force Drilling in the first place. Last Friday, two days after Niemeyer's death, he sent it to himself to Anhalt station, poste restante, and, what's most suspicious, he wiped it clean. There's a nine in ten chance we have the rifle that killed Niemeyer."

"Was the man taken to headquarters?"

"No."

"Why not?"

Grimm hunched his fat shoulders. "He failed to return home last night. His wife is in a state. 'Where is Roland Glantz?' I pressured her. Nothing. 'Where is Roland Glantz?' Nothing. She weeps, and – nothing. I'm heading to his publishing house now."

Roland Glantz was in the process of committing suicide in his office. This was the message Bora and Grimm received when they climbed the stairs of the tall, narrow building that housed – or had housed – the office of the Sternuhr Verlag. Probably none of the people who packed the stairwell actually worked for the publisher. Some may not even have been residents here. But the daily tension, air raids and the tiresome overcrowded conditions could make the sight of one so cracked as to take his own life rather entertaining. Bora's dislike for unruly crowds induced him, anxious though he was to get there in time, to let Florian Grimm overtake him. Using his elbows to shove people downstairs, the policeman pushed on like a salmon battling obstacles and gravity to swim upstream. Bora had to step aside and hold on to the balustrade so as not to be knocked off his feet by this or that tumbling body. In the confusion, he could not help thinking about his uncle, who – if Dr Olbertz had told the truth – had quietly done away with himself in the loneliness of his suburban home. Uncle Alfred had always been like that, a man of sound principles who did what he believed he ought to do, without fanfare. While Grimm single-handedly dispersed the mob on the landing above, Bora acknowledged that only a serious threat to his family or patients could have bent his uncle's will. *That's how we are, in our family: they have to kill us before we change our minds. Once they kill us, we can continue believing in what we believe.* Even if he could find the time to visit his cousin Saskia at the hospital while he was in Berlin, it was best not to do so; showing up at the clinic where she was hiding could make things worse for her.

These considerations distracted him for the short time it took Grimm to clear the way. Suddenly the landing was deserted, and the two of them stood before a tall doorway of bird's-eye maple, bearing a brass plaque with the name and logo of the publishing house: a twelve-pointed star set within a clock face.

Bora stepped in front of Grimm. As he turned the knob, the policeman urged him on from behind: "Is it open?" Inside the outer door, a wooden threshold formed a space delimited by a second door, in opaque glass, locked from the inside. Bora didn't hesitate, and fired a bullet into the steel lock to smash it; the ricochet missed him by a hair.

Inside, blinding daylight flooded a room lined with empty desks. The men's attention was drawn to a large window, wide open to the summer sky. "That's that, then," Grimm muttered, and stuck his head out to see what remained of the publisher after plunging down four storeys. He immediately turned back and cried: "He isn't there! The son of a bitch didn't jump."

"Is there a ledge below the window?"

"No."

"Where is he, then?" Bora turned and looked down a passage to his left which led to another office, and was alarmed to see a man jump off his desk with a noose around his neck.

"Halt, Criminal Police!" Grimm shouted as he sprinted in, as if the warning could stop a man who'd already hanged himself.

The bracket holding the rope, however, was not up to par. As the heavy-set Glantz plummeted, his weight yanked the hot-air duct from the ceiling, which fortunately wasn't in operation at this time of year.

Grimm rushed to the fallen man and grumbled something about a fractured hyoid bone or first vertebra. Glantz, however, at once started struggling against him, labouring for breath yet trying to keep the policeman from loosening the slipknot around his neck.

A step away, Bora had a mean urge to kick the unsuccessful suicide about.

Grimm carried a liquor flask in his coat pocket; he roughly handed it to the shivering Glantz, who – judging by the ease with which he emptied it – could not be wholly new to strong drink.

He'd struck his head in the fall. His left eyebrow was bleeding, and a bruise sprang up across his forehead. Only now did he seem to realize that he was facing a policeman and a lieutenant colonel. As Grimm sprang up with unexpected agility and pulled Glantz to his feet at the same time, Glantz saw Bora sweep a sealed envelope from his desk. "Those are private matters!" he protested. "Private matters!" But a wrestler's hold kept him from intervening.

"Not *that* private, judging from the audience you drew." Bora cut open the top edge of the envelope with Glantz's letter opener, which was shaped like a stiletto, the handle a dainty Florentine lily. "If we hadn't dropped in, the crowd would have smashed the glass door just to see you die." He unfolded the sheet and scanned it quickly. Then he handed it to Grimm without comment. "I detest amateurs," he said with a frown. "One look at those ducts is enough to know they could never hold your weight. The window was wide open: why didn't you use it, to make sure?"

Once free from Grimm's clutch, Glantz sheepishly massaged his neck. The stress, effort or compression of the windpipe had brought about a loss of urine, so that he faced two very unsympathetic men in embarrassingly stained trousers.

"Have you something else to wear?" Bora said sourly. "If not, take this." He tossed a grey dustcoat from the coat stand at him. "Compose yourself."

Once he recovered his grasp of the situation, Glantz seemed crushed. He fumbled around on the desk for his glasses, and tied the dustcoat around his waist by the sleeves. "My God," he groaned, "This is the most grotesque thing that could have happened to me." The way he looked at the open window in the other room prompted Grimm to go and lock it, but it was probably just a passing regret for his failure. "I imagine you were called in … the confusion … I am mortified, thank you."

"Wait before you thank us," Bora replied. "We are here to question you regarding the death of Walter Niemeyer, or Magnusson, or whatever the Weimar Prophet went by."

The words, connecting the events that led to the authorities' intervention like dots, petrified Glantz. "*What?* You certainly cannot believe —"

"We do believe," Grimm cut matters short. "You try to kill yourself only days after the murder of a man you argued with, and on top of that you leave this kind of note." He waved the sheet on his face.

"The note? The note has nothing to do with it —" The phone rang, interrupting Glantz's explanations. Grimm lifted the receiver, and when he heard something like a series of yelping sounds down the line, he let the publisher take the call.

"No, dear," Glantz said, rolling his eyes. "Nothing has happened. No, dear, no, it's not true. No. I'm here with two gentlemen. I'll tell you about it later."

After this brief exchange, he turned to the two men and said – as if the mention of Niemeyer were an unbearably sore point – "'For what I have not done' perfectly illustrates the way I feel, not having had the gumption to kill the Jewish bastard."

"Niemeyer was not Jewish," Bora observed.

"And anyway," Grimm chimed in, "here you wrote 'For what I *have* done'. Look." Glantz adjusted the glasses on his nose, read the note, and angrily burst out laughing. "As if going from tragedy to farce were not enough! It beats everything, that someone in my profession would leave a suicide note with a goddamn mistake in it!"

Bora said that he was not amused.

"Pardon me, Colonel, but who are you? You don't belong to the Criminal Police."

"Suffice to say, I'm the one who will question you." Standing behind the desk, Bora was methodically emptying its drawers, stacking objects and papers on top of it. "I have neither the time nor the inclination to waste time on chatter."

"Right." Grimm, meanwhile, was searching through the wastepaper basket. "Did you or did you not send yourself a Drilling rifle to Anhalt station, poste restante?"

Glantz stared at him with glassy eyes. "That I did. Yes. I didn't want to be tempted to use it on myself. The rifle belonged to my brother-in-law, a flyer who recently died in action. Yes, I *know* it is illegal to own weapons, thank you very much. All the more reason for me to hide it, after the murder."

"The method of Niemeyer's murder wasn't made public," Grimm whispered to Bora. Out loud, he asked Glantz, "Where were you during the night between the third and the fourth of July, and who can support your alibi?"

"I was nowhere near Dahlem, if that's what you mean. For the rest, what I was doing is my business: a private life is not yet forbidden, is it?"

Grimm's response was to stomp into the other room and throw the window open on those four storeys of empty space.

The threat deprived Glantz of what little energy he had. "May I ... I need to use the toilet," he whined.

"Looks like you already did," Grimm sneered, stepping back into the office. "If the john is nearby, I'll let you go, provided you leave the door open. And both hands on your bird while you do what you must."

"No, no, I only want to wash my face. There's a sink in the next room, inside a closet." Grimm followed him out of the office. Bora used those minutes to search through the papers he'd found in the drawers, mostly overdue utility bills, final notices and letters from exasperated suppliers.

Glantz returned with a piece of blotting paper stuck to his wounded eyebrow. Judging from the redness of his cheek, Grimm had used the brief interval to try to make him talk, or at least to make him pay for forcing him to race up several flights of stairs.

"What else happened to your face?" Bora asked, not because

he anticipated an answer from Glantz, but to inform the inspector that he disapproved of his methods.

The ownership of a rifle, compatible with the murder weapon to boot, was enough for an immediate arrest. Once they'd brought Glantz in, they could extract from him an admission of guilt. Bora cynically told himself that it was not what he wanted, because he couldn't be sure that it'd be the truth. *Now that Ida Rüdiger and the watchmaker are sitting on the back-burner of the investigation, as long as we don't find Kupinsky the publisher is our chief suspect. I don't know if Nebe expects a quick and handy solution from me, but if he does, he won't get one.*

"Can you write shorthand?" he asked Grimm, who hadn't expected the question and blandly said that he did not.

"Well, I can. Hand me some blank sheets from the desk, and get a chair for this man."

"Wait, Colonel." Grimm angrily took him aside. "This violates all the rules. According to regulations, interrogations are to take place at headquarters."

As he'd done with Salomon, Bora scowled at the ringed hand clasping his elbow, so that Grimm let him go. "The chief himself, Group Leader Nebe, has entrusted me with this case," he told him. "I make the rules. Do me the favour of finding a chair for this man, and let us begin."

It was difficult to say whether Glantz had expected to be questioned about the murder, now or any time. Uncomfortably seated, with the dustcoat still tied to his hefty waist, he soon admitted that he knew more details than those released by the press. He did not specify his sources, but it was possible that, as a former reporter, he had some police contacts, possibly in the Dahlem police. Bora planned to find out later.

"Tell me everything you know. I want all the details."

Glantz blinked several times. He had bulging blue eyes, and behind the lenses of his glasses one could see the white around his irises veined with red, as if he'd wept, or walked through a sandstorm. "I heard that he was shot with a hunting rifle, so I decided to pack the Drilling and leave it at the station in my name. It was common knowledge that we'd had a disagreement. I had already sued the bastard in a court of law."

Grimm could not help himself. "But why did you keep a Drilling in your home in the first place?"

Bora let him speak, because the same question had been on the tip of his tongue.

"Because my brother-in-law – his name was Flight Lieutenant Welzer, Seppi Welzer – brought it back from the front in North Africa. See, we'd been hunting together in the good old days, big game hunting was what we liked best. He'd been forced by an enemy fighter to crash-land west of Tobruk, and since the Drilling is a very fine rifle … well, he made out that the Drilling was lost in the incident. With help from a comrade – don't ask me his name, because I don't know it – he set it aside until his next furlough to the homeland. When he came to visit last Christmas he left the Drilling at ours, because he was a bachelor and had no other place to keep it. You understand, I couldn't very well go to the authorities, because I had already brought in all the weapons I owned. It'd have raised suspicions if another rifle cropped up, and one made for the Luftwaffe to boot."

Rapidly taking notes, Bora asked, "Why didn't you get rid of it altogether?"

"Get rid of it, Colonel? It's worth a fortune! It's a rare piece. Anyhow, after my brother-in-law died in a dogfight over Brunswick last February, the best thing was for me to keep it, that's all. Less complicated than explaining why I had it. Of course, when I heard about the murder, I realized how dangerous owning that rifle could be, given my run-in with the bastard. So I mailed it to myself, poste restante. I had no other plans."

"And in case the police were on to you, as in fact they were?"

"I would seem even more suspicious if they saw me throwing the rifle in the river or the canal. Don't you agree?"

Bora numbered the first sheet, and started the second. Nothing Glantz had said thus far exculpated him. When he added a shaky alibi (he was at home with his wife, who, however, had taken a sedative for her toothache and been deep asleep), his whereabouts during the night of the murder remained doubtful.

He lived in a small villa on Stendaler Strasse, north of the Spree; the absence of a porter on the premises allowed him to come and go as he pleased, the distance from Niemeyer's house was manageable by public transport, and as far as the curfew went even Grimm had to admit that it was occasionally violated.

Bora said, "You will admit that your suicide note is not helpful."

"Yes," Grimm echoed him. "It's practically an admission of guilt."

"I beg your pardon, it is no such thing. Aside from writing the opposite of what I meant to say – I wanted to die because I'm ruined, and did not have the guts to follow my first impulse, which was to kill the bastard. I'd even confided the possibility of murder to my wife, because the money I used to open my publishing business came from her family." Glantz rested his forehead against his open hand, as if the weight of his anguish were in need of support. "I committed the beastly error of offering Magnusson a huge advance to secure the exclusive publication rights to his *Encyclopaedia of Myth*. A massive opus, each volume was 1,200 pages long. The year was 1938, you understand, and the best editors in Germany were wooing him. Originally, the title was supposed to be *Encyclopaedia of the Occult*, but during the first draft, given the new laws on astrology and similar sciences, we opted for the term 'Myth' instead. Magnusson authored several articles on the subject through the years, both in his magazine *Beyond Ostara* and his quarterly *Siegfried Lives*. The encyclopaedia was to consist of twelve volumes in alphabetical order, plus an index, enriched with maps and four-colour illustrations. The entire set, in an edition of twenty thousand copies, was to be bound in Japanese silk, while a limited number of a hundred copies would have a parchment binding and lettering in pure gold. All hundred of these copies had already been reserved, you understand." Glantz's hand closed into a fist, which he banged against his forehead. "I was so sure of the deal that, God forgive me, I immediately acquired the silk from the Tomioka silk works in the Japanese prefecture of Gunma, not to mention the Italian paper – glossy 90-gram paper – bought from the Miliani paper mill in Fabriano."

Such an investment was inconceivable these days, when newspapers were down to four or even two pages. Bora's grandfather, the publisher, would have been horrified at the thought of such naivety. "The volumes would be published gradually, or together?"

"Together, Colonel."

"And was there a date agreed on, for the delivery of the text?"

"The twentieth of this month, for reasons – well, I don't want to say of an *astrological* nature, but Magnusson considered it the most propitious day. I anticipated that publication would occur on 20 April 1945 – in record time, given the war. The Minister of Propaganda himself was to present the first copy to the Führer on his birthday."

Bora did not want to stop to think where all of them, the Führer included, might be in the spring of 1945. "It is physically impossible to print twenty thousand copies of twelve volumes in nine months," he observed.

"Do you think I wasn't aware of that? Not even by using forced labour from the camps in Poland, which was my plan. I was ready to limit my ambition and publish the first three volumes in three thousand copies: *Aa* to *Baldur*, *Baucis* to *Celts* ..."

"I get it. What happened next?"

"What happened? The bastard never completed more than two hundred pages, that's what happened! Every time we met, he acted mysterious: he showed me stacks of typewritten material, letting me read only a few entries: *Asian Divinities*, or *The Medieval Wheel of Fortune*, or *The Swastika Cult in the East and West* … They seemed excellent. He was the Weimar Prophet! He owned a huge personal library, all sources were at his fingertips, why should I doubt him?"

"You should have at least insisted on a review of the entire text!"

Glantz's bloodshot eyes gave him a demented air. "You know, come to think of it I deserve to be arrested and beheaded, just because I let the bastard make a fool out of me."

Bora struggled to understand. "I have a hard time believing that you did not seek the advice of academics and other experts on the material he *did* give you."

Glantz put his chubby face in his hands. He rocked back and forth in that pose, moaning to himself. "You want to see what he gave me? You want to see it? It's on that shelf, in the sky-blue folder."

Bora gestured to Grimm, who retrieved the folder and handed it to him. Inside the cardboard cover, sprinkled with gold dust like a printed starry sky, Bora saw about a hundred pages, typed on both sides. The typing was faultless (probably a secretary's work), but the contents struck him as banal at best. Anyhow, the text came to less than a fifth of what would be needed to fill even one of the twelve volumes.

Staring at his feet, with his hands still on his cheeks, Glantz shook his head. "It was my good wife who convinced me not to commit murder, and insisted that I deposit her brother's rifle at Anhalt station. But thanks to my idiocy I ruined her life as well, see?"

"You can sell the silk and the paper," said Grimm.

Glantz looked at him wildly. "Gone up in smoke. I had them in storage, and the air raid of 21 June wiped them out. Gone! Fire finished what bombs had begun. My father-in-law was right, gentlemen. When you're a loser, you're a loser. I didn't even succeed in killing myself."

The policeman snorted. On his shirt front, the bright green of his tie resembled the skin of a lizard draped around his neck. He picked up the noose and put it on the desk, as evidence in a possible trial. "All the same, your alibi doesn't stand," he charged. "If your wife was fast asleep and there are no other witnesses to support your story, who says you didn't go to Lebanonzederpfad that night? The fact that the Drilling has been cleaned recently only makes things look worse for you."

Glantz shrugged. "Either way, my life is over," he said darkly. "I've lost everything. My house has been repossessed, in my pocket is an eviction order for this office, and if I ever had a professional reputation, the damn bastard destroyed it. Do you wish to arrest me for his murder? Be my guests."

"For now you're going to jail."

Glantz nodded towards the telephone. "Make the call then, quickly, Inspector, before they disconnect the service!"

Bora was still pensively reading the text in the blue folder. He glanced up to say, "You sued Magnusson: when was that, and how far have the proceedings got?"

He did not anticipate Glantz's show of hilarity. He laughed bitterly, and looked so ridiculous – with the blotting paper on his eyebrow, the dustcoat around his hips and his red eyes – that he gave the impression of a malicious clown. "How do you like the expression 'dead in the water'? I have no more money to pay the lawyers, and even if I had my day in court, Magnusson's fortune has disappeared. Oh, you didn't know about this detail? No funds in his name are registered within the Reich, and God knows he made millions through the years."

It was *not* a detail, and Bora was finding out only now. He turned towards Grimm, who was calling Kripo headquarters, and shrugged as if to say that he hadn't known either.

While they waited for the police van, Glantz asked to ring his wife. Grimm was against it, but Bora said yes.

"He could take advantage of the call to destroy evidence, Colonel!" Grimm's whispered objection irritated Bora even more.

"You had several days to search his house, and did not do so. What do you expect to find now? If there was any evidence, he disposed of it long ago." Bora indicated the telephone with a nod. "Make your call," he told Glantz, "but be quick about it."

After the police van from Alexanderplatz had arrived, taken charge of the suspect and left (it had been impossible to keep neighbours and passers-by from snooping around), Bora returned with Grimm to the Sternuhr offices to finish the search. He came away with some documents and the sky-blue folder; the rest of the paperwork would go to the Criminal Police stacks, while Grimm held on to the keys to the office for the time being.

They left behind boxed material related to the stillborn encyclopaedia, already addressed and waiting to be returned to Niemeyer (labelled "As agreed, to be delivered and stored in the garden shed" – not much of a depository for such a brainchild). Glantz's correspondence with the victim, however, was of some interest to Bora: sporadic in 1938, then more and more frequent, anxious and finally angry, it culminated in a storm of insults sent by registered post during the last three months. Niemeyer's replies on fine hand-cut paper, also on file, ceased in the summer of 1943. Magnus Magnusson (as was the name on the elaborate letterhead) displayed his annoyance at the publisher's doggedness. His last message consisted of a business card with his full name stamped on it, preceded by a solemn – and in Bora's opinion non-existent – academic title: "Doctor Professor of Cosmology and Applied Cosmography". Stapled to the umpteenth reminder sent by Glantz on 15 June 1944, it bore no date. The sole word on the business card, dashed in purple ink, was a less than esoteric "Arsehole".

Grimm loaded the Olympia with the Niemeyer paperwork and Bora's scant luggage, as if he already knew of his transfer from the Adlon, which was probably the case. While driving the officer to the Leipziger Hof, his account of the last hours indicated other reasons for his grouchiness than the absence of useable fingerprints on the rifle. "There was a call to the police headquarters from the Propaganda Ministry last night, regarding Ida Rüdiger. I got hauled over the coals about it." Grimm said it with a kind of pained surprise, as if this were the part he hadn't expected – a lack of support from his superiors.

Bora noticed it. *That means that Nebe usually backs his men up on controversial matters, and this time he chose not to. Why? For the same reason he contracted the case out to me? I don't know enough about Nebe to say whether he would stand up to Josef Goebbels or his close collaborators. But why wasn't I reprimanded? Goebbels loves to mortify the army.*

"We knew that might happen, didn't we."

"Hell, the Propaganda Minister himself vouches for the woman's alibi."

Bora had no reason to grin, but couldn't help it. "Frau Goebbels must be very pleased with Ida's hairdressing skills."

Grimm, mean-eyed, grunted through his short, upturned nose. "Also, I found out who it was that Ida Rüdiger paid to station themselves in Niemeyer's neighbourhood and spy on him. Private surveillance, nothing official. The name was Gustav Kugler, a former Kripo colleague of mine."

"'Was'?"

"Shot to death in Moabit on 1 July. Occupational hazard, in that line of work." They were now skirting the green area along Anhalter Strasse, in sight of the massive hotels around the train station. "He was wounded while on active service two years ago, and retired. For the past year he'd been making a living as a private investigator, no connection to us or other government agencies."

The timeliness of Kugler's death, given what he might have discovered about Niemeyer, deserved a comment on Grimm's part that never came.

"Was anyone charged with his murder?" Bora asked, eyeing a young woman through the open window, who was kneeling on the pavement and retying her high-heeled sandal.

"Nah. They fished him out of the canal under the railway bridge east of Bellevue station three days after he disappeared. What he knew, he carried with him to the grave: never was much of a note-taker. 'It's all in my head,' he used to say, and the hole they fired into it would have let everything escape, even if he had survived."

The girl's leg, her slender ankle, had the sheen of butter; no wonder the calico skirt slid back over her knee, exposing her thigh. She saw the officer watch her and smiled in a mischievous way. Bora, usually more serious than that, gave her an amused military salute in reply. To Grimm he said, "Do you have any *good* news?"

"Other than it's ten to one that Niemeyer's killer is already in our hands? Well, I tracked down the queer, Kupinsky. His house is being watched, so we can bag him any time you want."

Bora did some quick reckoning. He wanted to try Olbertz's number again, hopefully before the physician left the office for lunch. "I need an hour to settle into my new room and grab a bite," he said, "then we can go." He pulled a slip of paper with letters and numerals written on it out of his breast pocket, and laid it face up on the seat between them. "Does this tell you anything, other than that it belongs to a Berlin licence plate?"

Grimm darted a look at it while rounding a corner. "No. Why?"

"Find out who drives it."

"Any specific reason?"

"I'll know once I know who drives it."

At a walking distance from Kleist Park, the Leipziger Hof
contrasted both with the courts of law and other government
buildings on the green, and with the looming behemoth of
the Pallasstrasse bunker's tower, unbearable to the eye. The
façade of the four-storey hotel, freshly painted, stood out
against the otherwise faded block of houses. Its gilded sign
and revolving door belonged to an earlier generation, and
everything inside, from floors to light fixtures to furniture,
spoke of the late 1920s. Bora's room was already registered in
his name. He supervised the transfer of the Niemeyer boxes
to it, changed his sweaty shirt and ordered sandwiches with
"cold cuts" (the wartime menu of the day). His mid-sized
corner room had two windows that were advantageously
placed away from the bunker; the large bed and a bathroom
with a tub were definitely a plus, even though hot water – as
a notice explained – would be available only on Saturdays. As
in most respectable establishments, every room had a double
door, ensuring privacy for the guest and enough space to hang
suits to be cleaned, and set down trays after breakfast. The
door that presumably led to an adjacent chamber was nailed
shut, and its keyhole filled in. Bora quickly searched around
for listening devices, found none, then asked the switchboard
to ring Olbertz's office. This time, a nurse took the call. The
doctor was out, so Bora left her the hotel's phone number,
but not his name. Within minutes, the sandwiches arrived,
with a bottle of mineral water; he speedily disposed of them,
brushed his teeth and went downstairs to explore the building
before Grimm's return. Downstairs, judging by the presence
of cards and letters in the pigeonholes behind the counter,
there was no vacancy at the Hof. The wallpaper motif used
throughout was of stylized pineapples in tones of olive green
and pale yellow, with delicate crimson highlights. Woodwork

painted white gave a southern, fresh air to wainscoting and doors. Below street level were a panelled restaurant (crowded at this hour) and a cosy bar, whose far wall featured a giant sepia photograph of old Leipzig – the Pauliner church and the Café Français. Although the service could not stand up to the Adlon's, you could still be very comfortable here, especially if, like Bora, you had come from the front.

1:05 P.M.

Grimm's lunch left a stain among the red zigzags of his tie, due to the tomato sauce from the Anhalt station "Eyetie eatery", as he told Bora self-consciously. Bora wouldn't have noticed it otherwise. As for him, he had the gift of appearing fresh and well groomed, regardless of the weather or his mood, and relied on this to disguise how he felt.

Enquiring about the licence plate of the grey car now would make him sound overly anxious, something he had to avoid at all costs. He calmly got into the car and set the briefcase on his knees.

"Off to Kupinsky's, then?"

"I thought you were interested in the licence plate."

"Ah, yes. That, too. Any idea?"

Grimm didn't look at him. His small eyes remained fixed on a spot between Bora and the dashboard, yet Bora was sure that he was weighing the casualness of his reaction against the concern he'd manifested by asking in the first place, so he chose to modify it slightly. "Well, I *am* curious. Whose is it?"

"Car belongs to a retired general. His chauffeur drives it."

Bora had expected any answer other than this. He was ready to scramble an acceptable response, in case it involved the Secret Police, or the Reich Security Service. Not this, a pat confirmation of the concierge's story. "Yes, I thought so," he replied, finding nothing better to say.

Cemeteries dotted the working-class quarter between Tempelhof airport and the two long roads leading south-east, towards Zossen and the Schönefeld airstrip. *My way out of Berlin, if I make it,* Bora thought – and was surprised that he had thought it.

It was not a neighbourhood he knew. The aura of its riot-ous and impoverished past lingered, despite the dignified flats built for state workers at the turn of the century to improve its reputation. Dikta, however, had as an adolescent visited its notorious dance halls with her girlfriends, when on holiday from her expensive Swiss finishing school. Once, she and her best friend Luisa had avoided being arrested after a brawl by unhooking and re-hooking their silk stockings in front of the police, though she'd then quickly shown them her father's diplomatic calling card. "Otherwise," she'd told him, laughing, "they would have mistaken us for two cocottes!"

Once inside the building, Bora's melancholy grew. He always felt a pang of sorrow at the front doors of state hous-ing, flimsy like shutters, with glass panels whose vulnerability was lessened only by an etched pattern or thin drape. To this day, he believed that privilege can in part be measured by the impenetrable security of a front door. Grimm, who'd prob-ably grown up in circumstances like this, was unimpressed, and hammered on it.

Bubi Kupinsky opened the door, and stumbled back into his ground floor room mumbling a generic but abject "At your service", while Grimm slammed the door shut.

He bore little resemblance to the long-haired lad in the photo from his file. Aside from his lifestyle and the fact that he'd served time in prison, it was readily understandable why this 25-year-old was not in the army. At first, the way he limped made Bora think that he had a congenital defect (Goebbels' club foot came to mind), but as Kupinsky himself said, it was "a souvenir from the street fights" in Neukölln. He wore canvas shoes without socks, and, unprompted, showed them the three missing toes on his left foot. Only the big and little toe remained, creating a grotesque and painful sight.

As for the rest, a military haircut that left his temples and neck closely shaved gave him a stern and sad look. Bora and his men had shorn themselves similarly, at the start of the Russian campaign, so that they wouldn't have to waste any time on barbers during their fierce and unstoppable advance.

"Lieutenant Colonel – Inspector – I was not in hiding," Kupinsky pointed out. "I can prove it – as soon as I heard from my old landlady on Jägerstrasse that I was wanted, I reported to the nearest police station."

"The one at number 57?" Grimm intervened.

"No, further down, at 257. They didn't know what to do with me there, so I dropped the matter. Maybe – who was to say? – it was all a bad joke."

Bora took note of the surroundings. As he'd expected, the dreary room had two sources of light: the window onto the paved courtyard, and the fragile panel of coloured glass in the front door. The impression of vulnerability, prevalent in wartime, was particularly painful in the house of a man treated brutally ever since childhood. *Grimm loathes him; if he could, he'd snap his neck like a rabbit's. But I can imagine other scenarios, from the wretchedness of a political orphan to all that the SA Revoluzzer might have done to him when they had him in their hands.*

He said, showing none of his compassion, "You should have anticipated that someone would seek you out, after someone was murdered in the house where you occasionally worked."

"I thought of it. But it's one thing to make yourself available, another to go to the Kripo of your own free will." Kupinsky's eyes, of an intense violet-blue, no doubt were his principal allure; they reminded Bora of the colour of the ink used by Niemeyer.

The young man, perhaps unused to being formally addressed, stiffly watched the officer. However, Bora used the formal "Sie" with everyone, stepfather and grandparents included, on principle: if he switched to the familiar form of address, it was for reasons of extraordinary friendship or intimacy.

"I was to take care of Herr Magnusson's animals on the morning of 4 July, because he was expecting the gas workers. But there was a delay on public transport, so I arrived late. When I got there, it must have been past eight thirty – I spotted the fire service and the policemen, see, and kept well away. Then I asked the maid of the people who live on the corner, the lunatic asylum doctor —"

"Wirth?"

"That's the name, yes. She told me what had happened. The way she stared at me! See, a fellow doesn't have a dirty conscience, to … so I sneaked away, thinking that if the police wanted me, they could find me for sure."

"Right," Grimm interrupted, "as if Berlin were a one-horse town. Now you've come up for air because you've been out of work for days, and if you want to eat you must get a move on. The *other* profession we've taught you to keep away from."

Despite the hot day, the ground-floor lodging was dank; a star-shaped spider of cracks branched out from a hole in the plaster where there had once been a nail in the wall. Bora lowered his eyes in order to detach himself from the room. Much as he tried not to, the details of what surrounded him threatened to distract him. As usual, it wasn't so much the objects (like sounds and odours, he always noticed those anyway), but the more subtle and insignificant details that stuck, forming a whole that would stay with him. It was the way a shaft of daylight filtered through the half-shuttered window, bright and unbending; the shadow of a flock of dust in a corner and the veil of dust under a chair … He caught the absolute, and odd, centrality of these, as if a universe widened ceaselessly from this or that apparently insignificant point. Around each one, constellations of ideas wheeled; seconds were enough for him to elaborate an impression that for ever anchored him to this shabby interior, to the city punished by enemies all around it, and to the as yet obscure motive that had brought him here.

Grimm had just finished talking, and it was up to Bora now. Resting the notebook on his knee, he turned to Kupinsky. "Tell me about your job at Lebanonzederpfad."

6 p.m., at the Leipziger Hof. Dismissed Grimm early with the excuse of having to sort through the papers in my new lodgings. I can reproduce nearly verbatim what Kupinsky told us today, and not just because I took notes. He is a good observer, and if he didn't have the bad habit of trying to play coy (with males like Grimm and myself!) by wetting his lips and batting his eyelashes, he'd be undistinguishable from any other individual I interrogated.

He hadn't been in touch with Niemeyer for years, since the rise of the Weimar Prophet from the days of cheap advertising leaflets. Yet it was leaflets that brought them back together. Notwithstanding his limp, Berthold Kupinsky has for some time made a living distributing handbills (Grimm is convinced he's still selling himself, but that doesn't interest us now). Last summer, shortly after the air raid that damaged the post office and other buildings in Dahlem, Kupinsky happened to be in the neighbourhood, publicizing some attic-cleaning company or other. Niemeyer was sunning himself in the front yard. He recognized the young man from his characteristic gait, invited him into the house and, after a short exchange (Kupinsky was clever enough to understand that it was to Magnusson the Northman and not to Mandelbaum the Jew that he was speaking), offered him a position paid by the hour, tending to the animals and doing a bit of gardening. "I jumped into it head first," he

177

said. By the following autumn he was doing odd jobs for the entire neighbourhood, because "home owners prefer a lame German to hale foreign workers". Kupinsky was overjoyed: he was being trusted, received decent wages, even replenished his wardrobe thanks to his employer's hand-me-downs (which, incidentally, allows me to calculate that Niemeyer was of middle height and not overly thin). The sole fly in Kupinsky's ointment was Ida Rüdiger. The Party hairdresser despised him. She strove to surround herself with refined domestic help, untainted by a shady past like his. Before breaking up with her lover, she tried everything to make trouble for the Neukölln jack of all trades. Kupinsky gave examples: "She poured I don't know what on the rose bushes to make them dry up," and "She purposely left the windows open when the parrots were out of their cages." Kupinsky witnessed the furious arguments between Niemeyer and his girlfriend from the garden, and feared that his working days there were numbered.

But no. Before long, it is flashy Ida who packs her bags, after making sure that water is running from every tap in the house. Luckily for Niemeyer, water is supplied only at certain times during the day, so the damage to furniture and knick-knacks is contained. Still, some of the wooden floors are ruined. Workers come and go at the house, a few cases of pilfering ensue; the police are called, but Kupinsky is never suspected, et cetera, et cetera. The interesting thing is that, when Florian Grimm left the room (the beer he drank at lunch had to go somewhere) and I became insistent with Kupinsky, he looked at me slyly and pursed his lips, meaning that there was something he didn't want to tell us. My impression is that he did plenty of eavesdropping, and knows more than he says.

Even Grimm will admit that telephone surveillance does not discover everything. Besides, the listening devices were removed from the residence in February this year. By whose authority? Count von Heldorff's, no less, the Berlin police chief. That's all the information Grimm has on it. Should I deduce from this that Frau von Heldorff is one of Rüdiger's clients, and asked her powerful husband to ensure that her hairdresser's privacy was not violated? Possibly.

Rüdiger had Heldorff's calling card in her collection. This does not explain Kupinsky's secret. I rate myself an excellent interrogator, with Soviet colonels and generals in my bag: I trust that if I have another meeting with him – face to face from beginning to end, this time – I will have no trouble making Kupinsky spill the beans. But first I have to rid myself of Grimm's continuous presence.

Back to the question of Kupinsky's involvement in the murder. If I can believe all I hear, a few things are certain: a. the relationship between the prophet and the gardener was not of a sexual nature (though the gardener might well have wanted it to be); b. Niemeyer's privileged status granted him privacy, if not immunity; c. Ida Rüdiger broke up with him after tumultuous fights that included throwing dishes, burning underwear belonging to a young rival in the bathtub, and finally her hiring of Kugler, the late private eye. Kupinsky, like Frau Wirth, noticed the car discreetly parked in the neighbourhood. At first he thought it might be the Gestapo, but then he recognized Kugler, the former Kripo man, known to Kupinsky since the unfortunate Fritsch affair.

Unfortunately, when Ida Rüdiger put the capstone on her relationship, she also fired Kugler. We're talking here about the third week in May, thus in the last forty or so days before the night of his death, when Niemeyer was freed from surveillance and could invite whomever he pleased to his home.

Why then was Kupinsky included among the suspects? Because he has no alibi for the time of the murder (says he was at home, alone). As far as anyone knows, however, he did

179

not harbour any resentment towards the victim, and it seems unrealistic that a man of his physique could have crossed Berlin with a hunting rifle of any kind. We know Glantz owned a Drilling. Kupinsky never served in the army, and even though his father was a trigger-happy communist, he was only a boy during the Republic. Even if there is a remote possibility that he had access to a weapon, why would the victim open the door to him late at night? So far, he seems the least likely among the suspects, although I have learned not to readily believe appearances.

During the interrogation, there were moments when Grimm seemed tempted to wring Kupinsky's neck because of what Kupinsky was (or is). Yet the police make use of such people as informers. And not only the police. In Russia, at the beginning of the war, one of my commanders relied on information we received about the enemy from a Ukrainian transvestite named Ludmila!

Added later, at 6:17 p.m. Free of the policeman until tomorrow morning, I'm preparing to visit Maximilian Kolowrat, who lives an easy walking distance from here. What I know about Kolo comes from the *Berlin Illustrirte*'s biographical note, and what I recall from reading his books. He's fifty-three, from ancient Austrian stock, and has a law degree. After serving in the Great War as a company commander, he was briefly imprisoned by the Italians. Once repatriated, he left for South Africa, where he met his Afrikaner wife (the marriage lasted seven years, and ended first in divorce, then even more absolutely in her death during an epidemic). I'd call him a conservative nationalist, although as far as I know he abandoned politics years ago and then made his living as a widely published war correspondent (Spain, China, Mussolini's African campaign) and travel writer. Having lost his family fortune after Austria's defeat, he wrote for nearly every magazine published in Germany in the Weimar days, and thus painstakingly rebuilt his finances. Owned his own aeroplane when he covered the Ethiopian war (interesting photos from the air illustrate his chronicle).

Titbit: during the Berlin Olympic Games, he argued with our star filmmaker Leni Riefenstahl, which cost him his privileged seat in the terrace reserved for the press. I will have to summon all my strength in order not to show how nervous I am to meet him.

Note: before returning to the Leipziger Hof for the evening, although it was well out of our way, I had Grimm drive me back to the Adlon. My ostensible reason was that I'd forgotten the precious bottle of blue Pelikan ink. In fact, I went downstairs, to the dining hall – where the tables were already set for dinner, but no guests were around – in search of the head waiter. He's the same Alsatian from my good old days with Dikta, when handsome tips made him loquacious. Seeing me come in, he promptly approached to ask if there was anything he could do. I repeated my question about Salomon's whereabouts, which had gone unanswered at the reception desk hours earlier.

As expected (the concierge does not share information with the dining-hall staff), the head waiter didn't know that the colonel and I were not dining at the hotel, and sympathized with my having been stood up. He also said that Salomon's sudden departure from the Adlon coincided with additional demands on the kitchen, due to the arrival of several General Staff officers. Really? I was all ears. Imagine when, bless his heart, he saw no harm in adding that Salomon's vacated table had been occupied at midday by no less than the former chief of the General Staff. He beamed. "The Adlon is still the Adlon, Lieutenant Colonel!"

Yes, it is. So, Ludwig Beck is the retired general of the chauffeured car. I know him well by sight, and do not recall him among the officers dining at the Adlon. Two questions puzzled me as I walked out of the hotel: what's old Beck doing in the middle of Berlin, and why would he send his chauffeur to follow me? I thought that, after his resignation and his cancer surgery, he had withdrawn to his home in Lichterfelde.

I still have no idea of Salomon's whereabouts, but this piece of news will give me food for thought for the next several hours.

To Grimm, waiting for me by the car, I showed none of my perplexity. I even stopped to buy tinnies from a Hitler Youth boy, old enough to be destined for far riskier things in the next few months than selling propaganda pins for the Fatherland.

# 6

*Thirty spokes meet the hub, but it is the void*
*between them that makes the wheel.*

HEIDEGGER, *SOJOURNS*, CITING THE *TAO TE CHING* BY LAO TZU

## NEAR BARBAROSSAPLATZ, SCHÖNEBERG, 7:10 P.M.

*It's not the sort of place you routinely bring women to.* Along with an
aroma of pipe tobacco, after the briefest of introductions that
was the first thing Bora noticed about Kolowrat's apartment.
Small, if beautifully appointed (the books and sophisticated
artwork had to have come from a much larger place; there
wasn't a free space on the walls), you could encompass it at
one glance. Stepping past the bedroom to reach the parlour,
Bora glimpsed a spartan single bed through the partly open
door. *Made squarely,* he judged, *army-style. The kind of bed I'd sleep
in, if I had a place of my own.*

Boxed books, framed oils and sketches leaning against the
walls further restricted the useable space. The telephone was
on hand in the hallway – no wonder it'd seemed as if Kolowrat
had been sitting on top of it.

Dark-eyed and dark-haired, lean in a casual, English-looking
cardigan, Kolowrat preceded him along the hallway.

"Frankly, Colonel, he was a despicable man." The unexpected opening comment about Niemeyer came as they stepped
into the book-lined parlour. "How can such a despicable man
possess such a gift?"

It was a rhetorical question, which left Bora waiting for more.

"Saints ought to be equipped with supernatural qualities,
not be snake charmers who grow rich living off those so gullible

as to see the greatness of the gift and not the paltriness of the man behind it. There is a great injustice in all this."

Facing the guest in the space that now doubled as a study, Kolowrat had the appearance and easy manners of a world traveller, yet as far as Bora remembered none of the photos of his celebrated journeys to distant lands had portrayed *him*. Had he made the choice to consider himself a seeing eye, rather than a protagonist? It could be telling, and make a difference.

"I do not consider myself more cynical than most of my colleagues," Kolowrat now added. "But believe me when I say that I agreed to attend one of his shows only because some trusted friends insisted. After all, I was writing a series of articles exposing the credulity underlying our jazz age." He nodded towards a number of publications on the coffee table, next to a typewriter with a half-written sheet of paper in it. Because Bora chose not to sit down (there were only two small armchairs, one of them occupied by an old tabby), Kolowrat remained standing as well, with his hands in his pockets. "If you read my editorials, you'll know that I have a strong dislike for stupid, gullible women."

He didn't add *But I admire intelligent ones*, but Bora understood that this was what he was implying.

"And for stupid men?"

"Even more so. Like every man worthy of the name, I fought in the war. I travelled, seeing at first hand the misery and despair in places far away from here, and in places closer than we'd like to admit. The majestic sight of what we call 'unconquered heights and depths as yet unsounded' left me – how to put it? – impatient with the egotistical cares of many people. Not that I particularly scorned the Weimar Prophet, however wasteful with his psychic qualities he was. His unrestrained hedonism irked me. The young female dupe you read of in my article has no name, simply because she stands for hundreds of similarly affected sisters. Charwomen or field marshals' wives, all ready to see through someone else's eyes in order not to look with their own. All ready to pay for that privilege, although many could hardly afford it." Unlike many men who had faced him, Kolowrat gave Bora the impression of someone refusing completely and confidently to engage in comparison or challenge. He was wholly at ease with himself. "Before him, they said of Hanussen that he foresaw the burning of the German Parliament building, or else knew of it from simple hearsay and dared to speak of it. Well, the Reichstag burned either way, and Hanussen died."

"So did the arsonist Lubbe, by execution. Yet, credulous girls aside, it seems that both Hanussen and the Weimar Prophet were consulted by a male clientele from all levels of society."

"True, and more's the pity."

"You never had any use for his advice?"

Kolowrat laughed. "Absolutely not."

"But you attended his shows, and for a while you did frequent him."

"I was bored to death, writing society columns and crime news. It's true that I engaged him for a few days, in the hope of unmasking him."

"And did you succeed?"

"Yes and no."

Kolowrat invited him to sit, and Bora politely refused.

"I admit I was anxious to tear the Son of Asia – as he was known at first – to shreds. It was one winter, at Resi's on Neumannstrasse, that we were being treated to ghostly voices, fortune telling, messages from the Great Beyond … I watched widows and flappers swoon at his theatrics, laughed in my sleeve and took notes. Didn't his predecessor Hanussen turn a goat into a dwarf, and hypnotize a perfectly respectable lady into acting out an orgasm on stage? Well, under our man's spell a retired non-com laboriously laid a particularly large phantom egg, and a colleague of mine, materialistic to the core, sang the 'Magnificat' in a falsetto voice. You do well to smile, it was meant to make you smile." Gently Kolowrat eased the cat off

185

his armchair and sat down, so that Bora would do the same. "Miracle worker, my foot. Mine was the only open laugh in the astonished audience – well, imagine my surprise when he stepped up to me, stared at me and said in an undertone that before the end of the week news would reach me of the death of a woman who had once been dear to me in Africa! There was no way in the world he could have knowledge of my ex-wife's passing, Colonel. Not even through spies and informers unleashed across Berlin could he have discovered it, simply because it had not happened yet and no one knew it would happen. She was in perfect health then, and the epidemic that killed her in a few hours did so unexpectedly on the following Saturday. For me it was a philosophical turning point, I admit it. Not a psychological one, but a philosophical one, definitely. The Monday after, I sent for him. We sat in my Drakenstrasse study for over six hours, and at the end of the session I wrote him a cheque for a significant sum. He took it without batting an eyelid, as if it were due to him."

"And it wasn't?"

"Maybe." Kolowrat wagged his head. "Yes, it was. And I could afford it."

Straight-backed in his armchair, Bora was the picture of attentiveness, and yet he couldn't keep his mind from drifting. *Less than a year ago, seeking out my natural father's ageing lover near Kharkov, I closed one circle of family history. Today … Aside from my role in this criminal case, I wonder what my role is, vis-à-vis Max Kolowrat. Factually, he's nothing to me, and I'm nothing to him. Yet if Nina's life had turned out differently, he could have been my father, or at least my stepfather.*

"You see, Colonel, during those six hours packed with sleight of hand and melodrama, the man exhibited a knowledge of details so private that I'd never disclosed them to anyone; later, he shared with me episodes of my own life that I alone could know. And to think that I was determined to unmask him! To use an old Hasidic expression, I faced a *mirror of the soul.*"

186

In Berlin in 1944, few people quoted Jewish mysticism. Bora was quietly impressed. "May I ask why exactly you define him as 'despicable'?"

Without openly staring at him, he was memorizing Kolo's face and mannerisms – a professional habit that often was an end in itself, but not tonight. As for Kolo, he seemed perfectly aware that he was undergoing scrutiny and did nothing to elude it. His self-assurance held up without visible effort.

"Because he not only squandered pearls on swine: he also put a hefty price tag on cheap stage tricks. His serious moments were few and far between, and instead of prizing them, he held them in contempt."

"Magicians earn higher wages than saints," Bora observed.

"Precisely. Like Hanussen, outwardly Niemeyer was a show-man. Unlike Hanussen, he hankered after real power." When the tabby jumped in his lap, Kolo let it paw around until it found a comfortable position. "For instance, Colonel von Bora, wherever it is that you were wounded, I assure you that if you had met him beforehand you'd have been able to evade the place. He'd have described the location and circumstances so vividly that you could have avoided them."

Bora had not intended to frown, but did. "I might have gone down that Italian country lane regardless – minus my men, maybe, because I lost some of them in the attack. Are you suggesting that Niemeyer occasionally withheld details in order to let his predictions hit the mark?"

"I know it, yes. One example: having flown my own plane for years, I always pay attention to news of air crashes …" *Yes,* Bora told himself, *no doubt. Including Peter's, which deprived Nina of her youngest son, and gave you a reason to see her again.* "… Well, our Weimar Prophet was well acquainted with the Reichsminister and Inspector General Fritz Todt, and habitually advised him on his travels. So, when they wiped out Todt —"

"Forgive me. What do you mean, 'when they wiped out Todt'?"

Kolowrat's grin for a moment made him look younger than his age. "The air crash, of course, as he was taking off from the Führer's headquarters in East Prussia two years ago – you don't think it was accidental?"

"Of course it was." At risk as he was of liking the man, Bora went out of his way to mitigate his impulse, to the point of contradicting him for the sake of doing so. "The only reason that there wasn't an official investigation was that it was evidently an accident!"

Kolowrat did not reply. Without chasing off the tabby, he leaned forwards and began placing neatly cut strips of paper inside the magazines, as bookmarks. Bora was left to mull over the fact that a dead inspector general means an opening for someone else; that it was Todt's successor, Albert Speer, who officially declared the event a calamity, so that they could say "The king is dead: long live the king."

"According to your interpretation, Dr Kolowrat, Niemeyer could, by design or on a whim, choose not to warn Fritz Todt of impending disaster, or me about the partisan ambush. This makes him a dabbler in destiny rather than a prophet. Is this why some may have detested him enough to suppress him?" As he spoke, Bora felt his host's cool, searching gaze on him, and decided to stare back. *He doesn't know (or trust, or believe) what the real reason for my visit is, and is doing some analysing of his own. Naturally. I struggle to feel comfortable, or to appear more at ease than I am. In front of my stepfather, I am never at ease. Not even when I argue with him and win the argument.*

"'Suppress him' is an interesting choice of words, Colonel. Maybe. Whoever did it was someone who did not fear him. Yes, I say *fear* him: many of my once sceptical acquaintances were secretly unnerved by the showman's gift, and I myself never sat alone with him again."

"'Someone who did not fear him'. That is interesting."

"Or else someone impelled by an even greater fear. After all, there were those who thought him incapable of dying."

"They thought he was *immortal*?"

"Incapable of dying; I don't know if it's the same thing."

One of them would have to lower his eyes eventually, and it would not be Bora.

"Well, sir, he *did* die."

"So it seems." Kolowrat found a credible reason for looking away when the tabby jumped off and slunk out of the room. "He was gifted, privileged, arrogant and powerful enough to disregard critics and those who knew the falsity of his academic claims. For every friend he made, he made an enemy, in and outside the Party. Many owed him large sums, which isn't surprising. It was the same story with *Parteigenosse* Hanussen."

"There seem to be obvious similarities between the two." Having won the staring match, Bora felt a little ashamed. After all, he was the one imposing on Kolowrat. His long legs, an impediment in the crowded parlour, reminded him of the awkwardness of the circumstances. He, too, looked away, towards the framed photos of faraway lands. "What else can you tell me about Party Comrade Hanussen?"

Kolowrat followed Bora's glance. He leisurely left his armchair to straighten one of the pictures hanging at a slight angle. "Hanussen was someone I frequented enough to intuit that he'd become undesirable." He retook his seat opposite the guest. "On many counts. He was Jewish (but remember, even the Jewish press made a big show of despising him); he was an incautious lover; he was an investor, with none of the banker's discretion. Worse, he predicted the Reichstag fire less than a day before it happened. Grosser Marmorsaal, February 1933. I was there, Colonel, and heard it with my own ears. The question posed to him by the head of the SA in Berlin actually concerned the Party's odds in the coming elections. So where did the vision of flames come from? Anyhow, his nosedive began that spring, when some of his supporters were temporarily or permanently dismissed from office. Among them were Strasser, Heldorff, Schleicher …"

"The first and the last fell in the Bloody Purge of the SA a year later."

"Yes, along with their leader Röhm. Though not Count von Heldorff – or Lutze, who died in a car crash last year. We of the press wondered why Hanussen did not warn *them* of what was coming."

The evening was warm in the handsome little room, notwithstanding a breath of air from the open window that carried a faint wartime odour of plaster and brick dust. From the garden below – really a courtyard, which the westering sun did not reach and where shadows floated – the luxuriant top of a tall tree quivered lazily. Both men fell silent, each in his own way occupied by thoughts far removed from the subject at hand.

Bora couldn't shake the impression that tonight he was, if not liked, at the very least tolerated. *Having for years craved my stepfather's recognition, I have huge stores of respect for the general,* he reasoned. *I feel gratitude towards him for bringing me up as he did.* Yet affection was a sentiment that he had never experienced for the old man. *And though he* loved *Peter, his own flesh and blood, the General probably cares for me in his own way. Still, I was from the start his unwitting competitor for Nina's attention.*

"As for me," Kolo continued, "I'm content to say that I lived by our family's motto, *Et si omnes, ego non.* Even though all will do so, I will not. At times, I admit I stuck to it purely in the spirit of contrariness: if all behaved in a certain way, if something was all the rage, I kept away from it, out of principle. My drug of choice has always been risky sports, risky travels. To be honest, I allowed myself the luxury of malicious, biting clear-headedness, and kept myself at the same time in and outside things. Perverse bankers, infamous politicians, charlatans of all sizes, corrupt officials, young actresses pandered to by their mothers, the bourgeois starving for thrills ... Niemeyer was simply one of the many numbers performing under Weimar's big top."

"Corrupt officials. Meaning ... ?"

"Exactly what I said. One met them at all levels."

Kolowrat added nothing else. But the slight emphasis on the adjective "all" suggested that the leadership was not immune. It would be imprudent and rude to insist, so Bora didn't. "Speaking of Weimar's big top, did they ever find out what *really* happened to Hanussen?"

"Aside from the fact that he certainly wasn't killed where they found him in an advanced state of decomposition, out there in the fields around Zossen? No. And I heard from reliable sources close to the local government that 'rubbish is disposed of outside the city limits'."

"I imagine it was not difficult to find volunteers for such services, back then."

"It was very easy."

Bora decided to risk it. "Does the name Gustav Kugler mean anything to you?"

"No. Who is he?"

"Forgive me, but if you don't know or recall, I prefer not to say. I'd rather not influence you, in case his name comes back to you. And Walter Niemeyer, in those days ... ?"

"One might well wonder. Just then, as the Republic was ending, Walter Niemeyer broke the uncomfortable chrysalis of the Son of Asia to become Magnus Magnusson. As Hanussen's star faded, his began to rise. He published his second auto-biography, where he revealed himself as a pure Aryan and blamed Hanussen for having had to pretend Jewish ancestry in order to succeed on stage! The gamble could have gone badly for him; instead, the book was a hit. Have you read it? Cleverly worded – every line exudes *Heimat* and a Northman's pride." He dismissed his own comment with a wave. "Where Hanussen left off, the still comparably obscure Magnusson took over: prophesizing, miracle-working, moneylending ... Some even fancied that Hanussen had never died, or else his soul had transmigrated into his colleague, the new star.

As late as this June, despite the ban on fortune telling, many Berliners would go hungry rather than not be able to pay for Niemeyer's advice." The tabby silently re-entered the parlour, leaped back into its master's lap, and gave itself a thorough grooming. "You don't believe in any of these phenomena, Colonel. Do you?"

Bora had expected the question. "I believe in God."

"And in miracles?"

"I believe in God. Which is not equivalent to saying that I am rationally convinced that he exists. It only means that I believe in Him."

"But you set no store by prophecies …"

*More than you imagine*, Bora thought. *But this is neither the place nor the time to say that Remedios's prediction of my own end has weighed on me these seven years.* "Suffice it to say, sir, that as a soldier I have a strictly functional relationship with the future. My opinion of Niemeyer's talents counts for nothing in this investigation. My duty is to discover who killed him."

"And why."

"That, too. However, in the first instance *who*. The rest is up to prosecutors and judges. I must return to the front, and there's more than enough left for me to accomplish during my stay here as it is."

"Point well taken, Colonel. I knew Niemeyer's entourage better than most in Berlin, yet have no answer for you. I visited his villa on several occasions, on my own and when his parties lit up the night. Stop it, Krüger." Suddenly amused, Kolowrat waved the tabby's tail away from his face. The tabby then jumped on the table and busied itself with the sheet hanging from the typewriter. "Friends and admirers expected that he'd give his residence an exotic name, like 'The Garden of Delights' or 'Shangri-La'. Instead, he prosaically named it 'Villa Gerda', in honour of his mother. Even prophets have these philistine weaknesses, it seems. Women? Well, he *was* promiscuous. The mode of his death was not disclosed in the press, so I cannot hazard any theories regarding a culprit. A woman would likely use a small calibre, poison, a heavy object … Or a hired killer."

Bora kept mum about the details. "On the subject of Fritz Todt and his untimely death – were there other seances or stage performances where Niemeyer's insights assumed politically dubious contours?" The question was loaded with meaning, so he strove to mitigate it. "I ask because such visions would unquestionably draw people's attention."

"Unquestionably. Given his clientele, every statement could be construed as political. Until war was declared, there circu- lated in Niemeyer's milieu crazy whispers about this or that domestic or foreign plot against the Führer, whose miraculous escape every time was ascribed to timely predictions. What do *I* think?" Kolowrat shook his head. "I think the showman him- self initiated the bold rumours, by drenching his audience in alcohol, girls and cocaine at the Katakombe on Bellevuestrasse. I stopped attending his lavish home parties in '38, when, in my opinion – make what you will of this – the world began to need something other than conjurors and stage tricks. As you'll agree, the rumours in themselves were dangerous: for the gossipers as well as for the diviner."

Bora watched the cat play. "In view of this, can you suggest anyone familiar enough with Niemeyer for me to —?"

"Forgive me for interrupting: none who would talk, Colonel. No – that is a route precluded at this time, in this city. No lover, no servant, no client will tell you more than they feel safe to report. Remember, Niemeyer the social climber, bestselling author and trickster had little to do with the gifted sage. You could deride the first and dread the second. This is as close as you will come to hearing that the Weimar Prophet courted calamity, notwithstanding what befell his predecessor and rival Hanussen. Has anyone solved that blood-curdling murder? No. Eleven years ago, I uselessly tried to interview one Inspector Albrecht, routinely assigned to the case. All I was able to learn is that Hanussen was arrested just before one of his stage performances, and not by the police."

Bora kept up the appearance of impassibility, but wondered. 'Not by the police' – indicating what? The Gestapo, SA, a veterans' association? All equally conceivable. During his service with the Abwehr, rumours and predictions of conspiracies against the regime had surfaced constantly; he was peripheral to them, because of his work in counter-espionage, but as far as he knew – contrary to sarcastic comments in the international press – Hitler set no store by prophesies. Himmler, however, along with Rosenberg and others in high places, did. Yet the link between Niemeyer and those in power had existed for over twenty years, seamlessly extending from the Weimar Republic to National Socialism. During those two decades – like Hanussen – he could have been silenced many times. "Niemeyer was killed by a hunting rifle," he told him, on an impulse. "Possibly a Luftwaffe model."

Kolowrat's eyes migrated to the windowsill, onto which Krüger had jumped to perilously take up his grooming again. "Really? That is extraordinary! Discard a female culprit, then. No wonder he preached against hunting. At one of his parties at home, the Prophet literally kicked out a retired air force colonel because he habitually frequented a game reserve south of Grodno ... No, I do not recall the veteran's name, but I wager he and his family left for Poland in the autumn of '38."

Autumn of '38? A Jewish officer forcibly expelled after the Kristallnacht was an unlikely murder suspect. Bora had been interested for a moment, but gave it no further thought.

"Here." Kolowrat pushed the magazines towards him across the coffee table. "These are all the articles in the series *Stars over Berlin*. They may or may not be of help to you, but they faithfully portray a moment from our recent past. This long editorial, which – quoting *The Threepenny Opera* – I entitled 'Eat First, Moralize Later', will give you an idea of the world in which stage magicians moved at the height of the economic crisis.

Finally, this is a copy of *The Lucidity Factor*, my book exposing Weimar society, where I claim that diffusion, drunkenness and drug abuse created a 'floating world' in which the nation lost its way. Marginally interesting for you, maybe. Vitriolic, I'm afraid, but as a veteran I was undergoing an ungenerous phase."

Bora carefully stored the material in his briefcase. "I appreciate your time and observations, Doctor Kolowrat." He rose to his feet. "Should anything else come to your mind regarding Niemeyer …"

"Of course."

After taking the fat tabby down from the sill, Max Kolowrat closed the window. He then dug out a bottle and two cognac glasses from a glass-topped cabinet packed with gramophone records. "Before you go," he said, "unless you're on duty …" When Bora replied that he wasn't, he poured two glasses. "It's an old vintage. The last of its race. I'd share plum brandy from back home if I had some left, but Krüger here knocked it off the table three weeks ago."

Yes. It was not in France that Kolo had served as a war correspondent earlier in the war, but on the risky Balkan front. Bora cradled the cognac in his hand. The impression of a certain indulgence towards him on Kolo's part had only grown. Not fatherliness, but indulgence. *Why? Does he see in me a hopeless detective, a doomed officer of the front line, or – given my age and who I am – the offspring he could have had with Nina, if only she'd said yes? I'm wary of liking him, but he's not afraid to like me.*

Standing with the glass in his hand, he had a better view of the lush head of green outside – a linden tree, it was – whose leaves trembled in the evening breeze. Closer up, he noticed a deep fissure in the wall by the window; concealed from where he'd been sitting by the curtain, it ran from ceiling to floor as if a giant knife had tried to slice the room in two. *If I knew that Nina loved the general (that is, felt more than a dutiful and perhaps tender obligation towards him), my standing here tonight would be*

195

*close to unbearable. The fact that my visit feels anything but unpleasant must mean something.*

Kolowrat corked the bottle. Seeing Bora's attention on the structural damage, he amiably conceded, "A bit of a close call in late June. Less space, less comfort, fewer friends … We must move with the times, whatever happens. Unless unprecedented circumstances intervene, I will share Berlin's fate in this interesting phase of its history, and of the war." Again, he shrugged. "I'm an adopted Berliner, Colonel, there's nothing left of Austria-Hungary in me but a certain mocking affability."

Bora nodded. *Nina is the unprecedented circumstance he longs for. If I hinted to him that she needs him – I don't know if it's true, I surmise it as I'm surmising almost everything about this strange turn of events – something tells me he'd leave for Leipzig tonight, or on the first train that takes you there. But I won't say anything of that sort – because even with my mother I hold back, by replying "I'm fine", and in Russia, "Khan" Tibyetsky and I pretended to be no more than a Soviet general and an Abwehr interrogator, when in fact we were related to each other. Although he accepts me because I'm her son, I will not let Max Kolowrat know what I think Nina feels. I wouldn't do that to my stepfather.*

"To better days, Colonel von Bora."

"To better days, Dr Kolowrat."

Bora touched the mellow drink with his lips. It was excellent, smooth and consoling even on a warm night, and he sipped it carefully. Outwardly, he seemed to be paying a compliment to the preciousness of that last bottle of imported liquor. In fact, though, he was suddenly anxious that his visit would inevitably be misinterpreted. If he could have, he'd have said, *Please understand that I'm not here for pathetic reasons of jealousy or male control – we Bora men are not like that. But I had to come here, being the only one who knows Nina's secret, and you must appraise and gauge me as Friedrich's son, as General Sickingen's stepson, and especially as Nina's champion.*

All he actually said was, "My thanks for the loan, sir. I will return the material in good order as soon as I can."

"At your earliest convenience. I regret not to be able to help you more, Colonel. If I may suggest one thing, however: I doubt the stars have anything to do with Niemeyer's death."

"I agree. Should I phone before I come next time?"

"No." Kolowrat smiled, as if surmising why Bora had asked. "No need. Come directly, any time."

When he left Kolo's flat, Bora felt something that resembled tipsiness, something between melancholy and euphoria, impossible to ascribe to a single drink. He walked the short distance to Barbarossaplatz and found a bench, where he sat down as much to calm his confusion as to study the material he'd been given.

He remained there until it became too dark to see. Little by little, out of the gloom, the phosphorescent lines marking pavements and street corners emerged, near and far. In the spectral geometry that allowed Berliners to orient themselves across the blacked-out city, trams with shaded windows crossed the night, letting out a blue-green glimmer like *ignis fatuus* or the trail of glow-worms.

Bora put away Kolowrat's articles. He fully expected a police officer or a nightwatchman to walk by inquisitively, so he kept his documents and excuse ready for them. Out of light-headedness he'd come to a nearly unforgiving clarity of mind, which made him feel exposed and vulnerable.

Evoked by the reporter's intransigent, ironic pen, the 1920s let out small silent bursts in his mind, like soap bubbles whose iridescence leaves nothing behind. Red-clad pageboys at the Kaiserhof, the Adlon's slick-haired gigolos, caviar, pink gin, lesbian trysts at the Silhouette, underworld gangs known as Ever-Faithful or The Harmless Thirteen … How much Kolo had actually partaken of that drunken bliss was impossible to fathom; he'd surely frequented places where excess was on

197

the menu, but the clinical vein of his notes about illusion, crassness and spurious joy read like a list of diseases. *I have sat,* he reasoned, *in squalid mess halls and officers' clubs with the same quiet contempt, feeling adrift and alone. Kolowrat instead … it does not gall him to remember. He is like Polaris, fixed and untouched, and is capable of grinning at his own scorn.*

Overhead, so unusual in once-glittering Berlin, the sky was black and immense. Recognizable constellations – Aquila, Cygnus – soothed the eye with their apparent immobility. *There is no such thing as a fixed star,* Bora reminded himself. *It is a fiction of antiquity. In reality, everything in the universe travels, rotates, and only the slow interplay of orbits gives the illusion that we stand still. Even the word "Kolowrat" originally means "Wheel".* When, from a particularly dusky quadrant of the sky, a meteor detached itself, lighting up – it seemed as if a hand had tossed it like a rock into a pond – Bora watched its brightness as it grew in intensity, traversed the atmosphere and waned. That was it. Nothing more. To protect himself, he forbade himself all nostalgia, all recollection. *Every day is a day and I am who I am. If I had a choice I would be with my men in the Italian mountains, but I don't have that option. Six weeks ago I was in Rome … no.* He turned away from recent actions, recent thoughts. Regrets. Many things had happened since Rome.

*Order and disorder are the only two states of being.* By inclination he belonged to the first, yet he repeatedly found himself in the second. In between abided risk, a space he had to cross, back and forth. *In the end, I remain equidistant between the two states, forever in jeopardy.*

Now that Nina was safely away from Berlin, he was tempted to believe that the load on his shoulders would ease a little, if he could entrust her to someone in case of an emergency. Of course, he and Max Kolowrat had never breathed her name during their conversation.

Taking their leave from each other, they had merely shaken hands and exchanged a firm glance, as if passing a baton during a track relay. Both were devoted to the same woman, but they left her free to choose – and this was their quiet way of showing it. Bora could have broken every rule and risked telling him: "If Nina chooses you, love her." But there was no need.

Kolowrat loved her already.

It both pained him and filled him with hope.

Another meteor came down, small and flickering noiselessly, like a bead of water dropped on a hot surface. Clear, bombing weather.

*Everything moves, comes loose or falls apart. I spent the first twenty-three years of my life in the most absolute certainty. For the next seven years, I increasingly heard tearing noises; over the past two, I've witnessed pieces literally falling off, as if the common destiny of us Germans were dismemberment.*

Every day took something away from him. Only principles remained, like spokes of a wheel that kept going – speeding, at times – around a fixed point, the hub sustaining all. He called to mind the words from the *Tao Te Ching*: Thirty spokes meet the hub, but the void among them allows the wheel to exist. Yes. Only meteors, fragments of pulverized comets, crossed the slow westering transit like dust that rises and falls all around the fleeing wheel.

For a long time he'd felt alone with his choices. When he presented General Blaskowitz with reports that could cost him his career and his life, when he calmly took it upon himself to disobey criminal orders, when he pulled out this or that human life from the meat grinder of war. Even tonight he was alone, equally removed from those who might be plotting the unimaginable and those who would crush them. It was not true, as Salomon whined, that words like "oath" and "loyalty" had no meaning: they were simply concepts fraught with more ambiguity than one expects.

*To many, equidistance means safety, but for me it has always implied risk. The world of professional loyalty in which I function is*

199

made of commanders and subordinates; the private world is one of loyalty to fathers and stepfathers, and of loyalty expected from sons and stepsons. Where do I fit in? I'm a subordinate and a commander, a son and a stepson, but not a father.

*Or – not quite a father.*

The thought was unexpected and painful.

*God, Dikta's first, unborn child by me would be about five now. If he'd been in my place tonight and I in Kolo's, he'd have looked at me and judged me – how? The truth is that I was unable to save him or his two siblings, because I did not know about them. I should grieve for my unwanted sons. To this day, however, even after she and I parted on such bad terms, in retrospect my main worry is that Dikta risked her life during the abortions ... or at the very least risked being jailed, since the Reich punishes women who terminate a pregnancy.*

Odd, how even as he strove to detach himself from things and people, he occasionally blundered back into needing things and people, into needing *her*.

Equidistance could be an illusion, like everything else. In a lonely mood, Bora left the park bench. He followed Freisinger Strasse eastwards, in the direction of the Leipziger Hof. Twice they stopped him, twice he showed his papers, and finally a policeman insisted on escorting him with his torch.

LEIPZIGER HOF, THURSDAY, 13 JULY

Bora was already up at five o'clock. Nearly a week after his uncle's death, he'd awakened with a silly recollection from his childhood in Leipzig. It was in the autumn of '25, just after his twelfth birthday. While Berlin frolicked to the tune of American jazz, back home he'd evidently had his first erotic dream (if it *was* erotic – he remembered none of it), and Dr Reinhardt-Thoma was the sole person in the world he ever told.

*Well, Uncle,* he thought as he shaved, *thank you for not laughing at me that day. You were a fine man. Before leaving Berlin, I promise I will speak to your colleague Olbertz. He owes it to you, if his conscience still holds up, to tell me more about your suicide.*

Before long, a hotel attendant knocked with the news that the radio was broadcasting an air-raid alert. Bora, who was reading, came to the door in his shirtsleeves to thank him. He then left both doors open (the windows had been open all night because of the heat), but did not rush downstairs.

While grumpy guests filed past, bound for the cellars or the closest shelter, Bora finished studying Kolo's reportage on the Weimar occultism craze. Soon the ominous drone of the approaching planes, high and invisible from his corner room, was echoed by the staccato of anti-aircraft cannons around the city. Berlin might or might not be the main target this morning; still, a few bombs fell to the north-east. Through a gap between tall buildings, he saw smoke rising from the central quarters, a vast area that extended from the zoo to Alexanderplatz.

Still, since he could do nothing about it and did not believe in burrowing below street level, Bora read on. The opening of Kolowrat's *The Lucidity Factor*, so apropos, grimly amused him: "*Macht euren Dreck alleene*" – "Take care of your own muck" – the sneering comment blurted out by the King of Saxony in November 1918, in dialect, when he left Dresden to the revolutionary mob. *Definitely*, he thought, *we're all taking care of our own muck across the Fatherland.*

In an hour's time, the raid, anti-aircraft fire and alert were over. The wailing of ambulances and fire engines mounted in their place; smoke rose skyward like fingers from the damaged areas, as if reaching for the last quarter of a pale moon, still on the rise and already fading.

Downstairs, breakfast in the panelled hall (rehydrated egg yolk omelette) was a rushed affair, among faces weary with sleeplessness and anxiety. People thrown together by war, made meaner by it, grew impatient and rude; some, no doubt, cured their fear by spying and reporting on one another. Bora drank his ersatz coffee with an eye on those clients, sitting at other tables in their uniforms or civilian clothes, who might have been planted as informants, in this as in other hotels.

It was a nagging thought. *Whatever lies behind my orders to investigate, all I've exposed so far is myself. For God's sake, the moment my name was in the paper in connection with Uncle's funeral, everyone in Berlin who has a bone to pick with me potentially knew that I was here. I should wrap it all up by choosing at random one of the four suspects I was so graciously issued – well, minus Ida Rüdiger, perhaps, who has friends in high places – and presenting him to Chief Nebe. Glantz is the front runner, closely followed by Kupinsky. Kupinsky would be perfect: no one would miss him. Eppner's alibi is not above suspicion (they were all friends of his at the birthday party); besides, I'm sure I could make the little Russian girl, Paulina Andreyevna Issakova, swear to anything I want, and in so doing scuttle the watchmaker.*

Eight o'clock came and went, and still no Florian Grimm. Bora gave him the benefit of an hour, not knowing whether he was stuck somewhere due to the damaged streets, or the car had been lost in the air raid. Public transport, however, was functioning (a cause of pride for Berliners), so at nine he phoned Kripo headquarters to enquire. He learned that Inspector Grimm's house was among those hit by enemy bombs. No other information was available regarding him or his family. Unless the worst had happened, it could be hours before he reported for duty.

Bora hung up. He immediately formulated a way of benefitting from Grimm's absence. He wanted to see Dr Olbertz, who had never rung back even though his nurse must have given him Bora's phone number at the hotel. His medical office, however, was in the city centre, and even if it'd been spared in the raid it might be difficult to reach while they cleared the rubble. The other opportune target was Berthold "Bubi" Kupinsky.

Kupinsky did not answer the door. Bora waited a few minutes, then tried the handle. Discovering that it was unlocked, he entered without hesitation. He was met by the same squalor of his visit with Grimm the day before, starker because the open window flooded the front room with light. Nobody around. He stepped over a pair of pyjama trousers lying on the floor and walked into the bedroom. There, put away in a corner, leaned a rake, a shovel and a handful of other gardening tools. A few clothes drooped from coat hangers, the reek of cheap cologne mixed with mustiness and the stench of over-worn shoes. The bed, which had a coverlet with a loud floral print, had clearly been slept in.

Bora returned to the front room. It was possible that Kupinsky had gone out on some errands, but the hastily discarded pyjama trousers and the key left in the door told another story.

Looking out of the window (this side of the building faced a paved yard), Bora estimated that even a man with a limp could easily leave the house across the low windowsill. Yet if Kupinsky had sneaked out from there he could only have entered another apartment. No exits leading to external spaces or the street were in sight. Aside from a crumpled cigarette pack and a short stack of bricks against the wall, nothing else occupied the sun-soaked space.

In a few steps, Bora regained the stairwell. The coloured glass panel of the door opposite Kupinsky's trembled under his short raps. A strange shuffling noise from inside gave him the impression that someone stealthily crouching by the threshold was shifting back, in order to stand up and then approach the door pretending surprise. This, too, happened in Berlin: civilians bent double to pry unseen through the keyhole before cracking the door open for a visitor.

"Who's there?"

A heavily made-up little woman in her fifties peered out. She must have half-seen Bora's uniform, first through the hole and then through the opaque panel, so she kept her answers safely concise. The fellow at 17B? Been there only a couple of weeks, she did not know his name. To her, he was 17B. Someone had already come looking for him. Who? Men in civilian clothes. No fuss, though: the young man had followed them of his own free will. How long ago had this happened? Well, at about six in the morning, when her boyfriend went to work. "He's employed at the slaughterhouse, see. With those trainloads of Ukrainian cattle at seven and at two thirty, he's working overtime."

Bora made a quick calculation. It was out of the question that friends or acquaintances had come for Kupinsky. It could be plainclothesmen, Gestapo, Reich Security Service ... What if new evidence had surfaced and Kupinsky had been hauled in for murdering Walter Niemeyer?

"Very well," he said. "Thank you." He waited until the woman's outline faded behind the glass panel as she withdrew from the door, and returned to apartment 17B.

For whatever reason they'd seized Kupinsky at six in the morning, they had not searched the premises, which – depending on whether they had no real evidence against him, or needed none – could be a good or a bad sign. Bora took a few minutes to look through the young man's belongings. He discovered little of interest. A pencilled list of Dahlem addresses itemized garden work done or yet to be done in Niemeyer's neighbourhood: hedges and shrubs already pruned, flower beds to plant or dig out, upkeep of garden lawns ... The affluent Dr Wirth, Bora noticed, was marked as behind in his payments by two months. In the bedroom, among the hanging clothes he identified a good-quality summer suit, possibly one of Niemeyer's hand-me-downs. A fretwork bookend in the shape of an ibex sat on a dresser containing socks and fastidiously ironed, perfumed shirts. There were photos of actors and actresses cut out from magazines and glued to the wall; inside the drawer of the bedside table lay a quantity of sweets, cigarettes and what seemed to be – if the lessons on drugs and their effects Bora attended at the Abwehr were accurate – morphine suppositories.

Perhaps, as he'd heard from Grimm (who at this moment might be lying dead in the ruins of his house), Kupinsky truly was still carrying on the risky business for which he'd been arrested in the past. It was conceivable, all the same, that he was an informant, allowed to seduce men about whom the authorities wanted to learn more. The personal items were few. In the bedroom, they amounted to cheap cufflinks and shop-bought ties with Kupinsky's initials machine-embroidered on them. Bora's search shifted to another level: less than enthusiastically, he probed beneath the horsehair mattress and inside the pillowcase, behind the wood stove, inside the tins in the pantry, under the table, the few chairs and the worn rug. Nothing but sweet wrappers, ersatz coffee, small change. He ran his fingers along the window frame, in case any papers had been stuck between the wood and the wall. Nothing.

It was his habit to go beyond appearances that made him straddle the windowsill, step out into the paved yard, pick up the crumpled cigarette pack and look inside. It was empty. He could have ignored the short pile of bricks. Instead, on an instinct, he lifted them one at a time to look underneath.

He glimpsed a sealed envelope, neatly placed to fit into the shape of the bottom brick. On it, he read the typewritten initials of the receiver – E. D. No address. No heading, no mention of a sender. The high-quality hand-made paper resembled that of Niemeyer's correspondence with his publisher, found in Glantz's office after his failed suicide. Instinctively, Bora pocketed the envelope, climbed back into Kupinsky's apartment, and used the razor blade he habitually took along for a quick shave to slice open the flap along the crease.

Single, startling words can leap out of a text feverishly skimmed; and so they did now, to Bora. It was the double underlining of two sentences in violet ink, nearly tearing through the high-quality paper, that made his mouth go dry: "Immediate attention ... Reich Security Central Office ... the army ... vital interests of the State ..." Fear lay behind the impersonal neutrality of typed characters. He wondered how far into the chasm they had all fallen, if a soldier could break into a cold sweat on a summer's day because of something he *read*.

Niemeyer himself must have been in a funk while writing the text (there were typing errors and corrections), yet vengeful enough to plan to take everyone down with him if he fell. Bora could only imagine the recipient's reaction, if it ever reached him.

Was E. D. a friend, a solicitor, a notary? He hadn't come across the initials in Niemeyer's folder.

He replaced the letter in the envelope, folded it twice and slipped it out of sight into his left sleeve. For several minutes he paced around the room calming himself, trying to postpone unnerving conclusions until he felt collected enough to leave the apartment.

He'd barely stepped out when the sound of rough voices and a crowd of shadows darkening the door to the sunlit street froze him to the spot. Three hard-faced, hefty men, every one of them in an overcoat of the type that conceals the carrying of weapons, barged into the stairwell together. Caught short by the presence of an army officer, they paused, and their hesitation gave Bora the audacity to take the initiative and ask at once if they were here for the resident named Kupinsky.

The bulkiest of the three – all but a stand-in for Florian Grimm – grumbled, "What's your business with Kupinsky, Colonel?"

Bora took the calling card with Nebe's name on it out of his breast pocket, and showed it without a word.

The men looked at one another. "We're not here for Kupinsky," added the one who'd first spoken. "Please let us through."

Meanwhile, from upstairs came turmoil and noises; doors slammed, someone ran through the flat, a girl's strident voice rose and was immediately silenced. The three moved past Bora and ran upstairs; in the commotion that followed, it was safe to say that the doors to all the lodgings in the house but the one in question remained bolted. And even the door to the apartment in question, judging by the crash of broken glass, was yanked open by force.

The episode had nothing to do with him; Bora could simply walk away. Instead, he waited at the foot of the stairs for the conclusion of what seemed to be a full-scale arrest. Minutes later, the three scrambled downstairs dragging a man in an undershirt, whose nose someone had just fractured. He was white as chalk, and blood flowed onto his sweaty undershirt. He took a terrified look in the direction of the impassable officer while, lifting him by his armpits, they hauled him outside.

"I swear, Köpenicker Landstrasse 76 is all I was told," Bora heard him wail on the doorstep.

Unhurriedly – he meant to show neither an interest nor a total lack of it – he followed the foursome to the street door. Black cars were stationed up and down the street, manned by thugs wearing overcoats and felt hats low on their foreheads. In days of scarce fuel, the operation was too massive to concern a simple breach of the law, such as a robbery. Unless the man was a Jew, he must be wanted as a subversive: a pacifist, a communist, an enemy spy ... Now they were shoving him into a saloon that took off at once, followed by the other vehicles. The third car passed in front of Bora at a lower speed, and both driver and passenger stared closely at him as they went past.

For a minute or two he lingered on the lonely street, thinking *This could happen to any of us. This could happen to me. As early as the start of the war, when thousands daily gave themselves up as prisoners to us, I reasoned that this could happen to me.* He could imagine the dreadful lowing of cattle about to be slaughtered north of the river, how they must be rushing to finish off this batch before the second trainload came at two thirty. The asphalt was growing soft under the sun.

Bora could have left the neighbourhood at this point, but he re-entered the house and climbed to the upper floor. Blood drops on the stairs and on the floor tiles on the landing above led him to the right place even without seeing the shattered glass panel of its door. It was stuffier, smellier, as if the building were a carcass whose entrails sat here, up one flight of stairs.

Before Bora had time to knock, as soon as she discerned his outline through the broken glass a girl hurried to open the door. Her face was swollen with weeping and bruised, her lower lip cut and raw. *She uselessly tried to protect her man,* he reasoned, *and received enough to end any further opposition.*

She did not enquire why he wanted to come in. She stepped back into a parlour similar to Kupinsky's, except for the faded wallpaper. Bora saw family photographs, an unlit stove, and a shelf from which books and a dictionary had tumbled to the floor. Sheets, pillows, utility bills, various objects, even a small flowerpot with a sprig of mint, lay where they'd been thrown. A bloodstain on the jamb of the bedroom door might well mark the spot where the man's head had been shoved. You do not always need to bloody your hands to break someone's nose.

The girl had been in the process of filling a cardboard suitcase. A pair of rope sandals were still out, a white cotton bra and a petticoat with a torn shoulder strap lay on the bare mattress.

"What happened?" Bora enquired as if an answer were due to him, and the battered girl – she was no Ida Rüdiger, with her protectors and highly placed friends – muttered that the tenant "knew by sight" a couple of people arrested the previous week. An old excuse, that of casual acquaintance: even in Berlin, unmotivated police interventions were not a daily event. Bora understood that there was more. He noticed that she wore no wedding ring (though she could have sold or pawned it). "What's your husband's name? I might be able to enquire after him."

"He's not my husband, I just met him. I'm only subletting here."

It was probably a lie, but no matter. Bora reached for one of the utility bills on the floor and read the name on it. "Do you at least know what Anton Reich's occupation is?"

The girl, who would be attractive but for the blows and her cheap summer dress, did not know or did not want to say anything else. She furiously thrust sandals, bra and petticoat into the suitcase. "He does occasional chauffeuring, mostly for doctors of the Charité hospital – if there's a car to drive and fuel to drive it."

It did not sound like an illegal job, but a squad of plain-clothesmen doesn't come out with four cars without a good reason. As for the Charité, it was nowhere around Köpenicker Landstrasse, the address quoted by the man as they hauled him away. "He used to drive cabs, until his big mouth lost him his job."

She added the detail unrequested, out of frustration. Bora did not feel like threatening her in order to learn more. A big mouth usually meant merely griping about politics, not enough to call in the Gestapo. Anyway, whatever the fellow named Anton Reich had done to deserve arrest, it was of no interest to him. Bora watched the girl look around in search of something else to take along and – discovering nothing useful – snatch the sprig of mint, shake dirt from its roots, and put it in with her rags.

Bora left the house for good. He would have continued towards the closest bus stop, had he not glimpsed the object of his visit limping up the street with his hands in his pockets, from the direction of Hermannplatz. Bora turned back and hastily re-entered 17B, not to alarm Kupinsky and lose him again.

"Hello, Kupinsky."

Startled as he was, the young man gave up any attempt to escape; he stepped in, and after a glance up the stairwell (you could hear the girl sobbing upstairs), he closed the door behind him. Difficult to say what crossed his mind: he must have waved away at once any hope that the athletic army officer had come for reasons as shameful as they were out of the question. The second sobering thought, probably, was that more questions would follow, and he might as well fabricate something.

Bora saw through him. "It is best if you don't make anything up."

The less than subtle passage from the formal "Sie" to the rough familiarity of "Du" meant it would not be easy for him to wriggle through the interrogation. Self-consciously, Kupinsky drove his fists into his pockets, with the dark stare small crooks assume when they're under pressure.

"If it was you who turned in the fellow upstairs, Kupinsky, you came home a little too early not to raise suspicions."

"Me? No, sir. What are you thinking? I just stepped out —"

"Who came to fetch you this morning?"

"It's just that I'm out on parole …"

"I can easily check whether that is true or not."

Kupinsky tightened his fists in his pockets. His hooded eyes wandered to the window, in front of which Bora had positioned himself to conceal his expression from the brightness of the day.

"Well, it's all legal," he said. "I barely had time to get settled in this hole, and I'm told to observe and report on the fellow upstairs. There's no block warden here, and a man has to live."

Bora knew why he was staring towards the courtyard, and let the fear grow in him. *Of* course *the Gestapo would use him as a spy. Kupinsky has been dangling from a thread for years. Yet he*

*hid the letter from them as well; and now he doesn't know whether I
or they searched around and found it. He's dying to climb out and
see if it's still there. For all he knows, I too may be reporting to the
Gestapo.*

Kupinsky pouted. Unwisely, he tried to sidestep the officer
and reach the window. Bora blocked his way. "Closing the
window, with this heat … ? Mind you, I can tell when someone's
keeping information from me."

Now that his hands were out of his pockets, Kupinsky
seemed not to know what to do with them. He waved them
about as he walked around with an anxious grin on his face.
"No, no. I told you all I know, Colonel. I can't figure out what
else …"

"Tell me about 'E. D.'"

"Who?"

"Tell me about 'E. D.', and the questions end here. I know
the rest."

It was not even close to the truth, but Bora's claim drove a
wedge into Kupinsky's reticence. He stood there in his mix of
rags and costly hand-me-downs, teetering slightly, suspicious
and hopeful. "And that's all?"

"That's all."

"Jesus, I carried the load all these days, when I have nothing to do with anything."

"I'm waiting."

"There's hardly anything to it, Colonel. The day before his
murder, Herr Magnusson hands me the letter and tells me to
memorize an address on Herderstrasse, in Charlottenburg.
Ergard Dietz is the name. He also gives me the money to
get there on public transport, and everything. All I'm told
is that the letter is to be hand-delivered to a lawyer's office,
but wouldn't you know, he's out of town for a few days. Since
I was not to deliver it to anyone else, I took it home for the
time being. That same night, what happened at Villa Gerda
happened. I was scared stiff. I kept asking myself if I should

deliver the letter anyway, throw it away or keep it a bit longer. I just sat on it. When I had the courage to try the delivery again, there was a funeral wreath on the office door, a lawyer's office. How was I to know that Russian runaways cut his throat at his country place?" Bora did an appreciable job of concealing his surprise. "I never opened the letter or breathed a word about it, Colonel. I wish I'd never laid my eyes on it, that's all."

Bora agreed. "As far as I'm concerned, you never laid your eyes on it. It ends here."

"It takes a big load off me, Colonel."


11:15 A.M.

With the day still young, Bora meant to make the best use of it. From a public telephone, he called the Leipziger Hof to enquire whether Grimm had checked in. Hearing that he had not, he decided not to leave a message for him, in case he should turn up at the hotel. He then looked up Ergard Dietz in the directory, phoned his Herderstrasse office under an assumed name, and received confirmation of his death from a secretary. Sounding appropriately shocked at the news produced more information. Yes, she said, it'd happened on the night of 3 July. Poor Dr Dietz had barely settled for a few days of relaxation in his cottage near Grossbeeren, when murderous Russian fugitives broke in before dawn. Bora sympathized.

"Was it robbery?"

"That's what we think. Do you wish to speak with the firm's junior partner?"

"No, thank you."

Time to knock once more on Bruno's door for advice.

Despite German efficiency, that day it was not easy to reach the Beelitz sanatorium by train. The engine of the southbound train broke down near Kleinmachnow, and after half an hour of waiting in the overheated cars, the passengers were informed that repairs would take a long time. Bora alighted. He followed a dusty lane to the nearest village on foot, in search of a police station or an army post where he could secure assistance. All he found was a couple of Air Raid Warning Service non-coms, willing but unable to help. Despite being in the vicinity of the Bosch works, not even a calling card with Nebe's name on it could create a means of transportation out of nothing. He asked for a horse, to no avail. He was still nearly an hour from his destination, and the idea of going back to wait with the frustrated and overheated travellers was out of the question.

Having Niemeyer's letter on him added to his apprehension. When he succeeded in getting a ride in a decrepit farm lorry, Bora was glad for the dreary trip to Stahnsdorf, where he bought some periodicals and a ticket to the Beelitz Heilstätte. From the modest station, aware that even without Grimm the Kripo would not be long in providing alternative transportation for him, he called the Leipziger Hof on a hunch. As he'd expected, a driver named Trost had reported for duty at the hotel twenty minutes earlier. Bora skipped any explanation for his trip, and left instructions for the man to fetch him at 5 p.m. at the gate of the sanatorium.

Not far from the sanatorium, the SS and their shorn, vicious dogs had caught up with the runaway Russian prisoners. As Bora walked the last stretch to the gate, he heard from a farmer how the SS found them on the grounds of an abandoned farm and besieged them inside a barn, which they finally set on fire.

"Was about time," the old man grumbled, standing there with an unlit pipe in his mouth. "You wonder what took them so long to corner them, for Christ's sake. It's a scandal that the louts could have been running loose so close to Berlin."

Bora did not comment. Fugitives, Russian or not, could and did commit crimes: who better than them to take the blame for any wrongdoing? The acrid smell of smoke, and of bodies burning, was the same of Poland, Ukraine and, before then, Spain. *We are that,* Bora told himself. *We are also this. Or maybe this is all we are.*

The SS men drained their canteens in the shade; smoke dirtied the air but its shadow was delicate, nearly diaphanous; handfuls of straw and burning rags dangerously floated in the air, and could start other blazes. The farmhands blasphemed, tossing pailfuls of water on the hedge dividing the old man's property from the abandoned barn, to keep the branches from catching fire. The shorn dogs ran in circles.

Small, slender-winged hawks, merlins or stone-falcons shuttled around the barn skimming the ground, chasing field mice and insects as they fled from the blaze. They gave the impression was that in any case there was no escaping death, in any case.

# 7

BEELITZ HEILSTÄTTE, 2:40 P.M.

"What is this, Christmas in July? I thought you'd flown back!"

Bora laid an armful of newspapers and magazines in Lattmann's lap. "Something intervened."

"Well! Eva and our two older boys were here just now; you missed them by a hair. The wife would have been glad to see you."

"And I her. Sorry, Bruno." Bora sat down opposite his friend on the veranda overlooking the park. Hiding his anxiety from Lattmann was not impossible, but more difficult than with anyone else, including his mother. "You're a Berliner. Did you ever hear of the Weimar Prophet?"

Eyeing the headlines, Lattmann wrinkled his nose. "Who, the fellow who could 'mind-read and perplex the weaker fair sex', as the vaudeville song goes?" He glanced up. "All his shows sold out while I was growing up. Don't tell me he read it in the stars that you're to stay in town."

"I doubt it. His murder is the reason Nebe called me in."

Summarizing his task took Bora a few minutes, during which his friend looked alternately curious and baffled. "... So, you see, the groundwork produced a shortlist of possible suspects. I cannot reject it outright, although it skews my research. Given the ambiguous character of the man and the thousands he entertained in over twenty-five years, those four people may not represent all who held a grudge against him. I could be barking up the wrong tree."

"Why? Like him or not, Arthur Nebe is considered the shrewdest policeman in Germany, if not in Europe. If he came up with a list of suspects you can probably trust it."

"I don't deny that any of them, save perhaps Eppner, could be guilty." As was his habit, Bora discreetly surveyed the long, covered space. Few patients were around at this time, most of them preoccupied by their illnesses or visibly bored by inaction. Only the sullen man in the wheelchair – the same who had glared at him so insistently the first time – acted as if the visitor's presence, stirring him out of lethargy, were both intriguing and an irritant. From afar, Bora granted him an indifferent nod. "Still, Bruno, I wonder if they might merely be expendable. A fellow called Kupinsky is certainly … But more about him later, there's something I have to show you. Even a hairdresser to the rich and influential could be privy to dangerous gossip, and had best be put away. The others – a cuckolded watchmaker and a bankrupt publisher – I wonder …"

"Well, you have – what did you say – a week in Berlin? Do what you can, Martin."

"And that is another matter for concern. After he left the stage, the clairvoyant's 'private practice' turned even more lucrative. Many who would not be seen in public with him sought him in the privacy of his villa, or of their own homes. Did he keep notes? I'm sure he did. In Germany? Probably not. His trips abroad could have allowed him to stockpile embarrassing personal profiles and deposit his wealth in foreign banks."

When a buxom nurse's assistant placed a teapot and a cup on the wicker table next to him, Lattmann displayed an innocent grin. "Thanks for remembering that I like to take it out here. You're an angel," he told her. After she left, he voiced his objection to Bora's argument: "A showman doesn't enjoy diplomatic immunity. His bags could be checked at any time, coming and going."

"That's true. But as far as storing sensitive data, there are safes and vaults in Germany too, and trusty lawyers to keep them."

"To whom does his money go?"

"Don't know. No children, no immediate family. I read of distant relatives scattered around Hamburg. His bank account in Germany alone allegedly tops a million marks, although there's no trace of it." Bora paused while the invalid, staring ahead, wheeled himself past them with a singularly malicious grin on his face. "Bruno, I literally haven't the time for an investigation worthy of the name. What if I reach the conclusion that the culprit is not on the shortlist? I can't understand why on earth the Kripo would pick an ordinary lieutenant colonel to investigate a high-profile case. Nebe won't tell."

Lattmann rested the dailies and magazines on the table, next to the teapot and cup on their aluminium tray. "You're not exactly *ordinary*, and for all we know someone high up may have recommended you for a home assignment: counter-espionage does equip you for investigative work. That's where a good word from your fellow Leipziger Goerdeler would come in."

It was possible. Not informing him outright could have been a way to prevent his resisting reassignment away from front-line duty. Hadn't Nebe spoken of "young colonels, who dig their heels in like schoolboys"? And hadn't the succinct message in his Adlon pigeonhole read, "*It is necessary. At least come to terms with it philosophically, and good luck*"? The idea made Bora cringe.

"I will not leave the front," he protested. "I will not leave my men."

"You will if they make you. Drop of tea? Here they soak us in mint tea as if we were old ladies."

"No, no."

The patients – both those who could walk and those who had to be escorted – were leaving the veranda for an afternoon snack in the vaulted, aquarium-green halls. Lattmann waited until they were alone before becoming conspiratorial.

"Martin," he said, "you and I have been friends for years. A big part of our friendship, because of our duties, because of the 'Shop', has been not to ask questions. But the 'shop' as we knew it doesn't exist anymore." He touched the paunchy teapot with his fingertips, and once he'd made sure the liquid inside had cooled, he drank directly from its spout, holding down the lid with his forefinger. "I could always tell when you'd got yourself in trouble."

"Ditto."

"By association, though – unlike you, more by accident. Risk makes a man skittish and suspicious, no matter how he dresses up his anxiety in stoicism or humour, or whatever. We grew up in this system. It's all we professionally experienced, although sometimes we just couldn't go along with its demands. Watch out, I say. Act as though the suspects are *the* suspects, and find evidence that one of them carried out the murder. Now, tell me the *real* reason why you're here."

Bora had prepared for this moment, but did not answer at once. He chose one of the magazines he'd taken along – it was the June issue of Niemeyer's *Beyond Ostara* – and laid it in Lattmann's lap. "There are two. The first is that I lunched with Salomon yesterday: you cannot imagine what he asked me to do."

"Ha! Whatever it is, if the old codger is on an assignment in town the air raids have had all the time in the world to get on his jangled nerves."

Bora wagged his head. "It isn't that. I'm fairly sure he abuses Pervitin, Eukodal and sleeping pills, among others. But he did overhear *something*, over at the Bendlerblock, and now wants out of Germany. There, the monthly on your knees … Open it."

He watched Lattmann leaf through the magazine, see the letter found at Kupinsky's, read it, and go white. "Sent by Niemeyer to his lawyer the day before he died, but never delivered."

Now that the pink had left Lattmann's cheeks, freckles stood out like age spots on his skin. "Does anyone know you have this?"

"No one who will tell. You never saw it, of course."

"Is it the only copy, or are there more?"

"I have no idea. I bet on a carbon copy in Niemeyer's safe, although the Kripo found it empty. The lawyer died on the night of the murder, and Niemeyer's villa was torched."

Whispering was difficult in his agitation; Lattmann's voice sounded whiny and hoarse. "Jesus, Martin. What will you *do*?"

"I don't know. I'm trying to sort things out."

"And now you've got mixed up with Salomon? Stay the hell away from him!"

"It may not be possible."

"Fucking stay away. The fact that he sought you out is already a problem: what an inconsiderate, self-serving fool he is."

Bora deftly recovered the letter and slipped it into his sleeve. "I've read enough of Niemeyer's writing to recognize his style, let alone the paper and violet ink he favoured. He surely typed this. The question is interpretation. 'The deal is still ongoing', he writes. It suggests he was in the middle of an arrangement previously mentioned to his lawyer, who, however, might have ignored the counterpart's name. Niemeyer was evidently worried about the outcome, to the point that he considered 'the unfortunate possibility of a sudden demise'. In that case, Ergard Dietz should assume foul play and immediately bring 'the material entrusted to you in May' to the Reich Security Central Office."

"In a sealed box, yes. I read that. Does it mean the lawyer was not privy to the contents?"

"That's what I think. It seems the box was kept outside Berlin, because a trip is implied. It remains to be seen whether

Dietz expected a letter of the kind. To be sure, he fell victim to a bloody assault before having time to fetch the box and deliver it to the Reich Security Central Office. The worst of it is that Niemeyer's reference to the papers as having 'a literally explosive nature' might or might not be a metaphor carried too far."

Lattmann was slowly regaining his colour and his temper. He was on the point of reverting to the nervous habit of chewing his nails, so he tightened his fists to resist temptation. "Shit. Niemeyer must have had solid evidence in his hand, to declare an impending risk to the State – involving the army, no less. He couldn't realistically claim a vision, could he? The information leaked through 'a young female client under hypnosis' – how credible is that?"

"Credible, if the girl is as well known in Berlin circles as he suggests." Bora was thirsty. He poured some lukewarm tea into Lattmann's cup and downed it without even tasting it. "Why not? Niemeyer states he treated her for debilitating migraines over a number of weeks, in secret, because her friend – who *happens* to be the head of Berlin police, Count von Heldorff – would not approve of such a cure. We live in a paranoid world. Loose talk by women *and* men has brought a few to the guillotine already."

Lattmann folded his arms tightly, his fists under his armpits. "If Niemeyer does not hesitate to spell out Heldorff's name, it stands to reason that the head of police is in the middle of a major inquiry. Not concerning a *foreign* plot either, because that's not his purview ... Naturally he would not appreciate having his chatty sweetheart undergo hypnosis."

For his friend's sake, Bora hoped not to appear as careworn as he felt. The aftertaste of the artificially flavoured drink was unpleasant on his tongue. He said, carefully choosing his words, "Unless Count von Heldorff's involvement in the scheme is of a different nature."

"What?" Lattmann looked around the deserted veranda as if listeners could suddenly rise out of thin air. "That's *enormous*, Martin!"

"Is it? You cannot take over Berlin without having the city's police on your side. It would explain in part why Nebe chose an outsider like me to look into his colleague's doings. Police, even when they are SS group leaders, do not investigate policemen." Weary of sitting in the wicker chair, Bora ached to move around, but showing restlessness would not do. "Look, Bruno, it doesn't even matter whether we face a home-grown conspiracy, or only rumours of it. The SS or the Reich Security Service would have cracked down on it already, had a copy of the letter surfaced after Niemeyer's murder. Had Dietz not died in such a timely fashion, I'd have assumed that it was lost when the villa burned down." A slight dangling of his crossed leg was all he conceded to his anxiety. "What do you make of this lunacy, Salomon's included? You worked at Central Division. I need to know if we're thinking the same thing."

Lattmann cringed. At first, arms crossed and head sunk between his shoulders, he seemed altogether unwilling to run the risk. He came round quickly enough, but could not bring himself to speak the words out loud.

Bora watched him mouth "Hans Oster". The name of the former counter-intelligence chief of staff, sacked and bluntly discharged from the army months before, was what he'd dreaded to hear.

"So for once Benno von Salomon isn't making a mountain out of a molehill."

"Damn him, I almost forgot. Where is he now? He can't be trusted, going around on his own!"

"He left the Adlon before I did. I couldn't keep him from going, could I? If I track him down, I'll think of a way to handle him somehow." Bora took out cigarette and lighter, but remembering Lattmann's lung injury he immediately pocketed them again. "What to do about the investigation – that's another matter. By rights, I cannot keep the letter from Nebe, although I cannot exclude the possibility that it *could* all be just Niemeyer's vengeful invention, after the failure of a moneymaking scheme with Heldorff or persons unknown. It would not be an isolated case. As for Salomon's ravings, I don't know what's true and what isn't. But I need to hear all that you know."

"Blast, Martin. I'm not spelling it out."

When the devious Sister Andreas came within earshot, supposedly to shake out a towel onto the sunny greenness of the park, Lattmann reverted for a surreal moment to the most unrelated, crudest of chats. "Really? Really? Russki fugitives in our neck of the woods, no less! I'm glad they incinerated them. I was telling my boys, before you came ..."

Bora closed his eyes. From among the trees below, waves of summer air wafted to him. For once, after so many months, he felt exceedingly well. Physically, at least. If he didn't open his eyes, he could delude himself into believing that he was in a safe place at a safe time. Reality disappeared in the calming warmth of his closed lids, in the tender familiarity of bird calls rising from the old Beelitz trees.

Why did such a load of worry have to land on him at this time?

"Coast is clear: she's walked away." Lattmann's voice floated to him disincarnate across that flesh-coloured blindness, and then, when Bora looked, everything seemed green. "I will tell you what I know, but only if you swear you won't go and do something foolish."

"Have you ever seen me do something foolish?"

"I've lost count. Walk me over there while we're still alone."

Bora escorted him to a corner of the veranda where they could breathe the fresh air and also see who entered and left the place. They sat down.

"Remember when you came back from volunteering in Spain back in '38? In those days, those of us who were cranking out papers in the counter-intelligence's Central Division in Berlin seemed frazzled to you."

"Was that the word I used?"

"Something to that effect. Well, Martin, we had good reason to be. We had serious misgivings, because it was conceivable that a world war might follow the Reich's military provocations. The concern was, of course, that if you wave a stick at too many dogs —"

"I had volunteered in Spain, remember? I get the general idea."

"Yes, well. There was no doorbell we 'Oster boys' left alone, in or outside the country. Seeking diplomatic alternatives, possible agreements – you name it, we rang them: military, civilian, diplomatic, industrial, religious authorities. Even our old man baulked at some of the contacts we initiated."

Bora stood with his back to the railing, close enough not to have to raise his voice to be heard. "It explains some of the goings-on I saw in Rome during the Führer's visit later that year. But you left Central Division of your own accord."

"Two years later. Shortly before General Oster was called in and ordered to ease off, he was getting ready for a step I didn't have the stomach for. It's one thing to try to avoid a world war; it's another to leak information to the enemy that may cost the lives of countless of your own. It's true, Martin, so help me God. I came within a hair's breadth of resigning from the 'shop' altogether. I stayed because you stayed, but I have been keeping my nose clean since. The last I heard, those sensitive documents left the vault of the Prussian Bank in 1942. I'd give an eye tooth to know where they might be now." Frowning, Lattmann looked years older than the merry friend Bora knew in Russia. "Some colleagues talk too much, Martin. They talk to wives, girlfriends, who in turn lightly let things slip to others. Then there's chauffeurs, maids, orderlies … I was here on leave in September of last year – just in time to go back to the Russian front and be shot – when Ambassador Solf's widow incautiously invited a Gestapo informant – who passed himself off as a Swiss national – to one of her exclusive tea parties. You can imagine the rest. Two of those who attended regularly, Schwartzenstein and the industrialist Nikolaus von Halem, both close to our own General Tresckow from Army Group Centre and already arrested in '42, were sentenced to death a month ago."

"Tea parties may work for American revolutionaries, but not here. Berlin in 1944 is not eighteenth-century Boston."

"Maybe. Whatever that horse's arse Salomon overheard, it could be the same sort of talk Oster and the Abwehr paid dearly for: proposing a surrender, *or worse.*"

Bora expected it, but it still came as a blow. He had to turn away from his friend to regain his composure. Leaning on the railing, he lit a cigarette and took a couple of avid drags before putting it out, lest the nurses – who have a sense of smell like no other – detected tobacco smoke and came in to reprimand him. Salomon's trepidation, the edgy staff officers at the Adlon, old Beck coming out of retirement to visit Berlin, Niemeyer's last note to his lawyer … The pieces of the puzzle cascaded over one another, and the clairvoyant's death became merely a negligible detail of the riddle. All this, with the Americans in Normandy for the past six weeks and advancing into France. He returned to Lattmann's side.

"You left the Central Division in the spring of 1940, right? I'm glad no one sounded me out then."

"You were up to your gills in Poland, exposing the doings of the SS to the War Crimes Office; our Central Division wasn't looking for outspoken people then. Now, if they offer you a job in Berlin, take it. Or if the Americans do you the favour of breaking through across the Arno, go back to Italy as quickly as you can. Me, I'm ready to build a monument to the Russki who shot me and pulled me out of the game. I've decided I'm going to live through this war. For my family and for whatever will be left after this war is over. I'm not relinquishing Germany into the hands of whatever comes next."

Bora could no longer stand still. He went over to Lattmann's table to retrieve the magazines, as an excuse to discharge some energy.

"And you?" his friend confronted him, as soon as he was back.

"I'm reconciled to something else entirely."

"What does *that* mean?"

"Nothing." Unexpectedly, Bora smiled. "I told you I'll clam up if you push me."

Patients were meanwhile filing back to the veranda. When the mannish Sister Velhagen came to fetch Lattmann for "your afternoon check-up, Major", Bora asked her if he could smoke out in the park, and when she said yes he promised his colleague that he would wait outside, and not leave the sanatorium until they had time to say goodbye.

3:45 P.M.

Bora stood on one of the garden paths, angrily smoking.

There were moments when he longed for darkness, and not just physical darkness. *I don't want to see, don't want to know. I know enough.* Salomon's anguished, unshaven face, the shifty glance common to so many, fear nestling in men's eyes like rheum that cannot be wiped away ... For years, Bora had come to terms with fear. Seeing it in others always annoyed him, and occasionally alarmed him. Alarm, however, is not the same as fear. It is readiness to fend off the blow. If only he could believe that Salomon had nothing but personal reasons for his distress, he'd make an effort to understand him. But there was so much more, even before Bruno's revelations. He remembered his colleague Ralph Uckermann a month earlier, in the mountains east of Rome. How he vented his hatred for the regime – not expecting that Bora would react; it was not

225

like Bora to emote – and then commended his wife and sons to him, in case anything should happen to him "in the coming weeks". He made Bora swear on his mother's head, something that was unsoldierly and un-German. Bora had consented out of friendship, fully aware that Uckermann meant something bigger and worse than the impending retreat from central Italy. And weren't these "the coming weeks"?

He was beginning to trust his anger, to count on it as an antidote to discouragement. Waking up every day with a pang of hostility for the circumstances was definitely helpful. At times it was impatience that led to anger; other times something he witnessed, or heard, sufficed to make him see red. He kept up an apparent composure as a means of protecting his inner world, where he could keep his store of outrage undisturbed. What was odd was that he hadn't been this angry since childhood: those days it'd been a matter of feistiness, but even then he'd been able to conceal it beneath a veneer of compliance. Early sexual experiences had defused his anger, so that he'd been an unusually well-adjusted adolescent. At the university and in military school, they'd judged him to be level-headed, self-assured. Poland had been the turning point, and two stints on the Russian front after that. He fully understood what Oster and his colleagues found revolting about those experiences. But conspiracy was not his way. He'd made early use of his outrage by acting, whenever possible – often daily – in such a way that counteracted things. *If what they say about them is true, the SS have compiled a dossier on me that must be a mile long by now.*

"Am I speaking to Martin-Heinz von Bora? My name is Wilhelm Osterloh – we have Benedikta Coennewitz in common."

The man in the wheelchair had followed a gentle grassy incline, so that Bora had not heard him coming.

Being caught unawares nettled him. As for the name, Wilhelm Osterloh … Willy. "Willy from Hamburg" – that was how Dikta always referred to him. The last Bora had heard of him was that he had been working on the North-South Axis road project in Berlin, and that was months before the war started. He could have ignored the engineer, or pretended he didn't know of him. Instead, he said, "I *am* Lieutenant Colonel von Bora, and as far as I know Fraulein Coennewitz belongs to herself, not to either one of us."

"Well, we both shagged her, didn't we?"

The malicious words nearly made Bora lose control, a process so sudden that he was unable to guard against it. The idyllic garden view swam before his eyes as the blood rose to his head. *Either he thinks I won't strike a cripple, or else he hopes I will, thus creating an incident.*

Osterloh sneered when he saw him resist the urge. Settled with his wheelchair on the gravel path, he occupied the entire width of it.

"So." He lifted a pair of bloodshot grey eyes at Bora. "So, you *are* the stud who took her from me. What is it they say? 'Fancy meeting you here.' I knew it the day she came back from Leipzig seven years ago. I knew there was someone else. It bothered me, you know. She said nothing, but she'd changed. Then one day, after a row, she told me, 'I've fallen in love with someone else, and there's nothing you can do about it.' Can you believe that?"

Bora could. It was like Dikta to inform a man that he could do nothing about her choices; she'd done it to him in Rome, speaking of the annulment. Willy from Hamburg. That explained the long, moody stares the amputee had cast towards him during his first time here. Bora could not say that he hadn't been curious about Dikta's lover at the beginning, although the gist and extent of his conversations about him with her had been, "Will you leave him now?"

She'd bedded both of them off and on over a period of several months, eventually choosing Bora, as she said, because of "the great sex, your looks, your cleverness and your love of horses". Finding Osterloh here, in such a state, moderated the displeasure he'd anticipated feeling if such a meeting ever took place. Not that he cared about him, not in the least.

This side of forty, white with rancour and the long hospital stay, Osterloh kept his grimace-like smile. "We continued to see each other for a while, but I knew it was over. She was not the same in bed, and if that isn't a signal … She wasn't the same when we spoke, either. She treated me more and more like a stranger. 'He's a soldier, isn't he?' I asked her. 'I bet it's your usual jackbooted buck who makes women's heads spin. I thought you didn't like soldiers.' 'I like this one.' That's what she said. But we weren't thinking about a world war then. I said, 'You realize soldiers are always away. It doesn't seem the sort of relationship you'd like.' 'Well, I like *him*. I like him.' And then I found out – from Herr Dortmueller the industrialist, who met you in Leipzig at that time – that it was our young Baron von Bora, whom everyone talked about because he was such a great horseman and such a promising officer. I choked with spite, I admit. But I kept my sangfroid enough not to make a scene, much less try to get in touch with my rival. And I was far-sighted enough to warn Benedikta that she'd tire of you, too. I was right, wasn't I?"

Provoked as he was, Bora found the accumulated bitterness in Osterloh a sight that disgusted him, as well as making him angry. Knowing Dikta, the chance that she might go back to an old lover was nil. As of the most recent reports, she'd chosen to live in Portugal, away from the war and from men who get hurt in war.

"This conversation may be therapeutic for you," he snapped back, "but it annoys me. Please come to the point, if you have one, otherwise I will bid you goodbye."

The last thing Osterloh wanted was to throw away a chance to speak his fill. His inflamed eyes trailed away from Bora's figure and looked elsewhere. "The point is that I hoped she'd look me up once she got her annulment. To get even with you, if nothing else; believe me, I anticipated it. Foolish of me. She never called – and then the March bombs did *this* to me, so you can imagine ... If she left you after you lost a hand, imagine what she'd think of me, in the state I'm in."

"I don't want to imagine it, and I have nothing to tell you."

The accidental meeting had the unexpected power of stripping off whatever dressing time had placed on his grief over Dikta. Suddenly, Bora felt his loss once more exposed and bleeding like a fresh wound, nearly too painful to bear. He clung on to his pride to conceal it, even if it meant staying there instead of walking away.

Insects flying across the grounds from hedges blooming elsewhere speckled the air. When a ladybird landed on the armrest of his wheelchair, Osterloh squashed it with his thumb.

"With the war going as it is, Colonel ..." He wiped his finger on the tartan blanket covering the stumps of his thighs. "I have no illusions; what about you? I admit I find myself fantasizing that a Russian private might sooner or later teach our girl a lesson in humility." Vindictiveness was like a fluid that rose from Osterloh's maimed body to his eyes, brimming from them, making them narrow. The red in them was such that he seemed about to weep blood. "I can see it – Dikta back in Berlin: she in one of her Paris gowns, and a Russian with grubby underpants ..." He followed the movement of Bora's hand to his holster, and made a sarcastic face. "Here," he said, "Here," pointing with his forefinger between his eyebrows, hard enough to dig his nail into the skin. "Oh, *please*. You don't know the favour you'd do me."

Which, of all the reasons not to do it, was for Bora the sole, mean-spirited one that kept him from killing Willy Osterloh.

When the same nurse's assistant who'd served tea saw them confronting each other, she hurried over from the end of the garden path with an alarmed look on her young face. Osterloh told her everything was fine, and stayed her with a gesture. To Bora, whose telltale pallor he must have relished, he cooed provokingly, "I just wanted to know if it was you, the so-good-in-bed-and-in-the-saddle Martin-Heinz von Bora. Ta-ta for now." The smile left his face as he nodded to the nurse's assistant to come and fetch him. While she wheeled him towards the shade of a bird-filled tree, he continued to look back, craning his neck. And he was crying.


4:15 P.M.


After his check-up, Bruno Lattmann sat once more on the veranda, leafing through the periodicals Bora had brought him. He at once caught his friend's surliness and took it as a sign of deep worry about the political implications of his inquiry. "Well," he said, "I'm not going to let you leave while you're in this temper."

"I'm fine."

"Rubbish." Lattmann rummaged in the pocket of his pyjama shirt. "I scribbled it while you were out smoking." He took out a slip of paper, which he folded and refolded. "Remember the girl I mentioned the first time you were here – the one with the sick boyfriend, yes? Meet her, will you – what's the harm in it?"

"You're a lousy matchmaker, Bruno."

"Why? She's just a good girl who needs a shag."

"And I'm a good boy who needs a shag?"

"Tell me it's not true."

Bora had been furious since meeting Willy Osterloh, but Lattmann's well-meant concern was suddenly irresistible. "It isn't true that I'm a good boy," he told him. "But I do need a shag."

"Hallelujah. In case you're in the right mood, here's her phone number."

Bora's attitude changed the moment he unfolded the scrap Lattmann had handed him.

"This is the telephone exchange for the Reserve Army. Does she work there?"

"Remember the evacuation order for women and children; it's mostly those living in the suburbs, like Eva, or those with a place of employment who stayed behind."

This changed matters – a little, at least. Bora stowed the number away. "I'll see if I have time to give her a call."

"Wait. What day of the week is it?"

"Thursday. Why?"

"Because Emmy Pletsch comes to visit him on Thursdays. That's how she and Eva met. I bet she's still inside."

"Leave it be, Bruno. I'll call her if I have time. You're right about the other matter, though. I can't let Salomon run loose, and I must clear matters privately with those he supposedly overheard. Whom should I go and see at the Reserve Army?"

Lattmann's face had the expression of one whose well-meant advice has succeeded beyond his expectations. "Might as well seek an unofficial interview with Stauffenberg himself, if he will receive you." He pointed to the pocket where Bora had stored the phone number. "Ask Emmy Pletsch, she can arrange it."

As it happened, at that hour a handful of visitors, relatives and colleagues, were leaving for the day. "What a stroke of luck, it's her!" Lattmann nodded in the direction of a fair-haired young woman looking onto the veranda, and before Bora could stop him he was already waving at her to get her attention. "She always stops to say hello."

Bora saw that it would be easier to stick to business with her than he'd anticipated. She wore a uniform, and he didn't like uniformed women on principle. They were like the rest of his associates and subalterns, not at all objects of interest. He'd met young auxiliaries, pretty and more than eager – his secretary in Rome was only the last of a series – but those had been Dikta's days, and he hadn't even considered them.

Aside from the field-grey, however, he couldn't find much to dislike about Emmy Pletsch. Trim, fair-skinned, she was anything but ugly, and surely under thirty. His first, practical, thought was: *I'm slim but, as Ida Rüdiger puts it, a tall and sturdy lad, and she's rather small.* When she approached to greet Lattmann, she became more interesting than she'd been from a distance. Her right eye, Bora noticed, was of a shade of blue slightly different from the left one: the peculiarity gave her an unusual, asymmetric appearance, of which she was perhaps conscious, because she quickly looked away. A little mark on the bridge of her nose suggested that she wore glasses to read. Her hands, square and short-fingered like a farm girl's, contrasted with a pair of attractive, slender legs.

"Lieutenant Colonel – Major," she addressed the officers. "How are you today, Major Lattmann?"

"Ask something else, Staff Leader Pletsch," Bruno sneered. "No tobacco, no drink, no wife. I'd climb the walls if I could. May I introduce you to my good colleague, Lieutenant Colonel Martin von Bora?"

Her hesitation did not escape Bora. Hearing his name would hardly surprise her if she had merely heard Bruno or Eva mention it. Had she heard it spoken at Bendlerstrasse, like Salomon had? In any case, she rallied immediately.

"Colonel von Bora."

"Staff Leader Pletsch."

"The colonel will be in Berlin for only a matter of days," Lattmann explained.

"Oh. I wish you a good stay, Colonel."

"Thank you."

That was all. As she walked away, Bora had the impression of someone who no longer endures strain with patience, but with resignation. Even the touch of rebellion against one's lot that patience often implies had gone from her. Something about her shoulders and the way she held her head indicated a proud, quiet surrender. As for the rest – such details were unlikely to escape him even in pensive moments – she was shapely and petite (Bora still measured women according to Dikta's athletic build), not unlike Mrs Murphy in Rome.

*I scribbled a crazy note to Mrs Murphy, which said that I hoped to marry her one day, although she has a husband and a twenty-year-old stepson. I believed it when I wrote it, and I needed to assign myself a task to accomplish, to give me a reason to carry on. I still think about her, but more hopelessly than when we last saw each other.*

"Well?" Lattmann stared at Bora, who said nothing.

"Well?" he repeated.

"She wears a uniform."

"Not in bed, she wouldn't."

"Leave it, Bruno. You've done your good deed for the day." It would take more than a pretty girl to take his mind off the mountain of trouble facing him. Trying to sort out his priorities would require every ounce of concentration Bora could muster. He glanced at the watch on his right wrist. "Nebe's man will be here to fetch me any time now. I have to go."

Silent and immaculate, meanwhile, white-stockinged nurse's assistants were making the rounds of the veranda with their inescapable mint tea.

"The care of German heroes has passed from Valkyries to nurses serving dishwater," Lattmann grumbled at the sight. "Before they come here with my portion of slop, know that I'd have kept my mouth shut if you hadn't asked. You made me tell you what you're up against, Martin, so you, too, owe me the truth."

Bora slowly let the air out of his lungs. Maimed and injured men sat around, waiting for permanent disability, or death, or health regained and a return to duty at the front. Willy Osterloh was not in his corner. *I really would have done him a favour by shooting him,* Bora told himself. *But I'm not that merciful.*

"The truth?" He patted Lattmann on the back, an unusual show of sociability for him. "This assignment is the last drop, Bruno. Being shrewd, covering up my tracks – I'm no cleverer than those after me. You were right about Russia and Italy: I'd gone too far, and knew that I had. This is the 'something else' I'm reconciled to."

"Please, don't tell me it's as bad as all this."

"Let's just say that it's a matter of time. Like my late uncle, I can't blame anyone else for the bed I've made."

Lattmann swallowed. "Give me a cigarette. Blast, man, give me a cigarette. I'm dying to taste tobacco in my mouth, even if I don't smoke it." He snatched the cigarette Bora reluctantly handed him and sucked on it furiously. "It *can't* be this bad," he groaned. "What will your family say?"

"My family will accept things, as I expect them to do." Bora was so ashamed of saying this much, of revealing this much about himself, that he blushed under his tan and had to look down.

The awkward moment threatened to turn grim. Lattmann chewed on the tip of the unlit cigarette. "I shouldn't be telling you this, but eleven years ago, when my father had his own radio programme in Berlin, the gossip was that the SA or Heldorff had a hand in the matter of Hanussen's end. Heldorff became top dog in the Berlin police two years later. Father kept the story under his hat, especially as the Reichstag went up in smoke the day after the murder. Dangerous as the rumour was, about the death of a Jew who collected important debtors, it did not stack up to a national crisis … whether or not he could see into the future, like his Aryan replacement Niemeyer."

"If it's true, it took some gall on Nebe's part to saddle me with the task to expose his counterpart in the police."

"Can you think of a cleverer move? Come closer."

Forcing a smile, Lattmann pulled out three flat packets from his pyjama top and pushed them into Bora's breast pocket. "In memory of the old days, when back in Kharkov fear made us throw up or grow horny. For future use."

Bora did not want to contradict him. He silently buttoned the pocket over the army condoms.

4:50 P.M.

As he followed the path to the gate, halfway across the park and ahead of him he glimpsed Emmy Pletsch in conversation with Sister Velhagen near a tall, flowering hedge. The nurse was shaking her head at whatever Emmy asked her; no drama followed, only a weariness of stance and that controlled despondency perceivable even from afar. Ever so briefly, war seemed to Bora nothing but an unforgivable abuse committed by egotistical, unthinking males. *We are wounded, we die, and compel grieving women to stand about us, whispering.*

He waited at a discreet distance until the two women parted from each other, and then caught up with the auxiliary.

"Staff Leader Pletsch, one moment, please: is there a chance I could meet with Colonel von Stauffenberg later today?"

She turned around. Her eyes were moist, and when she saw him directly behind her she became a little defiant. "The colonel is not available today, Lieutenant Colonel."

"Tomorrow, then?"

"Sorry, unlikely."

Damn the bureaucracy. This was why he despised headquarters. Bora remained patient, because she evidently needed a moment to pull herself together, and he meant to reach his aim through her. "Will he be available at all during the week?"

"No. It is impossible."

The blossoming hedge along the path let out a balmy aroma; bees and golden flies swarmed above it. The fragrance in the air and her inflexible words oddly became one in Bora's mind, as if nature were trying to mitigate the refusal. The fact that she did not give or ask for details, but only said no, made him wonder: auxiliaries of her rank were more than just secretaries or assistants; the firmness of her denial suggested complete unavailability on Stauffenberg's part. She must have orders to that effect. Bora, who seldom took rejection well, physically loomed over her.

"Well, I have every intention of meeting him, with or without an appointment. Inform him."

"Yes, sir."


5:00 P.M.


Grimm's replacement had not yet arrived. Bora paced back and forth in front of the gate. Looking out, he could saw the site where the fugitives were caught and presumably burned alive behind a screen of leafy trees. Dove-coloured smoke rose to a certain height and then spread horizontally, as if an invisible ceiling blocked its further ascent. In Russia, in Ukraine, Bora would not have given a second's thought to such marks of horror. One met them daily, perpetrated by both sides. There, one told oneself, *This is the Eastern front; since time immemorial, we have butchered one another along these frontiers.* But here! Past the line of trees and the smouldering barn were gentle heights, and the shore of the Blankensee, and beyond was one of the old artillery ranges, south of Greater Berlin. The city limits lay only eighteen miles north of here. Pointless to wonder whether the fugitives were in fact Russian, or responsible for this or that crime (including the timely murder of Ergard Dietz). Bora was tired of steeling himself against bestiality.

And he was still angry. Osterloh's venom, followed by Bruno's well-intentioned meddling, renewed his bitterness (but it tasted like guilt more than bitterness) over losing Dikta. Angry with her as he was, he was angrier with himself for feeling so bereft. *I miss her now and always will*, he admitted. *As much as I try to convince others and myself that I make do, and have come to terms with the annulment, the thought of being for ever separated from her is intolerable.*

From the grounds of the sanatorium behind him drifted a scented, reassuring warmth. Yet during the cold season the same lofty trees had to rage and bellow in the wind.

Bora stood facing the gate, waiting, averting his eyes from the smoke and breathing slowly to compose himself, so he didn't notice the nurse until she was right beside him.

In her seersucker smock, Sister Velhagen had that appearance between a nun and a mess-hall cook that made some German nurses so sterile and unattractive.

"Do you have someone to pick you up, Lieutenant Colonel? And are you travelling to Berlin?"

When Bora answered yes, she asked if he would consent to share the car with three people. "They are an SS lieutenant who has a broken leg and hobbles on crutches, a Chilean radiologist bound for the Landhausstrasse Red Cross hospital in Wilmersdorf, and Staff Leader Pletsch of the Reserve Army. I wouldn't impose, but they have no other means of rapidly reaching the city."

It *was* an imposition. Bora wavered a moment and then replied in the affirmative, but not because Emmy Pletsch was among the passengers. The mixed company would justify his foray to Beelitz in the eyes of any Kripo man.

Sister Velhagen resorted to one of those quick, unamused smiles, without a show of teeth. "That is excellent. They've all agreed that it will be fine if you leave them at the Red Cross hospital – they can make their way from there."

At this point, an exchange of favours was only fair: "Sister," Bora asked (without really knowing why he did so; the idea had crept unwanted into his mind), "how is Osterloh, the engineer?"

"Osterloh, Wilhelm." The nurse glanced at Bora's gloved left hand. It was a habit with medical personnel, which he'd grown used to during the past year: to them, you are your wounds and scars. "Are you a relative? A colleague?"

"We used to have a mutual friend."

The sentence alone suggested nothing. Why was it, then, that she seemed to grasp what lay behind it, just as Bora had seen the unquenched fire beyond the screen of trees? *She perceives that we were rivals, and that – for whatever it's worth – I won.*

"The infections keep coming back," she said, "and they keep cutting his leg further. Medically, the doctors cannot make sense of it."

"And you?"

"I think resentment is eating him alive."

5:14 P.M.

The car was the same – the lovingly kept Olympia – but the plainclothesman at the wheel did not resemble Florian Grimm in the least. Slope-shouldered and lean, Trost gave the German salute with such officious indolence that Bora berated him for it and immediately wondered if it was a ruse to ferret out lukewarm officers. Nebe the SS man, if not Nebe the policeman, would not shrink from such methods.

What the policeman thought on, or might report from, the shared ride was the last of Bora's concerns. Waiting for his accidental passengers, he asked Trost about Grimm. He learned – in that order – that Inspector Grimm had suffered minor injuries, and would resume service as soon as possible; that the house destroyed in the raid was not his but his brother's; that both families were there at the time, and they were all trapped in the collapsed basement until midday.

When the time came to leave, Bora let the SS man sit in front, because of the crutches and bulky cast, while he less than comfortably rode in the back – with the physician, a swarthy Chilean named Ybarri, in the middle, and Staff Leader Pletsch on the Chilean's other side. The Chilean smelled strongly of phenol, an odour you don't usually associate with radiology but which reminded Bora of his hospital stays.

They had to roll up their windows when the road took them by the smouldering barn. Reduced to blackened stumps

238

in a bed of fat smoke, it reeked of death. From a safe distance, a handful of tow-headed farm boys contemplated the scene; their faces were blank, yet far from innocent. Bony and barefoot, they weren't any different from the Russian youngsters eating sunflower seeds while Peter's downed plane steamed in the summer heat with its dead flyer inside it. Lonely fields, smoke, stench: Bora still carried those inside him. *The boys are – what – twelve or thirteen years of age? War has been their life for the past five years. Next door, their mothers sell eggs on the black market; their grandfathers doused the hedge to keep the flames away and will later dig the ground to shovel what remains of the fugitives into a shallow hole. Their fathers have died at the front, or may yet die – and foreign lads will stand around them, gawking.*

From the corner of his eye, Bora glimpsed the passengers' reaction to the scene: the men stared with a kindred lack of expression; like an insomniac, Emmy Pletsch wearily rested her forehead in her hand.

During the trip, scarred by the usual showing of papers, halts and detours, the conversation in the car stayed sketchy, banal. The SS man, an avid sportsman, sounded very concerned about the state of his shin bone and kept badgering Ybarri for details on fractures and their healing. He was young, of the ambitious type that starts off sanguine but turns whiny as soon as he's hurt. Ybarri heard him out, answering non-committally and smoothing his pomaded head with his waxy left hand. Eventually the turn came for vacuous comments about the weather, the heat, the road, the season. Anything but the war. At one point, Emmy asked the doctor how he liked Berlin.

Ybarri turned to her. "Except for the air raids, very well. I'm obliged to you for asking." He admitted to suffering from claustrophobia, which precluded him from seeking refuge in underground shelters. Emmy said she understood: it was the same for her.

"Would you prefer the window seat, Doctor?" Bora proposed, but the Chilean declined. "No, no. *Muy obligado, coronel.* It's below ground that I can't stand it."

Bora was relieved. After Emmy's uncooperative answer to his request for an interview with Stauffenberg, he had no great desire to sit elbow to elbow with her. The truth was that Lattmann's dramatic disclosures weighed on him, killing off any interest in conversing. As for Trost, he now and then darted wary glances through the rear-view mirror.

Ybarri's halting German, on the other hand, had no effect on his loquacity. He asked Emmy Pletsch about the circumstances of her fiancé's illness, thinking, as he said, of transferring him for an extended round of X-rays to the Red Cross hospital, where he'd been working for months. Thus, Bora learned how Obersturmführer Leo Franke, an Old Warrior, had suffered a stroke on 20 April, after a ceremony honouring the Führer's birthday. At the NSKK barracks where he served as a driving school instructor, his comrades didn't realize until the day after that he'd gone from sleeping off the parade into a coma. Telling the story, Emmy passed no judgement; her voice was caring and calm. She gravely pointed out that Franke tried to save her father's life in 1933, when the old man died a "martyr's death" for the Party.

"Leo took the first bullet for him. He and I have been together ever since."

She could be no more than twenty-seven or twenty-eight now, which meant that she was probably sixteen or so when she'd started going out with Franke. Bora grew curious. He reasoned that "being together" covers a vast range of intimacy, and does not necessarily imply sexual relations. But when the engaging Ybarri enquired whether they had children, Emmy replied "Not yet."

*So she habitually went to bed with her head-bashing hero.* Bora turned to the window. *Does it necessarily follow that she needs someone else now?*

240

*

With most of the journey finally behind them, they made a detour through Grossbeeren, the area where the unfortunate Ergard Dietz owned his summer cottage. The sight of the needle-like memorial to the battle against Napoleon prompted the SS lieutenant to brag to Ybarri about a German victory. Bora, whose ancestors had fought there, kept quiet and watched sparse chalets file past the car with their leafy gardens. If Dietz never received Niemeyer's letter, there was no reason to think he'd delivered the unknown contents of his client's box to the authorities. He'd simply taken a few days out in the country, missing Bubi Kupinsky and the role history had set aside for both of them. Only the timeliness of his death at the hands of shadowy attackers, a handful of hours after Niemeyer's, made the coincidence implausible. After all, whoever killed Niemeyer could have found a copy of the letter on the premises. Provided he identified the addressee, he'd either have alerted the government or taken immediate action against the lawyer, in the hope that he hadn't received the original message.

Bora met Block's eyes in the rear-view mirror, a brief glance that said absolutely nothing. It was warm and uncomfortable in the car, a perfect metaphor of the quandary he was in now that the murder investigation and highest political stakes potentially coincided. *As for Russian fugitives,* he reasoned, *they are the scapegoat for the day: whatever happens, we can blame it on them. Why, I'm sure the State has a detailed plan for quenching revolt and disorder by blaming it on foreign nationals – or Germans. Niemeyer's murder in Dahlem was simply too egregious to pin on bloodthirsty prisoners of war, while out here, where houses are few and far between …*

A roadblock ahead indicated another delay. Kleinbeeren, where they now sat waiting, seemed deserted. The SS lieutenant dozed with his shorn head against the half-open passenger window. Ybarri prattled on endlessly. Emmy Pletsch limited herself to nodding occasionally to whatever he said, but her mind was elsewhere.

During the last leg of the trip, Bora had time to go from dismissing the plump, affable Chilean as a monopolizing encumbrance, to watching him play ladies' man as only southern men can do. And Emmy? Her absorbed, vulnerable profile gave the impression of reticence and at the same time of well-guarded fondness. Or something that Bora would not hesitate to term fondness. *It explains why Bruno thinks she needs a man. Well, it does show a little: she has that wistful reserve typical of good girls, really quite attractive.*

RED CROSS HOSPITAL, LANDHAUSSTRASSE,
WILMERSDORF, 6:32 P.M.

It's a fact: sometimes a moment is enough. Usually it is a moment that lasts a fraction of time beyond what we expected, and says many things. Or else it suggests just a single, unmistakable thing. Emmy Pletsch looked at Bora as she left the car – with a polite "Thank you for the lift, Lieutenant Colonel" – and something in the way she paused before turning away and reaching the pavement made his heart skip a beat. Bora realized that he held her glance as she was about to turn away, and although he did not intend to let Lattmann play go-between, he betrayed himself by staring at her that one instant longer.

Had Lattmann kept quiet, it wouldn't have happened. Exchanging glances with women was nothing new, at least ever since Dikta left him. But tonight there was that unexpected crumb of complicity in the way they looked at each other, as if to say: The two of us, among all others in the car, with their banalities, stand apart. How? It did not matter.

Bora was the first to avert his eyes, in his reserved, stern way. He told himself, *I will never see her again. The world is full* of glances, and this did not differ substantially from all the others. But it did, and suddenly nothing was as before.

No one else noticed, not even Trost. Ybarri helped the SS man climb the hospital steps, while Emmy Pletsch held the door open for them. Already she and Bora were ignoring each other, although he was unexpectedly glad to have her phone number in his pocket. *Why? She was neither friendly nor helpful when I asked her to set up an appointment for me, although I do plan to contact Stauffenberg with or without her. What, then? I don't care for women in uniform, let alone a girl whose lover is half-dead! Reticence, tenderness, the way her mismatched eyes send out different messages ... Purely my interpretation. Or is it because Bruno has a point? A point about my sexual needs, and the fact that she won't wear a uniform in bed. Right. As if she'd go for it. As if there were time enough. Well, there is, for a quickie. There comes a point during a war (and in life, I may add) when, as my stepfather told me once, everything accelerates. Our existence and the events around us accelerate, and so do our responses. Love and hatred develop and grow faster, your needs demand immediate attention, because as a soldier you cannot afford to waste time. I wonder where she lives. No. No. Hold back, Martin. She is a headquarters auxiliary you're also trying to use to obtain an interview. There's military etiquette, there are principles. Slam on the brakes.*

All Trost saw was a frowning young man who left the back seat and got in next to him.

"Where to, Colonel?"

"To drink something cold."

He'd given up hoping for it, but at his return to the hotel he found a message from Olbertz, setting up an appointment in a small café (La Scala was its name, no less) near Potsdam station. The concierge also informed him that a lady had telephoned, asking for him.

For a moment, Bora thought that it might be Staff Leader Pletsch – and immediately discarded the idea, since she couldn't have had enough time to set up an appointment for him to see Stauffenberg; besides, he'd never told her where he was billeted. His mother was back in Leipzig and Dikta lived abroad: both would identify themselves when calling. Ida Rüdiger, maybe?

"Did she leave a name, number or address?"

"No, sir. She did say she would call again."

Bora even imagined a ruse by Salomon, using a female friend to stalk him here, of all the hotels in Berlin. Unlikely – no. He decided not to worry about a female caller for now. He climbed to his room to shower and change his sweaty shirt, careful not to lose at any time sight of the tunic where he kept Niemeyer's letter. It was, all the same, unthinkable to keep carrying it around in Berlin. Even leaving it in the hotel safe was out of the question. Bora discarded the nooks and crannies in the room that he himself would be the first to search, as he'd done at Kupinsky's. Doors locked, curtains drawn, he emptied the boxes of mostly useless papers and cuttings from Niemeyer's house, and laid out the contents on the floor. For days he'd sieved through the material the Kripo had handed over to him, to the point of knowing at a glance what this or that folder contained. It was inside one of several nearly identical sleeves of assorted items that he clipped the letter to a sheaf of innocuous self-promoting fluff.

He then sat for a few minutes at the foot of the bed, tracing with his eyes the pattern of stylized pineapples on the wallpaper. They resembled eyeless, exotic faces with a wild knot of hair on their heads; a strangely calming, blind audience converging where the walls met. Before leaving, he opened the windows wide enough to let the air circulate, but not so wide that they let the evening warmth flow in.

Outside the hotel, Trost was waiting in the car. He jumped out to open the door for his passenger, and when Bora – instead of climbing in – deliberately pushed the door closed, he stood there, half at attention, half slouching. In his inexpressive face, scarred by small blemishes like a teenager's, his eyes were brown, round like chestnuts, warm for a German. He was dutiful to the point of obstinacy. Hearing Bora's demand for the keys, he baulked without actually saying no. He'd need permission from half a dozen supervisors, he claimed. At least.

"I was assigned Florian Grimm," Bora replied, as if speaking of an object handed out to him. "Not you. Until Florian Grimm returns, leave the keys here. Unless you have orders to keep me under observation – which is preposterous, since I am in charge of the investigation. Are there any objections," he added, "to my use of the car?"

Unconvinced, Trost remained silent. Judging by the oblique look he stole at Bora's artificial hand, perhaps he feared for the Olympia.

"Is that it?" Bora laughed openly, something he seldom did these days. "I perfectly manage driving up and down mountains with my one hand. In comparison, Berlin is child's play."

There was no way to change Trost's mind, however, before he'd had a lengthy phone conversation with his Alexanderplatz supervisor. In the end he sulkily relinquished the keys; while he turned the corner to catch the tram, he was still looking over his shoulder.

Bora had his reasons for wanting to take advantage of Grimm's absence, even if it lasted only ten or twelve hours more. For the moment, he did no more than park the car near the side entrance of the hotel. He chose to walk to the La Scala café, which was near the battered Potsdam train station.

7:45 P.M.

The lengthening shadows only accentuated the glare of the low sun. The crowded café was dim by comparison. Bora had never been to it. There were green upholstered benches along the walls, faced by rows of small tables: benches and tables, like everything else in a quarter familiar with air raids, had seen better days. Framed photos of opera singers and famous musicians – including Bora's father – hung in an arrangement that disguised the cracks in the walls. The autographs on them were forged, at least as far as the Maestro was concerned: Friedrich von Bora didn't sign portraits for just any of his devotees. At this hour, the place was filled mainly by women, office employees or shop clerks who treated themselves to the small luxury of a cold drink after work.

Bora found the secrecy of this meeting frankly excessive, but played along. He recognized Olbertz when the latter, discreetly moving aside a flat leather bag, had already made room for him to his left. An inconspicuous gesture, since there were no other free seats at this time. Two men who'd never met before might behave the same way. Bora nodded a greeting and sat down.

At first Olbertz looked at the partly filled beer mug in front of him as he spoke. "Let's get it out of the way, Colonel. Your uncle injected himself with a lethal dose of morphine. What else do you expect to hear?"

Bora found the introduction incongruous. "At the funeral you suggested that his act might not have been altogether voluntary. Let me at least understand if there were personal reasons, or —"

"No."

"'No' in the sense that the reasons were not personal, or in the sense that you decline to answer?"

"I decline to answer."

Impatience was something Bora reserved for other things. "Fine," he said. "Did my uncle's position on euthanasia play a role in his demise?" Silence was a reply in itself. "I take that as a yes," he said. "In combination with his having adopted a Jew, maybe."

"If you know the answers, you shouldn't ask." Smoothing the leather bag on his knees, the physician continued to face the table, as if the mug were his interlocutor. "All your uncle said is that he was ready to accept the idea of suicide, although it did not originate with him. I tried to talk him out of it. Half-heartedly, I admit, because it seems he really had no choice." The beer, some of which had spilled onto a cardboard coaster, let out a bitter odour Bora could smell from his seat. "This is not a good time for us to discuss this. Not a good time at all."

"Why are we meeting, then? You could have ignored my phone calls."

"I did. I am here for a different reason." A double snap of the buckles allowed Olbertz to slide his hand under the flap of his leather bag. Out came two sheets of carbon paper, type-written and stapled together. "A copy of the Weimar Prophet's post-mortem minus the omissions, which if I am not mistaken could be useful to you." Bora glanced over it. Saying that the existence of an unofficial report came as complete news would be pointless. "May I ask about their source?"

"Dr Wirth from the Charité hospital, where the autopsy was performed. Wirth heard that you questioned his wife about the night of the murder, and concluded that you weren't simply curious. He worries that you might have got an impression of hostility from Frau Wirth, so given that we both worked with your relative he encouraged me to bring you this. You can have it."

Bora was confused. He'd taken Olbertz for a friend of his uncle's, and here he was, carrying an olive branch from a Nazi physician. "It does not change my opinion of the Wirths," he said. The signature on the second page presented him with another surprise. "This is *your* name, Dr Olbertz!"

"So it is. When I ran into you at the funeral – not to mention when I was called to perform the autopsy – I had no idea you'd be investigating Niemeyer's death. You will find no significant discrepancy between the two accounts: two devastating shots … The first fired while the victim stood face to face with his killer, having been caught unawares in his own home … Falling on his face, he struck a small table, bruising himself … The second shot reached him when he was already lying on the floor, possibly already dead." While Bora browsed the text, Olbertz slipped another paper out from under the leather flap, which he lay face up on his knees. "The real surprise – which, given the Prophet's public role, had best stay untold – is that he was circumcised."

Bora had barely time to glimpse the photo before the physician put it away again. "I thought … an eyewitness spoke of an old episode when Niemeyer was exposed by two Jewish members of the audience, and found to be, well, 'whole'. How do you think … ? And *why*?"

Olbertz buckled the flap of his bag. "Well, there are a few reasons why circumcision is performed for medical reasons. Barring these, some research suggests that exceedingly promiscuous males run a lower risk of contracting social diseases if they 'streamline their tool'. In this case, I believe the operation was carried out in adulthood, clearly after the episode you mentioned."

"Who was Niemeyer's attending physician?"

"I believe it was Dr Karl von Eicken, a throat specialist – the best for singers and public speakers. He even treated the Führer once. But circumcision … Such an unpopular surgical practice must have been performed outside the Fatherland, during one of the victim's extended tours abroad. Italy, Greece or Turkey come to mind."

The specifics did not appreciably change things, save the unlikely case of an anti-Semite mistaking the naked Niemeyer for a Jew in the privacy of his own home. Bora credited such official censorship to the clairvoyant's popularity in high circles.

"Any details you wish to add, Doctor?"

"Yes, but not to my report." After a quick scan of the room (no one was minding them), Olbertz placed a morocco key case in front of Bora. "Here is the key to your uncle's office in Dahlem. Although he entrusted it to me, I don't care to keep it." He waited until Bora pocketed it, before adding, "If there's anything you'd like to salvage, I urge you to be there before half past six tomorrow morning."

Bora swallowed an angry question, whose political implications would surely fall on deaf ears. "The clinic is changing hands, I take it."

"You could say that."

It was to be expected. The stress of the day threatened to undo the punctilious control Bora exercised on his temper. He counted to ten, and then to twenty, breathing slowly. When a sad-looking waitress came to take his order, he asked her straightaway what was available, other than beer, to spare her a series of "I'm sorry, we don't have …" or "We no longer have …" followed by whatever drink he'd ask about. "Fanta," she said, and he declined. Olbertz emptied his mug. He meticulously set it in the middle of its cardboard coaster.

When a fly landed on a dab of foam along the glass rim, he seemed about to chase it away, but didn't. Under his breath, his eyes on the greedy insect, he told Bora, "You'd be wise to mind whom you frequent."

Bora found the advice of little use after meeting people of all kinds and persuasions in the last few days. Resentful of warnings in general, he replied, "The same may be said for you, Doctor." He meant Wirth and other politicized physicians, nothing more, yet Olbertz was startled. He tried to hide his reaction, but to no avail: Bora noticed it. Not that Germans lacked reasons to fear indiscretion in those days. Perhaps Olbertz regretted whispering those few words at the state funeral about a forced suicide.

Walking back to the hotel did him good. There was always a moment, for him, when the accumulation of anxiety met an invisible ceiling. Like the smoke he'd seen rising from the burning farm, it could only spread horizontally, finding its level. As long as he had pressing issues to resolve, fear took second place. The thing to do was not to look ahead beyond the immediate future, hoping for a welcome diversion now and then.

A diversion *was* coming his way. Leaving Karlsbadstrasse for Potsdamer Strasse, opposite the Elizabeth clinic, from the corner of his eye he glimpsed a girl at the tram stop who reminded him of Emmy Pletsch. It was not her, but the very fact of mistaking someone for her was indicative of something.

*It's because I like her smell*, he thought out of the blue.

What? Her *smell*? He had no idea where that impression might have originated. She used no perfume, as far he'd been able to tell; she seemed scrupulously clean, and besides, they'd never stood close enough. Could it be the same as for young animals, who scent each other out, and according to that scent choose and mate with each other? As always in his life, layers of self-control and observance of rules intervened (co-workers, secretaries and other men's women were always off limits). Motionless on the pavement, Bora noticed how the young woman at the tram stop cast a shadow that reached halfway across the pavement.

Just then, upon closer scrutiny, he was surprised to recognize that it was Emmy, after all, waiting for the tram, alone. It was after work hours; she was in civvies, and her hair was down. In a high-waisted, persimmon-coloured dress (Bora had heard Dikta call it a low-cut 'pinafore dress', something like a modern dirndl), a short-sleeved white blouse, and sandals with cork soles. All was prim, there was nothing vain about her.

\*

Bora impulsively crossed the street to the tram stop, just as the tram arrived. From behind, as she reached for the pole to step up, the clasp of her bra under the light cloth of her blouse formed a small knobby ridge between Emmy's shoulders. *I bet she wears cotton underwear, and the summer season allows her to go about without stockings when she is not on duty.*

Wherever she was bound, Bora climbed after her. The wide-hipped housewife blocking his way was unceremoniously pushed aside, an elderly couple holding hands separated as he pressed through the crowd towards her. This late on a weekday, every seat was occupied by a weary Berliner. Emmy stood wedged in the sweaty crush, her left hand circumspectly placed across the flap of her handbag. When Bora addressed her, she darted a surprised glance up at him and then looked away.

"Staff Leader Pletsch, I really must insist on securing an interview with your commander."

"My commander's schedule is taken up for the rest of the week, sir."

Once again, her uncompromising tone and words betrayed specific instructions in that regard. Bora ignored the hurdle. "Well then, it should be possible to meet him outside work hours."

"I am certain of the contrary, Colonel."

The packed floor and a jolty ride forced the standing passengers to cluster and bump, a trial for the senses in days of bad diet and scarce hygiene. The whiteness of Emmy's blouse seemed misplaced and oddly intact, like a patch of snow in a reeking broth. Bora could imagine, given the chronic lack of water and soap, the effort required to keep hair, nails and clothes in order. Being a head taller than most, he dominated his space and partially shielded her from the pressing mob.

Emmy testily kept her eyes on her handbag. "I assure you," she continued, "a meeting would be extremely difficult. Ninety-nine per cent impossible."

Ninety-nine per cent impossible is not appreciably better than one hundred per cent. A screeching halt unsteadied the crowd, allowing him to catch a passing whiff, or so he thought, of sweet almonds in her hair. Was that the smell he'd been thinking of?

They were now somewhere in the neighbourhood of Barbarossaplatz, not far from Max Kolowrat's flat. No one left the tram; if anything, a number of sweaty drudges heading for the Innsbrucker Platz train station crammed themselves in with their parcels and bags to catch the evening train.

Bora was seriously tempted to hop off as soon as possible. "Staff Leader Pletsch," he said quietly in her ear, a resolute closeness that might have seemed cheeky but for his words, "is it necessary for me to lie across the doorstep of the Reserve Army to meet him? I will if I have to."

She pushed away from him a little, lifting her right shoulder as if to reject him, but in so doing a wisp of her blonde hair actually grazed his lips.

"I will if I have to," Bora repeated.

Emmy wiggled to free her right arm enough to take a small notebook out of her handbag.

"Where are you billeted, Colonel?" she asked, and when Bora told her she wrote it down. "It's highly unlikely and I promise nothing, but I will be in touch if there should be news. Goodnight, sir." At the following stop, she left in a stream of other travellers, quickly, but not so quickly that Bora could not get off before the tram resumed its route.

He followed her discreetly, curious to see where she went. *It's just professional habit*, he told himself, *nothing else*. In her persimmon dress, Emmy Pletsch hastened on without looking back. Now that she was alone the burden of worry rested once more on her shoulders, stooping her but not slowing her down. She crossed Lauterplatz to Niedstrasse, where she turned right.

As Bora had expected, her destination was a former girls' school where auxiliaries quartered together.

Through the open windows, in the mild evening air, you could perceive bunk beds; ropes stretched wall-to-wall, items of women's clothes hung up to dry. Behind the ornate Wilhelmine façade the sky stretched bright pink, like watery blood.

Bora waited until she entered the building before resuming his way home.

LEIPZIGER HOF, 9:34 P.M.

Bora chose to dine at a corner table in view of the bar, with its giant turn-of-the-century photograph of the Pauliner church and the Café Français in Leipzig. He felt feverish and very thirsty. Mineral water not being available, he drank tap water, "carefully boiled", as the waiter explained.

Whatever his stepfather said about things accelerating during a war, the present day seemed to have gone on for ever.

Had it really begun with a tender recollection of Uncle Reinhardt-Thoma, and an early air raid? Like stills from a silent film, Kupinsky's rooms faded into the bloody-nosed man nabbed by the Gestapo, and this into Niemeyer's spooky letter to a dead lawyer, the Russian prisoners burning alive, Willy from Hamburg, Lattmann and Olbertz with their unnerving revelations … And then the image became Emmy Pletsch, Staff Leader Emmy Pletsch.

Bora was just in the state of mind he didn't like being in.

For weeks on the Gothic Line with the regiment, the sole feminine presence had been a pinch of farm girls, the occasional Italian refugee from the city, mares and she-mules. Having spent long periods of his life with other men, he was used to the lack of female voices and female glances, but missed them nonetheless.

With Nora Murphy in Rome – well, with Nora Murphy there had been nothing, he hadn't even tried. He'd fallen for her like a schoolboy, for whom a married woman (and an

American to boot) was totally out of reach. He'd desired her and censored his desire for her. After Rome came the frantic German retreat to the north and weeks of bloody mountain fighting.

Bora contemplated the sepia outlines of long-dead customers outside the Café Français, and thought of the last time he'd taken a woman to bed. Late March. Alcohol had played a role then. He did not recall her face, her body or her name. Yet the gap between the careful, elaborate uniqueness of his longing for Dikta and that mercenary fuck at the edge of unconsciousness allowed him to long for Mrs Murphy and now entertain an untimely, improvised interest for the girl with the strange eyes. *We exchanged glances when she left the car, as if we suddenly desired each other. Whether or not things accelerate, we're both lonely, and I'm in deep trouble.* Lattmann was right: not taking advantage of these few days in Berlin was madness. Well? Here in Berlin you only had to look around, like in Paris in 1940, or in Rome three months ago. The women who stayed behind all seemed ready for it. What other purpose did the two leggy brunettes now entering the bar have in mind?

Not so easy for an introvert, even less easy for a finicky, very sober introvert.

Once in his room, Bora made sure Niemeyer's letter was still where he'd hidden it. Lights off and windows open, he sat sipping water out of the bathroom tap from his toothbrush mug.

The race of thoughts in his head (a crime to solve, finding Salomon and securing a talk with Stauffenberg, preparing for the worst at his uncle's clinic in the morning) needed to be stilled before it triggered a new surge of anxiety.

Whoever said that water has no taste? Bora could taste the iron pipes in his stoneware mug, brick dust and the shame of Berlin under the bombs. He finished his drink and went to sit by the window: fully dressed, monitoring his overwrought senses.

Fever made him *feel*, with a raw intensity. Like many things that have a greater significance than they apparently deserve, even the condoms Lattmann stuck in his breast pocket (top-quality Blausiegel) seemed to take up more space than their size suggested, like a weight on his heart. He pulled them out and fingered their flat, unromantic wrappers.

Dikta objected to their use during and before their marriage, which was how she had become pregnant three times. Bora remembered insisting on using a prophylactic before leaving for Russia, because the front was dangerous, and making a child at that point too risky. Yet during his first furlough they'd reverted to the old freedom of making love without precautions. Away from his wife, he never allowed himself a reason to use a condom. And now, contrary to official propaganda, it was not a good time for fathering a child, and possibly an unwise time to bed a girl.

*It's not a matter of missing sex in general – at the front, I am used to that. I miss sex with her, with my wife. How can she not miss me? I know she misses me. It is a matter of size, rhythm, flesh and mutual need. We can stand being apart from each other, but not going without it.* After meeting Willy Osterloh, the idea of living *without it* was once again unbearable. All the more so that he should not see or hear from Dikta. He couldn't. He didn't want to know where she might be (safely in Lisbon, he'd last heard, with her mother), and yet she was the only barrier between him and wanting somebody else.

He, who never wept, had wept in Rome for his unborn sons, for his brother lost in Russia, for the war that never ended, and – he was ashamed of it – for feeling so bereft, after Dikta. For a hundred things he'd found reason to grieve, but not for himself. He hadn't been able to feel pity for himself until he'd left Rome at night with his men, a month and a half earlier.

It seemed like a life ago already.

Preparing to update his diary, he emptied his pockets before removing his tunic. The morocco key case to his uncle's office came to rest on the table side by side with Peter's lighter, the condoms and the steel fountain pen with the gold nib Dikta had given him. Then came wallet and change, the keys to the Olympia, the tram ticket … Bora tidily placed everything in the drawer, except for the pen and Uncle Reinhardt-Thoma's key.

Thursday, 13 July, 11:07 p.m. The key my uncle touched every day for years, and the visit I will make to his clinic early in the morning, bring back to mind the childhood memory I woke up with today. I report it below, not from self-absorption (I don't like myself that much), but because it shows the kind of man he was, and why we loved him.

Erotic dreams, and the concept of Eros itself, were unknown in our house. When I was twelve, I at most fantasized over *The Goose Girl* in my grandparents' summer parlour, a sort of Arthurian painting, or *Ophelia's Drowning*, in the style of Burne-Jones. I couldn't make up my mind between the sinking beauty and the naked girl turning into a feathered creature, but the extent of my reverie did not go past the possibility of kissing them. After all, we were still a month away from the day my playmate Waldo Preger and I would spy on the Polish girl, the seasonal worker breastfeeding her newborn in East Prussia.

Oh, yes. Communion every Sunday, and studying for Confirmation. They kept us boys so ignorant, that scary morning I'd at first thought I'd wet my bed, and then that I was ill. In my distress, I wouldn't get out of bed. It was Sunday, I recall, and my parents were out in the country with Peter. The General's orderly was worried enough to phone my grandmother, who phoned Uncle Alfred, at the time the head of surgery at St Jakob's hospital on Liebigstrasse. Kind as he was, he immediately motored to Lindenau, and soon I heard his voice downstairs, asking in his baritone, "Where's the patient?"

I think it took him seconds to understand what the matter was with me. Having started his practice in the barracks of nearby Gohlis, he knew enough of youngsters' reticence to say, in all seriousness: "You won't go blind if you do it." And because I protested that I hadn't done anything (it was true), he sat at my bedside and said, "Let's take a look."

I wouldn't let him, which of course confirmed his diagnosis.

Odd, how certain scenes stay with you in the smallest detail. It's as if I had the two of us in front of me, as we were then. Uncle Alfred wore a musketeer's beard those days, which in my eyes gave him a swashbuckling air. "Is it wet and sticky?" he asked. "Yes? Well, you're not ill, and won't die of it. It's called sperm, or seminal fluid. Feels dirty but isn't, and if you were female, it'd be blood." (Not what I wanted to hear – the entire thing was unnerving). "As I see it, Martin, you have two possibilities before you: you cultivate the practice with moderation, or else you leave no time for it, by playing sports and other healthy pursuits. Whatever you do, don't use it in a girl, because she might become pregnant."

Use it in a girl? I think I began to weep at this point, partly from relief that I wouldn't die, and partly because of what he'd just said, which horrified me. I felt miserable, and surely said something to the effect that I didn't know how to mention any of it in confession the following day. Uncle Alfred was a freethinker even then. "Why should you say anything?" he burst out. "Do you tell the priest how many times you sneeze? If you didn't do anything wrong, there's nothing to confess. No, no. It'll remain between us men." Today I wonder how he could keep from laughing. "But you must have schoolmates who are growing whiskers already, and you must have seen stallions mounting mares. How do you think colts are made?"

Whiskers, stallions and bleeding girls – one sounded worse than the other that morning. I'd been living in the blessed bubble of childhood and desperately wanted to stay there. The good doctor read my mind, or else I verbalized what I felt. "You can't," he said, "it's done now. The little pot is on the fire, and will brim over now and then." Brimming over? For God's sake! I was probably bawling when I begged him not to tell the General.

"I will not tell the General, or your mother. But now get up. You're not sick. Blow your nose, shower and go on with your life." In the time it took him to light a cigar, his eyes swept around the room full of my boyish things. Did he think over the advice he'd given me a moment before? "On second thought," he added, "my prescription is to remain a child a little longer."

I tried, but by the following year I grew to be 5'10"; at fifteen, I was over 6 foot tall, and I believe the only sport I didn't practise was ladies' gymnastics. The fire he spoke of was under the little pot, and it's been on ever since. As long as Dikta was on my horizon, I remained fairly good at keeping it under control. Without Dikta, there are times when I wish there were no little pots and no fires under them.

Nineteen years have passed since that Sunday in the Leipzig quarter of Lindenau, Uncle. I miss you, and mourn the fact that you had no choice in your solitary death.

# 8

*He who has learned to die has unlearned to serve.*

MICHEL DE MONTAIGNE,
'THAT TO STUDY PHILOSOPHY IS TO LEARN TO DIE'

## DOROTHEA REINHARDT-THOMA CHILDREN'S CLINIC, DAHLEM, FRIDAY, 14 JULY, 5:46 A.M.

Bora had never been to the place before. It was a stately mansion built in the 1920s, with steep gables of moss-green slate crowning the outline of a hipped roof. Pale grey stucco lent a fresh and sober appearance to the four-storey façade. A long L housing the wards extended perpendicularly from the back of the building, invisible to someone facing it directly from across the street. The ground floor, presumably occupied by the main office and Reinhardt-Thoma's office, had windows topped by low arches; upstairs, Bora identified the consultation rooms by their vast, uncurtained glass panes.

It surprised him that so early in the day (a dewy mist still hung in the air, the leafy trees along the street quivered with a richness of sparrows) an official-looking van and a lampblack saloon were stationed in front of the clinic. *But then,* he reasoned, *this is Dohnenstieg, where none other than the Commissar of the Reich, Heinrich Himmler, has one of his residences.*

What made him change his mind on the subject was noticing that the clinic's door was ajar, and movement was perceivable in the twilight of the interior, where electric lamps blinked.

Bora wasted no time hoping it might be employees of his uncle's, come to save what was salvageable, on Olbertz's advice. *Olbertz did not even want to meet me, he surely didn't risk —*

Any doubt ended with a crash of broken glass on the upper floor. A filing cabinet literally flew out, scattering in its fall a storm of folders and loose pages. A desk minus its drawers followed it in the plunge, and the drawers immediately after.

Brochures, rubber stamps, prescription pads snowed down.

At the first burst of glass, the sparrows surged from the trees, peppering the ground with their fleeting shadows. Bora followed with his eyes the ripple and twist of this or that piece of paper in mid-air, sailing and coasting upward as if in defiance of the law of gravity. But already another pane shattered with the clattering of smashed ice; chairs and examination couches, sheets and white smocks fell out, each landing in its own way on the grassy space below.

Between thought and intervention the interval often lasts only seconds. Bora could have asked (but what was there to ask?) the plainclothesmen sitting in the lampblack saloon. Instead – and no one prevented him – he went over to the house and stepped through the open portal into a waiting room unknown to him and yet somehow familiar: it was the prints of famous Saxon views along the walls, fleetingly seen while he raced upstairs, in the same way that landscapes fly backwards in the frame of a train window.

Compared to the dimness of the stairs, the consultation room was flooded by daylight. A handful of bareheaded thugs wearing Hitler Youth shorts were laboriously unhooking a metal shelf from the wall. A heady odour of spilled disinfectant and phenic acid rose from the slippery floor, strewn with glass shards and surgical instruments.

A young man in the black Special Services uniform of the same paramilitary corps led the devastation. Confronted by an irate Bora, he growled back, "What business of yours is it what we're doing? We have our orders!"

Thank God for hierarchy. Bora struck him a backhanded slap across the face, hard enough to make him stagger in his ill-fitting boots. The others, who were facing away from the room, didn't notice at first. None of them carried any weapon, save fanaticism.

Stunned, the young man in black steadied himself. He massaged his left cheek, up and down. Only when he realized that a lieutenant colonel was demanding the name of his direct superior did he seem to emerge from the blind fury that had filled him until a minute ago.

Standing stiffly to attention, he stammered in his Berlin twang, "Beggin' pardon, Lieutenant Colonel. We was in a hurry, we was told it was Jewish property …"

The bare-legged boys from his squad had the look of cats caught stealing. They grew pale when Bora said, "This clinic belongs to the late Doctor Professor Reinhardt-Thoma, whose state funeral last Sunday was authorized by the Führer himself!" Mentioning Hitler to the Hitler Youth was like bringing up the name of God. The young man in black didn't know what to do with himself. He identified a certain Schmitz, Corps Leader, as his commander, while he gestured for his companions to halt the vandalism. He could not think of a justification other than the one he'd given, but Bora understood that the orders must have originated with the Health Ministry. Perhaps even with its head Leonardo Conti, his uncle's bitterest foe for many years.

From the boys, Bora learned that the patients had left the clinic three days earlier. While today's action was fully authorized by Corps Leader Schmitz, neither the wards nor the ground floor were to be damaged in any way, because the new director would soon move in.

Below, Bora found the plainclothesmen from the lampblack saloon. They said they were from the nearby Cecilienallee police station, and asked a few formal questions which he had no difficulty answering. They did not seem to be aware that Bora was a relative when they blamed the disaster upstairs on the long friendship between the late owner and "the Jew

Goldstein". In fact, they were here waiting for Dr Wirth, newly appointed head physician of the clinic.

"And you were simply passing by, Colonel?"

"I do not believe a German officer has to account for his intervention when furniture rains down from windows in Berlin, and when an insubordinate member of the Hitler Youth dares to disrespect him!"

With local policemen, the point could be convincing. However, an official protest would make no difference, with them or anyone else.

Bora left the house. There was nothing there he wanted to rescue from Wirth, not even the prints of old Saxony. He had only come by to see what shape the changing of the guard would assume. The bitter fact that it involved Niemeyer's neighbour, too stingy to pay his crippled gardener and too cowardly to be here in person, convinced him not to tell his mother about this. Crossing the garden, he changed his mind, and leaned over to pick up a small, empty glass bottle for medicines as a keepsake.

Useless, and the object of least value there.

Along the street, the trees were once more loud with sparrows. Bora looked up at the frenzy of grey handfuls of them in the dwarfing tangle of branches. Odd, how trees had not seemed this large to him since he was a child; fringes of morning sun speckled their dark heads as he walked away.

At the tram stop, he decided against smoking when he already had a cigarette between his lips. He'd quit in June, on the principle that out in the field a keen sense of smell is a plus; he only carried a pack around as currency. But he was still struggling to give up the automatism of reaching for a cigarette when he felt under pressure.

He could count on the fingers of his one hand the times when he'd struck someone in adulthood. It was so contrary to his nature that the loss of control that generated that sort of aggression troubled him deeply. Nicotine would not help.

He grumpily had to accept that both episodes – the wrecking of the clinic, his slapping the Hitler Youth – were further signs that everything was falling apart, heading for dissolution. *If Stauffenberg refuses to see me, I may really have to lie in wait at the door to his office. Because if it is true, as Hölderlin writes, that even solid rock has a need of rifts, some things need to be said before it crumbles to nothing.*

Actually, he had no need to resort to such a drastic solution. At his return to the Leipziger Hof, while he breakfasted and drank something that resembled very bad coffee, the waiters told him he was wanted on the phone. The call came from the Reserve Army. It was not Emmy Pletsch speaking, as Bora supposed, but Stauffenberg's adjutant, Lieutenant von Haeften. Without preliminaries or details, he flatly invited Bora to visit the colonel's office at 2 p.m. that day.

"Good," Bora answered, just as curtly. "I will be there."

7:35 A.M.

Between now and the call at Bendlerstrasse, a little less than seven hours away, Bora had a list of chores to do. Not necessarily in that order, they included enquiring after Salomon at his office (if necessary with a plausible excuse), returning the material borrowed from Max Kolowrat two days earlier, and phoning Glantz's home in case the Kripo had released the hapless publisher. There was a question he had to ask him, on the surface related to the murder case but, as far as Bora was concerned, also addressing a more political concern. As sponsor of the *Encyclopaedia of Myth*, Glantz may know of a safe or a deposit box where Niemeyer kept his manuscripts or other important papers – including, perhaps, a copy of the letter meant for the Reich Security Central Division.

Geographical proximity and the early hour convinced him to begin with a call at Kolo's flat near Barbarossaplatz, incidentally riding the same tram he'd shared with Emmy Pletsch the night before.

Once there, Bora did not know what to make of the sight before him. Along the street, cleared of all vehicles but a service van from the Technical Emergency Service, a small group of people, including Max Kolowrat, were bivouacked on the pavement with a few of their belongings strewn around them.

In Kolo's case, it was a stool on which sat his typewriter, and Krüger sitting on top of the typewriter with the face of a cat subjected to indignity. The writer himself stood nearby with an unlit pipe in his teeth, looking up at the windows of his flat. He saw Bora approach and answered his greeting with a nod.

"There was a bit of a shift in the rear of the building overnight," he explained. "TeNo is checking all the apartments to make sure it's safe to go back." He pointed philosophically with his pipe at the other dwellers strung along the pavement. "There isn't much we can do. At least it's cool and shady at this hour."

Bora looked at the others. An elderly lady in a feather-collared robe and slippers was knitting in an armchair complete with antimacassar; a middle-aged couple sat playing cards on the back of a suitcase; a few steps away a man with the cropped hair of an army veteran cradled a potted fern in his arms. The unforeseen circumstance was welcome: Bora was embarrassed at the thought of speaking to Kolowrat again, so this pavement meeting invited the sort of brevity he preferred. He asked where he should leave the returned material, and Kolo told him to put it down on the pavement. "The technicians will be kind enough to bring it in, just as they took our things out."

He was facing him directly as he spoke, so that Bora couldn't get out of enquiring if he could be of any help.

"No, thank you. As you see, neither Krüger nor I are upset. He followed me around half the world, and it won't

be a morning on the pavement that daunts him. Rather …
Do you have a light?"

Bora took out his brother's lighter without thinking. Aware
as he must be of Peter's death, if Kolo noticed the Luftwaffe's
eagle insignia on it he tactfully pretended not to. He kindled a
fire in the briar's bowl, before saying, "The name you indicated
the other day, Gustav Kugler … I believe I know who he is."

Bora, who until now had been dwelling on a single dilemma
(*Should I think or should I not think that he likes my mother, and that
he hopes to marry her one day, just as I hope – or hoped – to marry
Mrs Murphy, someone else's wife?*), felt a bolt of excitement go
through him.

"Really?"

"Yes. Shady characters of the jazz age couldn't belong to
the Blue-Red Tennis Club or play at the Wannsee golf course,
but you may believe that they attended swell parties at the best
cabarets. Crime news was not my favourite subject; still, I did
take regular notes. The female reading public had a soft spot
for criminals like those you read of in Rex Stout's novels, or
the 'crooked policemen' you saw at the cinema. American
shotguns and sub-machine guns were the rage. After your visit,
I looked through my old records, and … As I said, I believe I
know who Kugler is. Well – to be precise, I don't know where
he is now, or what he's doing. But in the Weimar days he was
a policeman in the vice squad, not exactly corrupt."

Bora had cast his hook the other day, but he'd done it with
little or no hope that there'd be fish in the lake. He concealed
his enthusiasm by lunging to retrieve the knitting needle the
old lady had dropped (she graciously looked up to thank him).

"'Not exactly corrupt', Dr Kolowrat? That is —"

Kolo shrugged. In daylight, his face showed an outdoors-
man's web of little wrinkles around the eyes; the corners of
his mouth, however, reinforced the impression of someone
in the frequent habit of smiling. "That is … It seems he took
no money from panderers to look the other way, which some

of his colleagues did. If he grabbed the chance to have fun with a streetwalker while hauling her in, why, it'd only be seen as a minor infraction. No, the man was crooked in another regard: the gossip was that he 'removed' individuals whom the authorities considered expendable or wanted out of the way: callous criminals, double-crossing informants, God knows who else. I never met him in person. In a couple of instances, they pointed him out to me in the crowd, at a bar or during some less than formal get-together. Unnerving, isn't it? By now, he's been either dispatched by someone or has made the grade."

Bora lifted the Weimar-era material he'd lent him out of his briefcase, and placed it in an orderly stack near the stool. "Your first hypothesis is correct."

"Ah, right. Back then, in nine cases out of ten this would mean that his employers unleashed another killer after him." Like professors and lecturers Bora had known, Kolowrat underlined his words with small waves of his pipe. "That, too, is a way of disposing of rubbish. Not surprising. More than a few Berliners died that way, *during the Republic*."

The way he said this, the slight emphasis, made Bora suspect he was actually implying the opposite, a light-hearted irony you did not meet every day. All the same, his uniform and his role of investigator required that he take the statement at face value.

"He did not die during the Republic," he observed. "Kugler was killed a few days ago. He ran a private investigation agency."

"He did? Interesting. Was Kugler blackmailing a client or had he gone back to his old ways, and someone had orders to empty the rubbish bin with him inside it? One wonders whether a hired killer ever changes his habits." When a TeNo foreman with a yellow armband leaned out of a window to communicate the "all clear", Kolowrat nodded. To Bora, who was a step away from him, hanging on his every word, he commented, "I always thought little of contract killers. They're often no more significant than the weapons they wield, and occasionally just as little conscious of their actions. The rubbish collectors sent after them are less squalid."

Suddenly, Bora found himself brooding. He had more familiarity with the process of death illustrated by Kolo than he cared to admit – Russia, Rome ... first-hand experiences, best not to remember. The Abwehr called it "cleaning up". He said, "For me, the most interesting person of all is the instigator."

"Or instigators. Only in the case of strictly private murders for hire is the matter so simple as to entail no more than two men."


8:37 A.M.


So Kugler was rumoured to have been an assassin for "the authorities". Kolo's expression matched the one he'd used the first time they'd met, when speaking of Niemeyer's anteced-ent, Jan Hanussen. Then, he'd said that Hanussen had been liquidated, but "not by the police". After leaving Kolowrat and his dispossessed fellow tenants, Bora reflected on those separate but somehow related pieces of information. Was it possible that after leaving the Kripo the investigator had become a freelancer again? Max Kolowrat had assigned an unchanged disposition to the hired killer, although it was no more than a reporter's comment.

Grimm might be the man to ask, however touchy the subject might be for one who'd shared a professional life with Gustav Kugler. Until Grimm's return, the allegation added grist to the mill, but little more.

Bora checked the time. Army offices were open for business now, so he might as well venture to contact army headquarters at Zossen to enquire after Salomon. He chose a public phone he knew to be working to place the call, and truthfully identi-fied himself as a former officer on Salomon's staff. "I'm in town on furlough, and would like to say hello to him if possible."

The news that the colonel was on medical leave did not surprise him; but it deeply worried him. "Nothing serious, I hope," he said. "Has he checked into a hospital where I might visit him?"

No information was available about a hospital he might have checked into. Why not try the Adlon, where he'd been staying until recently?

Bora promised to do so, although he knew the colonel had left the hotel. As far as he knew, Salomon had no relatives in Berlin. He'd been estranged from his wife ever since the first Russian tour of duty; there would be no point trying to trace him through her. *Hell,* he thought, *should I bring him up with Claus von Stauffenberg this afternoon? After all, it's from him that Salomon heard about me. He might know.*

It was quickly growing warm. In the phone booth, Bora turned his back to the sun to leaf through his notebook. While interrogating Roland Glantz, he'd jotted down his home number – the same his concerned spouse had been calling him from. If he was back from Alex, Glantz was surely not in the best mood to chat, but would hardly dare slam down the receiver on an investigator.

The phone rang for some time (Bora counted seven rings) before his wife picked up the receiver. From her voice, he realized at once that things had got worse for the Glantzes. He expected that the publisher had not been released, but had to ask, and did. Frau Glantz started to sob. Through her broken words, Bora learned that Glantz was not only still under arrest, but had attempted suicide again last night. It was altogether possible, given the state of the man, although Bora suspected the immediate trigger could have been mistreatment at the hands of the Kripo interrogators.

It occurred to him now that although he'd given his name, he had not identified himself to the wife as the officer who first questioned Glantz. He did so, adding, "I was at the Sternuhr office when you phoned your husband on Wednesday. To your knowledge, is Herr Glantz still held at the Criminal Police headquarters?"

"I wish I knew," she moaned. "I'm afraid they'll take it for an admission of guilt on his part. He shouldn't have done it, Colonel, he shouldn't have done it!"

Bora agreed, in principle. What he said, however, was, "Can you confirm that your brother left something at your house before he was killed in action? I have a particular reason for asking."

"It must be that damn gun! I told Roland to get rid of it, after Seppi was shot down near Tobruk ... I could only convince him to put it away in a safe place, poste restante. Good God, he lost his mind after the trick Magnusson, or Niemeyer, or whatever his real name was, played on us ... I wanted to make sure he wouldn't be tempted to use it to avenge himself."

The rest of the call yielded nothing else of use. Frau Glantz had never heard her husband mention a particular repository where Niemeyer kept copies of his manuscripts, including the *Encyclopaedia of Myth*. On the point of hanging up, Bora tried a last card. "Did you ever hear of a solicitor by the name of Ergard Dietz?"

"No. Is he someone who could help my husband?"

"I'm afraid not."

"Can *you* help my husband, then?"

Bora had anticipated the tearful request. "What I can do is call in to enquire about his state of health, and perhaps learn where he is now. I will only ring back if I have any information to share with you."

An odour of warm asphalt and open sewers – the latter unthinkable in Berlin before the bombs – accompanied the rise in temperature when Bora left the booth. The third call would take longer, and was not to be attempted from a public phone. He returned to the Leipziger Hof and, from his room, dialled Arthur Nebe's personal number.

The SS Group Leader and chief was not in. Had he been sitting at his desk, he'd have answered his private line. Bora then tried the Kripo headquarters's central exchange and asked for Nebe's assistant. The man confirmed that the chief was out of the office, and gave no information about his routine for the day; to the question tactfully put by Bora about the detainee Roland Glantz, he replied with the annoyance of a bureaucrat who sees no reason why he should answer.

"What *about* the detainee Roland Glantz, Colonel?"

Bora explained briefly, although he doubted an attempted suicide inside Alex would come as news to Nebe's right-hand man.

"Ah, yes. He tried to hang himself again."

"And did not succeed?"

"He did not succeed in hanging himself, but struck his head in the fall and is unconscious. Our physicians at the infirmary fear he might not come to any time soon, if at all."

Not what Bora wanted to hear. "Is he still at the infirmary?"

"He is not … Look, Colonel, I don't know where they took him – there's a myriad of hospitals and clinics in Berlin."

This could only mean that Glantz had passed into the hands of the Gestapo. "May I leave a message for the Head of the Criminal Police?"

"You seem to have his private number. Try him tonight after six."

Two calls, two failures. Bora had a little more luck when he enquired about Florian Grimm.

It was Trost – he was apparently Grimm's subordinate – who picked up the phone. Yes, Inspector Grimm was quickly recovering, and expected to report for duty the following morning. (Bora was not enthusiastic about this; he'd hoped to have more time to himself, and the car at his disposal for longer.) He asked that Grimm bring along detailed information on the interrogation of, statements by, state of health and location of the detainee Roland Glantz, and hung up in a vexed mood.

He was rather hopeful about the next call, mostly because it was not strictly business-related. He took Emmy Pletsch's number out of his breast pocket. In the process, one of the condoms fell out, a small incident that might be telling but did not embarrass him very much. What he had in mind was to thank her, without adding any details: she'd understand that it was about setting up his interview with Stauffenberg.

A colleague of Staff Leader Pletsch answered the phone. Staff Leader Pletsch had just left her desk. Would the lieutenant colonel care to try again at ten?

Such recurrence of absenteeism made one doubt the much-vaunted efficiency of German office workers. Bora was disappointed but replied that yes, he would do so.

In the interval, he ventured another round of calls intended to discover Salomon's whereabouts. The Charité hospital had a reputation for the treatment of nervous diseases, so he began there. When that failed, he went down the list of other medical centres, military and private, that he knew to be still standing. Whether his interlocutors disbelieved that he was merely seeking his former commander, and would for that reason not release the information, or whether Salomon really had not checked himself into any one of them (having perhaps left the capital), Bora's effort availed him nothing. The sole element that kept it from being a complete waste of time was that it brought him up to ten o'clock.

Once more, he phoned Reserve Army headquarters.

This time Emmy was in. She responded in a not entirely terse voice to his thanks (he could imagine her face, looking as if her mind was elsewhere). Unwilling to let it go at that, on an impulse Bora took his plan one step further. He asked, "May we have lunch together today, Staff Leader Pletsch? I could come and pick you up."

She hardly let him finish. "No, Colonel. I don't think so."

Bora found that he was more frustrated than he had a right to be. "Very well, then," he said, and was about to hang up.

He was not used to rejection by women, and gave rather too much importance to Emmy's refusal. On the other hand, she could not be so naive as not to recognize a certain longing in the tone of his voice, underneath the absolute correctness of his words. Not taking no for an answer wasn't like him, so he couldn't believe that he actually said, "What about a cup of coffee?"

She did not answer at once, giving him time to regret his perseverance. Then she simply said, "Yes, thank you."

With an hour to spare, Bora sat in his freshly made room (a luxury he would soon forget, if he made it back to the Italian front) thinking over the news gathered thus far this morning. What he had learned from Max Kolowrat about Kugler's moonlighting as a semi-official assassin in the Weimar days threw a welcome wrench in the machine.

Grimm had told him nothing about it – but he might not necessarily have known or had any reason to see a connection between his old partner and Niemeyer's death. After all, when Bora had asked him about notorious Berlin murderers, the inspector had not hesitated to identify the S-Bahn murderer with Paul Ogorzow, his old SA companion. The Kugler lead was as far-fetched as it was intriguing. Still, even supposing that for whatever reason the investigator had played a role in the murder, he certainly did so on someone's orders. According to Lattmann, the gossip eleven years earlier pointed to the debt-ridden Heldorff as a possible instigator in the shooting of Jan Hanussen, whose place as a Party mystic Niemeyer had taken up afterwards. Heldorff was deep in city politics even then. Had Kugler been in his employ somehow, and continued to be? In its ambivalence, the mention of "Berlin's police chief, Count von Heldorff" in Niemeyer's letter had its significance. It was Heldorff's girl who had unwittingly fed Niemeyer with hints on a conspiracy by the army ... Bora drew a triangle in his mind, whose angles read 'Hanussen', 'Heldorff' and 'Kugler', and another labelled 'Niemeyer', 'Heldorff' and 'Kugler'; the third one, the one he was most hesitant to imagine, read 'Niemeyer', 'Heldorff' and 'Conspiracy'.

Of the three, this last one was fraught with danger, whether or not Niemeyer had made everything up, and whatever role Heldorff played in it: blackmailed debtor, sleuth or conspirator. If he owed Niemeyer money, as he'd owed Hanussen, the discovery (how? From Niemeyer himself?) that his girlfriend had leaked information about an ongoing inquiry into high treason offered the perfect opportunity to eliminate him. On the other hand, someone else could have been the object of Niemeyer's blackmail – members of the conspiracy, such as those whom the terrified Salomon had overheard.

Bora felt the sweaty army shirt stick to his underarms and stomach. He recovered Niemeyer's letter from the anonymous folder where he'd placed it, slipped it into a waterproof pouch along with his diary, and prepared to take a shower while keeping an eye on them, as in his paranoid Moscow days.

He unbuckled the prosthesis, a chafing nuisance around his wrist in the heat of the season. What if he was wrong? Niemeyer could have made up the contents of his letter, at least as far as his knowledge of an army plot. He could have passed off a vision or an intuition for a credible rumour, so that after his murder his enemy (or enemies) would be crushed. The words you leave behind in case of a violent death cannot lie. Or can they?

*I could burn the damn letter to ashes and be done with it. Bubi Kupinsky would never tell that he had it, or that I saw it. Should I mention it to Stauffenberg, or would that be my undoing? If I had no scruples, I could even use it as Niemeyer tried to. Except that I'm up to my neck in scruples.*

Bora stood under the gushing cold water, unspeakably anxious about his two o'clock meeting – oddly, for a completely different reason, also about sitting with Staff Leader Pletsch in half an hour. In fact, among the many questions he rolled around in his mind, there was an innocent one to himself, left unanswered: was he showering and changing for the deputy chief of the Reserve Army or for Emmy Pletsch?

At any rate, for good luck he would put on the tailored army shirt his mother had brought him from home.

Minutes later he picked up the prosthesis from the bedside table and contemplated it, a strange new part of him he still had to get used to seeing, to using, fiercely determined as he was not to think of his loss. During the withdrawal from Rome he'd thrown away all his musical scores, including those his father had composed or arranged for piano. On the Eastern front he'd been ready to die, so he'd never entertained the thought of mutilation, or of surviving it. True, with his right hand he could move or close the fingers of the artificial one into a fist, finely articulated inside the handsome black glove. In cold weather, when gloves were worn, it was at first sight undistinguishable from his live hand. Not so during the summer.

"You could have lost your forearm, or even the whole arm," they'd said at the hospital in Verona, trying to cheer him up. "Be thankful that it's only your hand that is gone."

Well, thankfulness took odd shapes these days. With his back to the mirror, Bora fastened the prosthesis back on. *I believe in fortitude,* he told himself, *and try to live by it. But what is this injury doing to me deep down, how does it affect my temperament?*

*Claus von Stauffenberg lost an eye and his right hand, and three fingers are all that remains to him of the left one.*

At the last moment, a quarter of an hour before meeting Emmy at a small, exclusive café off Bülowstrasse, Bora decided to take Niemeyer's letter with him. Dangerous as the choice was, he felt that – whatever happened with Stauffenberg – he had to find a better hiding place for it before nightfall. As he quickly went downstairs, he discarded his grandfather's apartment, which was out of the question just like his Uncle's clinic, whose key he had in his pocket. Not even banks, not even churches were secure, and at this point, many of his former Abwehr colleagues could not necessarily be depended on either; the people he most trusted he didn't want to put at risk. As he walked out to the car, Bora even thought of the Japanese officer he met at the Adlon, whose sense of caste loyalty could be relied on as absolute, and who was not afraid to die. He was his best bet, if he was still alive.

Enough brooding for now. He didn't want to meet Staff Leader Pletsch over coffee and abject anxiety.


DIE DAME CAFÉ, 11:05 A.M.

In the days Kolowrat wrote of, the café was called Kaugummi, and William Wrigley himself invested American money in the establishment, designed for the young and fashionable German consumers of chewing gum. The Brownshirts had devastated it and jailed its Jewish manager. Since the beginning of the war it had reopened, with Biedermeier décor, a bill of fare richer than most and a new management rumoured to have Hermann Göring as its secret shareholder. Its full name was now Die Fliegende Dame, after a large canvas depicting Europa riding a white bullock, but everyone knew it as just Die Dame.

"How beautiful," Emmy said of the painting. Seeing the choices available on the menu (Bora had chosen the place because of its first-rate service), she asked him, "May I order a cup of *real* coffee with *real* cream? I haven't had any in over a year. You'll think me provincial, but I do miss some of our tasty everyday things, like buttery *poor knights* at breakfast."

"You may order anything you wish."

She did not look straight at him, while Bora watched her closely. *I may be making her uncomfortable, but that's how it is. In observing her this way, I give the impression that I can afford to, because I'm not desperate. She praises a peacetime breakfast of bread fried in butter, yet in the end, if she said yes over the phone it's because she wanted to see me again.* He kept telling himself that he liked a different sort of woman, but it was a fact that at least two of those he'd fallen for – Remedios and Nora Murphy – were petite.

She put away her reading glasses. The delicate blonde down on her forearms reminded him of the girls in Russia and Ukraine, from whom he'd stayed away for Dikta's sake – and because their fairness and throaty singing had been dangerously attractive. The small watch on her left wrist was modest, with a strap of imitation leather. If she wasn't wearing a uniform at this hour, it meant that she probably had the afternoon off because of her boyfriend's illness. Her white blouse, devoid of embroidery except for a diminutive string of off-white flowers bordering her collar, seemed to him home-sewn, perhaps by a friend, or by Emmy herself.

The waiter came; Bora ordered coffee and cream for her, and iced coffee for himself. Asked if she wanted anything to eat, she glanced up, smiled and shook her head.

He wondered whether she slept poorly, or cried often. Possibly both. Under her eyes, there stretched a tender blue shadow that only youth kept from being a flaw. Yes, if she did not look at him, his scrutiny was the reason. *Am I doing something contemptible? Does she really believe I invited her to thank her? She might. I'm a lieutenant colonel, she does not expect to be flattered by me. I only wanted her to make amends for declining my lunch invitation, because an auxiliary cannot reply to an officer as she would to her equals.*

*Is she passive? Didn't her man teach her anything? No. She knows that, by her silence, she is forcing me to wonder about her. She asks nothing about me, not only because of her subordinate rank, but to lay claim to that small, untouchable feminine space of hers, that compels us men to try to break into it.*

"So, tell me about you," he encouraged her, once the waiter had left. "Where are you from, and what brought you to Berlin?"

"I don't sound like a Berliner, do I?" She smiled selfconsciously, still looking down. "I grew up near Breslau, which is where my family still lives. There isn't much to say about me: I was at secondary school and doing well, when my father, who headed the local SA, was killed. So I left school and took a typewriting course: the sort of career choice a girl from my background is likely to make, you'll say. Not that I lacked ambition, but Mother wanted me to stay close to home, and so on."

"'And so on'?"

By simply repeating her words, Bora had unexpectedly struck home. Emmy raised her asymmetric glance to him. It was as if two girls were spying from behind a narrow gap; the right eye, the lighter one, was innocent, naive; the darker one sombre, and something very much like desire came from it. "I usually say, 'and so on', in order not to add that I was already dating Leo, whom Mother did not approve of. Oh, not politically, Colonel, I must be clear about that. Because he'd been married, and was twice my age. So I left home at seventeen. Seems like a lifetime ago."

*Nina's age when she became engaged to my father*, Bora thought, and censored his thought at once.

Emmy rested her hands on the edge of the table, much as she must do in front of her typewriter, awaiting dictation. Her nails were short. A little wrinkle formed between her straw-coloured eyebrows when she looked down, as you sometimes see in unhappy or pouty children. She moistened her lips, before speaking again.

"Have you noticed how even the things that seem most cohesive start falling apart one day?"

"Yes."

"I often think about it."

"I do too."

Imagine. Suddenly they were in a place separate from everyone else, like the day before in the crowded car. Yet when the coffee was served *it* seemed the sole reason why Emmy had accepted the invitation – so happy was she to see it.

"Forgive me if I sip it one spoonful at a time, like a beggar or a little old lady." A sunniness had come over her. When she smiled, her upper lip curled inwards, baring her small regular teeth and her gums, an artless and childish smile Bora didn't usually like in women but accepted today. *In a way, I am imposing myself on her. Would I have done this even just a month ago? No. But things change. Things fall apart.*

Well, how had things actually changed? He wasn't proposing to Emmy Pletsch, nor making her understand that he wanted to take her to bed. He was as reserved as ever. Not insecure, but contrary. Or maybe insecure. *I have no more to offer her than she does me. We only met hours ago, but hours is all we have. All I have, at any rate.*

She contemplated the painting, on which the shapely nymph sailed with a smile over clouds and sea as if being kidnapped by Zeus in animal form were a welcome change. Carefully, self-consciously, she gathered every fleck of cream from the surface of her coffee, letting it sit in her mouth to savour it.

"It's even better than I remembered."

Men, mostly officers, sat at the other tables around the room, sipping wine or beer. Emmy eyed them, but spoke to Bora.

"What will they think of you, sitting here with a woman who acts so gawkily?"

"I usually disregard what people think."

Bora was surprised at his words. It was more than he wished to reveal, and, put this way, it could also imply a measure of contempt on his part. "Take all the time you need," he hastened to add. "We're not on duty."

He followed Emmy's glance towards the painting. Europa travelled from east to west, as the darkening sky to the left of the painting indicated. There, amid puffy clouds, a crescent moon and a shooting star or comet matched the bright sun on the right-hand side.

*Does she like me? I can't tell. She can see how seriously injured I am. I'm hiding nothing from her. Being attractive is nothing to brag about when the alternative is a comatose man. If Bruno says she is a good girl, it means that she has given no sign so far that she is look-ing for someone else. Yet he saw through her, as I do. So what? I have no intention to expose myself emotionally, or even just be told no, to something well beyond an invitation to coffee. Not that emotions would necessarily have a role in it. It all boils down to the question of whether I like her enough to try. I could simply let things run their course.*

The sweet, warm drink relaxed her. Emmy told him she moved to Berlin when Leo Franke, promoted to driving school instructor, was assigned to the NSKK office on Graf Spee Strasse. "That's how I found a job on Bendlerstrasse nearby." Titbits, small elements of life followed one another, in reply to his first question. It was as if she were talking about stran-gers, or an existence over and done with, and irrecoverable. "That's odd," she interrupted herself at one point. "I can't find much more to tell about the years we spent together. Yet we did things, we had plans, we grew used to each other. We were supposed to marry on 20 July."

"Because you're used to each other?"

She slowly put down the spoon, careful not to cause a tinkle when the metal met porcelain. It could seem a subordinate's awkwardness on her part, yet Bora read it correctly as a form of diligence and self-control – incidentally his own way of being in the world.

"Why, yes." She stole a glance at him. "I think so. Many people do it, and habit keeps most marriages going. My par-ents', my sisters'. Mother says that habit hurts less than love."

"This is absolutely true," Bora caught himself saying. Once again, he'd said more than he wanted. As an interrogator, he was trained to befriend prisoners to make them talk, but this situation was completely different. Or, no – different in a way: there were things he wanted to know *about* her, rather than *from* her.

"Thank you for facilitating my appointment with Colonel von Stauffenberg, Staff Leader."

"Yes, sir."

One small spoonful after the other, Emmy finished her coffee. What little lip rouge she wore left no stain on the edge of the cup, but she stared at the porcelain rim intently, as if something about it were wrong, or worrisome. In thanking her, Bora had meant no more than what he said. Why then that contrite pressing together of lips on her part?

She stared at her empty cup as Dr Olbertz had contemplated his beer mug the night before, a sign of embarrassment, or guilt, or fear. Sotto voce, she said, "I do not know you, but … Allow me to suggest that you cancel it, Colonel. For your own good."

Bora heard her words as if they'd been shouted at him. *She is saying one – no, two enormous things. That, as far as she knows, it's best if I avoid meeting Stauffenberg, when it is exactly what I want, and that she allows herself to think of my own good when she admits that she doesn't know me at all.*

He thought for an intense handful of seconds before saying carefully, in a similar undertone, "You are informed about what is happening, aren't you."

Her reaction startled him. Standing up suddenly, Emmy showed her entire figure, the figure of a healthy, good girl in a panic, who is not attempting to be seductive. "I must go, forgive me."

"If you go now, it means you really do know."

She sat down again, with an air of unhappiness. She seemed trapped, as often happened to Bora's prisoners who betrayed themselves during interrogation.

He did not pressure her. "Don't worry. I'm responsible, solid and tight-lipped. Especially for a Saxon." He grinned without any ulterior motive. "However, it will be best if I meet your superior, believe me."

"But my superior doesn't care to meet you."

"This will not keep me from turning up as agreed. I have nothing against being shown the door, but only after I say what I've come to say."

This was how things stood. Scrambling for a reason to leave, she switched to a voluble series of excuses (having to meet a colleague, to catch a train, to bring a change of clothes to Leo Franke on a day other than visiting day) ... Prisoners short on arguments rambled similarly under interrogation, tripping over their own words.

"Even though Leo doesn't even know I'm coming, really, I have the afternoon off, so ..." A girl owed it to her man, didn't she. It so happened that her best friend Marika was good enough to come along for the train journey, which was why she had to get going, and then, and then ...

Bora only feigned self-assurance. The dimensions of what was in the air, so frightening to Salomon, must be out of control if even young auxiliaries were involved in it. He uselessly struggled to concentrate on the girl sitting across from him; from her nervous wordiness, he only caught the tail end of what must have been a justification on her part.

"... please don't misunderstand what I said. About me and Leo, and not missing him ... He's there, he hangs on to life, and I will take care of him however long it takes."

*Why is she telling me this, and what else did I miss of what she said?* Bora delayed a comment, making her worry that her unrequested disclosure had annoyed him.

"If Franke was a habit for you," he then said, straightforwardly, "it's understandable that you don't miss him. One misses *other* things."

"Right." Her mouth and her innocent eye agreed. "You're right." The liquid blue of her sombre eye signified that she wondered what those "other" things were. "... It's just that I'm so sad for him. So hopelessly sad. Can you understand?"

"I believe I do. I lost my only brother on the Eastern front. My sister-in-law Margaretha would understand."

For the third time Bora stopped short. *Would* she? What was he saying? Margaretha was already dating someone else, as Dikta no doubt was. Things change. Well, what about him?

Wasn't he … no, this was not a date. What was it, then? … Having a cup of coffee with a girl in very dangerous times.

Opposite him, Emmy Pletsch was the very picture of discomfort. Perhaps she knew that Bora meant *love*, a word neither of them would pronounce.

"My friend Marika will be waiting for me. I really must go."

"Understood." Bora sprang up from his chair before she rose from hers. "I'll be in town only a little while longer. Will we see each other again?"

Not "may we", but "will we". It was a question – well below a request to meet her again.

"I don't believe so, Colonel von Bora."

Stretching her hand out to shake his across the table, she thanked him for the treat. Composure was coming back to her, now that she was free to go. Her light eye, the reserved and naive right eye, gave him a last look while she turned away. Clutching her handbag – it was the same straw pouch she'd carried in the tram – she left quickly, so that he would not attempt to see her out.

Bora remained at the table a little longer, thinking of what he would like to write in his diary but could not.

*If, as Emmy Pletsch says, Stauffenberg is reluctant to see me, there can be at least two reasons. In any case, I'm on the razor's edge. Officially, everything is as always, the army is faithfully united under its Führer. In fact, there appears to be no circle in Berlin where schemes and secret plans are not being whispered about. Perhaps some hearsay is being circulated intentionally, according to the principle that a true plot is not so foolish as to show its hand. But I started to believe that Salomon had heard right, even before I found Niemeyer's letter. And I think Staff Leader Pletsch finds herself in the same predicament, in and out at the same time, probably very frightened. She mentioned my "own good". What should I make of it? She doesn't know me, so she isn't speaking out of affection or self-interest. Her advice suggests that there's a potential risk in meeting the deputy commander of the Reserve Army.*

Driving back to the hotel, he kept thinking, with no solution in sight.

*Everything seems to turn like a wheel around the fixed point of Fritz-Dietlof von der Schulenburg, who hears about me from Stauffenberg. Why then is Stauffenberg unenthusiastic about meeting me now? Either Schulenburg, as son of the former German ambassador to Moscow and, like him, already under Abwehr scrutiny in 1941, told him not to trust me; or he learned from other sources – not excluding that foolish Salomon – that I have more trouble with the Party than most. Not that it makes much difference at this point, but I have to know. And I must decide what to do with Salomon, whose nerves could break down any day. If he weren't a German officer, and my former commander, I'd know exactly how to deal with him.*

*And Staff Leader Pletsch? The way she conversed and looked at me with that ambivalent sky-blue and dark-blue glance of hers … Has Bruno spoken to her about me? She could not seriously think that she could change my mind about meeting her commander. Not even if he sent her to me with that in mind. No, it's the other, much more basic thing. I've been around. I can tell she's interested every bit as much as I am, yet she holds back.*

*Too bad. I never had trouble denying myself to girls, but can't abide rejection – not even now. Especially not now.*

It was the type of personal reflection Bora might later note in his diary, except that what was at stake in Berlin today, more and more past the stage of idle rumour, dominated everything else. He was balanced on a tightrope between resolve and utter panic. Hadn't he felt a storm coming? The storm was circling overhead.

What he resolved about Staff Leader Pletsch, while eating a spartan and unimaginative lunch at his corner table, was typical of him: *so, early on in the process I'm giving up on a possible little story with Emmy. She likes me, but not enough to go to bed with me. I'm not attracted to her beyond my ability to resist, but more than enough to take her to bed. That's the difference between men and women, and it doesn't say much for us males.*

*Damn, though: women do this to you. Uncle was right, it's that little pot on the fire, spilling over once in a while. You deem yourself superior, put your trust in intellect, in discipline, and then it's enough for any one of them to sit across from you – no, not any one of them. If a woman has this effect on you, there is a reason, and it's not just hormones.*

*When I joined the army, for all my book learning I was little more than a lad. Our training sergeant, who loved to spread pearls of wisdom regarding women, used to tell us, "Some of 'em, lay them just to make 'em happy, and maybe you'll end up having fun yourself." The concept was crude, but in the end ... Who knows if, as my godmother told me in Rome some weeks ago, I am forever looking for more than just a lover? I am not so special. At times, I see myself as a frisky hound: following a trail, but not above going off after a new scent that distracts me.*

RESERVE ARMY HEADQUARTERS,
BENDLERSTRASSE, 1:54 P.M.

The Reserve Army headquarters occupied the same building where Bora worked while serving in the Abwehr, although the bombs had since damaged part of its structure.

Once inside, Bora went to the room of the day officer, who like most of his contemporaries on similar duty had an expressionless face and avoided any personal comment. He checked his register and neutrally observed that there was no appointment in Bora's name slated with the deputy commander at that time. Bora was about to insist, when a fair-haired young man – he introduced himself as Lieutenant von Haeften, Stauffenberg's adjutant – joined them from upstairs.

"Please, Colonel," he said, preceding Bora upstairs and towards a long waiting room, where in better days a row of five intact windows had created the luminosity of a country residence. Bora was aware that the door ahead, closed now, led into a smaller corner office, where Stauffenberg had his desk. But Haeften faced him, giving no sign he'd open the door. "Colonel von Stauffenberg is awaiting you on Tirpitzufer." A street number followed. "May I ask you to be so kind as to retrace your steps as you leave?"

"Of course."

Bora did not show how irritated he was. *They don't want me to wander down the hallway because I'd potentially be seen by the various colonels and lieutenant colonels who work here, who may or may not know what's going on. God forbid I might turn left and find myself face to face with General Fromm, who runs this outfit and whose office is only a sliding door away from Stauffenberg's.*

He patiently retraced the short distance to the entrance and left the building. Following the left bank of the Landwehrkanal eastwards, he walked past the navy headquarters, formerly the seat of Shell Oil, with its overly futuristic, wavy façade. He was bound for the spot once occupied by a double bridge. Removed already five years ago, in its place lay a wide platform resulting from the massive work involved in creating the North–South Axis road. Willy Osterloh might have thought it up. A meeting away from Stauffenberg's office, in what promised to be a private house, heightened its unofficial nature.

Under a perpendicular, unbearably bright sun (he was glad to have met Emmy just after showering), Bora felt the heat rise from the pavement, creating a closed circuit of sultriness. Strangely, however, he was not perspiring. He grazed his neck as he straightened his uniform, and realized that his hand was ice-cold.

During the walk, an idea – midway between an impression and a conjecture – began to clarify in his mind, much like a mirror image caused by heat on a summer's day changes, as you draw closer, into the solid object of which it is a mere ghost.

*Stauffenberg is one of a reduced minority that has direct access to the Führer. If there is a plan afoot, he must be the protagonist. If, as I believe, there's an explosive device involved, given the way the war is going the deed will happen not in Berlin but in one of the Führer's field headquarters. Christ, I had trouble filling a fountain pen with a single hand. How much more complicated would it be to prime a bomb with only three fingers left, and only one eye? Unless he plans to make damn sure by blowing himself up with the rest, it's sheer folly to hope to succeed. Unless all the heads of the dragon are lopped off, and I don't see how that's possible, a bloodbath is certain to follow a failed attempt. Then it won't be just neurotics like Salomon who'll confess the names of those who conspired under torture – and even those of many who did not.*

2:07 P.M.

Stauffenberg himself came to the door. The flat was a traditional one, in which the so-called "Berlin room" at the centre opened on to the other rooms. Light and shadow would chequer those interior spaces according to how much or how little of the daylight's glare the doors and windows let in.

The occasion, and the fact that they had much in common, made pleasantries unnecessary, beyond a greeting and a superficial smile. After nine years, Stauffenberg was at the same time different and wholly himself. Aside from the obvious injuries suffered on the African front, it was his cautious attitude that rendered unfamiliar the handsome, excellent rider Bora had beaten – by a hair – at the Heiligenhaus horse trial of 1935. He declared (or simply pretended) that he did not remember him, but Bora was prepared for this. His self-esteem needed no external validation, and too much had happened since those careless days.

"Colonel von Stauffenberg," he began, "I would not take you away from your duties if I didn't deem it indispensable. To put it bluntly, during my presence in Berlin of no more than four days, I have heard – from completely separate sources – *insistent, alarming* rumours concerning the mood within the

Reserve Army." The pallor and vexation that came upon Stauffenberg's face was another detail Bora had to ignore. "After eight years in Admiral Canaris's service, sir, be assured that I do not speak lightly, nor offhand."

The silence between them lasted seconds. Whatever was in Stauffenberg's mind, he guarded it well.

"Did Oster send you?" he asked in a controlled undertone. "Because if Oster sent you ..."

"He did not."

"Do you come from Goerdeler, or Gisevius?"

Bora did not know who Gisevius might be, and refrained from enquiring. "Not at all. I'm in town for a completely different reason."

Calling a spade a spade was risky. Somehow, dropping names without details afforded the two of them only a minimum of latitude.

"Then it was Salomon who sought you out." Stauffenberg spoke through gritted teeth. "A colleague told me that the fool walked in while something was being discussed in confidence."

The haughty comment came well short of denying the possibility of a plot. Bora's practice in confronting fear nearly failed him. What took its place was an acute pain at the base of his neck, hot and chilling at the same time. He stepped aside, where the glare of the sun gave way to partial shade.

"I doubt Colonel von Salomon would have 'sought me out' – and found me, by sheer coincidence – unless he'd heard my name from Fritz-Dietlof von der Schulenburg at the Bendlerblock."

It was as close as he came to suggesting that it'd actually been Stauffenberg, according to Salomon, who first brought him up.

"This would not present a problem," he elaborated, "if Colonel von Salomon were not in a state of extreme nervous tension, so much so that he jumped to the conclusion that I was aware of what is apparently being planned."

Stauffenberg rallied instantly, as a champion equestrian reins in the horse at the right moment and sidesteps the unmanageable hurdle. Standing squarely in the cruel afternoon sunlight (the window overlooked the canal and the Elizabeth hospital beyond it), he said, "An interesting allegation of imprudence, given the way that you have reportedly compromised yourself through the years."

The rebuff left Bora remarkably indifferent. However, the margin within which he could manoeuvre grew so narrow that he had to leap and clear the obstacle. "Through the years, I acted as I did because it had to be done."

"Or so you judged. Didn't it occur to you that your exposing yourself in that way might appear intentional, to avoid being enlisted when the time came?"

"I didn't care to wait until someone *enlisted* me."

"Oh, a worker bee and a wasp in one." Stauffenberg had taken exception to his words. In the small study, his head nearly touched the prisms hanging from the lamp. So similar to Bora in size and bearing as to provide him with a reflected image of his anxiety, he seemed pained and provoked at the same time, under pressure to the point of physical suffering. "It won't save you, you know."

"I do not expect to be saved."

A stormy pause told them that they were pointlessly embittering each other. But, as happens when two equally skilled sportsmen have gone too far to concede the race, Stauffenberg chose to drive the spurs in.

"You are played out, Bora. We have no use for you."

Bora hated himself for blinking. In the dreadful days after surgery, a flicker of the lids had been his way of confronting agony under medication – the response would not be lost on the ailing Stauffenberg.

"The fact remains, Colonel, that Salomon's self-control is close to nil."

Stauffenberg paced up and down, now blocking the sun,

now letting the shafts of light flood the room. With a tightly folded handkerchief, he dabbed his empty eye socket under the leather patch; the three fingers he had left on his hand moved quickly, like a spider inside a glove. "Where is he now?"

"I wouldn't know. He left the Adlon Wednesday morning."

"You must track him down."

"Must I, Colonel von Stauffenberg? I'm assigned to another task in Berlin. And as you say, it is best if Salomon is not seen in public with an officer as politically compromised as I am."

"It's not what I *meant*, colleague."

There was no more hiding behind innuendos and half-spoken words. A growing sense of impatience made them sweat in their handsome uniforms; nevertheless, Bora paused before answering.

"I hear you. But I have no intention of doing away with my former commander."

"You would, if you knew the stakes, and cared about what we plan to achieve afterwards." So it was true. Salomon's gibberish at the table, whispered just before Bora forcibly led him to the men's toilets to recover; before then, his colleague Uckermann's oblique hints in Italy, Bruno's warnings ... and Niemeyer's undelivered message to his lawyer, aimed at destroying them all. Something told Bora not to show Stauffenberg the letter, to make no mention of it. The pain at the root of his neck for a moment nailed him to the sport. He held his breath until the sting passed. Salomon had rambled on about the plotters as determined men standing before the abyss, or something to that effect. Show-jumping practice, however, teaches you to discover who will clear the last hurdle and who will not, even among champions. Since Stalingrad, Bora had in that regard made himself unreadable by others; he'd given himself up for dead, and – depending on his mood at a given moment – now either appreciated or simply tolerated each new day as a useful one in the pursuit of duty, whatever its end might be.

With a sinking heart, he realized that the proud officer before him, ready though he may be to take the risk, wasn't planning (or didn't have permission to plan) to die in the act. Stauffenberg's belief that salvation lay beyond the abyss increased rather than reduced the jeopardy he was in, and this made him vulnerable. Bora saw in it the mark of coming disaster.

Under old man Canaris, there had always been two kinds of officers in the Abwehr. There were those who, from the first days of war, readily intervened to counter the excesses of the SS in the field and of the Gestapo behind the lines, gradually accumulating a list of ideological trespasses. And then there were those who, feigning loyalty, entertained strange and sometimes objectionable connections inside and outside the army, in a game of chance that gradually became an end in itself and threatened to make them lose touch with reality. These were officers of the old school – including the youngest among them – who implicitly trusted one another to the extent of speaking openly and too much; a seemingly untouchable caste. Even Admiral Canaris, who was the epitome of astuteness, in the end placed esteem for his colleagues before prudence, and paid for it.

Bora was not among this latter kind. Notwithstanding his stepfather's influence, or perhaps because of it, he belonged to the new world of those who behaved as soldiers employed by a regime ought to behave. When he was in the Abwehr, he'd belonged to the first kind: determined, sometimes impertinent, but skilled in political dialectic, not inclined to familiarity and, as far as army rules were concerned, fastidious nearly to a fault. He chose his words carefully.

"Colonel, in little more than a year's time I've executed two human beings with whom I had no personal quarrel and who nominally were on our side – for service reasons, of course, but that's beside the point. One doesn't know what killing is until one kills in cold blood." He did not add the obvious:

*Assassination entails juggling with ethics, a unique brand of resolve and the willingness to forfeit one's existence if need be.*

Stauffenberg understood Bora's motive for the disclosure. "Sometimes, you will agree, preserving one's life is imperative."

*No, no, no.* How warm it was in the room. Bora felt the cruelty of the hour like an additional burden: a foretaste of purgatory and a sign that none of them would be spared, come what may.

"Speaking only for myself," he said, "I've reached the conclusion that it is best not to have personal stakes in *any* future benefits."

Stauffenberg crumpled the handkerchief before pocketing it. "What, you separate the act from its successful outcome? You remind me of the Boeselager brothers, the swashbuckling mentality of the cavalrymen on the Russian front; Curtius the Roman knight, who sacrificed himself in the bog for the sake of victory! Speak frankly, colleague: does the idea of high treason itself trouble you, or are you afraid?"

This time Bora couldn't help but betray his anger by blushing. "If I were afraid, I'd have kept quiet or turned to someone else, instead of coming to you, Colonel von Stauffenberg. I have been trained in intrigue and, whatever my personal view of the matter, I am duty-bound to tell you that the many rumours that are circulating are full of details, and unless the odds are with you the deed mustn't even be attempted."

Had he been someone else, Stauffenberg would probably have grown furious already; but instead, what Bora read on his face was utter frustration and an unwillingness to listen to reason.

"Permit me to argue the point," he pressed on. "Making the attempt and failing in it would be a catastrophe. This late in the war, unless you have support from outside the Fatherland, even in the unlikely case that you are successful, such an act will convince no one. It will not keep the Russians from reaching Germany ahead of the Americans – it *will not* – I have family and friends in the east, I know whereof I speak – and it will not save Germany from abject defeat *and* an unconditional surrender. We both know it. Unless avoiding these is *not* the practical aim that has led our brother officers as far as to conceive of high treason —"

"I can't believe it." These, or something like them, were the words that Bora heard the exasperated Stauffenberg whisper.

"You forget the army's honour."

"That's long lost, unfortunately."

"What about individual honour?"

"After years of acquiescence, that is now lost as well. The western allies don't trust any of us. It's a fact. And we can't blame them."

"Not true." Stauffenberg paced the floor, his booted tread echoing on the bare wood. "You forget the forgiveness of sins."

"After millions of victims?" Difficult as it was for him to keep his voice down, Bora had no choice but to whisper. "We're both Catholic. I haven't forgotten, and I'm not denying the forgiveness of sins: but there are limits to the right to expect forgiveness from the good Lord. Or from the enemy."

"The hour of repentance is never behind us."

"In the privacy of our souls, yes, but that doesn't avail Germany. Practically speaking, your chances of success against the Party are – what? Did you work them out? Seven to one? Eight? *Nine* to one? For God's sake, Colonel! It irks me to use the word, but I *beg* you to reconsider."

"Are you mad? Either you're mad, or you are an officer impervious to disgust."

Bora was losing hope that he'd be able to make himself heard. "I am impervious to disgust in the sense that it is the souring of something we've previously enjoyed."

"Don't think yourself a saint."

"I don't. Nor am I, for all my faults, a repentant sinner."

"But your kind proposes no alternative: your alternative is to do nothing!"

Bora was left to wonder what "his kind" might be: he hoped it meant officers extraneous to the plot, rather than cowards, or worse. "Speaking in clichés is unworthy of us, Colonel von Stauffenberg. Have we really no other arguments? There's much that can yet be done, on a daily basis – even if it's a thankless job."

"I will hear no more of this." In his agitation, Stauffenberg missed the handle of the door the first time he reached for it. "Go. This is the end of our conversation. And I warn you, Bora, whatever you or other doubting Thomases may have in mind – know that nothing and no one can stop what has been set in motion."

"God help us, then."

"He will. In this life, I think that we have nothing more to say to each other."

"I agree."

At the last moment – the door had already swung open – something in Stauffenberg's demeanour caused Bora to anticipate and dread what he might be about to add. It came upon him with such heart-rending certainty that he actually had to fight back tears.

"Don't offend me by asking whether I can be trusted to keep the secret, sir. You very well know that I shall."

Outside, a breath of wind made it easier to breathe in the hot air than it had been in the suffocating room. Bora walked to the parapet by the canal in a daze, climbed down the steps and lit a cigarette on the bank, staring at the water's lazy flow.

The moment he snapped out of his bewilderment would be so painful, that he tried to hold on to the numbness produced by his confusion. The image of Salomon bobbed out of the chaos of ideas swirling in his mind, Salomon vacillating between betraying his brother officers by revealing the plot, and committing high treason by keeping the secret. Now, in his current anxiety, Bora could gauge what his old commander must be going through. It would be a miracle if he hadn't already cracked under the load. Stauffenberg was right: finding him before someone else did was unquestionably the priority – and close to impossible.

He deeply inhaled the cigarette smoke, to keep his queasiness under control. The last time he'd entertained the thought of "being spared" was before Stalingrad. Yet as early as 1942 he'd got wind of unofficial meetings, secret personal contacts that had nothing to do with the demands of the war … The subtle spoor of rebellion trailed by officers like Oster or General von Tresckow had reached him long before Lattmann had mentioned them. Bora had not tried to learn more, nor would they tell him anything: he was already too exposed to be useful to them. As Stauffenberg had put it, he was played out. He'd burned his bridges, it was true. But he recognized the familiar, pungent whiff of smoke, and knew that something else – and somebody else – was burning now.

What he'd just heard had come as a terrifying confirmation, rather than news.

*At this very moment, the afternoon cargo train from the east is disgorging animals for the slaughter. How fitting.* It was one of those times when Bora would have been grateful if someone had put an end to his life by shooting him from a merciful distance. Not for the act in itself, but for oblivion: being there, and suddenly not being there. Not even "pulling away from things" was helpful at times like these. Helplessness was something he denied himself; in the past, he'd wiggled out of it no matter how desperate the situation, but there was a limit to one's ability to deny reality. He could see no way out of the bind. Whenever he felt overwhelmed, his usual next step was simply a *physical* next step. So he paced along the bank of the canal, asking himself whether terror tasted of anything, and whether you could recognize its taste in your mouth.

# 9

*Every truth is twisted.*

NIETZSCHE

## HOTEL ADLON, 4:16 P.M.

Bora had to make an effort not to stare at them: a cluster of General Staff and administrative officers – and he was sure that a few of them were the same he'd seen days earlier in the same lobby – stood around, with document cases and travel bags at their heels. The same tense air of expectation hovered about them, as if a long-postponed examination were underway.

A mechanical greeting was all that Bora exchanged with the group as he walked to the desk. There, he had to wait until a showy girl in a red turban had finished complaining about a bar of soap disappearing from her room. He doubted that it could happen at the Adlon; more likely she'd pocketed it and now wanted more. She'd never have dared the trick with the concierge, and it didn't seem to work even with this sly-eyed young clerk.

Even before she had walked away in a huff, Bora had changed his mind about enquiring if Lieutenant Colonel Namura was still at the hotel. His curiosity might attract attention, and that was exactly what he wanted to avoid. He climbed the stairs to the floor where he had been staying until Wednesday, intending to try his luck directly.

It was still early in the day, and most officers assigned to military and diplomatic duties would not leave work before five o'clock, or later. Unless the late-November air raid had razed it, the seat of the Japanese legation in Berlin would still be adjoining the imposing Italian embassy on Tiergartenstrasse, a short ride away in a taxi.

*If Namura leaves his workplace punctually at five, he won't be here before five thirty, but I can't wait more than half an hour.* Bora knocked on his old neighbour's door, knowing that it was probably a waste of time. As expected, no one answered. *What if he's moved out? If he has moved out, or worse, has done away with himself, I could be waiting here until doomsday. Someone else might be occupying his room now. Worse, the hotel detective downstairs might wonder about me, and lie in wait for me with questions, if he thinks that I've stayed upstairs too long, given that I don't have a room here.*

At ten past five, Bora met Namura just as he was about to go back downstairs.

"Namura-Chusa, good afternoon."

This form of address, placing his army rank after the surname, was formally correct. Few, if any, westerners used it, and Namura showed by a flickering of his eyelids that he was surprised to hear it.

"Bora-Chusa," he replied. "I thought you'd left the Adlon."

"I'm here to see you, if you have a moment."

At any other time but wartime, the request would seem unusual, even overfamiliar. Could the interval they'd spent together smoking on the top step during the air raid have changed the rules of etiquette for them? Namura frowned, but after a second grunted the short assent so typical of his culture. He preceded Bora up the flight of stairs and to his door.

The room, so similar to the one Bora had occupied that it could have been the same one, was impeccable. No personal items in disarray, or even in view. The sole exception was a large, framed wedding picture on the bed, propped against the pillow. Even without stepping closer, Bora recognized Namura sitting with his knees far apart and the beribboned hilt of an elaborate ceremonial sword in his hands, and his bride standing at his side in a traditional costume. He looked away with embarrassment, being all too familiar with the fetishes of a man in love. Until a month ago, he'd carried Dikta's photographs with him. Only after disposing of them had he used his teeth to remove the wedding band from the ring finger of his right hand.

"*Dôso.*" With a small gesture, Namura invited him to sit down. However, Bora declined, explaining that he had come on a private and urgent matter. Not knowing whether there were any listening devices in the room, he asked, with a bow of his head, for permission to open the window. Being a military attaché, Namura immediately understood. He threw the window open himself, and waited for his German colleague to join him there.

"Namura-Chusa, I have a favour to ask you, as a brother officer," Bora began. His face was so serious that Namura once more saw through him.

"And as a man who, too, wishes to die?"

"Yes."

Before meeting Stauffenberg, Bora had placed Niemeyer's letter, in its envelope addressed to E. D., inside a larger, unsealed Manila envelope, which he now handed to the Japanese officer. Without looking at the contents, Namura sealed it, walked to the desk against which he'd rested his briefcase upon entering the room, and added the envelope to his papers. There was no need for any comment. Namura closed the window.

"You told me the other day that your honourable grandfather served as consul in Japan," he said. "Was his stay a fruitful one?"

"It was a fruitful one, Namura-Chusa."

"Let us speak of it sometime."

Meanwhile, Bora had scribbled on a page of his notebook, *How long can you keep the envelope?*

In perfect western longhand, Namura wrote below it, *I will occupy this room till the end of the month.*

*

Bora walked into the Leipziger Hof at ten to six, with every intention of getting in touch with Arthur Nebe by telephone at the appointed time. Handing him the room key, the concierge informed him that a lady had once more called and asked for him.

"She would not leave her name, Lieutenant Colonel, no. I took the liberty of suggesting that she try again after nine in the evening."

Bora looked at the hand-coloured photo of the Underground Fair Hall in Leipzig hanging on the pineapple-strewn wall behind the man. "You did the right thing. Did she ask for my room by number, or … ?"

"No, sir. Naturally, I would not divulge the number of your room to an outside caller, especially one who does not give her name."

*So, whoever she is, she knows I'm billeted here, but no more than that.* He had to make sure that it wasn't Emmy Pletsch. "A Silesian accent, would you say?"

"Oh, no. No accent to speak of, but if I were to hazard a guess, I'd say Rhineland or thereabouts." Not Ida Rüdiger either, then, Bora's second-best bet. The nonplussed expression on his face encouraged the concierge to venture further hypotheses. "If the lieutenant colonel will allow me – the caller sounds somewhat impatient."

"Not so impatient that she would leave a name by which I could identify her," Bora answered drily. "Should she phone again while I'm out, tell her from me that I will not take anonymous calls. If she's this reluctant to give her name, I must at least have a number where I may reach her."

"It will be done."

At six o'clock, Arthur Nebe's private phone number rang on and on. If he hadn't left for the day, he was away from his office. At the Kripo headquarters' central exchange, they told Bora that the chief would definitely be in early on the following day.

"The chief has your number. Should the chief choose to return your call, he will do so. But it isn't generally done."

Bora replaced the receiver in its cradle. Why was he trying to contact Nebe, anyway? He had no valuable update to report. One reason was to gather information on Gustav Kugler's past as an enforcer in Berlin. But after all, Grimm would be back in the morning, and if he was as willing to gossip about his former colleague as he'd been in the case of the S-Bahn murderer, he would satisfy his questions.

The dark heart of the matter was Niemeyer's letter. Safe for the moment in the hands of his Japanese colleague, after his meeting with Stauffenberg Bora could no longer mistake it for the ravings of a frightened and vengeful man. Blaming the conspirators, or Heldorff, or all of them, Niemeyer provided culprits and a solution Bora was not ready to trust. Much less could he turn it over to the chief without unleashing a witch-hunt in the military.

Thank God his cold-bloodedness was back. On his way out of the Adlon, he'd enrolled (and tipped) the Alsatian head waiter, asking him to discover if anyone in the hotel – chambermaid, valet, porter – knew where Salomon might have moved to. The old man promised to find out and send word either way.

There wasn't much Bora could do between now and nine o'clock, when the mysterious woman might or might not seek him a third time. That afternoon, before leaving Die Dame, he had drained a bottle of Apollinaris water, which had cost him an outrageous sum. Astride her white bullock, Europa had seemed to smirk at him from the painting, as if to say *You are a perfect fool for letting Emmy go.*

The windows in the room faced west, so the heat of day was coming through them. Closing them did not appreciably improve things; Bora compromised by leaving them open but drawing the blackout curtains across them. He didn't need to look out to be reminded that the trains to Paris, and via Leipzig to Vienna, were less than a mile away, beyond

Potsdamer Strasse. Paris was still in German hands, presumably much as he'd last seen it four years earlier, when he'd been under orders to trail that wayward patriot, Ernst Jünger, and to oversee the execution of a German deserter in the beautiful "City That Does Not Look at You" ... No point deluding oneself; the Americans would reach Paris before long. As for Leipzig and Vienna, well, he didn't want to think about their prospect of survival, as cities of the Reich in the Red Army's path. Just like Berlin.

Bora reclined on the bed with his boots on; the only concession to form was that he laid a newspaper on the pale yellow counterpane before resting his feet on it. If he wanted to function in the next hours, he had to get Stauffenberg's words out of his mind. And Emmy too, whom he'd made talk about herself while he himself had told her so little.

Propping the pillow behind his head, he tried to relax his shoulders. He'd always been laconic. It was a fact. Not because he had nothing to say, but because he was cautious, and had been trained not to trust too readily. But, Christ, he did it in order to protect others – if it came to that – not himself. Jünger, his off-and-on correspondent since their French days, did not think twice before sending him troubling letters. They were hand-delivered and sealed, yet Bora found such a cavalier disregard of caution inappropriate. Ernst Jünger provocatively writing about the need for a "larval life" was not all that different from Oster, let alone Claus von Stauffenberg. *These men behave like officers of the old imperial army, a privileged class that was allowed a certain amount of rebelliousness because it belonged to the same milieu as its sovereign. This isn't the way you prepare a coup. We are all brother officers, but even among brothers there can be betrayal, or a weak link that breaks under threat, or torture. As in physics, the forces of resistance ought to arise from attrition, cohesion, weight and acceleration ... How many of them can the conspirators claim? If I ferret out Salomon, I may have to kill him.*

*

He woke up after eight thirty, and the sight of *Magnus Magnusson: Clairvoyant from the North* in his lap told him that he'd fallen asleep while reading it. It was not like him to nap during the day, so it must have been the recitation of Niemeyer's fictitious Norse lineage that did it. Sunlight still filtered through a gap in the curtains, hanging limp in the absence of any breeze. Bora went into the bathroom to wash himself. As always in the past ten months, there was that first moment of surprise at the fact that he could no longer, strictly speaking, wash his *hands*, which then became acceptance. The face in the mirror looked back at him, stern and boyish; there was a certain resemblance to Stauffenberg, the younger Stauffenberg of nine years earlier. In the stifling room over-looking the bridge, he'd felt (and feared that he seemed) a lad compared to him. Commanders occasionally judged him to be younger than his thirty years, which he minded a little. He'd known suffering, for God's sake. Perhaps not as much as Claus von Stauffenberg (or Willy Osterloh), but he'd known suffering – and how! He quickly shaved for the evening, and avoided catching his eye in the reflective surface.

9:02 P.M.

"Lieutenant Colonel, a telephone call for the Lieutenant Colonel." The waiter's message came barely above an obliging whisper, but had the power of startling Bora. He had to control himself not to rush from his chair (in the dining hall there were no phones that could be brought directly to the table, like in other Berlin hotels) to one of the private phone booths off the lobby.

"Martin, this is your sister-in-law."

Without those words, he might or might not have recognized Margaretha's voice, as he hadn't seen her much.

"Duckie!" he said. "Is everything all right? Where are you?"

"I'm in town."

The concierge was right, she sounded impatient, and not overly friendly. Bora thought of Nina's words about her having become embittered after Peter's death in Russia.

"Is everything all right?" he repeated.

"I want to see you."

"I'd like to see you too, it's been months."

She didn't reply. It'd actually been close to two years. Bora had last been in Germany on furlough early in September 1942. Her stand-offish tone, the fact that she hadn't identified herself to him by name – much less her nickname – and now her silence, made him anticipate some sort of bad news.

"Are our families all right?" he urged her. "Your little girl?"

"Yes, all fine. I want to see you."

"Well, if you wish I can leave now and come to you, Duckie. Where are you staying in Berlin?"

"Let's meet in front of St Matthew's, on Matthäikirchplatz, in half an hour." Margaretha was not obliged to tell him where she was staying, but her reticence gave him pause. Bora tried to visualize the map of Berlin: no hotel of consequence, that is, of the type an industrialist's daughter would choose even in wartime, looked out onto the church square. She was Catholic, but the church was a Protestant one. She may be a guest of relatives, or family friends ... Then he remembered that the Air Force Ordnance Inspectorate was there; hadn't Nina said that Duckie was seeing one of Peter's colleagues, now assigned to a desk at headquarters?

The distance from the Leipziger Hof was entirely manageable on foot. Bora left word for them to leave the table set for him (he was hungry), and started out for the quarter south of the Tiergarten, near the Bendlerstrasse and the place where he'd met Stauffenberg only hours earlier.

The very last shadows were long and crisp, of a muted lilac tinge. The greenness of the vast park north-east of the zoo mellowed the sweltering heat of the fading day. A scent of blooming shrubs – and of trees splintered by debris during air raids – rode the ghost of a breeze. If one closed one's eyes, Berlin was as Berlin had ever been. Bora turned away from the canal at the corner of Tirpitzufer, where the water ran silently and slowly. So much in the last few days had happened within walking distance from here: the Potsdam and Anhalt stations, where he'd gone with Grimm and the policeman to recover Glantz's rifle; Leipziger Strasse, where a bomb had gone off shortly after his arrival; the Adlon was fifteen minutes away, and so were the Japanese embassy and Ida Rüdiger's beauty parlour.

Bora was apprehensive about meeting his brother's widow; on the phone, she had spoken to him as to a stranger, but that could be because he and Dikta had parted ways. He didn't know whether to hope or not hope that she might be carrying a message from his ex-wife. His agitation grew so much that he placed a lid of self-control on it.

The striped, pseudo-Gothic church of St Matthew's cast a vast shadow. With its pointed steeple, in the low sun it gave the impression of a tall creature, halfway between a red-and-ochre llama and a giraffe kneeling by a blue pond.

Few people were around at this hour, strollers returning from the park mostly. If Bora remembered correctly, his uncle's colleague Dr Bonhoeffer, who'd attended the funeral, had a son who was or had been an ordained minister of this parish. As he proceeded into the square, he caught sight of the young woman standing there alone, dwarfed by the building behind her.

At first he hesitated, because Margaretha was unrecognizable. Bora recalled her as she was on the day of her wedding to Peter, a credulous and tender twenty-year-old, as if she hadn't yet grown up. Traditional, without ideas of her own, madly in love. She was close to twenty-four now; the endearing chubbiness of the earlier years was gone. And there was a meanness in her eyes.

The first thing Bora noticed was that the wedding band and Nina's ring, the heirloom once denied to Dikta, were gone from her right hand. More than a sign of freedom, that naked hand (the left one wore a summer glove, and held the other glove like a scrap of lace) seemed to him a rebellion against the world she had known.

They greeted each other civilly, without seeking an embrace, and she explained how she had traced him through Bruno Lattmann, to whom she was distantly related. Bora readied himself for some sort of grievance, but was taken aback by the way she embarked at once on a tirade which she must have been thinking about right up to the point she saw him arrive. The argument was about Peter, of course.

Keeping at arm's length from him, she at once berated Bora for her loss – as if, instead of keeping mum on the phone about her reason for wanting to meet him, she'd indicated to him that she would tell him exactly this. Bora felt guilty as it was, because at the start of the war with Russia he'd enthusiastically shared with his brother every success they'd met on the way east.

He decided to let Duckie have her say. After speaking to his mother, he had expected a reproach from her, and unless her recriminations became downright offensive, he was ready to sympathize. Apologies, on the other hand, were impossible and futile.

"… He loved me but he *adored* you," she raged on, as if her jealousy, delayed and then finalized by death, were too strong to remain unspoken or be mollified. "Don't deny it. His eyes lit up whenever he spoke of you. It was 'Martin, Martin, Martin' all the time, as if he'd made himself a pattern of you to follow. When you went missing in Stalingrad, he was so crushed that he nearly forgot that I was *pregnant* and he should take care of *me* and think of *me*. We were supposed to be happy, buy a house and have five children, and be happy!" She spoke with venom in her voice, as if Bora had wilfully kept that future from happening, or didn't care at all. Yet he'd written her a long letter after Peter's accident, and anyone with an ounce of sensitivity would have read in it how shattering the bereavement was for the surviving brother.

He let her speak without interrupting her, shifting his gaze between her angry figure and the placid church beyond. So far, she'd only spoken about herself. He asked, somewhat provocatively, "Did you know that Nina was in town last Sunday?"

"For the funeral? Yes. I'm not attending funerals anymore." Right, and she wasn't wearing mourning clothes. She'd donned a bright, flowery silk dress and a straw hat with a heart-shaped brim, fashionable but unsuitable for a wartime city. "Speaking of which," she said, "I want Peter's lighter. Give it to me."

It was the only keepsake Bora had of his brother. "I lost it," he lied.

"That's not true. Peter's father let you have it, so give it to me."

"I lost it in September, when I was wounded."

"It's *mine*!"

"Well, you can't have it, it's gone."

The excuse was plausible, and – given their strained relations – Margaretha would not ask his mother about it.

Bora had never envied Peter for having a wife of whom his parents approved. Now that he saw how mistaken that approval was, his stepfather's dislike for Dikta seemed tragic. Still, he could not bring himself to censure anyone today, not even this warped incarnation of a former sweetheart.

"When did you last see Nina and the General?"

"It's none of your business. *You* were never home. Peter volunteered for Russia, not once but twice, because you did. He could have fought on a different front, if it weren't for you."

"He could have died on a different front, Duckie."

The only thing that remained of the girl he'd once known were her dimples. Yet now they showed because she pursed her lips in a stiff grimace, not in a smile. She aggressively jutted out her chin.

"Only if *you* fought on that other front. If it weren't for you, he'd have listened to me and to my daddy and transferred to the High Command." (Bora cringed at the thought of such family manoeuvres. *Not Peter*, he thought.) "My daddy and I would have made him see sense." She actually stomped her foot like a spoiled child, and her heel clacked on the pavement. "Don't you see? You ruined everything for me. Our life was perfect, and you ruined it!"

If one could tolerate a twenty-year-old with a mediocre knowledge of English addressing her father as "mein Daddy" in the American style, in a wife and mother the expression sounded infantile.

"Flying was Peter's life," Bora reminded her. "If you don't understand that, you never really knew him."

"Ha! Listen to you. Damn you, you never even understood your own wife!"

Why was he talking to her? The childish bickering tired him. Worse, it threatened to turn to anger and disgust in him, at hearing someone sputter whatever came to their mind out of resentment or fear. Bora patiently raised his eyes to the steeple, standing whole in its pretended antiquity while so many venerable buildings lay in ruins.

"Leave it, Duckie. Good luck to you in preparing your next perfect life."

"What if I am? I *will* have my husband, and my house, and my five children!"

Bora glanced at her scowling face, and then had to look away. She spoke as if those plans were expensive toys she'd been promised and which she would get one way or another. How could sweetness turn to utter poison? Dikta's cruelty, when she'd told him that she was leaving, had tasted less acrid. True, it was Dikta who had exerted the most influence on her sister-in-law, teasing her with her talk of sex, provocative underwear and egotism. In a strict household, the two girls might have bonded and eventually become alike, although Margaretha's spite betrayed an overindulged upbringing all of her own. Distantly related as she was to Bruno Lattmann, Bora was glad not to have asked his friend about her.

"Well, I wish you the best in securing what you want. Only remember that we're at war."

"As if I could forget!" She took him by the arm so that he'd look at her, burrowing her dark and burning eyes into him. "Do you know why I wanted to see you?"

Bora slowly freed himself of her hold. "No doubt because you meant to give me a piece of your mind."

"That, and to tell you that Dikta and I used to read your letters to each other at night, and then get into bed to masturbate. She *taught* me. Oh, I learned so much, practising what you wrote to her!"

There followed a moment when, in a splintered image in his mind, Bora saw himself striking Duckie with his fist, smashing her teeth, making her fall backwards and leaning on her to thrash her. It was so true to life that he could even smell blood. He saw her prostrate and disfigured, instead of standing triumphantly in front of him.

He really didn't know what held him back – by now, whatever he had to lose was no more important than what he had already lost. He managed to control himself somehow. And not only to control himself: to take leave, and walk away from the looming church, placing between himself and his sister-in-law the minimum distance needed not to retrace his steps and kill her.

14 July 1944, 11:38 p.m. Written in Grandfather Franz-August's ruined flat, where I came to have some peace.

I can take anything. I am convinced of it now; I only wish I knew how it is that I do it, so that I could share it with all those in this city, in this nation, who will suffer more than I and need to learn how to take it. The fact is that endurance cannot be taught. Today, perhaps – though I was barely conscious of it – I told myself that the real tragedy was having lost my brother, not listening to his widow vomit venom. I used to worry that Dikta might be a bad influence on her, and so she was. Whether Dikta did it because the General disliked her, or because she simply felt like it, it does not change things. What's worse, it does not change the physical nostalgia I feel for her. The letters I wrote to her were not meant for anyone else but her. I should be furious, and yet … It is as if I were ill with her, and the only way I knew how not to become even more ill was by not seeing or hearing from my wife.

In the dark library around him, soft cracking sounds rose from the battered shelves. A green, sweet scent from the plants of the nearby Westerwald pushed through the broken window. Bora turned off the torch he had been writing by, and opened the curtains onto the night. This could be the old family home south of Leipzig, with the linden tree in the garden planted by Luther's wife, Katharina von Bora. This could be a world where people and ties still held fast, where Niemeyer still charmed the crowds, and everything was still possible. A time of wholeness and confidence, when you could safely ignore the storm clouds.

He awoke shortly past one o'clock, uncomfortably curled up in his grandfather's armchair. If he'd come here to seek peace, this wrecked library and this old piece of furniture were the wrong place. He'd dreamed of Dikta, of that fateful night he'd met her at the army ball, in a gown cut dizzyingly low at the back, unsuited for a 21-year-old but capable of making him lose his head in April '37.

What did his sister-in-law know about him? Margaretha could pry into all his correspondence with Dikta, and never understand.

Wearily, Bora unbuttoned his tunic, rummaged for the cigarettes, found them, and lit one with his brother's lighter. He wondered if women (except maybe Remedios) had ever understood him. Then, as now, he didn't like to be touched before he was excited. He had to reach a restless anxiety first, a need to be aggressive that suffered a woman's touch as long as it didn't try to slow him down.

He'd never seen himself as capable of rape, never. Of rough sex, not least if he was thwarted, yes. It'd happened once in Borna, in the summer of '38, after Spain – after Remedios, the young peasant witch who'd taught him so much about love in the mountains of Aragon. A furlough spent alone with Dikta, in a room where the old linden tree in bloom filled the air with its heady scent.

"Let's pretend I don't want it," Dikta said, laughing.

"No, Dikta. Better not." He was feeling aggressive (after Spain, after Remedios), and disinclined to test his self-control. Although she tried to charm and insist, he left the bed; he went out onto the balcony, to watch the stars and breathe the oily fragrance from the dark, unruly head of the linden tree.

"All right, love, come back. I'll be good." Even as a girl-friend she was a liar. She led him on and played rough and exasperated him; then she pushed him away, kicking, biting and laughing. But even as she laughed, things got out of hand. Afterwards they were both exhausted. Bora had scratches and teeth-marks that the uniform would luckily conceal, and on the delighted Dikta, a medical examination would show that some force had been exerted.

The bruises on her inner thighs anguished him. "Let's not do it again, ever, Dikta."

"Why? I enjoyed it. It was fun." But for the next two days she was too sore to make love, which troubled him even more.

The two nights that followed, Bora would not sleep in her bed. In the library, he sat up reading and drowsing in his grandfather's armchair. The third night, Dikta walked in. She sat in his lap and kissed his bruises, and he kissed hers.

To this day, it was the episode in his life that shamed him most. Bora could not think about it without blushing. Yet he knew himself well enough to discern that physical aggression was all but beyond him.

After the event, he was sure the military chaplain would not give him absolution, but the savvy priest – a veteran of the Somme – didn't sound shocked, and took the opportunity to lay on him an extended homily on the bliss of wedded love in the service of procreation. Bora walked away with the feeling that for the Roman Catholic Church it'd be all right even to ravish your girlfriend or your wife, as long as you made her pregnant. So he'd given himself a penance: in lieu of Hail Marys, for a whole month he denied himself lunch, took cold showers and did without alcohol and cigarettes. He never told Dikta about it; she'd have laughed at such nonsense, just as she did at the profusion of flowers and apologies from him.

"Will you stop, Martin? I never enjoyed such a glorious, achy tumble. I'll marry you for it one of these days, silly."

And so it had come to pass.


SATURDAY, 15 JULY

By six in the morning, Bora was at the Leipziger Hof. Grimm was due to report at eight, and Bora had every intention to be seen sitting at breakfast by then, in the hall with the sepia Leipzig scene. Ever since waking up in his grandfather's library, an oppressive awareness that danger was at hand convinced him that Stauffenberg would act today, wherever and in whatever form. It was nothing but a hunch – although hunches were what he often had to thank for his survival. *I'll keep my eyes open, not for omens but for signs that something is happening.*

The first news was good: at 6:45 a.m. (Bora was in the lobby, jotting down his list of things to do), an errand boy cycled over with a verbal message from the Adlon head waiter. It seemed that the colonel (meaning Salomon) had requested a cab when he'd hastily checked out of the hotel early on Wednesday morning; the luggage he left behind had been forwarded to the Elizabeth hospital on Lützow Strasse.

The large Protestant hospital, near the Office for Foreign Trade, occupied a city block off Potsdamer Strasse. Because of its religious affiliation and vicinity to the Reserve Army headquarters, Bora had placed it at the bottom of his list the day before. It'd been the final call he had made, and he distinctly remembered hearing that there was no patient there by the name of Salomon. What if the good deaconesses granted asylum to desperate runaways?

He decided to drive to the hospital personally, confident that he would be back in time for Grimm to see him drinking ersatz coffee at his corner table.

Bora's pretext was that he wanted to return a book to the colonel – in fact, none other than Niemeyer's *Magnus Magnusson: Clairvoyant from the North.* He paced the waiting room for twenty minutes (an eternity, given his apprehension and haste), before learning that Salomon had been admitted briefly but was no longer on the premises.

The young foreign doctor, probably a Dutchman judging by his speech, said, "It was a mere case of gastrointestinal trouble. He was dehydrated and we detected an irregular heartbeat, so we kept him under observation overnight. In the morning we needed the bed, and dismissed him."

Thursday morning. Two days' advantage that could make all the difference. Bora acted disappointed, while in truth he was indignant. "Do you have an address – or at least a forwarding address, to which I can send the book? I hate to leave town without returning it."

"Can't help you there, Colonel."

"It's a matter of principle. If I leave the book here with you, is there a way that it could reach the colonel?"

"I don't see how. He explained that he was going home on medical leave, which is all I can tell you. If you know where the colonel lives, of course, you can send him the book."

Aside from his long-lost property in Masuria, Bora didn't know where Salomon might be. Another round of calls might secure a forwarding address, but the odds were ten to one that the colonel was not travelling in its direction.

He returned to the Leipziger Hof in dire need of something that had caffeine in it.


LEIPZIGER HOF, 8:00 A.M.

Bora kept a discreet eye on the hall, half-filled at breakfast time. Grimm would turn up at any moment, and he would have to summon all his energy not to betray any agitation: those trained to detect it underneath a show of self-control are seldom taken in. As often happens when you await someone, his eyes anticipated the bulky image of the policeman, his cheap suit and outrageous tie, automatically discarding newcomers who differed from that description.

Thus it was that he at first ignored the jowly fellow in a dust-coloured trench coat, even if his bulk was comparable to Grimm's. When a second man followed, however, it became obvious that they were two of the three men he'd met in Kupinsky's building. Bora raised his defences. The duo searched with their eyes here and there, but it was just pretence, because it was him they wanted, and they had recognized him right away. They did not show their badges to the obliging waiter; one of the two gestured a denial, but no different from that of any visitor who has no time to sit down and eat.

Bora finished the sip of coffee substitute he had in his mouth, and rested the cup, monogrammed with an "L. H.", on its saucer. Seemingly impassive, he prepared to smile – just as he was prepared, if needed, to point the gun at his own chin and fire.

To his right, a flight lieutenant stood up with faked indifference, but he forgot his sunglasses on the table, and the napkin slipped from his knees and fell under his chair. Bora caught his awkwardness out of the corner of his eye. A moment later, the two were standing in front of him, and he had to find a way to confront them.

"Good morning. May I help you?"

There was no way of knowing whether they'd expected his move. Anything, Bora knew, could have happened since he left Stauffenberg the day before. Thoughts of Niemeyer's letter, Salomon, the Alsatian head waiter, milled in his head like bits of foil.

The heavier-set of the two, his face grumpy under the rim of his hat, said yes.

"A work-related question? Would you care to sit down?"

"No."

*This is how they do it.* He had seen them do it, through the years. They counted on their threatening silence to intimidate those they arrested and interrogated … *No, I cannot afford to smile, much less show that I have a hundred reasons to suspect why they are here.*

"When did you last see Berthold Kupinsky?"

Well – *this* he hadn't expected. Bora wasted no time wondering how the Gestapo had found him here (that was the least of his problems). The important thing was to understand whether they had already nabbed Kupinsky and squeezed him until he told them about the letter. A reverent silence had fallen on the hall. Those still sitting at breakfast were doing so only because leaving hastily might arouse suspicion.

Bora said, "On Thursday morning, while you were busy with his upstairs neighbour, Anton Reich."

It was so outrageous of him to suggest that he knew what their duty was that day, that there was a fleeting glint of admiration in the eyes of the second agent, who was less massive and perhaps less brutal than his partner.

"And what do you know about Anton Reich?"

"Nothing. He does not appear on the list of murder suspects I received from the chief, SS Group Leader Arthur Nebe."

They did not ask him about his investigation, which could mean something, or nothing.

"Why then are you familiar with the name?"

Bora was bathed in a cold sweat, but replied with a serenity that surprised even him. "I did not find Kupinsky at home, so I knocked on the door across from his and learned he'd gone out at 6 a.m. After your arrival, I went upstairs and glimpsed the name 'Anton Reich' on an envelope in the man's apartment."

"And why did you go up to Anton Reich's?"

"Because I heard someone weeping."

The answer was disarming. Had Bora known that the Reich's fate was linked to the arrest on 76 Köpenicker Landstrasse of three enemies of the State about to meet with Stauffenberg, he'd have swallowed his tongue before answering. Fortunately for him, the men – communists who'd been on the run since January – had been seized for reasons unrelated to the plot.

The Gestapo agents did not order Bora to stand, so Bora remained seated, with the coffee substitute cooling in his cup. *Whether he likes it or not, Kupinsky has become a Gestapo informant. Why don't they ask me about him? I cannot show excessive curiosity, nor disregard.*

"In case it's of any help," he said, "Kupinsky had nothing to add to his earlier deposition."

It was a colossal untruth. Bora was scared to say it, and the fact that the two did not react meant nothing. They might know everything about Kupinsky, Niemeyer, even about Heldorff and whatever role he played in the larger scheme of things. They might know enough about him to arrest him now. Bora thanked his forethought for making him unlatch the holster before sitting down to breakfast. The only thing that really mattered was not to let them take his gun from him.

Where was Grimm? The electric clock on the wall showed ten minutes after eight. Bora said, raising the cup to his lips, "Forgive me if I finish this, I don't want it to go to waste." *Then, if they do not arrest me, I'll run upstairs to vomit into the sink, because I feel like throwing up my guts.*

Just as they had drawn closer to his table, the two did an about-turn and left without saying goodbye. Bora took out a cigarette and stuck it in his mouth in the hope of controlling his nausea: he would never make it to his room before vomiting his coffee. He'd taken a first drag when Grimm showed up at the door.

He somehow found the brazenness to observe, "Ah, there you are. I expected you fifteen minutes ago, Inspector."

"A pit bull after a dog fight" was a good simile for the way Florian Grimm looked when he walked into the dining hall. When Bora asked if he cared for a cup of coffee, he said no, and stood there with scuffed hands and a bloodied sticking plaster on his meaty head. The tie for the day matched the colours of his bruises, with the aggravating circumstance of a bold paisley pattern. He took a hesitant step forward, like a slow-witted schoolboy called to the blackboard. Bora furtively latched his holster and leaned back in his chair. *Grimm might reply, "I don't butt in when there's Gestapo around," or he might pretend ignorance. Both reactions would indicate that he means to keep his distance from the Secret Police. But if he says, "I saw you had company," he's informing me that he knows very well who I was with, and simply chose to wait outside.*

"I saw you had company," Grimm said.

Bora nodded casually. "Glad to see you're all in one piece. Are things well with your relatives?"

"Yes, thank you."

Asked about the air raid, Grimm gruffly summarized. Both families escaped with minor injuries. Although the house was a near loss, relatives in Neukölln were able to shelter his brother, wife and children. He did not enquire about Trost's dismissal in his absence or about the Olympia, openly parked in front of the hotel. He waited for Bora to rise from the table before handing him a few stapled sheets.

"The transcript of Glantz's interrogation, Colonel."

"Ah. Is he alive?"

"He's alive. Has a shattered jaw."

Not exactly the injury you'd get falling while you tried to hang yourself. Bora had seen his share of dislocated and cracked jaws on prisoners in Poland and Russia, and wondered if Glantz's cell was on the third floor of the Gestapo-run Alex.

"He's confessed to the murder," Grimm added, prompting Bora to flip quickly through the sheets. "A signed confession is a signed confession. You may see for yourself what motive and details he gave."

Bora glanced up from the paper.

"Did he confess before or after breaking his jaw?"

"As far as I know, he was injured when he struck the floor of the cell. He signed his confession half an hour earlier. The fact is that the Gestapo has him now. The chief is trying to have him released back to us. He's confessed, and he's ours."

It could make only so much difference, Bora thought. The document, typewritten by a clerk and signed by the prisoner's own hand, covered four numbered pages. Bora placed it on the table and read. It detailed the reasons behind Glantz's plan to murder Niemeyer: personal bitterness, economic loss, damage to his professional image, profound stress; it tried to justify his act by insisting that Niemeyer was actually Jewish and for years had swindled the German public on that account. The publisher gave direct evidence of the fact: during an outing in the country in 1942, after a stop in a beer hall, both he and Niemeyer had heeded a physical urge; in the bushes, "without malice of any sort", Glantz's eye had fallen on the part of Niemeyer's anatomy that "showed evidence of circumcision". Niemeyer's response had been to turn away immediately, but, as Glantz declared, "I saw what I saw."

Three of the four pages contained a venomous list of the Prophet's offences against him. From the last paragraph of the third page onwards, there followed a concise but credible reconstruction of the actual murder. Bora caught details: the back door unlocked – the disassembled rifle previously concealed in the shrubs – wiping off fingerprints from barrels and stock ... Glantz showed familiarity with the villa and with Niemeyer's habits, but showed no repentance.

While Bora read, the flight lieutenant returned to the hall; with a muttered apology to no one in particular he retrieved his sunglasses from the table and left again. Grimm crabbily looked after him as he left.

"It boggles the mind that Niemeyer got himself snipped after being shamed by real Yids," he commented. "Have you heard about Kupinsky, Colonel?"

Bora took the briefcase from the chair on the other side of the table and placed Glantz's papers inside it.

"No." He spoke with the cigarette in his mouth. "Is there any news?"

"He's missing again. On Friday, when the local policeman went to check on him as a matter of routine, his clothes and personal items had gone. At dawn a pair of shoes, one worn in a peculiar way along the sole, turned up at the foot of the Warsaw Bridge. They might belong to the queer."

So that was why the Gestapo had come asking about Kupinsky. Preceding Grimm out of the hall, Bora kept dragging on the cigarette to keep the nausea down. He said,

"The drowned eventually surface on the bank by the Treptow observatory, don't they?"

He sounded callous, but in fact he doubted that Kupinsky had killed himself. He was hiding somewhere, and as far as Bora was concerned, it was a good thing.

"Let's go to Glantz's place, Inspector."


## STENDALER STRASSE, MOABIT

A hurricane seemed to have gone through the house. Even Grimm looked mystified as he ran his eyes around: not one piece of furniture, not one object still stood in its place. It was an upper-middle-class interior, once quite luxurious. Many furnishings were clearly missing: no doubt scavengers had rushed in to loot the place after the couple's arrest. The disappearance of hunting trophies from the walls (only the brackets remained) made little sense: what could Berliners do with stuffed animals these days? Only sell them – if they found a buyer, who in turn could do nothing with them. More understandable was the removal of the bed sheets and table linen, whose handwritten labels remained on the depleted shelves.

Echoes of the devastation in Grandfather Franz-August's flat, and Reinhardt-Thoma's clinic. Bora had seen enough. Head down, he moved aside this or that fragment on the floor with the tip of his boot.

"Husband and wife ended up on the third floor because of the Drilling rifle," Grimm said, as if expecting the question from Bora. "But he owned up to the murder before the transfer."

"What else did he say about the Drilling, other than that it belonged to his brother-in-law?"

"He said, as he'd told us, that he killed Niemeyer with it."

Yes, maybe. Or rather, yes, of course. Unless owning up a crime he had not committed was his desperate way to avoid more violence. Or a transfer to the Gestapo, for a political crime. Bora told himself he had to ask Nebe, if he ever found the head of the Kripo at his desk. No guarantee he'd receive an answer, however.

"Case closed, then."

"Looks that way, Colonel. But we need Glantz back in our custody." With his heavy footsteps, Grimm walked in and out of rooms, trailing the odour of the iodine used to medicate his scalp. "Are we looking for something in particular?"

Bora swept up a photo of a mild-looking, hefty woman from the floor; she was the physical counterpart of her husband. "What about Glantz's wife?" In the fur coat of the portrait, she resembled a she-bear emerging from a winter sleep.

"They would have hauled her to the third floor even if he hadn't admitted the murder. They've moved her to the women's prison on Barnimstrasse awaiting trial. After all, the rifle belonged to her brother, and she let her husband keep it at home." At the foot of a built-in cupboard lay scattered brochures announcing the upcoming publication of the *Encyclopaedia of Myth* "by the eminent Dr Prof. Magnus Magnusson". Bora retrieved one and read its grandiloquent text. Had Niemeyer maliciously taken advantage of his publisher, getting money for a job he never meant to carry out, or had he simply promised what he could not deliver? Compiling an encyclopaedia all by himself! How could Glantz have fallen for it? Max Kolowrat spoke of members of the magician's audience being subjugated to the extent of making themselves ridiculous. But it's one thing to mesmerize someone during a show, and another to swindle a professional publisher over many months, if not years. Glantz *could* have killed him. And no, they were looking for nothing in particular.

"I'm curious to hear what you think about all this, Inspector."

"It depends on whether we get him back and on the judge assigned to his trial," Grimm commented meaningfully. "In the case of murder, a death sentence is a foregone conclusion. Otherwise, if they find extenuating circumstances, though I don't see how, it's labour camp for life. Which is always better than having his head lopped off."

Was it? According to some reports, there were labour camps where a prisoner survived an average of only two months. The war, however badly things were going, would last longer than two months. Bora wouldn't give a penny for the lives of the Glantzes.

"You asked what I think. The book-man could have killed Niemeyer, that's what I think." Grimm brooded, straddling the wreckage. "By his own admission, he carried the Drilling piecemeal to the victim's property, and we saw by the way he packaged it that he knew how to disassemble a rifle. Says he found the back door open. It is possible; we found no evidence of a lock being forced. At the beginning, he said he learned through the grapevine that there was shooting involved, a detail we never made public. Perhaps he knew, simply because he *is* the murderer. Didn't he try to hang himself when we came on the scene?"

"A culprit would have destroyed the rifle instead of shipping it to himself poste restante."

"Not necessarily. Believe you me, Colonel, murderers have a thousand reasons not to make a clean breast of it until they get pummelled, hardened criminals and cowards who pulled the trigger on an impulse alike. Here we have someone who talked before they roughed him up on the third floor, which is what they're doing with the watchmaker. Oh, yes … It did Eppner no good running his mouth off about being a lieutenant in the Foot Guards. He violated several laws by hiding a pistol in his toilet and keeping a Russian servant at home."

Bora stared at Grimm's tie, a maelstrom of violet, purple and lilac, with spots of bright orange and magenta.

"How long has Eppner been in?"

"Since Tuesday last, the eleventh."

"Why didn't you inform me?"

"His violations have nothing to do with this case. Besides, if Eppner invents a plausible excuse for the pistol and the

Russian, and finds a good lawyer, he might get away with a few years in a labour camp."

"Let me guess. He is not by any chance being transferred to a camp …"

"He wasn't until yesterday."

In the car, as they headed south, Bora tried to make sense of the latest developments. Tedious Gestapo interference could be the reason why Nebe had saddled an outsider with the case; Niemeyer's political connections, especially in the past, warranted that sort of attention. If so, a professional investigator would find himself in a bind. A soldier in that role might defuse the conflict between the two institutions. Or not. *Why do I go on searching for other leads and suspects, Kugler included, when there's already someone in jail who has confessed to the murder?*

Out loud, he only said, "A convenient arrangement is not what General Nebe expects."

"Meaning what, Colonel?"

"I don't know yet."

Bora rolled down the window. The morning light rained from a sky so clear and sparkling, enemy bombers would be foolish not to take advantage of it. The electric lines and telephone and telegraph exchanges that were still functioning were merely waiting for the next raid. The moment he allowed his concentration to stray from the criminal case, a foreboding of what this day may bring was like a hand around his throat. It might be only his impression, but there seemed to be less evidence of police at street corners; if true, it was something that he didn't know how to read. Or didn't want to.

"That former colleague of yours, Inspector, the dead investigator – what can you tell me about him?"

In this once Red quarter of workers' housing, they were driving down a short street renamed after Herbert Norkus, the young Party saint whose martyrdom had taken place nearly twelve years earlier. The question was appropriate to the neighbourhood.

Grimm glanced at him. "Kugler? Not much. We weren't serving in the same department when he was injured and retired. You know how it is with pals you knew when you were young. In recent days, we've had no reason to look each other up."

"But you associated with each other during the Republic."

"You're damn right, Colonel. Those were the days. He was a tough one, Gustl. See the bruises I got on my head in the air raid? That's nothing! He and I got our skulls bashed in every other week, and you can be sure we reciprocated, with interest. I had some five stone less on me then."

"Well, it was a logical next step, then, for both of you to enter the police, keeping order ..."

"Yes, but I wasn't cut out for the *Sittenpolizei*, the vice squad," Grimm said, unbuttoning his coat and removing his badge, as he always did when he didn't need to display it. When he'd put it away in the glove compartment, he reached for his Trommler cigarettes. There were none left, so he crushed the pack in his hand and grunted a "thank you" when Bora handed him his Chesterfields.

"American stuff?"

"American stuff."

Grimm pinched the artificial silk of his tie. "I favour some American stuff, too, from the old days."

In the small park coming up on their left, called Norkusplatz these days, girls were watering a rich crop of vegetables, presumably blessed – like a working-class version of the Gardens of Adonis – by the boy's blood.

"The vice squad, that's where Kugler served for some five years." Grimm blew cigarette smoke as he spoke. "He had the stomach to deal with whores and pimps every day, and all of it without being on the take. Say, Colonel, are you really curious about all this? You must have been a whippersnapper then."

Bora chose not to take the comment as a reminder that *he* hadn't helped build the new Reich.

"Definitely. A whippersnapper in Leipzig." His eyes lingered on the gardening girls, and the liquid, silvery tongues that rained from the watering cans. "Back in Saxony, it was not unusual in those days for police officers to moonlight, the pay being low."

"The pay is *still* low. But it depends on what you mean by 'moonlighting'. Gustav Kugler took no money to look the other way, and neither did I."

"No offence meant, Inspector."

"None taken. Just so that you know."

It matched what Bora had heard from Kolowrat thus far. They were crossing the Old Moabit boulevard now, heading for the Spree's curvy bank. *It's easy for me to pass judgement, not having lived through those troubled times.*

"The worst thing," Grimm continued, "is that he leaves a widow and three children. If she's the same girl he was dating then, she's no brain either."

Bora sympathized. The question of moonlighting, however one understood the term, remained unanswered, but he did not insist.

"Where can I buy some aspirin?" he asked instead, a request his visible injury justified.

Grimm indicated a pharmacy at the next street corner, where they stopped. Returning to the car minutes later, Bora noticed across the street a small tavern of the type Norkus had known, identified by number rather than name, and suggested they go and have a drink there.

Soon they were sitting in a sun-baked court at the back, under a canvas awning camouflaged with hand-painted blotches of grey and brown.

Over water and beer, respectively, Bora extracted more nostalgia about the revolution from the policeman, although Kugler's name was not mentioned again.

"After the Great War, my stepfather headed a Freikorps in Saxony," he contributed to the conversation. "Nothing like the Berlin street fights, but still …"

Grimm agreed, but remained tight-lipped about the details. Bora was restless. This oaf was a thorough Party minion; he wouldn't get anything out of him that he meant to keep to himself. It seemed ages already since he'd vainly sought Salomon at the hospital, ages since he'd heard from Stauffenberg what he'd rather not have heard.

He returned to the safer subject of Glantz's and Eppner's detention. One relevant titbit he ferreted out was that a minor wrangle over Frau Glantz's captivity had occurred between the Gestapo and the Criminal Police, the latter being resentful of political interference in a case of murder.

"See, Colonel, the Niemeyer case is within our purview."

Bora, who was toying with the rectangular tin of aspirin on the oilskin tablecloth, readily agreed. "They asked me about Berthold Kupinsky at breakfast."

"So *that*'s what it was about."

"Yes. I couldn't have added anything about Kupinsky if I'd wanted to." Bora deftly balanced the grey tin on its narrow end. "Why ask *me* about him?"

"The Niemeyer case is within out purview."

"Precisely. I see no reason why the secret police should develop an interest in it." There were moments when Bora pretended awkwardness, and others when he let it be known how adroit he really was, his injury notwithstanding. With his thumbnail, and without upsetting the balance of the tin, he tore the paper band with which it was sealed. "As a matter of institutional correctness, I will report this morning's conversation to the Chief."

Grimm watched Bora tap the tin flat on its back, flip it open, fish out two tablets and swallow them with a sip of water. "It's the right thing to do, Colonel."

When a rare breath of wind entered the courtyard, the canvas awning overhead heaved like a sail. Bora looked up.

"Especially considering that I should be with my regiment right now, instead of doing my own brand of moonlighting in Berlin."

The large mug Grimm had in front of him was empty but for a frothy residue. It'd take five more at least before he loosened up, so if he now hung his beefy head, it was for a different reason. The gauze on his scalp, brown with iodine, sat among scars Bora had never noticed before. Some had been stitched up, others left to heal as best they could.

Grimm slowly said, staring up at him with his small, slanting eyes, "I don't know how it was for you in Russia, Colonel —"

"For me it was Stalingrad," Bora drily interjected.

"For us, it came down to sweeping the place clean of Reds and Jews, in front or behind your swanky divisions."

Even a "yes" would be saying too much. Bora refrained from any sign of acknowledgement.

Grimm squinted. "Am I proud of it? No. Am I ashamed of it? Even less. It had to be done. We killed hundreds at a time, of all ages and sizes. Hundreds? Thousands. Stark naked all, sweaty or shivering or pissing themselves." With his chin, he pointed at Bora's gloved prosthesis. "Let me ask you: what did you feel when your hand was blown off?"

"I don't remember. I usually say I felt nothing."

"See? And *I* felt nothing. After the first week, that's how it was. Kill, move on. Routine. What the fuck, it makes you wonder." He tutted. "At times I'd go rummaging through the heaps of their flea-ridden rags to see if I could feel *something*. Nothing. Nothing. It's odd, isn't it? Useful but odd."

A tilt of the head, and he disposed of the last beer suds. "Why did you ask about Kugler? His moonlighting days were long behind him."

Afterwards, Grimm didn't ask where they should go, and Bora didn't tell him. They drove silently until the next checkpoint, where a tram accident required a detour. So they went back to Old Moabit, past St John's cemetery, and they had to wait there too. Grimm kept out of the sun behind the wheel, while Bora stepped out. He needed to move, to give himself, by walking around, the illusion that he was drawing close to a solution. Things – murder included – might be simpler than he was making them. His Abwehr training might be getting in the way of accepting the confession of a man who had both motive and opportunity to kill Niemeyer.

This was a neighbourhood he knew well from his school and service days in Berlin. Ahead, the sullen block of the criminal court crouched like a watchdog, back to back with the army's Staff College and the largest military complex in town.

Keeping to the little shade available, he paced along the wall of the garrison barracks across from a secondary school. There, something caught his strained attention. He could swear they were shouting assembly orders inside the compound. At this unusual time of day? Did it mean anything? Everything else was tranquil. At the end of the street, sitting in the car, Grimm was listening to the radio; the tinny sound of a popular song rose and fell, like an invisible, irregular wave that wafted out of the Olympia and at some point in the air met the echo of the same song from a high window.

Bora marked the time: *11 a.m., 15 July 1944.*

In twenty minutes, they had cleared the hurdle. Bora had elaborated an imperfect but feasible plan.

"Inspector, how long would it take you to fetch the Eppner papers? They may be irrelevant to the case, but I need to see them. Who knows, we might discover that the reputable vicar and the other guests lied about the birthday party at the watchmaker's. We could end up with not one but two self-confessed murderers."

True to his profession, Grimm showed no appreciation for

the irony. "It won't take more than the time to go to Alex and back," he answered, flatly. "Longer, if Eppner was transferred elsewhere, or if the chief orders me to fetch Glantz back from the Gestapo. He confessed, and he's ours."

"Fine. Let me off here and go. I'll walk the rest of the way."

"It's nearly two miles to the hotel, Colonel! I could leave you at the underground stop."

Bora pretended more irritation than he felt. "You know, it annoys me when people treat me as if I were crippled. I will *walk*. See you at the hotel when you get there."

No sooner had the Olympia started eastwards than Bora took the underground to Kugler's office, seven stops away on Mainzer Strasse.

MAINZER STRASSE, NEUKÖLLN, 11:46 A.M.

In that quarter of immense working-class apartment blocks, a gloomy porter with a wet rag in her hand told Bora that he'd find Frau Kugler in the office. "Couldn't pay the rent, so she relocated here, where her man used to work."

It had a yellow façade, wedge-shaped, like a slice of non-descript cheese between two modern multi-storeyed slices of bread. One on top of the other, there were two ugly metal-framed windows with panes painted dark blue for curfew, which surely forced those inside to turn the light on even in daytime.

To the right of the door, the nameplate (in fact, Kugler's business card) had been altered. The title "Private Investigator" was crossed out, and Kugler's first name, Gustav, had been replaced by Witwe, "widow".

Bora rang a disturbingly loud electric bell, and before the echo died out the door opened. He faced a bony, weary-looking little woman of uncertain age, with a kerchief tightly wound around her head and tied above the forehead. Wisps of hair, of an undefinable drab colour, mostly like mud, had escaped the cloth at her temples.

She said at once, "The agency is no longer in business," and even before Bora could explain he was not exactly a client, she began to sniffle without weeping, with all the dignity she could muster in such a miserable place.

"I'm sorry for your loss, madam. May I come in?"

"Can't see why you'd want to come in, but come in."

She threw the ground-floor window wide open when he entered. At a glance, Bora reckoned there were two rooms in all, one above the other: the bedroom was presumably at the top of a spiral staircase, and this here was Kugler's old office. His work desk was now strewn with turnips and various kitchen items. On the wall, the month of June still showed on the calendar, probably untouched since the man's death.

An invented tale of family ties explained Bora's visit, in search of private papers gathered by the late investigator. Frau Kugler stared blankly at him. She seemed too discouraged and exhausted to raise any objections. Her three children were nowhere to be seen, so Bora imagined they'd been sent out into the country, as many young Berliners had. "In the country", he knew, was a euphemism that often meant that the alternative to burrowing underground during air raids was to labour in the fields for brutal employers who saw in you a cheap drudge, or – if you were a girl – even worse. It took close to a minute for her to digest the question and come up with an answer. She used the hem of her apron as a potholder to remove a ramekin of boiling water from the top of an iron stove, roaring even in this heat.

"Be my guest," she said. "Whatever you're looking for, if it's still here, you'll find it in the archive."

*If it's still here.* Bora eyed the kindling in a cardboard box at the foot of the stove with concern – mostly pieces of discarded furniture, varnished and foul-smelling, but also rolled-up folders and shredded files.

"Archive" was a lofty word for the filing cabinet against the back wall. Bora had no idea of the volume of work Kugler might have garnered in wartime, and with clearly reduced means. The top two drawers were empty. Opening the third, he realized that Frau Kugler was methodically burning the files, from the letter A onwards. He anxiously pulled out the bottom drawer, where no "Rüdiger" was featured under the letter R. His only hope was that Kugler's papers were filed under the names of those he'd been watching, not his clients'. In the third drawer, the letter M was empty. Bora searched through the file labelled N, from which several documents seemed to be missing. Of the folder concerning a certain Neumann (spousal infidelity), only two pages densely filled with dates and addresses remained. Who knew, it might be the same case that cost Kugler his life. Bora was heartened to find the Niemeyer file still in place.

Frau Kugler, unmoved by the discovery, cleared a space on the desk for him, between the turnips and a short stack of chipped plates with a gilded rim. She had in the meantime put on a pair of galoshes wholly unsuited to the weather.

"Today it's the bread queue," she announced. "I have to go. When you're through, please pull the door shut behind you."

How Berlin had changed. Never before would the lower middle class, so faithful to principle and self-respect, have allowed a stranger to step into this squalor, and allow the same stranger to remain alone in the house to rummage around at will.

However, the circumstance suited him, because Kugler was altogether a capable organizer. Bora made sure the surface of the desk was clean before resting the folder on it. The first item was the contract signed by Ida Rüdiger with a flourish (Bora could imagine her vengeful spite as she penned it). A series of cards followed, paperclipped in sets of four. They chronicled the stake-outs near Villa Gerda: day, hour of arrival and departure, remarks. A handful of envelopes contained other papers and photographs. Bora could not skip over anything; it would take him at least an hour to go through the contents. He decided to take along the cardboard folder to do it at leisure. In exchange, he left a couple of banknotes under the stack of plates. Having given neither his surname nor his address, there was no way for Frau Kugler, were she so inclined, to return the money.

As he was about to leave, he stumbled over the box of kindling, and from the folder he held under his arm a sprinkling of small photos came loose and fell on the floor. Intrigued, Bora picked them up. They'd been taken from a distance, probably from the shrubbery by the edge of the pond, where a strip of public land bordered the gardens. The rear entrance to Niemeyer's villa, which he'd seen portrayed in the Weimar gossip sheets, was recognizable in all of them. Niemeyer, less impressive than in his official portraits, was peeking out of the door, or else was pictured in a smoking jacket or sports outfit standing next to a tall young woman.

She could not be Frau Eppner, because the watchmaker's romantic wife was well over forty. It might be the lover whose gowns Ida Rüdiger (so said Kupinsky) set on fire in the bathtub. Bora returned to the desk to flip through the photos. In one enlargement, where the girl appeared from an advantageous three-quarter angle, her face was obliterated by ink. He wet his forefinger and tried to wipe it clean, to no avail. He'd try later with soap or alcohol.

On the back of every photo were pencilled the date and time of day. All had been taken at about the same time, 3:30 p.m. or 4:30 p.m.. In all but the two enlargements, the girl was wearing a hat that partly hid her features, and round sunglasses. She was bareheaded in the close-ups, made for unknown reasons quite useless by Kugler's ink. But perhaps there were *good* reasons. Bora shoved the folder into his briefcase. Before leaving, he thoroughly searched the desk drawers. He also climbed the spiral staircase to the darkened upper room, where a frameless mattress lay on the floor and cardboard boxes contained clothes and whatever else the widow had brought along.

When he walked out of Kugler's place, there was no one in the wide street; the old working-class apartment buildings lined it battered and mute. The shade lay in pale, narrow strips, and a sweltering heat rose from the pavement. Bora filled his lungs with the stagnant city air. He'd suffered scorching summers in Ukraine, and in Spain before then. Now he ran hot and cold, and if he was sweating, it was a chilly sweat.

He found a spot to collect his ideas, inside a modest but cool eatery along Jägerstrasse, until the war an Italian restaurant much frequented by air force cadets and their girlfriends. He ordered a bottled lemonade and was left alone.

15 July. Written at Mutti Maria's. Thank God Kugler's loopy widow is the orderly kind. One more day and fire would have reduced what's in front of me to a handful of useless ashes.

Two very interesting things: the photos (16 in all), portray the same young blonde, who apparently visited the victim at about 3:30 p.m. one day a week, leaving after one hour. The calendar in my notebook tells me it was always a Wednesday. The visits are recorded from mid-February to Wednesday, 17 May (Kugler was dumped by Ida Rüdiger the following day). Two enlargements are from photos shot, I believe, from inside a car parked along Lebanonzederpfad. In both the girl is shown to be alone as she walks towards Niemeyer's property (you can see the Wirths' garden behind her). If only I could wipe off the ink concealing her features … Kugler pressed the nib of his pen on the paper while he blackened it. We'll see.

The most stimulating detail, however, is that three of the surveillance photos date from the first half of February

(1, 8, 15). Kugler's contract with Ida Rüdiger bears the date 23 February. Must I assume that he was shadowing the girl before the papers were officially signed? Or rather that he'd already started the surveillance of Niemeyer and his visitors on his own? Why? On whose orders?

I can't put forward a precise theory. She could be anyone. But why erase her features? To benefit (or out of fear of) whom? Ida Rüdiger would have no use for a scribbled-over image. Nowhere does Kugler identify the girl, unless I can infer something from the address of a modelling agency in Pankow.

Another question: why was the hour of the meetings so regular, week after week? It reminds me of the appointment you make with a physician, a dentist, a masseur.

Lovers' trysts are carved out of the day whenever one can make it, especially if there's a jealous lover still on the scene.

What follows is pure and hasty conjecture on my part, but I am pressed for time (the week is nearly up). Nebe will not keep me here for ever, and I could be called back to the front at any time. I try not to dwell on it, but that's what I'm dying to hear: I am consumed by anxiety for my men. My place is in the field with them. They know I didn't want to leave, no matter how fond I was of my late uncle.

As I say, it's pure speculation, but here is what I think:

The girl in the photos is the same I've heard about elsewhere

– Bora did not write that he had read about her in Niemeyer's delirious letter to his lawyer –

She regularly visited Niemeyer once a week (for a hypnosis session?)

Kugler's interest (or rather the interest of those who really hired him)

– Bora omitted "possibly Heldorff, or others" –

predates the contract with Ida Rüdiger, and may have the same motivation (jealousy?), or a completely different one

It's crucial for me to stop by the hairdresser's today. I would be wise to phone her beforehand to make sure she's home, but I don't want to give her fair warning and risk that she stays away on purpose. 12:34 p.m. – time to go, before Grimm gets back to the hotel.

# 10

*Survival is just one aspect of the struggle.*

HANS BERND GISEVIUS, *WHERE IS NEBE?*

LEIPZIGER HOF, 1:32 P.M.

Sitting in the lobby with his back to a fissured and expertly
patched-up bow window, Bora knew from the way the sunlight
bothered him that he was running a high fever. For years, he'd
been somatizing anxiety; if premonitions had been merchan-
dise, he could have sold them wholesale. Grimm should have
been here already, but was still away on his errand. Eppner
might have been transferred from Kripo headquarters, or
Kupinsky's body fished out of the Spree ... However, Bora
was ready to discard the excuse of bureaucratic snags. What,
then? His misgivings did not go as far as that. Despite being
practised in mental censorship, he kept bumping against the
same troublesome consideration: meetings at the Führer's
headquarters never began before midday, and usually lasted no
more than one hour. Should Stauffenberg act today, it should
be over just about now. Apart from the activity he'd imagined
more than detected behind the wall of the garrison barracks,
nothing in fact warranted his feeling of alarm. SS and army
vehicles were around, but not in a state of alert. The officers
he'd seen did not look apprehensive. Civilians went about
their business as usual. Hard to tell what happened inside
army schools. They were great, impenetrable, silent buildings.

*Still, if today is the day, after the fact they need to take the city,
block all communications and neutralize the SS and police. Only the
army can do so, but it will need reinforcements from outside Berlin.*

*This would require two or three hours, which dilutes the surprise factor. Of course, you can give the alert early and disguise the movement of troops as an exercise.*

The north-western Berlin quarters teemed with barracks. There were the army schools at Potsdam and Döberitz, the Prussian Military School, the Reserve Army troops ... By marching left and south from its quarters on Ziegelstrasse, the Greater Berlin Military Police Battalion could head straight for Unter den Linden. The Berlin Guard battalion Grossdeutschland was housed in Moabit, a bit further out on Kruppstrasse, where he himself had attended the army's Staff College, north of the Olympic Stadium.

Who headed up the battalions these days? Politically aligned, they did not strike him as the kind of outfits that participate in a coup: unless you convince them that their armed intervention (against other Germans!) serves to *prevent* an overthrow. It'd happened a decade earlier, when the SA was beheaded in one fell blow, with the excuse that they were plotting a rebellion.

Bora tore himself from such subversive thoughts. Unless Grimm had been maliciously sent from pillar to post by the Gestapo, he was grossly overdue. Did it mean anything? And would any conspiracy succeed in consigning the police to their stations and headquarters? The bright yellow fabric of the sofa danced before his eyes. He'd take a quinine pill, if he thought he could keep it down. He forced his mind back to the subject of Walter Niemeyer.

*Keep your sights on him, Martin. It's all about what happened that evening. Imagine the scene. Gifted or not with second sight, Niemeyer is calmly leaving his evening bath when he finds a hunting rifle pointed at him. How could it happen? Easy.*

*Whomever he worked for, a man like Kugler could find his way in; any policeman or former policeman, SS man, Gestapo agent or intelligence officer knows how to open a door without forcing it. I'm capable of it, too. I, too, have done it.*

*It all happens so quickly, Niemeyer has no time to react. The first shot brings him down (so says Olbertz), the second finishes him off (or is unnecessary). Then it's just a matter for the killer to sneak out (with or without stealing or searching for something first). That same night, Ergard Dietz dies at the hand of Russian runaways, so useful because we can hang on them all sorts of crimes. And what about the faceless blonde, with her migraines and compromising revelations? She has already left Berlin – unless they've eliminated her. Possible? Possible. Dr Olbertz, Uncle's friend, grew very alarmed when we exchanged barbs about dangerous visitors.*

Bora's mind wandered to dangerous subjects again. Could Olbertz, too ... ? How many officers, how many civilians in Berlin were somehow peripheral to the great wheel of a conspiracy? *Nebe could have picked me to penetrate the plot and beat his colleague Heldorff to it ... or to prove his implication in it. But even if I am external to the intrigue, I cannot betray my brother officers. How can the chief of the Kripo not suspect me? Goerdeler, on whose recommendation he supposedly chose me (?), has been accused of political unorthodoxy for years. In that case, Nebe's game could be even more nefarious.*

Three minutes to two o'clock. Bora could no longer sit still. He wasn't hungry, but went to have a late bite in the deserted Leipzig hall, after which he left the hotel on an errand of his own.


LANDGRAFENSTRASSE, 3:16 P.M.


Ida Rüdiger was dressed to kill. The plunging neckline dropped so temptingly between her breasts that it was impossible for Bora not to steal a glance. A wide-brimmed hat with a cluster of silk poppies sat on her coiffure; in her hand, a hatpin with a garnet head seemed long enough to stab him in the heart, if she got that idea.

"I didn't expect to see you again," she huffed.

Bora apologized. *I thought she was on her way out, but she's just come back. She's overheated, there's perspiration on those impressive teats of hers.*

"Only a couple more questions, please. Herr Niemeyer held private hypnosis sessions at his home, isn't that so?"

Perhaps because her lover's duplicity was her obsession, she saw through his enquiry. "Yes, but not for women."

"What does that mean?"

"It means that his hypnosis sessions were reserved for male clients."

"Why?"

"Why?" Ida Rüdiger dabbed her bosom with a tiny handkerchief. "Because I insisted on it." She nodded towards the stack of magazines on a shiny credenza. "Open any of those at page 6, where the advertisements are."

At random, Bora chose a periodical whose coloured cover featured a winsome girl scaling – God knows why (if not to show her thighs) – a street light. The advertisement in question occupied the entire bottom of page 6. It announced hypnotherapeutic sittings and consultations "on professional matters and matters of business, debility, mental fatigue, et cetera". A note in bold specified: "Only for a distinguished male clientele."

"It does not say who the therapist is," Bora observed.

"Of course not. It would be gauche for Dr Prof. Magnus Magnusson to run his advert next to those for depilatory cream and hair lotion. You'll notice the address and phone number correspond to Villa Gerda's."

"Yes, I see that."

"Call it a small victory, Colonel. We'd broken up, but Walter kept to the rule, at least officially."

Bora nodded. If so, it was even less likely that just any girl could be a client in that sense. Was she well known, which was why Kugler erased her features? Or rather, was she the wife or lover of a powerful man? He wondered whether Kugler had shared the photos with Ida Rüdiger (he didn't think so), and for the moment he made no mention of them.

"May I keep this announcement?"

She looked at the back of the page to see if there were any articles she meant to save. "Not this one, but you can tear the page from another magazine. The advertisements are all the same."

Bora did as she said. Ida watched him awkwardly tear out the page with one hand.

"You know, I put the fear of God into that minion of yours," she said.

It was easy for Bora to smile (and he knew the effect his smile usually had).

"But *I* do not suspect you in the least, madam. I recognize my mistakes when I commit them."

With enviable precision, she tossed her hat across the hallway into a dainty armchair.

"Are you trying to tell me, then, that there was one woman in particular? Was Walter killed by one of his sluts?"

Her reaction suggested that Kugler had kept the photos to himself.

"I mean to find out. Incidentally, why did you fire your investigator only in late May, if you'd met Niemeyer for the last time on the sixth?"

Grown impatient with his fumbling as he tried to fold the page up with one hand, Ida Rüdiger snatched it from his fingers and did it for him.

"Here." She eyed him knowingly. "Questions, questions. You're army intelligence, aren't you. Or used to be. See, I've known men in power for a long time; you don't pull the wool over my eyes."

"I'm not army intelligence. Why did you fire Gustav Kugler only in late May?"

"Because I was still curious about Walter's doings, but Kugler was getting nowhere. In three months, all I got were five lousy pictures of a brunette meeting Walter at this or that café. Her, I knew of. She is an extra at the UFA Studios. The same who left her underwear behind, which was a pleasure to burn in the tub of the guest bathroom – just as I burned her pictures."

It did not sound like the girl in Kugler's photos. In a wig, maybe …

"Tall?" Bora asked.

"What do you mean, tall? She's little more than a midget. I don't know who killed Walter, but one thing I can tell you: with or without women, he'd started getting in trouble from the day he passed himself off as a Jew."

The unexpected comment made Bora think of a question so impertinent that he hesitated to pose it. But she was a worldly-wise woman. It was enough for her to hear a neutral "Speaking of which …", to take up the subject.

"Naturally. If, during the autopsy, they wondered why he had that ugly job done to him, know that it happened in Cairo, before the war, because of an infection he got who knows from where. Jews have nothing to do with it."

"Well, his first autobiography was rather convincing."

"*Up from the Shtetl*? Rubbish. You don't really think I'd fall for a Jew! Walter did say that he really had lived that life, though. Another life, understand? A previous life."

Bora didn't comment on the fact that Niemeyer had carefully avoided the subject in his amended autobiography as a Scandinavian sage.

Before he could step away, Ida Rüdiger cheekily walked around him, as if to judge his haircut.

"Starchy *and* hidebound," she taunted him. "If you discover that it was a female who killed him, let me know. I want a front-row seat at the trial."

Only the modelling agency whose card he found in Kugler's folder (Thulestrasse, on the corner of Schönhauser Allee in Pankow) was missing from his list. Bora, still annoyed by Ida's familiarity, chose to call from a nearby telephone booth. He introduced himself generically as the admirer of a girl who had given given him that number, adding that he hadn't heard from her in some time.

"I was wondering whether she's in."

Laughter came from the other end of the line.

"We don't run a boarding school here! We take fashion photos; lots of girls come and go. What's the name of yours?"

"Well, she never did say. We only met one evening."

"Can you describe her, at least?"

Bora did his best, based on Kugler's photos. "Please understand: I *have* to see her. I'm going back to the front tomorrow."

"Sorry. Your description fits several of our models. Without a surname, there's no point. Maybe if you give me yours …"

Shamelessly, Bora continued the fiction. "She doesn't know it, either. I said 'one evening', but one *night* is actually what we spent together. I'd love to see her again before I leave."

Which, thinking of another girl, was the only detail that came close to the truth.

This time, there was a sympathetic pause. "Well, there *was* a girl who left without notice, but she's been gone from Berlin over a month. She didn't even pick up her cheque for the last photo shoot. Not that she wanted for money, if you get my meaning. I don't wish to disillusion you, but the young lady did not need the job. She came to work in a private chauffeured car. That is … if I were you, I would not get my hopes up. No, I can't give you her name, the information is private. If you care to have some pictures of hers as a keepsake, buy the June issue of *Berlinerin*. I think she's featured from page 16 to page 19. Sorry. Good luck at the front."

Bora hung up. A private car? In Kugler's surveillance notes, he'd read *private car – different chauffeurs – leaves her at the corner of Lebanonzederpfad – picks her up 1 hour later, parking no less than a block away.* That was all. The number of the licence plate was not recorded: why? An investigator would always jot down a foreign or diplomatic plate too. Unless, of course, the car bore an unnumbered plate, the privilege of ministers and top officials.

He walked to a newspaper stand across from the telephone booth. The June issue of *Berlinerin* had sold out, but the seller indicated a better-equipped stand not far away. Bora went over to it, and once he'd secured the magazine he flipped it open on page 16.

The title of the photo story was "Do You Really Know Her?"

How fitting. The girl was no doubt the one shadowed by Kugler. Posing under flattering lights, she enjoyed the sort of exposure one was able to admire in peacetime periodicals, and even in *Signal* and other military monthlies at the start of the war. In July 1944, such extravagance seemed very much "after its time". Nineteen black-and-white poses occupied three full pages. In every one of them, the same unnamed model – between twenty and twenty-five years of age, Bora estimated – wore different make-up and headwear, from a toque to a tiara to a farm girl's chequered kerchief. In one, she sat with a thread of pearls around her forehead, like a woman in a Renaissance portrait, in another she mimicked Marlene Dietrich, in a third one she reminded Bora of the Soviet film star Lyubov Orlova in *Volga, Volga*. In these days of drastic paper shortage, publishers would not grant such space to just any girl.

Bora put away the magazine in his briefcase. *Damn*, he thought, *if fair Helen's face "launched a thousand ships", this could be the face of someone who in her imprudence can send us all to the gallows. Forget Bubi Kupinsky, drowned (or not) in the Spree! If what Niemeyer wrote to his lawyer is only half true, not even the bones of this dumb blonde exist anymore.*

Bora then phoned his hotel. Still no Grimm, and no messages from him. He left word at the front desk that if Inspector Florian Grimm or anyone else came looking for him, he could be found at the Catholic church on Winterfeldtplatz.

ST MATTHIAS'S, SCHÖNEBERG, 4:18 P.M.

He did not pray, did not think. He simply sat in the refreshing twilight of the papist church Bismarck had allowed them to build in arch-Protestant Berlin, until now spared by the war.

Years earlier, while attending the Military Academy and when he worked for Canaris, he used to come here to listen to organ music. Today, a handful of elderly people were kneeling in the first rows, whispering the rosary together.

Bora stared at the main altar without seeing it. Nothing could keep him from thinking about the storm circling oppressively over their heads. Even without the enemy at the gates, out there Germany's fate was being played out – at least, the attempt was afoot. He didn't know what to wish for.

When an elderly priest approached him and asked if he was waiting for confession, Bora realized that he'd been sitting opposite a confessional. He shook his head without opening his mouth. *I cannot tell him that I haven't the slightest desire for it.* In Rome, he'd gone back to attending mass and taking communion, mostly because he worked as a liaison with the Vatican, and churchmen make you buy a ticket if you want to talk to them.

The priest slowly shuffled to the main altar, genuflected in front of it and joined the rosary group. The muttered Latin words reached Bora like the droning of bees. "*Stella matutina … Foederis arca …*" – as if the Mother of God really were a star heralding daylight, or the repository of an irrevocable, eternal pact.

*What is irrevocable? Everything is falling apart.* Bora made the sign of the cross – deliberately, unlike most men, who are furtive about it – and left the church as disquieted as when he entered it.


LEIPZIGER HOF, 5:34 P.M.

As it turned out, Grimm phoned ten minutes after Bora walked back into his hotel. There'd been a delay, the policeman said concisely, this was the earliest he could call. Unwilling to conjecture the cause of the delay, Bora kept his part of the conversation down to monosyllables. He waited for Grimm in the lobby as if he'd done nothing else all day, with a selection of newspapers around him. To his left, elbow to elbow on a small sofa upholstered like all others in bright yellow, sat three laughing Bavarians of the type that would not lose their job or good humour, not even after a coup d'état, the perfect fellows to be found chatting with.

Only after more than an hour did Grimm enter. In a bad humour, and with the look of a battered draught animal expected to show up for work even with a broken head, he explained that a practice alert had held him up. He added no details, and Bora did not ask for any. Once he'd blamed his tardiness on the service, Grimm did not apologize for leaving the officer without a car and without information, but the awkward gesture with which he handed him the Eppner papers did it for him.

"A fine state of affairs. You left me without a car and without information. I wasted nearly an entire day." Bora knew when to play the Prussian. He jumped up from his seat, put his cap on and grabbed his briefcase by the handle. Brusquely holding it out towards the policeman, he said, "Carry this, at least."

A contrite Grimm preceded him out to the car. "Where to, Colonel?"

"Where *can* we go, at this time? I have to review the watch-maker's file. What about Glantz?"

"The chief himself is seeking his release back to us tonight. There's news about Kupinsky as well."

Bora's antennae went up. "Did you find him? Dead or alive?"

"I wish. Looks like the queer faked his suicide, and is on the lam. We got a tip-off and missed him by this much." He pressed his fleshy thumb and forefinger tightly together. "It's only a matter of time before we catch him."

It was not the news Bora wanted to hear. *Now there's a poor bastard I should have killed, to save everyone worse trouble.* Kupinsky in the hands of the law, or God forbid the Gestapo, could unravel matters more quickly than Benno von Salomon. "Are there new charges against him, other than that he's escaped while on probation?"

"Fleeing while on probation is indicative of something." Grimm sat at the wheel, waiting to be told where to go. "I wonder if we underestimated him."

In his view, Grimm had a point. By comparison, Eppner's deposition was bizarre. Bora read how, unlike Glantz, the watchmaker at first succeeded in pleading his case for possessing a pistol and keeping it concealed in his house, thanks to the presence of a former Foot Guards official at Kripo headquarters. The question of the foreign worker Paulina Andreyevna Issakova, staying at his residence against all regulations, proved harder to resolve. However, what complicated matters was the sworn statement by one of the guests at the birthday party that —

"What?" Bora interrupted his reading. "Someone decided not to support Eppner's alibi?"

"Worse. It seems Eppner made some disparaging remarks about our air force that evening, and not only that."

Bora read on. During the party, due to the conviviality and bootleg alcohol, the conversation around the table became unguarded. Complaints were voiced by everyone whose house or business (or both) had been bombed in June. Everyone had probably pitched in, but once news of Eppner's arrest had surfaced, a guest rediscovered his patriotic strain and spontaneously showed up at Alexanderplatz to help to sink him. The Luftwaffe was only one of the branches of the armed forces berated by the host, and the government itself hadn't been spared.

"At the moment," Grimm said, as he loosened the knot of his ugly tie, "he's out of our hands at the Sachsenhausen concentration camp."

That, too. What an idiot Eppner was, and what a can of worms … Bora put away the folder, feeling unhappy. Two days to go, nominally at least, and no solution in sight. He was dying to know what had delayed Grimm at headquarters, but the policeman seemed intent on keeping mum about it.

"Back to Kupinsky, Colonel – now that we know that he isn't feeding the fish in the river, we can't deny he's the cleverest of the four. Why, the communist queer could be a sly cold-blooded killer. I've seen my share of murderous weaklings."

"Yes, well, at this point anything is possible."

Grimm seemed to be angling for ideas that would be welcome to the officer, or cheer him up at least. "Should I drive to the watchmaker's main shop, in the city centre? We're running late, but it's on Krausenstrasse, and we might catch Frau Eppner behind the counter."

It'd be a miracle if she hadn't been arrested too, and their three shops requisitioned. Convinced that there were too many trees, and that barking up any of them was turning out to be a waste of time, Bora said yes anyway.

The shop – which he recognized after Grimm parked in front of it, because he'd gone there once with Dikta, who'd fallen in love with a gold watch in the window and then typically changed her mind about it – was about to close for the day. Grimm sprinted with unexpected zest from the Olympia to keep the shop clerk from rolling down the shutter all the way.

When Bora joined them, he heard that Frau Eppner had moved to Nassenheide to be closer to her husband. She'd engaged Ronge to plead his case and save the family business from being seized, and that's all he knew.

Ronge (one of the intimidating names in Ida Rüdiger's calling-card collection) was a star-quality lawyer, likely to cost the Eppners all they had anyway. With an annoyed wave, Bora recalled the inspector, and off they went the way they'd come.

Shortly after eight Bora ordered Grimm to leave the Olympia with him. Grimm could not object.

"Just in case more exercises or bombs intervene. Is there enough fuel?"

"The tank is nearly full, Colonel."

"Good. See you tomorrow, at eight sharp."

It was little more than a pulling of rank on his part. But if, as he believed, the practice alert had signalled a last-minute scrapping of Stauffenberg's plan for the day, Bora was curious to go see what went on among the General Staff officers who might still be housed at the Adlon. He waited until Grimm's tram chucked away, and drove to Pariser Platz.

Right away, he noticed that Namura was still out. The key to his room was hanging behind the concierge's desk. Downstairs, a glance around confirmed a sparse presence of officers having dinner. At the table, so full of brass in the past few days, sat four colonels with a blank look on their faces, as if a train long awaited had left without them. If it hadn't been a real practice alert, unrelated to the conspiracy, theirs was the despondent attitude of men whose hopes have been dashed or once more delayed.

What could have gone wrong? Hitler was famous for changing his schedule. His chief ministers – who would have to be wiped out with him to achieve any real success – might have been absent from the meeting. Bora replied with a mere glance to the head waiter's welcome, signalling with a gesture that

As always, Bora checked the locked door leading to the adjacent room. He then went to sit in the bathroom in order to be able to keep the light on and reread Kugler's notes. It was true what Grimm had said, he wasn't much of a note-taker. Photos of the girl, dates of her visits to Niemeyer and a few additional words: everything else he had to figure out on his own. The post-mortem report Olbertz had given him was the next document he took in hand. A decision to omit Niemeyer's circumcision from the official version – irrelevant to the case – would have been taken at the highest level, per-haps even higher than the Kripo chief's. Grimm himself was clearly unaware of the detail, as the victim had a towel wrapped around his waist. The original autopsy contained all that was summarized in the second version, plus the shameful detail and the victim's fall against the small table. Bora remembered the gaudy elephant-shaped brass fixture from the photos of the scene of the crime. Shining the torch on a close-up, he could detect small traces of the victim's blood on one of the elephant's tusks – not that a bruise on the face would make a difference to a man who was dead before hitting the floor.

The second brandy came, which he poured into his tooth-brush glass with the first shot, giving back the empty glass. It was too early to go to bed. Taking advantage of the availability of hot water on Saturdays, he took a long shower, shaved and got dressed again, though he didn't put on his boots or button his tunic. He then filled the tub with water (it took for ever, the tap was only flowing weakly) to make sure that he had enough in the morning, in case the service was suspended overnight.

Towards eleven thirty, the three wails of the first air-raid warning sounded. At the same time the power went out across the neighbourhood. Waiting for the second alarm, Bora patiently followed the routine, making sure that the windows and doors were open. He still felt feverish, disin-clined to leave the room, and resolved not to take alcohol or medication before lying down in his bed. Quinine brought about sweating, and a ringing in the ears, neither of which he looked forward to.

The frantic triple whine of the second siren (bombers were drawing near) brought about the shuffle and footsteps of the hotel guests descending to the air-raid shelter. They'd recently built one under the hotel, Bora knew, but the safest choice was the monstrosity not far away, across the square on Pallasstrasse. By this time, the German Women should have gone home, unless their celebration had ended after the curfew. In this case, they were still at the Leipziger Hof, and he could imagine a troop of possibly tipsy skirts entering a shelter where men and women huddle together in the dark. Instead of amusing him, the idea made him melancholy.

When he heard a rap on the door, Bora did not catch himself thinking "Gestapo" only because he'd had it in mind for the past three years and was aware that the next knock on the door could be the last one. He readied himself to make an excuse for not going downstairs. Nevertheless, he flicked on the lighter's flame, because it was his habit to look into the face whoever came into his presence, especially at this hour.

It was Emmy Pletsch, in uniform. Emmy Pletsch, whom he'd thought of during the day. Emmy Pletsch, who lived far from here, and who suffered from claustrophobia.

"I can't go down to the shelter, Colonel. Do you mind if I stay?"

He remembered he'd given her his room number in the tram, when he'd asked for an interview with Stauffenberg. Was she a member of the German Women's Association, surprised by the air raid in the hotel? Very likely. Still, she'd come to *his* room.

No mistake, no accident. It was night-time; there was only one bed. Nonetheless, Bora said, "Please", and stepped back to let her into the room. Careful not to show that he understood perfectly, he offered her a chance to think it over and change her mind; that was all.

Emmy was panting a little, from running up the stairs – or maybe not. Avoiding his eyes, she stepped in and sat on the edge of the bed. Out in the hallway disgruntled and harried people were still hastening past the door, so Bora blew out the flame of his lighter and sat next to her.

A minute or two went by, during which the building became deadly quiet. Outside, through the open windows, searchlights fingered the dark, their unbending shafts moving like northern lights, or soundless summer lightning.

Bora had to watch himself, because the girl's closeness excited him and he was tempted to try a direct approach. When she asked if she could wash, he grew hopeful but kept up the pretence for her sake.

"Yes, of course. There's hot water tonight, or there was until half an hour ago. The tub is full."

"Thank you."

Emmy stood up and moved easily in the dark, accustomed, like most Berliners, to frequent power outages. Bora thought back to his wandering through the house at night as a child, playing a game of dexterity that would become so useful later, during the war.

Through the open bathroom door, he heard her taking off her clothes. He avidly recognized the nearly imperceptible rustle of the discarded jacket and blouse, the quick whisper of the skirt zip opening. Women undress in a meticulous fashion, thus Bora could make out the progress of her disrobing. The question was, how much would she take off? No other sounds followed, so she was not bathing. She must be simply standing there.

His mind followed one route, his body another. Prudence met desire head-on. Everything slowed down, became dense, it was like finding himself in a fluid that lazily flowed against him, through which he advanced, mentally numb, while the physical part was anything but asleep. Whatever might follow the air-raid warning, death included, this was here and now.

Bora closed and locked both doors to the hallway, pulled the blackout curtains across the windows. Quickly, he removed his uniform down to his underpants, which he habitually slept in. He felt for the condoms in the bedside table drawer, took one out and rested it on the marble top.

Barefooted, Emmy came back lightly, sure of the few steps between the bathroom door and the bed. She once more sat down next to him. Bora would be able to tell by embracing her whether she still had something on, but he waited for her to move close enough to graze his thigh. She, too, wanted to know if he was still dressed. All he had to do then was run two fingers around her shoulder and, without hesitating but also without hurrying, down to her hip, to realize that she'd removed her underwear as well.

*How good a girl is she?* He circled her waist with his arm and let her rest her head on his chest. They remained that way for perhaps half a minute, during which their breathing accelerated. *Is she ready for it?* Bora took hold of her by the hollow of the nape – just below her hairline, in the very place, he absurdly thought, where a sudden twist of the neck can kill someone on the spot. They started kissing, and to his surprise Emmy was a good kisser – this at least she'd learned from Leo Franke.

It went on for maybe a minute more, during which he became increasingly impatient at her simultaneous lack of resistance and reluctance to give in, her shivering and unwillingness to go beyond kissing.

"Please," she said at one point, "do you have anything strong to drink?"

Bora knew exactly where he'd placed the brandy on the bedside table, and stretching out his hand he found it nearly at once. Their hands touched when he gave her the glass. He heard her anxiously gulp down the liquor, like someone unused to alcohol. He tasted the woody aroma on her tongue when he kissed her again.

All Emmy did was snuggle up to him. Wasn't she a proper girl, and he a decent man? Bora felt far less well behaved than usual, but knew that women – except for Dikta – often did not like to be rushed; so he timed himself according to her breathing. Gently, he laid her on her back, and leaned over her to keep kissing her.

The all-clear sounded, but he did not hear it. The room was hot. Both were sweaty – Bora feverish – but perspiration can be apt and even pleasant, at certain times. Emmy was awkward, all knees (Bora thought he must have been like her at fifteen), and lay there with her ankles tightly crossed. Rather than presume that she was ready, he judiciously let his hand slip down her body to ensure that, physically at least, she'd gone past her mental reservations. He was by now eager enough not to want to think beyond tonight. His underpants were the last to go. He felt the first moisture, and it was time to wear a prophylactic. He hadn't used one since losing his left hand, but this, too, he had practised. With his teeth, he carefully tore the package of the *Blausiegel* army condom, which was dry and felt dusty and only slipped into place without effort because he was already damp with excitement.

Unpredictably, as soon as he entered her she had an orgasm, so he had to start her all over again, mindful that he had to hold back in order not to turn aggressive. She tasted like sweet almonds when he kissed her, when he ran his tongue down her neck.

He recognized a girl untaught by her lover beyond kissing, perhaps on purpose. Emmy was submissive and clumsy, as some female students he'd made love to in his university days. It was possible she had never had anyone before or since Leo Franke, before tonight. Well, what a surprise: she *was* a good girl. Bora kept it simple and was patient, which was a change from Dikta and unexpectedly pleasant; rewarding, even. He heard himself telling her, "Easy, easy. Just let me," as one would with a skittish mare before a hurdle. When, after a while, she grew more adventurous, he could afford some vigorous insistence without scaring her. *I am not corrupting her, I am teaching her. Perhaps Dikta thought the same when she spoke to our sister-in-law.*

If he thought of the immense, deadly trouble he'd got himself into, the best thing he could do was lie without love alongside this appreciative girl. Without love, it was still gratifying. That she wanted a man was reason enough for her, and for him it was a release of tension after his drunken binge in Rome, when he'd taken – to this day he didn't know whom – into his hotel bed. What a consolation to lie here and simply do it because both parties needed it. *I must not think of how accomplished it was with Dikta, it's over. That lovemaking is over.* But Emmy smelled and tasted like sweet almonds, a pleasant scent and such a lovely flavour.

Was she thinking of Leo? She whispered "my love" a few times, but in the throaty, careless way women do when they're in bed, even with a stranger. Bora certainly didn't. Dikta was the only one he'd called "love", in or out of bed. It'd take more than an hour or a night together for him to use the word with another.

Energy, experience and a good dose of frustration made him perform well, and the dark helped. Not just because of the hand, as Lattmann had imagined – the rest of him more than made up for it, and German women would have to confront their men's wounds as a fact from now on. No. It was because in the dark you can make the kind of physical love that doesn't encourage looking at each other. Dikta and he had made love looking into each other's eyes, loving each other first with their eyes, as they'd done from the beginning. The warning in the gospel, that looking "on a woman to lust after her" was already adultery, had surely been true of Dikta and himself. *If it ever happens again,* Bora thought while this naive young woman clung to him, *I'll know I'm over Dikta. Until then I will make love in the dark, or not look them in the eye.*

\*

Afterwards, she fell asleep next to him. For her, too, this must be the epilogue of many sleepless nights. Bora left the bed. Reserving the tubful of water for Emmy, he washed himself thoroughly (he'd learned how to wash well with little water), and disposed of the used prophylactic. Dustbins in Berlin must be full of Aryan sperm these days, whatever the Führer preached. It seemed as fitting a commentary as any on their collapsing world. Everything made sense around him – it was once more this place, this night, and in between there had been a sexual encounter that had done him a lot of good. Something like a veil had fallen off his ability to concentrate.

Bora went back to bed. He slept little but well, and when he awoke at dawn Emmy was still slumbering. In the twilight of the room, she lay on her side with her left hand between her thighs, in a protective pose, or – on the contrary – as she'd fallen asleep on many nights, perhaps, fondling herself to calm down.

LEIPZIGER HOF, SUNDAY, 16 JULY, 6:20 A.M.

Decency required that he went downstairs before her, giving her time to get ready and follow discreetly. Bora noiselessly unlocked both doors and left the key for her on the bedside table.

He did not expect to find, at this unsociable hour, Benno von Salomon standing outside his door in a dressing gown.

"May I come in?" The same urgent tone, midway between an order and an appeal. Relieved as he was to see him at last, Bora found the intrusion unacceptable.

"You may not, Colonel."

"Is someone there with you?" Bora's face indicated that he would not say, so Salomon grew demanding.

"Why, is there someone in your room? Are you meeting with someone? Who is it? Let me in."

Bora interposed his full height, pulling the inner door closed behind his back. *Imagine if he were to find a girl in my room who he might have seen, of all places, at Bendlerstrasse ...*

"I prefer not to, Colonel."

Suspicious and agitated, Salomon might make a scene; Bora swerved him in the direction of the stairs. "I assume you booked a room here, sir: let's go to your quarters."

For a moment, Salomon baulked.

"If we must. My room is down the hall. Follow me."

Bora followed him closely, to keep him from raising his voice and allowing them to be overheard. The colonel's room – windows closed, curtains pulled across them – was still dark. Salomon switched on the screened bedside light. "They think I'm gone from Berlin, but I've been hunting everywhere for you for days."

"You have? I was under the impression that you were making yourself unavailable."

"Look, there's no time for recriminations. Time is awfully short and I absolutely need to get out. Out of Berlin, out of Germany. I need to do it *today*." He stood there with his short, greying hair uncombed, spiked by sleep and sweat, like dog fur. "If you know what's good for you, you'll find a way to get me out."

Any appeal for help rightly belonged with the plotters. Did Salomon fear that *they* would silence him for good? Bora knew he'd have to act on it soon, one way or another. What was intolerable was the arrogance of his demand. It insulted him. "Are you still in the regular employ of the German army, Colonel? Because if you are, to speak in these terms is treason."

"Oh, do me a favour, leave these lexical idiocies alone!"

"It was you who asked me whether I knew the meaning of terms like loyalty, and so on. I *will not* help you defect, Colonel von Salomon."

Salomon must have anticipated these formal objections.

"Yours is a family with diplomatic ties," he pressured him. "The embassy of a neutral country will do, a foreign legation … Must I spell it out for you? If I do not leave German soil, *no one can depend on my keeping silent.*"

Frowning, Bora faced him, caught between egotism and a crushing sense of duty. The unwelcome meeting threatened to mar his euphoria after the night with Emmy. She would soon wake up and go down for breakfast, and he wanted to be there. Christ, he hadn't felt so well in many months, and this tormented man had shoved reality in his face. Far from feeling anything that resembled pity, for a remorseless moment he contemplated the feasibility of shooting Salomon there and then. Expedient and definitive, yes, but highly impracticable. It could not be done.

Yet he could not risk losing track of him again.

"I trust you." Salomon held his ground with an energy born of despair. Pacing at the foot of a bed identical to the one Bora had just risen from, he repeated, "I *trust you.* Should anything go wrong with the scheme … should they miss their target … the pressure is unbearable. I'm in your hands."

Bora squared his shoulders. "Very well," he said, after a pause that seemed what it was not – a prelude to acquiescence. "Meet me tonight at eleven at the corner of Lutherstrasse and Augsburger Strasse, in front of Horcher's." As he gave him the restaurant's address, Bora had no clear plan as yet; or rather, he only had one, chilling in itself. "Come in civvies, alone."

Salomon repeated the address like a hopeful schoolboy. "In civvies. Alone. Does that mean you will help me?"

"For the moment, it means that between now and then you must refrain from asking questions, and from meeting anyone else."

"Promise me you'll help, and I will not leave this room all day."

"If you trust me, Colonel, there's no need of promises."

Staff Leader Pletsch came down for breakfast with other young auxiliaries and members of the German Women's Association. Seated at his corner table, Bora nodded a greeting to her group. She was as reserved as ever, with that face of a girl whose thoughts are elsewhere. Her companions seemed particularly solicitous towards her this morning. Why? Had she told them anything? He was determined to take his time and have a word alone with her as soon as the others left the table. Grimm would not be there before eight, so there should be time enough.

Bora made his ersatz coffee last for ever. Within half an hour, when Emmy was the only one left behind, he joined her with his all but empty cup. "Good morning."

"Good morning."

"May I sit down, Staff Leader?"

"Please do."

The dining hall, down here below street level, was lit artificially even in daytime, but the slight redness around her lips, from kissing, was so telling that Bora thought, *I could bed her again, if she let me.*

"Are you off to work?" he asked.

She looked down as he spoke.

"Not today. And you?"

"In twenty minutes."

They were once more addressing each other formally, sitting across from each other as they'd done at Die Dame. Both were blushing. Except with Dikta and Remedios, Bora had always felt a little ashamed after making love. *She and I may be facing each other properly, but she knows what's in my breeches, and I know what's in her pretty cotton knickers.* But he liked to rise after a night of sex as he did from the table, with some appetite still unappeased. *Yes, I could bed her again if she let me.*

He was unprepared for what Emmy told him next. "Leo died during the night."

Her lips went a little tight as she said it, the corners of her mouth drawing downwards, like a child about to cry.

"When during the night?"

"It doesn't matter. Whenever it happened, I wanted to be where I was."

"I'm very sorry, Emmy."

Using her first name created that little intimacy again, although neither of them knew what use to make of it now.

"The worst thing," she said, "is that in ten years …" Her tears came down without sobs, she was disconsolate. "I haven't even made a child with him. Now I have nothing."

They were whispering to each other. In wartime, you saw many such moments, when emotions come through in conversation; the handful of uniformed men sitting around the hall paid no attention to them. Bora watched her with the peculiar sense of helplessness men feel when women weep.

"I understand," he said. "Far better than you can imagine." He did not consider that his next words could be misconstrued – or perhaps he did. "Is there anything I can do?"

Words have power. Emmy stopped crying like a little girl nursing a hurt, and held her breath. The hall where they sat seemed to fall away, along with the tables and the handful of uniformed men in their chairs, the sepia images of the Pauliner church and the Café Français … When she looked up, Bora saw that the source of her strangeness, the subtle colour difference between her eyes, was nearly gone. Reluctance and yearning no longer divided her against herself.

"Yes," she said slowly, returning to him the key to his room. "Yes. There is."

Bora felt dazed. He could imagine his friend Lattmann telling him, "That's not what I meant, when I brought the two of you together. Are you out of your mind?" *Well, yes. Things are falling apart, and I am out of my mind.*

"I very much would like to," he said.

A number of latecomers were entering the hall for breakfast, including the matrons of the German Women's Association. Bora and Emmy left the table separately, only to stop on the stairs leading up to the lobby. They exchanged an army salute, and then, overcome by a desire to kiss, they did so quickly, with that crazy promise between them. They did not want to change their minds, so it had to be done soon, as soon as possible.

"Before noon," she said in his ear, "because after that I no longer have a reason to postpone my reassignment from Berlin. My train leaves shortly thereafter."

Bora could think of nothing else in the minutes leading to Grimm's arrival. He did not reason beyond the act in itself, as if there weren't a host of possible consequences other than the one he and Emmy had in mind. As if impregnating a girl whose thighs he'd had to coax open just hours earlier (*delightful, delightful*) were not the most untimely and inconsiderate proposition he'd entertained, aside from fantasizing a marriage with the very much married Mrs Murphy. Eleven was the time they had agreed on, the place being the room a colleague of Emmy's had moved out of two days earlier, at Marika's house a block away from one of the Charlottenburg train stations. Bora would go there now and wait for her, were he not carrying the burden he'd been loaded with by Nebe on the one hand and the conspirators on the other, with Salomon's fate on top of it all.

At any rate, his fever was gone. There had been a moment during the night when he actually felt it leave his body. As if sexual relief had the side effect of opening a deadlock in the investigation that had kept him physically burning until now. A chink in the oppressive, airtight circuit of Niemeyer's murder had become a gaping door while he lay fully relaxed at Emmy's side. How had he not seen the solution? It'd been right in front of him for days.

It was high time. Risk – of the deadliest kind – was something he was prepared to brave in the next few hours to prove his point. Fantasizing about leaving something of himself in the belly of a willing girl placed the seal on his readiness to die. Lieutenant Colonel Namura would approve.

He walked out to place a call to the Adlon from a public phone, with enough time to spare to have Grimm find him standing in the lobby with a cigarette in his mouth.

The inspector looked like someone who'd come bearing news. He immediately claimed the Kripo's success in negotiating Frau Glantz's and Gerd Eppner's release from the Gestapo. Before nightfall, both would return to their Alexanderplatz cells.

"What about Roland Glantz?" Bora enquired, while Grimm opened the car door for him. The day was already sultry. At this hour, Emmy Pletsch was riding in the crowded tram, with that blonde nape of hers a little damp with sweat, and with her secret. "Eleven o'clock, at Marika's," she'd repeated, running up the stairs from the breakfast room. "Don't forget." As though he could.

"What about Glantz?" Bora repeated, censoring his thoughts as if Grimm could read them. At most, as a henchman trained to read men's faces, he could sense that he'd had sexual intercourse from the different and diminished quality of his tension. But lovemaking was not yet forbidden in the Reich.

"Not yet," Grimm admitted, as he wedged himself behind the wheel. This morning he wore a tie that exceeded all others in garishness, with blotches of bright blue and green, and ink-black outlines of tropical palms. "The chief is still working on it. It is *our* inquiry," he groused, although it remained to be seen what more they could squeeze out of a man condemned to die.

Inside the Olympia, the heat was intolerable. Seat and backrest felt like fire, and so did the wheel, judging by the way Grimm's paws tapped it a couple of times before grasping it firmly.

"There's an additional piece of news, Colonel," Grimm said, even before the usual "Where to?", and Bora understood that it had to be something significant.

"Tell me."

"It came in just minutes ago. They fished out a body along the Osthafen. Male, twenty-five to thirty years old. No shoes."

"Kupinsky?"

Grimm shrugged to indicate that he didn't know. "That's his old neighbourhood. It'd be best to go check."

Despite the open car windows, his overheated bulk let out a fat man's reek. No matter how clean they are, Bora thought, the obese still have that smell, and they're the first to be conscious of it.

From Kleist Park they took Göben, heading east. It was a daily trial finding one's way among closed thoroughfares, recent cave-ins, working crews busy repairing gas and water mains. You forgot how quickly you crossed Berlin on the underground, or skirted its limits on the train without delays or stops.

Bora didn't know whether he should want the drowned man to be Kupinsky. The last time he'd seen him, edgy but thankful to be rid of Niemeyer's letter, he'd judged him ready to sink back into the anonymity of wartime Berlin – though not literally.

"Was he the sort that was likely to commit suicide?" he asked.

They were driving past the massive turn-of-the-century gasometer, for the past two years used as an air-raid shelter.

"Nah," Grimm said, without moving his eyes from the road. The gauze taped to his head threatened to come loose in the heat. Sweat implacably streamed down his face, so that he had to keep wiping it with the hairy back of his hand. "But you can never tell for sure."

Bora nodded. He saw his partner in a different light this morning. He felt he understood him more, and no longer needed to wonder whether he could trust him. Both had experienced Russia, even if in different ways. There, one learned the value of human life, even when that value was nothing.

From Hasenheide, they turned left onto Pannierstrasse, past the Catholic church and the city warehouses. In front of this or that shop, queueing housewives fanned themselves or quarrelled, and old men sat on benches blandly staring. The river port Grimm and Bora were headed for lay beyond the Treptow bus depot, where long brick buildings stood in various stages of decay. The Spree wharf north of the small public park had been severely hit during the past winter, even though the number of civilian casualties was almost equalled by the loss of lives among the enemy flyers. Here and there, green spaces that had been well kept until the air raid were now overgrown with weeds (poppies, mullein) or had been seeded. In a long, fenced bed, lettuce and graves vied for a place in the sun.

A police car and an ambulance were visible on the bank. The rank stench of the water and swarming insects welcomed them at the spot where the body had become anchored. A policeman reported that an employee of the nearby rails had discovered it at seven in the morning.

"Must have been in the water for a couple of days, so it isn't easy to figure out where he fell in. He had a letter in his pocket."

Without betraying himself, Bora felt his heart leap. What if there existed other copies of Niemeyer's letter to his lawyer, or other dangerous messages? If the dead man was Kupinsky – if Kupinsky carried such letters on his person – it could spell disaster. He furtively looked at Grimm, to see the expression on his face.

"What sort of letter?" the policeman enquired, impatiently.

"The water's nearly destroyed it. It was handwritten."

"Where is it?" It was Bora who asked this time, and the policeman handed him a limp sheet of paper which the sun was quickly drying.

Grimm looked over Bora's shoulder. "Did you find it inside an envelope?"

"Yes, but the envelope was open, and there was no address on it."

The ink, black veering into brown, had nothing to do with Niemeyer's distinctive purple. Bora breathed more easily. The text was brief, a few lines, scrawled and illegible. Likely a farewell note or an explanation. Not even the signature was readable.

"Did he have other papers on him?"

The policeman led them across a patch of debris-strewn earth to where the body lay.

"Only a train ticket and a frilly pocket comb."

"Could be Kupinsky." Grimm quickened his step.

But it wasn't. It was an emaciated young man in undershirt and trousers held up by an army-style two-pronged belt. His shoes were missing, and so was half of his face.

"He must have floated against the jetty's cement beam as he emerged near the bank. There, Colonel, see."

Bora wondered whether he was feeling sad. Ever since Spain, and without ceasing to kill as a soldier, he'd been melancholic in the presence of death. Every time, it had seemed a waste to him, if not a tragedy. At least, that's how it'd been until Stalingrad. In Stalingrad, he had lost count of the dead, and nearly his sense of pity.

"He's not the man we're looking for," Grimm told the policeman. "Ours is missing three toes on his left foot."

"Ah … Well, if he's a cripple, it stands to reason that he'd kill himself," the policeman said, unthinking. Bora pretended that nothing was amiss, even though Grimm warned his blundering colleague with a glance.

In fact, Bora hadn't taken any offence. He was so relieved that, for now, no other compromising letters were floating around, that the quip came to him spontaneously.

"Some cripples can swim. Those will have to shoot themselves."

\*

Back from the Osthafen, any remaining sense of humour left Grimm and Bora when they punctured a tyre. Grimm worked on it, wheezing like an ox, after removing his shoulder holster and rolling up his shirtsleeves. As if that weren't enough, they were stuck for nearly an hour on Dieselstrasse, where the Landwehrkanal bent southwards, due to the discovery of incendiary bombs in the debris. Impatiently, Bora left the car to find out more from the working crews and stayed away a good half an hour, during which Grimm saw him wander among the ruins.

Out of the blue, while they waited with wide-open doors in an absolute absence of shade, Grimm said, "Are you feeling all right, Colonel?"

"Yes. Why do you ask?"

"You seem – I don't know, a bit under the weather."

Now, if there was one thing Bora was sure of, it was that he did not look under the weather. It'd take more than a night of sex to make him look peaky the following day. He judged it a gratuitous and spiteful remark, which might have the magical effect on others of making them actually feel tired.

"I feel just fine," he snapped back. "And, unlike you, I don't suffer in the heat."

But he probably *did* look anxious. He couldn't wait to call Emmy and confirm their eleven o'clock date, and needed to find an excuse to get away from Grimm. As minutes trickled by, he betrayed himself by constantly glancing at the watch on his right wrist. He obviously had a choice between being asked whether he had an appointment somewhere, and openly volunteering the information. In the end, he said, crossly, "I must place a personal call."

"Let's go back to the hotel, then."

There was no complicity in Grimm's tone, nor could there ever be. No solicitude, either. Had Bora told him he needed to buy matches, the policeman would have commented in the same tone of voice.

"I don't see how, the road is blocked."

"I'll drive you to the closest underground station."

Emmy's girlfriend lived in the neighbourhood of the clinic on Sophie Charlotte Strasse, at the northern edge of Charlottenburg, so Bora did not care to return to the hotel, which was quite far away from it. "Take me to the nearest working phone booth, please."

The girl whom Bora only knew as Marika – a nurse – answered the call. She fretfully told him that she'd tried to reach him at the hotel for the past hour. Emmy's train had departed earlier than expected.

"She'll be leaving about now, Colonel ... From the Westend station, that's where."

Bora called up the station. It wasn't a large one, but he could imagine Emmy being called to the phone over the loudspeaker, in the confusion of people coming and going ("Calling Staff Leader Emma Pletsch ..."), and her hastening to a phone where she could talk to him.

At the other end of the line, her voice was so broken with tears that he could barely make out what she was saying. He understood that her train would move out at any moment; her trunk was on board already, there was no time.

"Oh, Emmy. I'm very sorry, Emmy."

They were the same words he had spoken in the morning, only now he meant them.

"Don't forget me," she sobbed, and hung up. The girl in uniform, whom he wasn't supposed to like, the awkward girl with the strange eyes who was as irrationally ready to have a child as he was, was leaving Berlin for God knows where. *I'll never see her again*, Bora told himself, full of sorrow. *And we will both forget last night, and each other.*

Berlin looked lonelier and emptier; death felt closer than it had five minutes ago.

\*

He was despondent, but didn't want Grimm to see him like that. It took him a few stormy minutes to regain his inscrutable demeanour, but he knew himself all too well – sexual frustration had already played tricks on him (in Poland and Brittany, and elsewhere), and the aggression he normally kept under control was rising dangerously close to the surface. He could say the wrong thing, or do something foolish. What kept him lucid was wondering if Emmy had been spirited away from Berlin because the coup was imminent. A national alert could be declared at any time, and he would be caught in the bloody repression to come, regardless of whether the coup was a success or failure. After all, Salomon was still footloose, and was threatening to squeal.

In his flustered state, he switched from thinking *At this moment, I should be making a son with that girl,* to *A catastrophe could happen any moment now. Forget Emmy Pletsch.* Still, Emmy Pletsch was foremost in his mind; how she must be feeling, boarding the train without seeing him again. *She'll find another. If that's what she wants, another man to make a son with, she is sure to find him. But it could have been the two of us. Against all reason, Emmy and I could have been each other's life.*

When he returned to the car – parked in the shade, Grimm standing next to it with the knot of his tie loosened and a lit Trommler in his mouth – Bora was once more master of his nerves, and had made up his mind about the next step.

"Did you get through, Colonel?"

"I did, thank you."

"Roadblock's been cleared."

"Good."

Before they resumed their way, Bora stored the briefcase he so seldom parted with in the boot of the car.

At the intersection with Braunauer soon thereafter, he prevented Grimm from asking where they should be heading. "You know," he said in a conversational tone, all too aware that his aggression longed to find a target, "I am re-evaluating some of my ideas about the case. You and I may still have some doubts about Glantz's guilt, but the fact remains that he confessed."

"That's what I think, too."

"But there's a possibility we've disregarded so far."

Grimm looked over at him. "Are you thinking of the watchmaker?"

"No."

*Emmy is travelling away from Berlin. Before nightfall, we could all be hanged.* How many times had he chosen to keep colleagues and co-workers (or prisoners being interrogated) in suspense, with his way of hinting and not telling?

Grimm was too shrewd to fall for it. "Well, Colonel, if you have someone in mind, out with it. We've been at this for a while."

"I was thinking that we've kept Gustav Kugler out of the list of suspects."

"*Kugler?* What does Kugler have to do with it?"

"I'm not sure. I'm simply considering the possibility of his involvement, that's all."

"Excuse me, but I fail to see how he could be involved. Aside from Glantz, remember that Kupinsky disappeared from circulation. Considering that he breached his probation, the queer must have had a good motive for scampering off."

"I agree."

"And if he didn't jump into the river, Colonel, then he's holing up somewhere. As a matter of fact, if he's hiding, for whatever reason, I think I know where to find him."

"You do? Why didn't you tell me before?"

"Because I thought Kupinsky was the drowned fellow."

As far as Bora was concerned, the best thing would be for Kupinsky not to surface at all. Once in the hands of justice, he could prattle nearly as dangerously as Salomon. It might be wise to follow Grimm's lead.

"Enlighten me."

Grimm spoke of a once famous hideaway used during the chaos at the end of the Republic. "Reactionaries and communists kept visiting it off and on even afterwards, and later it became an occasional shelter for Jews and other kinds of criminals."

"Why don't you tear it down, then?"

"It stands on the grounds of an old imperial estate; folks from the art school or whatever kept us from demolishing it. We nailed the entrances shut, but you know how these things go. You can't control every inch of the territory."

"Let's go, then."

"I should tell you it's a ways out of Berlin."

"Do we have enough fuel?"

"As for that, we do, plus an extra can in the back."

The Köpenick area, enclosed by long lakes and the meandering river, had long been a mecca for vacationers. Before her marriage, whenever she was in Berlin Dikta used to come boating here with Willy from Hamburg. Puschkin Allee had kept its charm; the villas and summer bungalows deep in their green gardens, thus far spared by war, belonged to a different planet. But Bora's was a soldier's view of the world. In this or that large house, he anticipated the setting up of a German (or enemy) command post; in the monuments – one the solemn and ugly Bismarck Keep – he saw landmarks to dismantle before Russian infantrymen used them to orientate themselves. The peaceful vistas only spoke to him of war.

As for the Reds' hideaway that had galvanized Grimm's interest, it was in fact an eighteenth-century observatory at the edge of the old Köpenick forest. The place was appropriately (and literally) called Sternwarte, a lookout for the stars. Generally, Grimm said, they called it the Tower, because such was its aspect. More than anything, it resembled a stubby belfry with ornate and pointless late baroque string courses.

How many constellations the amateur astronomers of two centuries earlier had hoped to survey in the foggy climate of Brandenburg, it was hard to fathom. Perhaps the building had merely been an Italian-style *capriccio*, allowing its visitors to gaze at the horizon, at the red-roofed, tall-domed skyline of old Berlin.

It sat isolated in a deforested area, bordering a property of the type broken up into smaller estates at the end of the eighteenth century, and possibly turned into public space after the Great War.

It belonged to a hunting lodge, rather than a chateau, on which an enemy bomber – back from a raid with one of his engines on fire – had randomly dropped the load still stored in the belly of his plane. This, Grimm explained with some satisfaction, had not saved the pilot. He pointed the skeleton of its fuselage out to Bora, already half-buried in wild creepers. At the far end of a long patch of cleared land, from here it seemed an elongated, humpbacked ridge.

Of the hunting lodge, only the ruined walls remained. Neatly cut ashlar and other architectural fragments had been hurled more than half a mile all around the crash site. Bora did not doubt that the observatory, long abandoned, served all kinds of rendezvous. The political ones were probably not in the majority. Given its nearness to the shore of the lake and the moorings for leisure boats, it'd been – and most likely still was – a haven for quickies, not necessarily between members of the opposite sex.

"The entrance seems to be barred," Bora said, preceding Grimm towards the construction. "There's a window in the rear we could climb through."

As it turned out, the window, too, was nailed shut. Bora, who out of habit didn't like having someone standing behind him, stepped aside so that he could watch the policeman's shoulders.

"Kupinsky would never be able to scale the structure to the second-floor opening, and the grid wouldn't let him through."

Standing knee-high in tall weeds which had evidently not been disturbed in days, Grimm grumbled, "Waste of time."

In the ruins of the hunting lodge, they did find traces of recent occupation: the ash of small fires lit in the nooks of the walls, discarded prophylactics and human excrement. Grimm looked around with his nose to the ground, flipping this or that rock with his toe, as if someone could be hiding underneath it. The sole object of any interest – but useless to their search – was a handsome metal plaque with the Köpenick municipality's seal on it: two fish facing right and left of the key of St Peter, with the seven stars of the Pleiades. Whatever it'd been nailed to once, bombs had yanked it out without destroying it.

# 11

*As above, so below.*

SAYING ATTRIBUTED TO HERMES TRISMEGISTUS

1:45 P.M.

It was close to two in the afternoon by the time they resumed the trip towards Berlin, after a stop in Marienhain to have a bite and secure some bottled water. Then Grimm remembered that they had recently caught runaways and other undesirables in a raid in nearby Rotberg. It turned out to be another wild goose chase; and that's how they found themselves on a lonely gravel road under a pitiless, vertical sun, still outside Berlin, with only a railway crossing for company.

Grimm was pouring water into the radiator. On both sides of the road stretched rapeseed fields just past their bloom, which must have seemed like a pale golden sea two months ago. Bora didn't know where they were, or how far out of the city. He forced himself to control his breathing, slowing it down to calm himself as he used to do before school tests and horse trials. As he relaxed he grew hot, but strangely not hot enough to break out in a sweat. It seemed centuries since he'd sat across from his mother at the Adlon, and since Willy Osterloh had insulted him (though not nearly as much as Duckie had, later). Emmy would soon be far away from him, and not only physically. The Italian front seemed furthest away of all, in time as well as space.

When Grimm had ensconced himself once more behind the wheel, Bora casually said, "Honestly, Inspector, if we weren't colleagues in this investigation I'd begin to suspect

371

that you've taken me far away from Berlin in order to get rid of me."

Grimm had been busy blotting the sweat from his face before starting the car. He must have heard Bora, because his eyelids flickered. But for a moment he didn't look at the officer.

"Is this a joke?" he said then, neither turning towards Bora nor addressing him by his rank. "If this is a joke ..." But he remained sitting there, without starting the motor.

Bora smiled, giving the impression of half-joking camaraderie. "Well, I sensed that my mentioning Kugler offended you. I understand, we all feel a certain esprit de corps. Of course, I would be well advised to fall into line with the idea of Glantz's guilt. We have his weapon and his signed confession, and he's destined to lose his head anyway. Between you and me, though, I believe that your ancient colleague could be the real culprit."

"Now *that*'s a joke."

"Why? He was watching the victim for some time, and knew his routine, and given his profession I imagine that he knew how to pick a lock without anyone seeing him."

Even without closing his eyes, Bora could imagine Emmy's clean scent of sweet almonds.

"Last night, things became clear to me. Kugler could definitely have killed Niemeyer. Not with the Drilling rifle we recovered, of course, but with a comparable weapon, of the same calibre – say, a Mauser G98 of the GeCa or GeHo type, modified into a twelve-gauge, common in the Weimar days – but one which we may never find. Unfortunately, his death leads us into a blind alley, which we can only get out of by going back the way we came."

As Grimm listened, a thick odour of sweat rose from his body; its sourness, however, was different from the one it'd had on previous days, or even that very morning, and it had nothing to do with the exertion of changing a tyre. Insecurity and fear give sweat an acrid quality. Whatever his thoughts were, he brooded on them as he tapped the steering wheel. Bora remained on this side of friendliness but kept an eye on the glove compartment, where he knew the policeman stored a second gun.

"I don't know about that," Grimm said all of a sudden, after sitting there for a while like a volcano about to explode. "Come to think of it, it *is* a possibility. As you say, we have Glantz's confession, though in a way it would make sense if the Rüdiger woman were behind it. She hired Gustl Kugler, and even if he lost his life in an accident, we've got *her*. The thing is, what with her friends in high places and good lawyers and all, she may be untouchable. I see why you'd go with Glantz. But I thought you said you would not present the chief with a merely convenient solution."

"Sometimes we have to say things we don't mean."

That was the extent of Bora's reply. Grimm, who had expected specifics and received none, leaned back in the driver's seat as far as his frame allowed. Bora watched him attentively as he took a pack of Trommler from the glove compartment, pulled out a cigarette and put it in his mouth. With a nod, he asked Bora if he would care for one, and Bora said yes.

Outside, the daylight was blinding, yet at the same time washed out; it was too hot for birds or insects to chirp in the rapeseed fields. There was a solitude that both men remembered from Russia. They smoked in a leisurely way, looking away from each other like two people who find themselves in a confined space without having anything to talk about. Grimm stared at a spot somewhere between himself and the fly-spattered windscreen. Bora gazed out of the window without taking in any landmarks or other details. It was like looking into an oven, yet he felt something like a vein of ice forming inside him. He remembered a quarter in the outskirts of Kharkov, inhabited by artists after the October Revolution; his father's old lover spying on him from behind a silk screen. It was in her garden that he had stopped to chat with her

Russian maid, the young widow whose upper lip was so prettily beaded with perspiration. It was in her garden that he had killed in cold blood.

Even with the windows open, he could smell the reek coming from the whale-bodied Grimm; but he didn't hold his breath. He had a hunter's instinct, even if he had never hunted animals. *Or perhaps not*, he told himself. *I have a* predator's *instinct. The fact that I am occasionally mistaken for prey does not change things.*

Tossing the still burning cigarette butt out of the window, Grimm took up the conversation again. "I don't know how you could ever prove Kugler's involvement, Colonel. If it really happened as you say, I'd be curious to hear how you came to such a conclusion."

Bora leaned forwards to extinguish what remained of his cigarette under the sole of his boot.

"I'm suggesting that it wasn't Ida Rüdiger who hired Kugler – or, rather, that she did not hire him to do what he did."

That was all the explanation he gave.

Grimm was losing patience. "Well?" he snapped, "Christ, I've been driving you around for days all over Berlin, looking for a solution. I believe I have a right —"

"I will present a complete report only to the chief."

"But I don't get it. Any one of the four suspects, the queer included, is a better candidate than Kugler!" Grimm cleared his throat, and kept frowning at that spot somewhere between himself and the windscreen. "Anyhow, Kugler is dead. Without a motive, a weapon or a murderer who can be prosecuted, you have nothing. An expert policeman like SS Group Leader Nebe will never accept that."

"Somehow I'm convinced that Chief Nebe will hear out my hypothesis."

"Whatever makes you think that?"

"Let's just say that I am further along in this investigation than you think, Inspector. It is a known fact," Bora added, though it was something of an exaggeration, "that in the Weimar days Gustav Kugler did the quick-and-dirty work for the establishment."

Grimm forced a laugh. "Is that what you meant by 'moon-lighting'? I don't know where you dug up that story, but you still lack a motive – the ABC of police work!"

"As for that, I believe the motive was unknown to Kugler *and* to the man sent after Kugler to clean things up. *Selbstreinigungsaktion* – 'cleaning up after oneself' – isn't that what they call it?"

"This is pure nonsense. With great respect, Colonel, I can't begin to think why the chief chose an outsider like you for this job … You're just scrambling for ideas."

It seemed to Bora as if he could touch death if he reached out his hand, and he felt unspeakably serene. "Why didn't you tell me that there was another version of the post-mortem? I know there was, I read it."

"So what? You read that Niemeyer had the Jewish cut done on his dick? Glantz told us that too. It was decided to omit the detail because he'd been so popular in political circles – there'd be a scandal if word got round."

"That was the one point that got my attention, actually." The friendly expression on Bora's face remained unchanged. "I should have paid more attention to the other omitted detail: the cut on Niemeyer's face. I don't believe that he struck his jaw on that tacky brass elephant when he fell. I think he was surprised in his own home, defended himself, and his assailant punched him. When he staggered back, he was shot at close range with a twelve-gauge slug capable of slaying big game. The second round was unnecessary – he was already lying dead on the floor."

"Surely you read in the post-mortem that his blood was found on the brass elephant?"

"Please! You're a professional. A practised killer only needed to dip two fingers in the blood and smear the sharp angle of an object to account for the injury." Bora took a deep breath. "If, as you said, Gustl Kugler's moonlighting days were over, that is not to say that yours are. What if I tell General Nebe that Kugler did it and you cleaned up after him, like in the old days?"

"*What?* You can't be serious! You forget I'm an official in the Criminal Police. I never even met Ida Rüdiger before this investigation!"

"It's interesting that you should point this out, instead of denying that you killed Gustav Kugler."

"Enough is enough. If this is not just idle talk, I won't stand for it, Colonel von Bora!"

"Which is not a denial."

Grimm flushed angrily and blasphemed, something that never failed to annoy Bora. "What's got into your army head? I did not kill Kugler. Kugler was a has-been, killed by some whoring husband in a back alley. Admit it, Colonel, you're at your wits' end and haven't the faintest idea of who killed Niemeyer."

"But I do."

"Of course – *Kugler.*"

"No. I said he *could* have done it. His guilt is plausible; his death points to there being an organizing mind behind it all. The alternative is that *you* did it. Either way, from my point of view the only snag is that you cannot provide me with any useful details. You were simply following orders."

"Now you've overstepped the mark."

"And what will you do – shoot me? *That'll* take some explaining to General Nebe!"

Lightning-quick for a fat man, Grimm swept out the gun from under his coat, only to feel, by its weight, that it must have been emptied – including the round in the chamber – while he changed the tyre. He then reached for the reserve Mauser HSc in the glove compartment; discovering that this, too, was empty, he dug into his pocket for his PPK. Bora let him.

"Inspector, isn't it enough that you had to play the role of the man who sweeps up after the horse parade? I've done it myself, and it's no fun even when you're told why. That's how things stand. That is the low opinion they have of you. You could shoot me and toss me in a ditch, but I am not exactly a Russian peasant, or a former pal, or an illusionist who once pretended to be a Jew. If you shoot me, you'll have no excuse for your superior, who entrusted me to you. You could run, hide, kill yourself. But you could never go back to Alexanderplatz."

"Ha! Get off your high horse, Colonel. Regimental commanders with the Knight's Cross are a dime a dozen in Berlin. They won't even miss you. You know the routine: start by handing me your gun."

Bora's plans were less fully elaborated than he cared to admit. He could only try to gain some time.

"That gauze plastered to your head," he demanded to know, "is there really a cut under it, or was the bomb hitting the house merely an excuse to spy on me unseen for a couple of days? I think you were at headquarters, manhandling Glantz so that he'd confess, and that you struck him in the jaw just as you did on the day of his first failed suicide – only more violently. That deadly gold ring of yours does plenty of damage and draws blood ... just like the blow you inflicted on Niemeyer before shooting him."

"*Hand me your gun!* By God, if I can waste a fake Jew with millions in the bank, I can waste a crippled army fuckwit. But not in the goddamn service car."

It was just like a Party minion not to want to mess up a service car. Bora slowly edged his hand towards his holster and unlatched it.

"No, wait. I'll do it." Grimm's thick fingers lifted the Walther P38 by the grip and tossed it on the back seat. With the stubby barrel of his PPK, he gestured for Bora to get out of the Olympia. "And don't try to run."

Bora did as he was told. The brightness and heat of day dazzled him. Unknown as the place was – an ordinary rail crossing, along an ordinary gravel road – there was something familiar about it that he tried to recall. He had no idea what. Grimm kept the gun on him as he came around the car, squinting in the sun. *If he drove all the way here to shoot me, it's because he understood that I was on to him. For all I know, he foresaw that I would be on to him even before I was. Is that what I'm trying to remember?*

"Do you have any notes on you?"

Obviously Grimm meant material about the murder case, in addition to what he expected to find in Bora's briefcase *afterwards.*

*He could just search my body after shooting me,* Bora thought. *It has to be that last scrap of respect for uniform and rank that makes him ask me to hand them over myself. I have no notes on my person. It's all in my diary, or in my head.*

"Yes," he answered nonetheless. "In the inside pocket of my tunic."

Grimm did not trust him. Chest and armpit were the perfect place for a hidden holster. He approached Bora without letting go of his gun. "Unbutton your tunic," he ordered him. "And now take it off."

A moment's delay on Bora's part caused Grimm to change his mind: after all, even without a holster, a handgun can be easily stored inside one's clothes. He lunged at the officer to prevent him from trying anything while he removed the garment.

There was no hidden gun, but it was the opportunity Bora had waited for. He struck Grimm's wrist with the edge of his right hand, a blow from below violent enough to send the small, ugly PPK flying. They both dived and scrambled for it, where it had fallen on the tracks to the left of the crossing, where the rails were slightly raised above the road. They crashed hard onto the rock-filled trackbed. Bora came down on his left knee, which had been wounded months earlier and never quite healed. Such blinding pain shot through him that he came close to blacking out, and in the dimness of things he wondered how anyone could be hurt so much on the tracks of a German line, groping for a gun. He clung on to consciousness to keep Grimm from getting past him, because nothing would keep Grimm from opening fire.

They rolled around, bruising themselves on the merciless spikes and edges anchoring the rails, driving each other face down on the splintered sleepers and the sharp rocks piled up between them. His build and height usually spared Bora from having to play the role of the underdog, but Grimm was heavier; Bora could not gain the upper hand. He struck and was struck back, and was viscerally enraged by the pain, as if what depended on this scuffle was not the solution of a crime (what did he care about Walter Niemeyer? Less than nothing) or even his life, but the destiny of a whole generation, his generation of disciplined yet rebellious young men. He and Grimm didn't want the same thing: Grimm wanted to seize the gun so that he could fire it, while Bora merely wanted to wrest it from him. *I must remember, I must remember ...* Excitement and numbness alternated, made worse by the ringing in his ears brought about by the quinine. He wanted to grab a rock and smash Grimm's head with it, but had to use his right arm in an effort to avoid being killed. Before, too, during other frantic moments of extreme duress, there would come to him the sense that there was something he urgently had to remember, yet there hadn't been always actually been something for Bora to recall. He caught sight of the PPK, wedged barrel-down in the ballast, where Grimm could easily reach for it, so he strained to turn the policeman over on his back like a gigantic insect. In so doing, he fumbled for, found and grasped his obscenely loud tie. It was a risky move, because his left arm, hindered by the prosthesis, could only keep Grimm at bay, not restrain him. Hastily, Bora wrapped the artificial silk around his right fist, at the same time pulling at it with a jerk that would break any man's neck.

Not Grimm's. His bulk resisted both the yank on his throat and Bora's attempt to overturn him; it was like trying to subdue a bull intent on destruction. Bora suddenly found himself in even greater difficulty when the policeman shifted the massive load of his right leg over him, nailing him to the ground – the situation seemed desperate, and fatal. Holding on to the tie as to an animal's leash was all that Bora could do. He inched his hand up the twin lengths of cloth, twisting them together, closer and closer towards his adversary's gullet. Still, he was unable to prevail. Winded, drenched in sweat, Grimm crushed him with all his weight, all the while creeping closer to the gun. Bora could only hang on to him and try to slow down the policeman's crawl. *I must remember ...* He found it hard to breathe; a well-placed kick would send him tumbling down the railway embankment. Were it not for the excruciating pain in his left knee, he'd already have slipped into a semi-conscious state, and then anything could happen. A blow on his temple made his head ring; blood droned in his ears; he felt the heat of the steel track under his cheek, the nauseating odour of grease, dirt, metal, wood. Crawling over him, Grimm came within a hair's breadth of the gun.

It was then that Bora let go of the tie. The sudden release made Grimm recoil enough for Bora to beat him to the gun with a thrust of his right arm. He could only just reach the gun, but it was enough to enable him to toss it away. He didn't know if it had landed on the other side the railway crossing, or perhaps somewhere else behind him. He only knew that he'd snatched it from under Grimm's fingers and thrown it.

Numb, fatigued by the heat and the pounding they'd given each other, they collapsed to a stop. But Bora was younger and – if that were possible – the angrier of the two. *I must remember, I must remember ...* He rummaged for and finally got hold of a rock from the trackbed, the most primitive of weapons. The action of raising himself on his knees to strike triggered such agony in his left leg that the blood drained from his head. For an instant he went cold, and everything turned black; when he could see again, Grimm had raised himself to a crouch, holding another such weapon in his powerful fist.

Both, however, wanted to get hold of the pistol, rather than stone each other. *I must remember something ...* Severed from all that had been until this morning, and all that ever would be, Bora hazily understood – as if it mattered, at a time like this – that only if we grasp everyday reality can we truly perceive ourselves. Without it, we're incoherent and adrift, filled with pain and anger, and we wouldn't even know what it is that they are filling. He knew that his left knee would give way the moment he attempted to put his weight on it. Helplessly, he watched Grimm skulk along on the tracks searching around for the gun, sniffing with his bleeding nose and sucking on his bloodied lips, until at last he sighted it, on the other side of the tracks.

Bora crawled after him. He despaired of being able to outdo him this time, when he couldn't even overcome the pain enough to pull himself up. He perceived neither landscape, nor sky, nor anything else around him – only the deafening roar of his blood pumping in his ears, and a complete indifference to anything other than Grimm. Grimm rose to a crouch again, letting go of the rock, and stretched towards the place where the gun lay.

*I must remember something ...* Bora made a frantic effort to stand, and stumbled back.

The pressure wave and the ear-piercing racket of the train barrelling past a few inches from him knocked him down again.

Flying rocks, dust, heat, the shock of hitting the ground at the foot of the bank – Bora would have wept with the pain, if he could have. In a hallucinatory flash, he imagined that he saw the fluttering of the variegated American tie disfigure the air; but there was nothing there. He slumped down by the trackbed, whimpering through his teeth while the terrible butcher's cars from the Ukraine, laden with animals bound for the abattoir, took Grimm away, leaving him alive.

He averted his face so as not to see the train thundering by. Not because it was running over Grimm, but because it was carrying innocent animals to slaughter, as millions of human beings had gone to slaughter in the past five years. *I'm a witness – I'm a witness – I'm a witness …* said the din of the train, scraping along the steel tracks, drowning out everything else.

He dragged himself back into the Olympia. He couldn't estimate the seriousness of his knee injury. The joint wasn't broken, he knew that much. The tendons? The ligaments? It hurt like hell, and as his tension relaxed his left arm also began to ache. *It will pass,* he told himself. *It has to pass.*

Handfuls of dust and an unbearable heat entered the car from the open windows, from the open door. Sitting in the passenger seat, Bora was embarrassed to find that regaining his breathing was proving such a challenge, and also about the anguish that came upon him. The tracks up ahead seemed like the edge of a world, upon which Death had literally placed its seal. Whose bloody wax was what remained of Florian Grimm, chewed up and dragged along the tracks that led to Berlin.

Providing a nearly unbearable contrast, delicate wild flowers grew at the edge of the trackbed. Wild chicory, hawkweed. The same blooming weeds also grew in Poland and Russia, along mass graves that Bora had photographed unobserved, sinking to his ankles into the soft earth, where taps and roots were intertwined with human hair. Beyond, like a sight inconceivable until this moment, lay the landscape in which he found himself: a serene, undulating horizon, sparsely dotted here and there with houses. He made no effort to try to understand which villages they might be, or which outer suburbs on the city's furthest periphery.

He closed his eyes. While at the sanatorium, sitting across from his friend Lattmann, the blinding glare had been benign, but now there was no comfort in not being able to see. His next moves, crucial as they were, seemed as out of this world as this sunlit, green area of cottages and fields. *I could remain on this side, and not cross over.* But going beyond things was what he'd always done, not caring about boundaries.

When he looked up at the sky again, a high, cottony cloud lazily approached the sun; soon it would conceal it, obfuscating for a moment the splendour of the day. The tips of the wild flowers barely vibrated; his breathing, though not the pain, was under control.

Only now did Bora realize that his cap was lying on the gravel road, where he'd lost it earlier. It seemed miles away, but once he was able to bear the pain, he would reach it in four or five steps. Now that the train was speeding indifferently on to its destination, silence fell like an enormously heavy tent collapsing. From the car, Bora detected shreds of red mush and cloth, a shoe, and a more recognizable tattered something ten or so yards further along the railway crossing. He was ready to wager that the conductor, a Ukrainian prisoner of war or ethnic German, dog-tired after the endless trip, hadn't noticed that he had killed a man. He fought against crying out as he got out of the car. Once he had retrieved his cap, he hobbled around the Olympia to reach the driver's door, tossed the sweaty cushion on which Grimm had sat into the back, and took his place behind the wheel.

Wearily, he buttoned his tunic. He felt around for and recovered the P38 from the back seat; he then removed this and that object from the glove compartment, pocketing one and tossing the other out of the car.

*God help me,* he thought, *the 2:30 westbound train was what I was trying to remember. Did I count on it, subconsciously? There was nothing else I could count on. Ever since Kupinsky's neighbour told me about her boyfriend working overtime at the slaughterhouse, I've been thinking of those daily trainloads of Ukrainian cattle, at seven and at two thirty ...* Bora was suddenly horrified by all this. *Does Nina know that there are moments like these in my life? How can she not loathe sitting across from me? But maybe Nina loves me because I am bad, loves me only because I need to be loved.*

Clenching his teeth against the pain, he started the engine and drove across the railway crossing, and followed the road signs for Berlin. *It is by no means certain that I will live through the night,* he admitted to himself. *Not certain at all. However, the thing must be brought to a head.*

The impending storm whose threat he had felt even before landing at Schönefeld stifled the afternoon air. Caught up in all too concrete matters, Bora had tried to ignore it during the last few days. Now, heading for a hospital to have his injury checked, the sensation surged back again. What in God's name would he tell Nebe? Until this morning, he'd been able to visualize how he'd begin, once he was standing before the man who'd charged him with the investigation: "I have come to the conclusion ..." Now, try as he might, the necessary report refused to yield even a first word.

Before re-entering the city limits Bora stopped by a farmhouse, because he spotted a soldier in the yard, an old-timer in the Emergency Corps's blue-grey uniform. The fatherly type, with a second worldwide war under his belt. Boldly, Bora told him that he needed to clean himself up and straighten out his uniform. Whatever excuse he came up with ("an accident" covered a multitude of credible scenarios when you wore a lieutenant colonel's collar badge), his appearance spoke for itself. The old man let him in and supplied him with water and towel, and even volunteered to brush his sorry-looking tunic for him.

While he stood by a rickety washstand, washing himself thoroughly with home-made laundry soap, Bora overheard the wife tell the farmer-soldier in the other room, "Poor lad, think what the war has already done to him."

The earnest words hit home, without offending him. *It's not defeatism when they feel sorry for you. If these folks only knew where I was half an hour ago! In the same day, I have gone from being a crippled army fuckwit to being a poor lad. It has to mean something.* The wife made ersatz coffee, which Bora drank gratefully, remaining on his feet. His knee was beginning to swell, and sitting down to drive the rest of the way would be a challenge. Before leaving, he asked the old man to help him transfer some of the extra fuel from the jerrycan into an empty water bottle, so that he could use it later to remove grease and grass stains from his uniform.

Crossing Friedenau, a police patrol stopped him in Schillerplatz, only to let him go again at once. They'd seen him with Grimm before – the licence plate might be known to those guarding the roadblocks and have been given special clearance. His papers and passes did the rest.

Although it was Sunday, at the Red Cross hospital on Landhausstrasse, in Wilmersdorf, Dr Ybarri was on duty. The only sign of his Latin hedonism were a couple of young nurses, better-looking and more sociable than nurses usually were. When he heard that the officer who gave him a ride a few days earlier was waiting outside his door, the Chilean immediately let him in.

Even more than by his frazzled appearance, he was surprised by the fact that Bora addressed him in Spanish. The Germans who had fought in Aragon and Castile during the Civil War had seldom learned to speak it.

He replied, in Spanish, "*Que pasó?* What on earth happened to you?"

Bora gave him a somewhat modified account of what had happened, describing it vaguely as an accident. Without adding any details, he said that he'd got hurt in a fall, which to a certain extent corresponded to the truth.

Ybarri studied the bruises on his knuckles. Looking him directly in the eye, he said, "That ecchymosis on your thigh …", hinting – though he wouldn't say so explicitly – that he doubted the ridiculous excuse of a fall. "What were you carrying in your pocket?"

Bora was not about to tell him that he'd stored the PPK magazines and chamber rounds there, to hide them from Grimm.

The radiologist didn't insist on knowing more. He personally radiographed Bora's left arm and leg, after which he gave him the usual talking-to physicians had reserved for him ever since September: "Don't tax your knee; there's a limit to what you can do while you're convalescing …" – things Bora knew already, and advice he ignored as soon as he could.

He gathered that he had a bad contusion on his left elbow ("But if it goes back to hurting in earnest, it'll be because of the mutilation") and a battered and sprained knee.

"It will hamper you for a while, colleague. Ice packs and rest is what you need. I'm going to inject you with a painkiller, and apply a bandage that will allow you to function as best you can. But when you go back to your command, or wherever it is that you work, make sure you see a specialist."

Nodding in agreement, Bora was already thinking of his regimental surgeon, whose speciality in civilian life was gynaecology.

"Thank you." The need he had for something to make the pain abate did not keep him from asking, "What's in it?" when Ybarri readied the hypodermic needle.

"You need it."

"Yes, but what is it?"

"I'm sure they gave it to you after *that*." Ybarri pointed at Bora's prosthesis with his chin.

"Does it have a name? I need to function in the next several hours."

The needle went in. "It's pethidine, and you'll function just fine."

Minutes later Ybarri, who wanted to step out for a smoke, escorted him out of the radiology ward. Before they left each other he asked Bora, using the confidentiality of their shared Spanish, "*Dígame, colega* ... have you heard anything about the little blonde we shared the car with – Staff Leader Pletsch?"

"No."

"She's a pretty one." The Chilean tutted. "I was hoping ... *Bueno*, I gave her my phone number, but she never called."

Bora answered in German, with a German's stolid seriousness. "Well, she may be a good girl. There are some, you know."

The hospital dispensary was his next stop, to secure more aspirin. That was what Ybarri had advised, although Bora, of his own accord, also enquired about pethidine.

"Dolantin?" the medic at the counter asked. "It's an opium-based analgesic, Lieutenant Colonel. It works well, but I wouldn't drive after taking it." Was that really true? It meant that Bora had better get into the car before the medicine started to have its effect.


4:55 P.M.


Bora entered the Leipziger Hof doing his best not to limp. With a scowl, he silenced whatever question might have been on the hotel clerk's lips. Lifts were unreliable in wartime, so he had to climb to his fourth-floor corner room, where he washed thoroughly, careful not to dampen his bandaged knee. Aside from the bruises on his hand, impossible to conceal, he was presentable; the welt behind his left ear, where Grimm had roundly punched him, would evade a cursory glance. The problem was that the pethidine would start working within minutes, and he was beginning to feel nauseous and numb. He put his head under the running cold water in the sink, if nothing else to wake himself up. His day was like a tightly woven piece of cloth, in the middle of which a ragged hole represented what had happened at the railway crossing. He couldn't go there with his mind, if he wanted to avoid panic. More than anything, he had to avoid thinking altogether, because three unavoidable rendezvous still lay ahead. They would require every ounce of psychological energy that he had.

*I must be mad. Only this morning I was ready to impregnate a girl I'd barely met, to leave something of me behind. I will leave nothing behind.*

After changing, he spent almost half an hour monitoring his nausea (was it the painkiller? Was it fear?). It worried him that his clarity of mind was starting to wane along with the pain. He knew enough about the effects of mind-altering substances to realize that they varied greatly. In the next hour, he could fall asleep or turn hyperactive (or belligerent). He had to keep calm, to stop thinking about the day. He sat by the window, nervously leafing through his diary, until he stopped at a random page written nearly two years earlier, when things in Russia were still going well but he must for some reason have been homesick.

In the photo of her first wedding, I remember, my eighteen-year-old mother looks like a little girl. But a serious, grave little girl. At forty-eight, my father looks like Tsar Nicholas II or King George V, Nicholas's cousin. Thick, impeccable dark hair and beard. The picture taken five years later, at her second wedding, shows Nina still looking serious, and exceedingly beautiful in my eyes. My 47-year-old stepfather beams in his new uniform of a major general – he'd just been promoted. Bareheaded, his cropped hair is already grey. In both cases, a whole generation separates the bridal couple. I'm thinking of how Max Kolowrat might have fit into the intervening years; according to his biographic note, he was only five years older than Nina. When Dikta and I, on my parents' insistence, celebrated our religious wedding eleven days after the civil one, war was already in the offing. My friend Bruno, who acted as my best man, took the only photograph of the ceremony – I have it before me – as we walked out of the army chapel: Dikta in a pearl-coloured gown, myself in my cavalry captain's uniform (that, too, a recent promotion). Sunday, 27 August 1939. Although she is blonde, Dikta and I strangely resemble each other, as if we were brother and sister. I never noticed that before. We are apparently smiling for the camera, when in fact we'd just told each other something extremely intimate, which we were in a hurry to try out.

Had he really written such things? The firm, quick handwriting read like the last will and testament of a bygone world. Everything, everything falls apart.

Bora felt better after throwing up in the toilet bowl. He then turned to the first available blank space (he could not afford to waste even half a single page in a nearly full diary), and wrote:

16 July 1944, 5:58 p.m. I'll keep any comment about the case entrusted to me for later. Most importantly, even if everything else falls apart, I cannot; I have to remember that. I reproach myself all the more for seducing Emmy, in a fit of male egotism – a poor girl who was too embarrassed to open her legs and had to have a couple of drinks to muster her courage before coming up to my room. It's not surprising that she fell fast asleep afterwards, which is generally the post-coital prerogative of the callous male. I only hope that she will give herself to someone who is worth it.

This morning, back from the Osthafen and wandering among the ruins, I discovered several lumps of white phosphorus, which had leaked from incendiary bombs. It's surprising how harmless they seem, resembling amber. There's a lesson in all this. I carefully stored a couple of them inside the small medicine bottle I've been carrying since my last visit to Uncle's clinic.

And as for taking "something", I'll be damned if the pain in my knee is not coming back. I'm alert, but running at 50 per cent of my normal lucidity.

At 6:15 p.m., he had the boxes containing Niemeyer's papers loaded into the boot of the Olympia. At 6:30, as requested by Bora during his call from the phone booth that morning, Namura stopped by to return the letter he'd entrusted to him. They parted ways wishing each other good luck, without believing in it. By 6:40, Bora was ready to sketch a first draft of the report for Arthur Nebe. At 7:00, he phoned downstairs for a typewriter. He refused the hotel typist (not only because of the nature of the report, but because the last person he wanted to see was some girl who'd remind him of Emmy Pletsch). He typed the text himself, quickly enough, but in his haziness making mistakes and having to start over again.

At 8:16, he was done. Grimm usually came off duty at 8 p.m., so it'd be some time before they missed him at Alexanderplatz. Surely, his wife had no ready access to a telephone; accustomed as she must be to his absences and delays, she would not ask his colleagues about him until the following day. When Bora rang Nebe's office, his number was busy. At the switchboard, one of his assistants answered. Instead of forwarding the call to the chief, he walked away from the phone, so that for several minutes Bora had good reason to fear all sorts of dramatic consequences.

He was, on the contrary, given an appointment for 9 p.m., as on his first evening in Berlin. No advice on what precautions he should take or which entrance he should use. Bora slipped the report inside an unused folder he found among Niemeyer's papers, and left the hotel.

Outside, the sultriness had not given way, despite the evening hour. In Italy, under this arcing light, cicadas refined their chirring calls and scents intensified. Here, the city air smelled of soft asphalt and quenched fires. In the clear, dry, paper-white western sky, anvil-shaped clouds rose vertically to a great height. Who knows where they came sailing in from. Before nightfall a violent rain might pour down from them, onto the western quarters.

A surprise awaited him at Kripo headquarters. General Nebe was still busy, no interviews with him were possible before one in the morning. *One in the morning*? Well, there *was* a war going on. Bora was glad to walk away without having to answer questions about Florian Grimm. Only after he got into the Olympia with his stiffening, sore leg, did it occur to him that at this very moment Nebe might be ordering raids on the workplaces and homes of defiant officers and politicians. A terrifying prospect, yet nothing he could avert or control. He would plod along until someone stopped him. Spreading along the western horizon, the tall clouds covered the sinking sun, in an anticipation of dusk that dissolved shadows only to create a deeper twilight.

Bora went back to his hotel, reopened the folder with his final report, and then restlessly dozed until the time he had to go and meet Benno von Salomon.


CORNER OF LUTHERSTRASSE AND
AUGSBURGER STRASSE, 11 P.M.

At this hour, there was no one loitering in front of Otto Horcher's famous restaurant. In the narrow glare of the head-lights, Salomon stood in the same civilian clothes he'd worn at the restaurant days earlier, as well as a boater which, from its tight weave and buttery colour, was evidently Italian. With him, he had a small and seemingly brand-new suitcase. For some reason, although they'd agreed to meet alone, he hesitated when he saw Bora on his own in the car. *No witnesses*, he was probably thinking, which would make him apprehensive. Bora motioned to Salomon to climb into the back seat, but as soon as he had placed his suitcase there, Bora reprehended him with a sharp politeness: "No, Colonel. Get into the front, with me."

A jittery Salomon obeyed. He was sitting where, for days, Bora had ridden at Grimm's side. He immediately rolled up the window, as if fearful that someone might grab or hit him from outside. A scent of blooming trees, deeper now that it was night and a gentle rain was starting to fall, continued to flow in from the wide-open window on Bora's side.

Starting out, he had the itinerary clearly in his mind; having travelled the route only once before, years ago, he was nevertheless sure that he had to get to Tegel and cross the Fliess to head north, skirting the city limits. Aside from the damage wrought by bombs on the city streets, for his purpose it was best to avoid the main thoroughfares, which were more likely to be patrolled. An alternative – unlikely because of its length – was to follow the old army route to Döberitz, south of the Olympic Village, take the state highway in Staaken to the crossroads north of Spandau, and head north-north-east. In the less populated periphery of the city, Lattmann said, it was possible to run into shady characters, escaped prisoners, or fully armed individuals who took it upon themselves to make the rounds of their neighbourhoods. None of them alarmed Bora in the least. Being pressed for time did.

"Where are we going?" Salomon tried to sound confident, but his voice was barely above a croaky whisper.

"Trust me."

"Yes, but where are we going?"

Bora would not say. He was in pain and had no time to lose, and did not feel like pandering to his passenger. There had been other times – the last time was outside Rome, at the end of March – when he'd found himself driving at night with a terrified man at his side. It all came down to creating an emotional distance between himself and his actions.

"Take a tranquillizer if you wish."

Salomon's heart must have sunk at the contemptuous words. He gloomily searched his pockets, then kept mum for ten minutes or so, trying to make out familiar landmarks outside his window. When he lost his sense of direction, he could no longer contain himself.

"We're definitely leaving Berlin. We're leaving Berlin, aren't we?"

In fact, it was one of the suburban woods, although it resembled open country. No more pavements or street corners marked with phosphorescent paint. Their reasonably smooth progress was the only thing that suggested that they were still following a well-maintained gravel road. Bora stubbornly kept himself to himself. He would not allow any questions. What he'd do next, he himself hadn't really decided yet, save the fact that he would not take Salomon back.

"We're leaving town – definitely. Definitely." A short pause, and then the colonel removed his boater. "My good-luck hat," he mumbled, as if by way of an apology, and carefully placed it in the back with his suitcase. Whatever he added was inaudible, a mere attempt to fill the agonizing silence between them. Bora knew Salomon was afraid of him, and ignored him. Focused on keeping to the route in the dark, he thought of things very remote from here. He thought he'd emerged from his drug-induced numbness, but his sense of direction was severely affected. Fragmentary recollections floated inside him, impossible to make out. The slaughterhouse cars speeding on, Grandfather's forbidden books, light and shadow contraposed in the room where Stauffenberg stood … Emmy, who left without having a chance to make a son with him. *Would I be feeling better tonight, if we had done it? Probably not. Probably – no, surely – I would start worrying about her already, and God knows I have no need of that.* When, at the tail end of a convoluted series of unspoken thoughts, Salomon muttered, "I was joking when I said that I was on to you in Ukraine: I know *nothing* about you, nothing about what you might have done," Bora slammed on the brakes. Although they were not travelling at high speed, the sudden halt jerked the colonel forwards, so that his forehead struck the windscreen.

If he had ever considered pitying him, Bora now confronted a demented urge to kill. He physically ached with it, pain on top of the pain he already felt. For a moment, he needed to kill just to stop hurting.

"Hand me your papers," he ordered him. "You furlough papers, your travel passes, your pay-book – everything. Do not make me ask twice."

"But – I can't get around without them."

"You will *not* get around."

Bora hadn't taken into account the possibility that Salomon would try to fling the door open and jump out into the night. It was by accident that, sliding on the wet road as it braked, the car had come to a halt at the edge of the road, where a large tree blocked the passenger's escape. Salomon kept pushing at the door in vain.

"*Hand me your papers.*"

Dejectedly, the colonel took out a batch of documents held together by a rubber band. Bora told him to hold them up one by one. He shone his torch on them to make sure none was missing.

"I'm a dead man without them," Salomon protested.

"You're a dead man with them, Colonel. You're a deserter."

Until now, they'd avoided this indisputable fact. At any roadblock or railway crossing, a uniformed man driving after curfew with a colonel in civilian clothes, whose furlough papers indicated a destination different from the one they were following, would raise immediate suspicion. Depending on those manning the block, it could mean immediate arrest or being hanged on the spot, for both travellers. Salomon sank into his seat. As for Bora – under the lingering effect of the medication he was angry and lacking the lucidity he needed. *But it's because I'm not lucid that I'm doing this in the first place.*

Following country lanes, through a lonely spot he assumed was somewhere in the Tegel forest, he realized he'd taken a wrong turn. Twice already he'd had to back out of side streets, having missed the turn-off. Outside it was pitch-dark; the headlights caught the rainfall in a weepy, reduced field of vision, as when you're squinting. Bora engaged the reverse gear, without knowing whether they'd fall off the side of the road, into a ditch or the Havel, in this moist flatland criss-crossed by canals, ponds, sparse woods.

Whatever concoction Salomon had gulped down, it seemed to have made him fall asleep, but when the car trundled over a rocky swell in reverse he sat up with a start. He looked right and left, but he couldn't see anything. A clump of pale, dripping young trees swung in front of the car when Bora veered off course. A few insect sounds came faintly through the open window. They could be a hundred miles from the closest inhabited place. Not a home in sight. A wooden fence surged like a set of long teeth from the shadows.

Further on, a solitary road sign alerted Bora that they would soon come to a bridge, certain to be patrolled at this hour. Once more he reversed. Salomon buried his face in his hands: a motion desolate enough to arouse compassion, had Bora not known him in Russia only a year earlier, with his shot nerves and absurd superstitions. The man now acting so helplessly was the same commander who had made him oversee the hanging of partisans and saboteurs. Onegin, one of them was called. Bora still begrudged the day. Summer of '43, his brother had just died, and the unwelcome order of executing a Russian peasant had soiled his bereavement and his grief with a redress not his own.

Hermsdorf. At last, they were travelling once more towards their destination. Bora confidently navigated the suburban lanes and byways in the wooded landscape, until the time came to reduce the speed; he proceeded slowly, as if on the lookout for a special spot, slowing down more and more, and then came to a complete stop.

Salomon was too unsteady to control the pitch of his voice. "Where are we? Bora, where are we?"

"Get out of the car," Bora instructed him. When there was no response, he alighted and walked around to open the passenger door. "Now, then, Colonel. Out of the car with you."

"No." Salomon baulked. "I will not get out. I will not."

"I'll pull you out if you don't."

Salomon refused to budge. Crumpled and stiff in his seat, it'd take two men to drag him out.

Bora said, "As God is my witness, I will count to three." What he meant to do then, Salomon understood when the muzzle of the P38 met his ear. Petrified, at this point he would not even fight to save his life. He slumped there, feeling horribly sorry for himself.

Bora yanked him out by the arm. "Do not make a spectacle of yourself." With his left shoulder, he pinned Salomon to the car so that he could not sprint away, took out his torch and switched it on.

Above them, out of the wet, scented night, stone spirals and bizarre animal shapes floated into view, marking an archway both exotic and monstrous, the entrance to a ghoulish graveyard. From the dark beyond the gate, high up as if suspended in air, a second torch winked back. Then both were turned off.

"This is the Frohnau Buddhist Centre, Colonel. They will take you in. See that you don't stick your nose out before the end of the war," Bora said, coolly. In fact, he was so angry he could hardly contain himself.

The gate noiselessly opened from within. Salomon wiggled like a fish, the moment Bora stepped back; in the wink of an eye, he was safely past the threshold; he even forgot to take his suitcase. When Bora tossed it after him, he suggested, "Maybe, depending on how things develop … in a few days, I could …"

"Colonel, I have someone posted outside, ready to shoot you if you try to leave before the end of the war."

It was a spur-of-the-moment fiction, but Salomon completely believed it. He started uphill in the gloom, stumbling along the path that rose to the solemn Buddhistische Haus.

Bora exchanged a few formal words with the gatekeeping monk, thanking the abbot for agreeing to his request when he'd called him up earlier, and then returned to the car.

He didn't have to try hard to remember the motto of the House, knowing all too well what it said: *What we are doing, anybody shall be able to see. What we are saying, anybody shall be able to hear. What we are thinking, anybody shall be able to know.*

None of it had been true of him, for years. All of it seemed to be true (or about to be true) of the conspirators. He only hoped he would not have to regret letting Salomon live. Sometimes an imperfect solution is preferable.

Suddenly, just for one moment, he felt too exhausted to face the rest of the night. But there was no time, not even to sit here and close his eyes.

*Who knows where Emmy went,* he wondered. *Somewhere safe, I hope, where she can await the end of the war. I am already forgetting her. My body has already forgotten hers, because it had no time to grow used to it. We were two thirsty people offering each other a drink. You don't recall the cup, nor its contents. All you know is that, afterwards, you feel no more thirst.*


KRIPO HEADQUARTERS, MONDAY,
17 JULY, 0:55 A.M.


Somewhere on the way back, Bora tossed Salomon's good-luck hat into the night. Returning by a direct route through Wittenau and Reinickedorf, he reached Alexanderplatz with no time to spare. It hadn't rained here. He turned into

Dircksenstrasse. Leaving the car, he felt a sharp sense of failure, as if he hadn't solved the case.

Everything sank into a vast sea of disillusionment. *Here it is*, he told himself. *My generation, sworn to sacrifice, sees its beliefs fall one by one, and even though failure does not belong to it alone, it has to share in the immense failure of New Germany.*

It was unbearable. He had to shake himself out of his anguish and believe that something could still survive the disaster. "In a few days ..." the hopeful and imprudent Salomon had said, once he knew his life would be spared. The attempt would take place any time now. What if it succeeded? After all, Niemeyer had been silenced before he could blackmail or betray anyone. The thing *could* succeed. All the same, Bora felt great sadness for the men who secretly laboured to change that world. *What does it say about us, if the way out passes through high treason and contemplates the loss of human lives?*

Eight hours after the Dolantin had entered his system, he ached but was lucid again. He would not let exhaustion interfere with his penultimate task in Berlin. His horizon did not stretch beyond this. He was so focused on what he would say that he only dimly perceived the circuit of halls, corridors and stairs he went through to reach Nebe's office.

Despite the late hour, Nebe was reading a stapled document, or pretending to do so. With a small gesture of the left hand, without raising his eyes, he invited Bora to approach. To Bora's weary eyes, the milky glass shade of the desk lamp had a green tinge, soft like a sea-froth medusa; you'd expect it to be soft to the touch. Palm up, so as not to show the bruises on his knuckles, Bora laid the folder on his end of the desk.

Nebe underlined a sentence in the document. Still looking down, he pointed at the folder with his pen. "On the phone you mentioned a final report. Is this your final report?"

"It is."

Not having been invited to sit down, Bora stood. It was all right by him – his knee ached less when he didn't have to bend it. Nebe did not urge him to sit. It was probably his way of forcing subordinates to speak up for themselves, to take full responsibility for what they said. Consequently, the opening sentence Bora had prepared was nothing like the words that came out of his mouth now.

"As a soldier, Group Leader, I can be stolid. It's one of those potentially negative qualities that turn into assets under fire. As a counter-intelligence officer, I have developed other skills, some of which are morally ambiguous but very useful. Whether you sought the soldier or the operative in me, from the start I confronted the question I wasn't allowed to ask: why would a professional, *the* professional among the German police, entrust me with a murder case? I had nothing to offer that his team of detectives does not possess tenfold."

Nebe's pen (Bakelite government-issue, nothing fancy) drew a straight, thin line under the typed text in front of him. "Well, did you answer the question?"

"Possibly." Palm up, Bora slid the folder towards Nebe with the tips of his fingers, until its cardboard edge touched the sheet in front of the lieutenant general. "The murder case of a celebrated and controversial man is in itself a predicament. Given the victim's political connections, it made sense to call an outsider to investigate, guaranteeing a neutrality of sorts. The time allotted for this inquiry seemed pitifully limited, but then there were four providential, credible suspects already on the table." Bora watched Nebe move the folder aside so that he could continue working on the stapled document, flipping the page and underlining a new sentence. "One of them, Ida Rüdiger, was difficult to implicate, due to her connections with the Propaganda Ministry. Fortunately, I didn't discard her altogether, because as a jilted lover she actually played a relevant role through her private investigator, a fellow by the name of Gustav Kugler. Two other suspects, Eppner the watchmaker and Glantz the book publisher, both under arrest at this time, had good reasons of their own to hate Niemeyer.

Both concealed weapons at home; the publisher eventually confessed to the murder. The fourth suspect, Kupinsky, is a disabled drifter. Possibly manipulated to slander our own General Fritsch eleven years ago" – Nebe, irritated, glanced up at him – "and recently engaged by the Gestapo to spy on his neighbours, he harboured no apparent enmity towards Walter Niemeyer, but like the other three he had access to the house. An embarrassment of riches for an amateur investigator otherwise short on time and real evidence. As late as this morning, Inspector Florian Grimm reproached me for lacking a culprit, and it's true that for nearly a week I groped in the dark. Today, though, I felt that I had the solution in my hand, and told him that much."

The only sign that Nebe was marginally interested was that he lay down the pen without replacing its cap.

Bora shifted his weight onto the hale right leg. "Tonight, however, when I started drafting my official report, it occurred to me that something – an element, a significant element – was still missing from the picture. *You* would never countenance a weak or partial solution! I came close to panic, I admit. It's understandable, I'm just a soldier, not a detective. Worse, thanks to my family's involvement in publishing, I grew up with a high tolerance for imaginative scenarios – hardly an asset for an investigator. So I thought: Niemeyer had as many enemies as he had friends. What if he fell victim not to a single culprit, but to group retaliation? It was within the realm of possibility, and I had a ready-made cast of characters. I envisioned Ida Rüdiger spying on her lover's routine; Eppner's unfaithful wife leaving the back door open; Kupinsky the gardener hiding a weapon in the yard; Glantz the ruined publisher firing the fatal shots. A plot of bloody retribution, where all are guilty and no one is, which reminded me of a British novel published by Goldmann ten years ago in my hometown, Leipzig – *Der rote Kimono*, whose original title was, if I'm not mistaken, *Murder on the Orient Express*. Does that mean that the solution had been provided to me from the beginning? Yes and no. Things did not go exactly as I described, Group Leader, but near enough. Somehow, it *was* group retaliation."

Bora hoped for a sign of acknowledgement, even just a wave of impatience, but Nebe's reaction did not go beyond replacing the cap on his fountain pen.

"My theory," he forced himself to go on, "concerns a strong-willed Frau Rüdiger, morbidly jealous of her lover. She caters to the ladies of the Party, freely exhibiting their powerful spouses' calling cards. One day she confides in a good client of hers, Frau von Heldorff, and asks for the name of a reputable private eye. Frau von Heldorff, on the advice of her husband, head of the Berlin police, suggests Gustav Kugler. Kugler, formerly a member of the SA and a former police officer, is actually someone whom Count von Heldorff wants to shadow his latest flame, a pretty blonde who coincidentally frequents Niemeyer's home." When Nebe reached for his pen, Bora feared he'd lost his audience. The head of the Kripo, however, simply returned the writing implement to its brass-and-marble holder. "Thus Kugler is serving two masters. For now, Group Leader, let me only add that the nameless blonde, whose migraines Niemeyer treats with hypnosis, reveals facts that mustn't become public. Ida Rüdiger does not learn about the blonde from Kugler, but knows enough about Niemeyer's other trysts, including the one with Gerd Eppner's wife. I imagine she and the wronged watchmaker meet to commiserate; they plan their revenge, and eventually involve Glantz in their clever scheme, the unfortunate publisher ruined by the Weimar Prophet. Kupinsky is extraneous to the plot, although he is by chance able to provide logistical support. So far, so good. They can all contribute something, and once Ida dismisses Kugler, the field of action will be clear. Eppner, the former lieutenant in the Foot Guards, will supply the ammunition, and – more importantly – a copy of the key to Niemeyer's back door, used by his wife to enter her love nest. Glantz, in contempt of all the laws of the Reich, keeps a military Drilling rifle at home, and firmly intends to kill the clairvoyant with it.".

"Guesswork."

Or a working hypothesis. It took all Bora's resolve not to. It took all Bora's resolve not be disheartened by the flippant comment. "The first obstacle to the plan is how to transport a rifle to Villa Gerda undetected. Glantz takes care of it, by agreeing with Niemeyer – I saw the boxes ready in his office – that he'll return the draught material for the stillborn *Encyclopaedia of Myth*, which is to be deposited in the garden shed. In fact, that's how they intend to transport the weapon, piecemeal. It'll be up to the publisher, a big-game hunter in happier days, to sneak into the property at night, reassemble the Drilling, and carry out the murder."

"Glantz confessed that much." It was the first, sneering signal of annoyance on Nebe's part. For a moment, Bora feared dismissal.

"Under duress, General," he nonetheless added, "and minus a couple of items. The first is that, unbeknownst to him, the phone lines of all those involved were tapped, at least after Ida hired Kugler. Inspector Grimm told me just the opposite, but I believe that's how he learned of the plan, and of his old partner Kugler's activity as well."

Nebe could not possibly miss the implication of Bora's statement. For an uncomfortably long time, the silence in the room had an intact, sealed quality. Never mind that right and left, above and below this muffled space, stretched the meanders of the vast police headquarters, with its archives, interrogation rooms, prisons in the cellar and Gestapo-run third floor. They were two men facing each other in the eye of the storm.

"Well? You're wetting your lips, Colonel. Are you nervous?"

Bora looked up from the folder. "I'm beyond nervousness, sir. But fear does not prevent me from formally accusing Florian Grimm of Niemeyer's murder."

"'Formally accusing Florian Grimm' … Sit down."

"I'd rather stand, General."

"Sit down!"

It was an order, and Bora obeyed. Fear had an odour and a taste; Grimm reeked of it in the car; now Nebe wanted him to taste dread, and to feel powerless.

"Finish your report."

Bora squared his achy shoulders. Thank God for pain and fatigue; buffering his panic, they anchored him to his body and allowed him to rally, whatever tonight's outcome. He watched Nebe place the folder over the document he'd been underlining, face down, as if to deny or neutralize its contents.

"Like Gustav Kugler, Group Leader, before joining the Kripo Grimm was, as you know, in the SA and then in Count von Heldorff's Berlin police. He is an old fox. Once he learns every point of the vengeful plan, including the weapon chosen by the aspiring murderers, he beats them to the punch. Child's play, for one with his Eastern front experience. In his profession, he has ready access to an arsenal of the proper calibre, including Great War Mausers modified into twelve-gauges, and other shotguns seized in years past from gangsters and left-wingers. Well! No one is more surprised and terrified by the news of the murder than Glantz, about to ship the Drilling to Niemeyer's garden shed. After he hears through the grapevine that the ammunition used is consistent with two out of three of the Drilling's barrels, he suddenly loses heart. He stupidly repacks and sends the rifle to himself, poste restante, at Anhalt station. He may be a coward, yet he redeems himself in the end. When, under arrest here at Alex, he's beaten up and then – against the wishes of the Criminal Police – hauled to the third floor and into the Gestapo's custody, he takes the blame without involving his co-conspirators Rüdiger, Eppner and Kupinsky."

Nebe pursed his lips in a way that could conceal any number of reactions. "You spoke of *two* elements left out of Glantz's confession – what is the second?"

"The most important thing, unknown however to the publisher: that Walter Niemeyer tried to profit from what the blonde said under hypnosis. He approached Count von Heldorff, and possibly others, asking for money or other benefits; or else he promised to divulge the dangerous content of his sessions with the girl. Understandably, from the Berlin police chief's point of view, it's enough to sign his death warrant. Once Niemeyer is dead, along with the solicitor he directed – in writing – to expose the truth in case he should meet with a violent demise, all could be well. *But the letter to E. D. – Ergard Dietz – is never delivered.* I suggest that Grimm found it inside a sealed envelope in Niemeyer's home (he told me the safe was empty, which isn't very likely). Once Heldorff read the copy, he immediately disposed of the lawyer and ordered Grimm to torch the villa, to destroy other possible repositories." *How wise the human body is,* Bora thought. *Pain chases off fear, and weariness chases off the pain.* "The problem is, General, that although Count von Heldorff played a primary role in this incident, it was not on his direct orders that Niemeyer was killed." Weighing his words, Bora was crazily tempted to drive his forefinger against the milky glass shade, sure that it would sink like a jellyfish. "I am sitting, worse luck, in front of the truly ingenious master of the game. It was on your orders, sir, it fell to Florian Grimm to execute Niemeyer. I can make my case."

Nebe's only response consisted of a small, brusque movement of his leg, which he attempted to conceal by shifting in his chair. The odourless, sterile atmosphere in the room thickened between them. The few items on the desk – penholder, an indelible pencil, the framed photo, a telephone – sat as if immersed in a syrup, and the yard of distance separating the two men threatened to solidify like glass. Silence was all it was, but it showed Bora what a "wall of silence" meant. When Nebe decided to speak through it, his tone was unruffled.

"*Execute.* You can make your case." It wasn't a question – there was no curiosity behind it. Like Bora's words, it was a statement of fact. "You better had, Colonel."

The last, harrowing hours were beginning to make themselves felt. Bora sat stiffly in order not to let himself slump; he'd have gladly stretched his smarting leg and rubbed his neck, but he could afford no sign of weakness before Arthur Nebe.

"It's been very difficult. The four suspects – it was nothing short of genius – were more than simple decoys. They actually fit into the scheme. Grimm ... ah, Grimm was beyond suspicion. Why should I mistrust the jolly veteran policeman placed as a partner at my side? He discovered the body, after all. And what fun he had, telling of Niemeyer's tawdry start as a self-styled Eastern Jew, and how the audience roared when he was exposed as being uncircumcised! That's what the official post-mortem said, too. Had I not gained access to the extended autopsy report purged from the official file, I would have never caught on. The autoptic detail I should have paid attention to did not concern circumcision, but the bruise on his face which the Charité physicians mistook for an injury incurred by Niemeyer when he fell forwards. It could arouse suspicion: best leave it out of the official document. I'd seen how Grimm's bulky ring tore the flesh when he struck Glantz, the day we 'saved him' from suicide. I suggest that Grimm punched Niemeyer, when Niemeyer surprised him in his house. I'll go as far as to add that the recent contusions on the inspector's hands may not have come from digging his family out after the bombs, but from working Glantz over under this roof, in good old police fashion, so that he'd say what he wanted him to say."

"All this concerns Grimm, not the head of the Criminal Police."

"Except that Grimm carried out someone's orders. And for all that we're unquestioningly disciplined in our New Germany, I kept wondering about that, until I understood *what* singled me out for this task in your eyes. A relevant, and for me alarming, fact: it was everything that you know about me, as a high-ranking SS officer and an acquaintance of Leipzig's former mayor, Carl Friedrich Goerdeler. I am under no illusion about it, General Nebe: I have been more than once called to answer for my so-called political unreliability. This being the case, why would the head of the Criminal Police initiate an inquiry by telling his ersatz investigator that if he couldn't solve the case before leaving Berlin, *so be it?* Was the Niemeyer case, then, not all that egregious? It couldn't possibly be a desirable outcome, if it wasn't solved!"

"You're rambling."

"Quite the opposite. If I hadn't learned that, long before spying for the jealous Frau Rüdiger, Gustav Kugler had done dirty work for the State, I would have never associated him with Niemeyer's death. But in the old days Kugler also associated with Grimm, who told me so himself. Kugler led to Grimm; Grimm led to you. From the start, General Nebe, Grimm and I were pitched against each other. If Grimm won the day – well, accidents happen; in the fifth year of war, lieutenant colonels are just as expendable as everyone else is. Alternatively, Grimm could be charged with killing me: a superb excuse to remove an assassin who might grow troublesome. After all, he unquestioningly eliminated Niemeyer because the head of the Kripo judged it necessary: it was office work, routine. Much as on the Russian front, I'm sure Grimm felt *nothing* while shooting Niemeyer." Bora heard himself speak as if someone else were explaining things through him with more clarity than he could.

"As long as I stuck to the four suspects, although I did not conceal my doubts about such a ready-made list, the investigation must have seemed to Grimm as merely pro forma. He might have resented me because I was an outsider, not part of the police force, but he was otherwise at ease. Day by day, his anxiety grew in proportion to the time I spent looking elsewhere for a culprit. My linking his old pal Kugler to Niemeyer, and to the murders he carried out for the authorities during the Weimar days, alarmed him. He must have started to wonder what would happen to him if I solved the case. Towards the end he knew he'd been found out, a realization that fuelled his anger. If I proposed a solution that implicated him, directly or indirectly, or if the Gestapo started meddling because of the way I led the investigation, he was done for. No wonder that he had the bright idea today of driving into the open country to dispose of me. Grimm might have been an old fox, but I'm a young one."

Nebe sat motionless, like a photograph of himself, devoid of any depth. "You realize that one of you two has to die."

"That, Group Leader, has already been taken care of." Bora's battered knuckles came into view when he took out and placed Grimm's badge on the desk. "If you need it, the rest of him is scattered along the tracks east of the railway crossing." Next to the badge, he placed a map that had been folded and refolded, on which the spot was marked in blue ink.

A long pause ensued, during which Nebe stared into space, and although Bora was sitting across from him, it was not Bora he contemplated. Small spasms ran through his ugly, seamed face, the face of a labourer in the employ of justice and death. It was like spying on him as private emotions succeeded one another, forcing the muscles of his cheeks and brow to reveal at last the man behind them. As for Bora, he trusted he was unreadable as usual, even by an SS Group Leader. A small advantage, but an advantage where none other existed.

Eventually, with some effort, Nebe slowly said, "That is … good."

It was one of those instances when a word meant not even remotely what it had been created to signify. Tonight nothing around them, nothing about them, was *good*.

Goodness was as far from this room as the airstrips from which swarms of enemy bombers took off to hammer Berlin.

It was, in fact, the end of everything both men – each in his own way – had believed in.

Nebe opened a desk drawer, stretched his right hand towards Grimm's badge, and put it away; after tossing a cursory glance at it, he did the same with the map. This was probably the one office in Berlin where there were no listening devices; still Bora wouldn't say anything more, until Nebe spoke.

"And did you learn the motive for Niemeyer's death?"

"I learned the *real* motive, General Nebe. During our first meeting, when you disparaged 'young colonels', it was not to me that you were referring. I could sense it. As for Doctor Goerdeler, who has known my family for years, he would not have recommended me to you, as I believe he did, if he had not seen in you a counterpart to his political feelings. A former mayor in disgrace and an SS Group Leader do not bump into each other by accident, especially *these* days."

Twice Nebe unsealed his mouth, as if in need of a deep intake of air. Bora, who had met him only once before tonight, had the impression that he'd aged years within minutes.

"I cannot let you depart from Berlin, Colonel. You understand that."

"With your permission, it was clear to me the day you summoned me here."

"And ... ?"

"I deeply resent it, since I had every intention of going back to my regiment. In my selfishness, I blame my predicament on you and your confederates." *Confederates*, not *colleagues*. It was not the SS or the Criminal Police that Bora meant. Nebe understood perfectly, and was shocked. In his place, a civilian would have run a nervous finger around his shirt collar to loosen it. "I may be flattering myself, but I think that you knew I'd solve Niemeyer's murder. That was not what you wanted of me, but you couldn't be more direct. It'd be high treason."

Nebe mechanically drew back in his armchair. He gave the strange impression of being equally about to shout and about to fall into a stony silence.

"When it comes to selfishness …" He began the sentence and then stopped, but only for one bitter moment. "When it comes to selfishness, that isn't something *my confederates* and I lack." He slowly pushed the indelible pencil aside. "Did you find the letter?"

"Yes."

"Where?"

"Forgive me for quoting you, but that is the one question you may not ask."

"Goerdeler said you'd find it. Give it to me."

"I do not have it on me."

"Give me the letter. It's not safe to leave it anywhere."

Bora's boyhood insolence came back from an unexpected, deep and desperate place. "For the moment it's safe where it is, General Nebe."

What time was it? Bora had lost all notion of time. Suddenly he had a primitive, animal desire to sleep. Across from him Nebe sat back, avoiding the glare of the desk lamp, sunk in semi-darkness. To Bora, familiar with interrogation techniques, that avoidance of the light indicated a shift in the balance between them, a subtle recapturing of the upper hand.

"What about your unreliable colleague?"

No names, and Salomon was Bora's superior in rank – yet Nebe could mean no one else. Bora had not anticipated the question, but wouldn't lie outright.

"Of all the competencies useful for this assignment, those linked to my Abwehr training served me best: I can be without scruples, and if needed I will kill in cold blood."

Nebe scowled. The words were not wasted on him. With his chin, he pointed at Bora's left hip, where he wore his holster. "Lay your sidearm on the desk, Colonel."

Bora did so, turning its grip towards Nebe. Next to the P38, he placed the extra magazine. At any moment, Nebe could pick up the phone and have him arrested. He only hoped it would not happen before he'd said all he had to say.

"The reason for picking me is that I was judged *safe*, and a disposable lure. You were biding your time until a drastic change in the government of the Fatherland would make Niemeyer's death irrelevant. All along you contemplated, as you still do, the success of your *enterprise*. In that case, Niemeyer's elimination will appear timely and beneficial. He callously tried to profit from his silence; alternatively, he would vindicate himself in death, exposing a bona fide plot against the Führer. He had to be stopped, and was deservedly brought down. Speaking as a soldier, his was a brilliant strategy, which only another genius could frustrate. Yours was a major retaliation in lieu of minor retaliation: as above, so below. In the event of failure, General Nebe, the Niemeyer case will be the least of your problems." Bora watched Nebe's hand move within reach of the telephone, only to remove an invisible speck of dust from it. "Your confederates, barring perhaps Count von Heldorff, neither know nor would approve of your method of handling possible traitors: I'm sure Ergard Dietz and Heldorff's girlfriend followed Niemeyer's fate. Yet Doctor Goerdeler and others – forgive me if I mention no one else, I *am* a soldier in our New Germany – agreed with you that I could be useful in Berlin this week, drawing attention to myself, scuttling as I did from one end of town to the other. Plainclothesmen, hotel detectives, even the chauffeur of a retired general kept an eye on me. It was when I began to *understand* and draw close to the truth that I became not only expendable, but potentially dangerous, in case the Gestapo got to me first. And if I hadn't prevailed on Grimm at the railway crossing, I'd have vanished without a trace."

Only Nebe's forearms and bony hands emerged from the twilight on the other side of the desk. "Yet you don't have all the details."

"Well, I don't know where Niemeyer's riches went. The money is gone from his German accounts. Either our spend-thrift Count von Heldorff secured it, or the Reich did. I don't know if Bubi Kupinsky, the sole member of the foursome who was not directly involved in the plot, escaped with his life or went the way of the lawyer and the blonde. I can't be sure whether Gustav Kugler was eliminated by Grimm, in the old Weimar way, or died for work-related reasons."

"The truth is that none of you matter at all."

The indelible pencil on Nebe's desk (a tool for sentencing without leave to appeal, for the reckoning of deaths that had already happened) was blunt. Bora noticed it out of the corner of his eye, and found meaning as well as comfort in the detail. "The most important element I don't know, sir, is *when* you will act. Something went on, the day before yesterday, a dry run or a 'go' scrapped at the last minute, and I'll wager there were other false starts. Admiral Canaris trained me well. I'm one of his boys, after all."

Bora's sidearm, lying between them, became the focus of both men's attention.

"I should kill you now," Nebe said.

"You probably should."

*Now Nina will never cast off her mourning clothes.* The thought came oddly painlessly to Bora's mind, as if it weren't *his* life that was in such immediate danger. *Yet Nebe imagines that I'm in such dire straits that I could risk it all, open fire on him and expose the plot.* They sat across from each other, unmoving, staring at the gun. Still, it was precisely that quiet detach-ment, the exact opposite of resignation, which made Arthur Nebe lower his eyes, and in doing so notice the useless, blunt pencil. Irritated, he cleared his throat, as if the loss of a sharp tip and Bora's composure placed a niggling obstacle in the way of his threat. He placed the P38 and magazine into his desk, out of reach.

"If it were only up to me, I would have already had you shot."

411

This meant that others – Goerdeler, or Stauffenberg himself? – had opposed the idea. Understanding this mitigated Bora's animosity a little.

"The letter, Colonel."

"The letter is in the folder in front of you, General Nebe."

The folder was empty save for Niemeyer's letter. Nebe scanned it carefully under a magnifying glass before tearing it to shreds. These, he lit with a match inside an empty inkpot. Before meeting Salomon, Bora had done the same in the sink of his hotel room with the Kugler material, Olbertz's post-mortem and his carefully typed final report.

"However it goes, Colonel – and you are mistaken, the enterprise *will* succeed – you'll share neither the remorse nor the glory of it."

He'd heard the same notion from Claus von Stauffenberg. Tight-lipped, Bora thought, *I have remorse and merits of my own. Those of others do not belong to me.* When Nebe stood up, Bora promptly surged from his chair, as always in the presence of a superior, despite his tiredness. He was perfectly aware that, whatever the lieutenant general promised, between the centre of Berlin and any one of the airports surrounding it, he could be put to death a hundred times. The tunnel still had no light at the end, or perhaps there was only a blind wall there.

Nebe, in fact, was far from being done with him. His next words were the first tonight that Bora hadn't expected. "Make sure you leave Colonel von Salomon's documents here. We would not want anyone to think he was a deserter, or that you aided him in his attempt to become one." He took in Bora's surprise as if it were due to him. "Had you been drinking? My men thought so, by the way you ran around in circles tonight before you found the Buddhist Centre in Frohnau." He gestured to him with his half-open hand, asking for the papers. "Your former commander died an hour ago. They will find him in the next few days in the woods, on the shores of the Hubertus lake. Officially, he will have shot himself in a bout of despondency over the deteriorating state of his nerves, medically certified since 1941. Unless of course any suspicion arises that he committed suicide after shooting the male prostitute – what's his name, Kupinsky? – he met in that solitary place. Don't look so crushed. It's because you are one of Canaris's boys that I had to take these precautions. As you say, you are and remain a soldier. That's your limit."

Bora's less than perfect plan had been to hide Salomon and hold on to his documents for an indefinite time, or until the situation cleared. Now, as he sorrowfully turned in the papers, he saw that the elastic band holding them together had frayed and snapped. "It's a limit I thank God for every day of my life."

Nebe now had the upper hand. "By the way, did you come in the staff car? Good. I imagine you also brought back the Niemeyer boxes entrusted to you. Good. Leave the Olympia here. Hand in the keys."

Did this mean that Bora would not get out of Alex alive? Or did Nebe expect him to walk across the whole of Berlin at this hour of the night? Bora was too worn out and sickened to ask questions, but claimed a crumb of self-respect for himself.

"I will leave the Niemeyer boxes here, General, but not the car. I'd rather drive myself back."

The proposal was midway between unprecedented arrogance and a legitimate request. Nebe evaluated the question with a frown, and then agreed.

When they parted ways, Bora responded to Nebe's stiff arm-raising with the army salute.

"Soon one of the two greetings will prevail over the other," the general grumbled, and pointed to the door. "They'll come for you tomorrow."

Bora left, ready for anything. It could be a bullet in the back of the neck or a thank-you note, or an insult. Nothing of the kind followed. Despite the season, Berlin was almost cold now, just before dawn. The stars were still out, but before long the sky above the buildings and ruins would take on that pale, fleshy tinge, which in Spain had reminded him of naked women. He saw himself as he was then, climbing up from the river, up the steep side of Riscal Amargo, in days when believing had not yet been painful. Now both believing and not believing hurt. But he was accustomed to pain.

He knew they would follow him. All the same, once he left the police headquarters and travelled across the city's centre, he did not take a left on Potsdamer Strasse to reach the hotel but continued south-west towards Dahlem.

Uncle Reinhardt-Thoma's clinic loomed in the twilight of dawn. It would be days before it reopened under new management, but Bora was ready to wager that Wirth had already moved his things into the ground-floor office.

Even though his knee hurt badly, he alighted quickly from the Olympia. Fatigued as he was, he acted automatically, but was aware of his every move. Meanwhile, the Kripo's unmarked car slid silently along the shadows of Dohnenstieg and parked across the street with its headlights off. Bora used the key Olbertz had given him. The lock had not been changed, so he had no problem getting in.

Crates and boxes of papers waiting to be filed away crowded the office floor. Bora set the torch in a corner, so that he'd have just enough light to work by. He began by pushing the heavy desk towards the oak panelling of the end wall; with his right foot, one at a time, he shoved and crowded the boxes all around it. All but one of the brand-new cotton curtains, folded and still partly wrapped, came to rest on the desk, along with folders from the drawers, two chairs and their stuffed pillows. Bora picked up a screwdriver – which had fallen when they'd moved around the furniture – from the floor and stuck it in his belt. He then lifted out of his briefcase the water bottle he'd filled with petrol in the home of the old farmer-soldier. He'd stopped it up with the surgical gauze Ybarri had used on his knee, and already added to it the amber-like lumps of white phosphorus he'd found when he'd rummaged through the debris. He set briefcase and torch on the threshold of the front door. Standing there, he kindled the petrol-drenched fabric with Peter's lighter, and tossed the bottle with all his might against the desk.

He left shortly thereafter. He locked the front door and stuffed the remaining cotton drape under it, to keep the smoke from filtering out too soon. Before stepping down to the front yard, he broke the key inside the lock with a sharp blow of the screwdriver's handle. Flames were rising inside when Bora walked back to the Olympia. He carelessly walked by the police car, where two plainclothesmen fretted, debating what they should do.

He drove to the Leipziger Hof without even glancing in the rear-view mirror to see if he was being shadowed. Once in his room, he ordered a schnapps to gulp down a painkiller, which he immediately threw up. It went down better with a glass of water from the sink. He instantly fell asleep, still half-dressed; in his agitated slumber, he thought he heard – but perhaps it was the first air-raid warning – the wail of a fire engine speeding in the dark towards Dohnenstieg.


17 JULY, 5:50 A.M.


In the morning, he remembered nothing of the day before. It was a complete blackout. He knew he was in Berlin and why, but could not explain the bruises on his right hand or his contused, stiff knee. His scant luggage was ready, so he must be about to leave. A vague image floated into his mind, of being in the car with Florian Grimm somewhere. The rest was a painful void.

It'd happened only a couple of times before, after major drinking bouts at the German embassy in Moscow. But that

415

was before the war, when the Soviets made young military attachés drink too much in an attempt (failed, in his case) to loosen their tongues. A very unpleasant sensation, which he tried to remedy by reading through the diary entries of the last few days. Piecemeal, through the reticence and self-imposed censure of his own words, he began to reconstruct the events, at least in part. Like clear-cut blocks of ice emerging from a flat sea, the endless hours just behind him surged back. Grimm, Nebe, Salomon, Kupinsky. They struck him as a sequence of infinite horror.

Still, they belonged to another life, as if he'd died and this morning a different Bora had come into the world, utterly indifferent to risk, remorse, fear, pain. He was once more aware, recalled every detail, and felt exceptionally calm.

Whatever his destination, Nebe would soon send someone to pick him up. Only as he shaved did the thought of Salomon being dragged away from the Buddhist Centre hit home. Silent tears rolled down his cheek, and he had to look away from the mirror so as not to see himself weep. *He was my commander. He trusted me. How frightened he must have been, how he must have believed that I betrayed him.* Darkness, the lonely lake-shore, the bitter odour of water – he could sense them as if he were there. And Kupinsky, once again the weak link, destroyed for ever.

At 6:30 a.m., the sun was red and enormous, four fingers above the horizon. As he stood by the window, clasping the horn button of his collar, it seemed to Bora the image of a giant wheel, like the one described in the *Tao*. Ah, yes. Didn't Max's surname, Kolowrat, mean "wheel"? The same ancient term indicated the sun's disc, the swastika, all that revolves around an immutable hub and creates or destroys as it goes.

When he left the hotel, there wasn't an iota of all that he had done and experienced during the past week that he did not recall.

\*

Outside, an unmarked car waited for him. It was driven by an auxiliary, whose orders must have been to reply in monosyllables.

In the back seat, Bora found his P38 and the extra magazine, the only sure sign that he would not be executed this time around. The day was beginning; enemy pilots were revving their engines for the next raid over Germany. Of all the times Bora had left a city without the certainty of seeing it again, this was the most melancholy. However things went, to *this* Berlin he would never come back. It wasn't just written with a blunt pencil: it had been written in ink long before. There had been other leave-takings like this one in his career: without advance notice, crude extractions from the mandible of Time. Paris, Moscow, Rome ... little more than names now in his inner geography.

The auxiliary did not look into the rear-view mirror; between the shoulders squared by the uniform, her neck was delicate. A neck easy to break, and just as easy to pull back in a kiss. Bora thought of Emmy, who was travelling to her next assignment, if she hadn't already arrived there. Bora looked at the girl's shiny hair, gathered under her army cap; not because he was interested in her, but to keep from looking outside. He did not want to memorize the quarters effaced by war, risking a comparison with what they had been, and what they would become.

*How long can we last, whether or not this plot succeeds? Nine, ten months at most. Then the Russians will come. Uncle Reinhardt-Thoma, forced to do away with himself, escaped before the catastrophe. But my parents, like the rest of Germany, will be spared nothing.*

The solution was to pull away from people and things. Colleagues, brother officers who had meant so much to him, receded not from his care – he would die for them – but from his attachment. As for material objects, he owned few that were exclusively his own, aside from books and what boyish belongings remained in the family rooms he'd inhabited as a boy in Leipzig, Borna and East Prussia. Did the awareness of

417

this make him feel free? No. The first and last time he'd felt free had been in Spain.

At Schönefeld, unexpectedly, an army surgeon awaited him with a first-aid kit. Bora saw what was coming, and immediately said, "I'd rather not. I don't react well to painkillers."

"Frankly, Colonel, we don't care."

A massive dose knocked him out for the duration of the flight. When he landed in Italy, a second shot woke him up quickly, after which he was functional again.

Thursday, 20 July 1944. 5:30 a.m. Note: today, had the Weimar Prophet kept his word to Glantz, the *Encyclopaedia of Myth* was to be delivered for publication. God knows where the Glantzes (and Eppner, and his Russian Ostarbeiter) are today!

I write for the first time since my return to Italy. The men were thrilled to see me back, especially Luebbe-Braun. He was relieved to hand me back the responsibility of command, which I had occasion to exercise at once.

Hyperactive as the second shot made me, I immediately started visiting the outposts up and down the line; the situation is such that it will keep us busy day and night. The knee bothers me, but never mind. Here at least I can comfortably get around in army shorts, and when I mentioned a "minor car accident" in Berlin, nobody here asked for details.

Speaking of minor accidents, a personal note: in Trakehnen, the same year Uncle Reinhardt-Thoma told me the facts of life, Peter and I had the great idea of accelerating the dismantling of an old barn. I suggested to my younger brother that we use fire, so, thanks to my (scant) understanding of chemistry, we combined petrol siphoned out of a tractor with phosphorus used as a fertilizer in the fields. All went inside a makeshift container, an empty vodka bottle left behind by the Polish seasonal workers. Once we'd stuffed its neck with sackcloth, drenched it with fuel and lit it, I threw it hard against the barn to see what would happen. The outcome surpassed all expectations, as the conflagration all but destroyed the rye field behind the building.

I needn't report the difficulty of explaining it to the General, whose comment to Nina on that occasion was that unless I joined the army, I'd turn out to be a perfect delinquent as an adult.

Anyway, punishment aside, the idea seemed a good one. Nine years later in Morocco, I merely perfected it for my Foreign Legion comrades bound for Spain.

What other use to the common cause could an arch-Catholic German lad be, a greenhorn Abwehr volunteer fresh out of military school? In Aragon, holed up as we were between a farmers' cooperative and a depot of broken-down trucks, we mixed white phosphorus and fuel inside bottles of Afri-Cola and corked them up with rags. They provided our chief ammunition for nearly a week, allowing us to halt the advance of the enemy and temporarily borrow from him the saying "No pasaran". I'm actually not proud of the invention, because it's a desperate weapon and a cruel one, especially for those caught in burning vehicles. But that's the way it went.

Yes, contrary to later claims by others – the Finns, the Soviets – it was we, Francisco Franco's legionaries, who first used the so-called Molotov cocktail against Russian T-26 tanks in Spain. The nickname signified our intent to counteract the communist coalition supported by Stalin's foreign minister, the wily Vyacheslav Molotov. In Stalingrad, towards the end, as long as we had fuel to spare, my men and I again resorted to it. Four nights ago, it came in very handy in Dahlem.

It's because of such dubious exploits, and because I have the reputation of being a lucky commander, that my men are irrationally optimistic. But I – I simply wait. I wait as if I am lying in the dark and a noise from somewhere in the house has alerted me: who is it, what will he do, and when?

I see myself all too clearly as a soldier in our New Germany: restless but loyal, ruthless but upright, involved in that which suffices to make me guilty but not to damn my soul. Saving my soul is all I can do, until the vice tightens once more. All I can do is hold my breath.

"Holding his breath" wasn't easy. Doing so without showing it tasked him. An hour after putting away his diary, Bora blessed a fierce enemy attack on his position, because it took his mind off his expectant worrying, off the conspiracy.

It was only late that night, through army radio and official communiqués, that he learned of the failed attempt on Hitler's life, and of the first executions. Stauffenberg (and surely Haeften) had been the first to die. In the weeks and months to come they would be followed by thousands more, including Heldorff, Olbertz, Dr Bonhoeffer's son – pastor of St Matthew's – the two Schulenburgs. Arthur Nebe, too, and even the old and ailing General Beck, whose chauffeur had shadowed Bora through Berlin streets.

The day had been bloodily won in his sector, so much so that congratulations from divisional headquarters came down the wire. Before sharing those, Bora had to read a pre-written note condemning the conspiracy, first to his dumbfounded officers and then to his soldiers, who after hours of fierce fighting seemed less concerned with the Führer's life than their own. He ignored as unreadable the discretionary addendum that had been wired in, verses by a Leipzig-area poet:

> *The People and its Leader are linked as one,*
> *Firm as a rock stands the Third Reich,*
> *Closely knit, tow'ring in the rays of morn,*
> *Glimmering like the costliest Holy of Holies,*
> *My Führer, lit up by your God-sent smile!*

*

Around two in the morning, Bora sat outside his tent, inactive for the first time in twenty hours. Of all the members of his regiment, he was the least surprised by what had happened, yet his grief for the way things had gone had power enough to stun him. At the foot of the cliff below him, a deep hollow swarmed with a sparse luminosity resembling fireflies, although it was too late in the season for fireflies. Whatever it was, it gathered in clusters like will-o'-the-wisp, or *ignis fatuus*, such as floats over bogs and shallow graves. There was no still water on the thirsty mountainside; but both armies hastily dug graves every day. Bora looked into the hollow in order not to raise his eyes to the sky, an unusual reluctance on his part. He knew which constellations spotted the night above him. It was the crumbling arc of meteors, the ineludible destiny of shooting stars he'd rather not see. Shooting stars are short-lived. But at least they move, while the firmament lets you believe that nothing will ever change.

He felt sick at heart, lonely and loveless and for once completely adrift. Four days later – though he didn't know it yet – the Hitler salute would become mandatory in the armed forces, an unprecedented humiliation. Hundreds – thousands – would die in Hitler's purge. The war would go on. The Russians were days away from East Prussia. Six months at most, and, casting an ever-wider net, the SS would get at him, too. Bora was grateful for this scrap of Italy he was still defending; if he could, he'd kiss every rock and ravine and high-perching trail of it.

In his tent, at the bottom of his army trunk, where he replaced it whenever he stopped reading it, Bora kept Niemeyer's first autobiography, written as Sami Mandelbaum (and salvaged from the material returned to Nebe). He'd for some reason memorized the opening sentence: "Ever since I was a child, I knew I was different from everyone else. My gift was such that I tried to smother it, so that I would not see, would not perceive what the future had in store for me.

421

My dear late father's name was Isaac; my esteemed mother's name, Perl —"

*We destroyed that world,* he thought tonight, *which Niemeyer falsely claimed for himself as long as it suited him; now we are destroying our own world. Thanks to men like Nebe, whatever his late repentance, we have brought devastation everywhere. What can we expect in return? My stepfather told me once that mine is a generation of vipers. If so, who laid the eggs from which we were hatched? Only from vipers is a viper made. Sergeant Major Nagel, hard as steel, whom I have known these four years, including in Stalingrad, was the only one who had nothing to say after the news of the failed attempt. I supposed that it was because of the magnitude of the event (Hitler is a father figure for many of us). Instead, a while ago he took me aside and whispered, "I'm so glad you came back, Colonel." My God, he'd feared for me, as if in his loyalty to me he understood everything! At that moment, his words meant more to me than anything else in the world.*

When, out of the dark, the same Sergeant Major Nagel noiselessly approached bringing a canteen half-filled with coffee, Bora thanked him, and took a sip. Tilting up his face to swallow the lukewarm drink, he closed his eyes, as if in so doing he could shut out and cancel the star-ridden night.

§

Arthur Nebe, with his good friend, co-conspirator and biographer Hans Bernd Gisevius, managed to escape the first wave of arrests. However, while Gisevius was eventually able to emigrate to neutral Switzerland, thanks to American support, Nebe remained in hiding in Germany. At first, thanks to his skills as a policeman, he succeeded in staging his own death. The Gestapo, however, caught up with him and executed him at Plötzensee Prison for his role in the 20 July plot, the same prison where he'd jailed so many through the years. He died by hanging on 21 March 1945, eight weeks before the end of the war.

§

Nina Sickingen decided to remain at her husband's side in Leipzig until the end of the war, when the city fell to the Americans after a fierce battle, immortalized in Robert Capa's action photographs. It was in their house that he shot the famous set of pictures of the American G.I. felled by a Nazi sniper. Before Saxony was handed over to the advancing Red Army by the western Allies, Nina and the surviving members of her family moved west to Bavaria, as her eldest son had advised her to do. Following the General's death in 1951, she accepted Max Kolowrat's marriage proposal and eventually made her home with him in Munich.

§

As for Max Kolowrat, following the promise he'd made to Martin Bora, he stayed in the German capital during the torturous last weeks of the conflict. He was among the city dwellers who bravely, even if to no avail, tried to protect their quarters from the Soviet onslaught. During the post-war occupation of Berlin, his facility with foreign languages and writing talent earned him the position of interpreter in the British Sector. In due course, even before marrying Nina Sickingen, he reverted to his role as a successful journalist and travel writer.

§

Emmy Pletsch met and married a young army surgeon in September 1944. He went missing in action on the doomed Italian front a month later. Although she suffered from loneliness and privation living in the vicinity of her native town, her advanced pregnancy saved her from being raped during the battle for Germany in the spring of 1945. Shortly thereafter, she gave birth to a son in a Soviet-run army hospital. After reuniting with her husband in 1946, she shared the experience of all Germans living behind the newly erected Iron Curtain. Incidentally, of the two children born to her in the early 1950s, she named the younger boy Martin.

§

Roland Glantz was still awaiting trial when the war ended. He was liberated and miraculously reunited with his wife. In the following years, fate partly compensated the publisher for his losses. The boxes of esoteric writings by Walter Niemeyer still in his possession provided him with enough material to create a successful series of journals on astronomy and predictions, eventually resulting in considerable pecuniary success.

§

Ida Rüdiger really did have friends in high places. She escaped from Berlin just days before the Red Army reached the city limits, and reached Patton's forces on the border with Czechoslovakia. The widespread presence of female personnel among the western Allies allowed her to quickly reinvent herself as a make-up artist. She eventually created her own line of cosmetics, christened "Ostara" in memory of her old lover Walter Niemeyer.

§

Gerd Eppner was not so fortunate. A few days after Germany's unconditional surrender, having survived arrest, internment and liberation, a stray soldier attracted by the precious watches he carried robbed and murdered him. What made it worse for the once proud second lieutenant in the Foot Guards was that his killer was not a drunken Russian but a German straggler on his way home.

§

Lieutenant Colonel Namura returned to Japan before the fall of Berlin. In the terrible days after the nuclear bombs that fell on Hiroshima and Nagasaki, ill-advisedly but knowing exactly what he was doing, he joined the conspiracy of army officers who opposed the unconditional surrender of Japan. During the night of 14 August 1945, the rebels unsuccessfully tried to storm the Imperial Palace and secure Hirohito's recorded message of surrender. Dictated as it was by an exasperated patriotism, the revolt failed, and the leaders of the conspiracy committed suicide. The German-Japanese copy of *Chushingura*, the legend of the Forty-Seven Ronin, was found in Namura's pocket.

§

Dr Wirth and his wife perished in the last, devastating air raids on Berlin. The same fate met Willy Osterloh in his native Hamburg, to which he had decided to return. One survivor was Peter's wife, Margaretha, who naturally got her way and all that she wished for – a husband, a house and five children. In time she grew bored with it all, but that's another story.

As for Paulina Andreyevna Issakova, she vanished at the end of the war. In this, she shared the fate of countless labourers from the territories of the USSR under German occupation. Her name does not appear on any document, either in Germany or in the Russian Federation.

§

On the night following Stauffenberg's unsuccessful attempt on Hitler's life, Martin Bora added an entry to his diary which revealed his feelings, and reflected on what would befall him in the months to come:

There is that saddest hour before dawn, which resembles evening gloom. We sense no intimation that the day is at hand. A good number of us, I believe, have lived in this dusk for years. We do not take a look around, for fear we might discover that there is no sign of light in the east, and that, conversely, a dark night is coming on.

All true, save perhaps the excessive pessimism of the last few words.

# AUTHOR'S NOTE

*The Night of Shooting Stars* is a work of fiction. However, the failed attempt on Hitler's life of 20 July 1944 is a historical fact. Nebe, Canaris, Beck, Oster, Goerdeler, Heldorff, Tresckow, Bonhoeffer, Olbertz, Haeften, the two Schulenburgs and Claus Schenk Graf von Stauffenberg are real characters. All of them paid with their lives for their conspiracy against the Nazi regime, some immediately, on the night of 20 July, many others only towards the end of the war, after suffering torture, trials and imprisonment. In the novel, Martin Bora's conversations with Nebe and Stauffenberg are fictional; however, I tried to create them based on what we know of their world views, especially regarding society and Germany.

Countless historians (Hoffmann, Molloy Mason, Benz and Pehle among others) point out that the conspirators, largely from a military and aristocratic background, dramatically differed on matters of politics, ethics and personal outlook. Such contrasts transpire from the memoirs by two men who resisted, Hans Bernd Gisevius and Philipp von Boeselager – two of the few who survived the purge.

In light of this, it is fair to wonder whether internal conflicts and operational differences, added to a touch of narcissism and the well-attested occasional cases of careless indiscretion, contributed to the failure of Stauffenberg's coup.

Historians do not agree on the subject. My personal belief is that we may never undo this historiographic knot.

At any rate, as Gisevius writes at the end of one of his memoirs, *To those whose ashes have been scattered, let us at least leave their unsullied faith in a better world.*

# ACKNOWLEDGEMENTS

My research before and during the drafting of the novel, especially as regards Berlin in 1944 and the context of the 20 July plot, owes much to many, in many countries. My gratitude goes to the Deutsches Bundesarchiv (Section R and Section MA), to the Gedenkstätte Deutscher Widerstand, to Robert Kirchner, Ernest Gill; and, for their studies, to Norman Ohler, Richard Bassett, Mel Gordon, Robert P. Watson and Danny Orbach. Additionally, a heartfelt thank you to the staff of Libreria Militare in Milan, to General Giorgio Battisti, Barbara Biagi, Marina Pagnussat, Silvia Musso, Marco Patricelli, Lia Beretta, Mariano Del Preite, Francesca Marcelli, Paola Pallottino, Giorgio Galli, Cesare Carrà, and to the best supporters: my translator from English, Luigi Sanvito, and my literary agent, Piergiorgio Nicolazzini.